DAPHNE BRUNO

By
ERNEST RAYMOND

CASSELL AND COMPANY, LTD
London, Toronto, Melbourne and Sydney

First published *October* 1925.
Second impression *November* 1925.
Special Edition *October* 1926.
3/6 Edition   *January* 1927.
Second impression *May* 1931.

Printed in Great Britain

DAPHNE BRUNO

CONTENTS

DAPHNE BRUNO

THE END OF THE LONG PROLOGUE

I

MR. THOMAS TENTER BRUNO, sitting beside his writing-table, with the revolving arm-chair swung round so that his legs could stretch past the drawers and his arm rest along the blotting-pad, stared musingly at the wall. The pained set of his mouth and the lift of his eyebrows showed that his thoughts, though they might often graze afield, were none the less tethered to a fixed anxiety.

Had he been sitting with the grace he assumed in public rooms, instead of so relaxed a port, his appearance and his surroundings would have excellently suited a presentation portrait of T. Tenter Bruno, Esq. For on the writing-table were sheets of paper, a silver ink-pot and a pen—the very symbols of his craft; and in the background rose shelves of books, the finished product of his kind and the true setting of his life. On one shelf was a row of fifteen volumes, with fifteen titles, over one author's name—"T. Tenter Bruno." Above them and below them, and on either side of them, were the works of Hume, Johnson, Burke, Bentham, Hazlitt, Lamb, Landor, De Quincey, Mill, and all the other critics, essayists and economists in whose company Mr. Tenter Bruno considered that his books might without presumption take their seat.

In these days (two decades before Victoria died), when men wore side-whiskers or moustaches and double-breasted frock-coats, Mr. Tenter Bruno wore a trim, pointed beard and a short-coated grey suit, perfectly tailored. The grey suit was almost as constant as the beard. In daytime, at any rate, Mr. Bruno was as likely to be seen with a shaven chin as in anything but a grey suit. It was hardly

1

Daphne Bruno

that he dressed the part of a literary artist, since he affected to despise those unpublished brothers who could only be known for great men by the length of their hair, the languor in their walk, and the lawlessness of their ties. The perfect precision of his grey suit, the uprightness of his tall, slender figure, and the neatness of his beard were a challenge to nincompoopdom. But (he admitted this to no one, not even his wife) it was best to have *some* sort of professional appearance—something that differentiated you from the unfamed multitude—something that the Press-picture left firmly on the memory for the paragraph writer to harp upon and foolish women to gossip about. To his wife the beard had been explained as necessary owing to the excessive tenderness of his skin (a tenderness which no man yet regarded as anything but a credit to him); and the grey suit was attributed to a very nice taste.

In reality Mr. Tenter Bruno's creation of his private and, as it were, patented exterior was rooted in his contempt for the crowd. There was no doubt whatever that a platform appearance and other food for the literary chatterer were commercial assets; and if people were such fools as to buy a writer's books more readily after tattling about his clothes, any wise man would keep their tattling green. At one time he even played with the humour to be a vegetarian and a teetotaller, but his love of comfort was more than his desire to have these interesting things written about him. As he put it to himself, the occasional paragraph was a pleasant thing, but an assured and adequate dinner every day was a greater.

There was a knock at his study door, but he decided not to hear it, remembering that he was anxious. Not that his anxiety was humbug, for it was very real indeed; but, since it was there, it might at least have the credit of its full dimensions. So he let the servant knock again.

"Oh, come in," said he patiently; and there entered a big-hipped, comfortable servant of about forty-five years, in a dress of powder-blue cotton and a plain apron.

"Now, excuse me, sir," begged the woman pleasantly, "but won't you have a cuppa-tea? What I mean to say is : a nice little bit of breaden-butter with a potta-tea. I'll bring it to you here, sir. It's after four o'clock, and we're having ours in the kitchen; and we couldn't bear to think of you

2

sitting here, and sort of—what I call—having nothing. And I'm sure you ate nothing at lunch."

Mr. Bruno had heard the tea-bell and ignored it, and now would have liked a cup of tea, for his mouth was unpleasant; but this good woman's doubts whether during an emotional crisis he would take tea prompted him in a moment of weakness to reject the offer.

"No, thank you, Hollins. I don't think I'm wanting anything just now."

He saw all that was happening in Hollins's mind. The good woman, while persuading herself that she was disappointed at this refusal, was really pleased that her master's suspense should be so interesting. And along with her conviction that persistence was the interesting part for her to play went a real desire to minister to him.

"Well, I should, sir, if I were you. Just a nice little cup, and a thin slice a-breaden-butter. I mean, you want to sort of—what I call—keep up, sir."

"Oh, well, oh, well," agreed Mr. Bruno, swinging his chair so that he faced his papers and his pen, and taking up a sheet and dropping it, "bring it along." He thought that perhaps he would drink it and perhaps he would leave it untouched to provide an interesting topic of conversation in the kitchen.

"That's right. And I'll just make it a little comfortable in here. Why, you've almost let the fire go out."

He glanced obediently at the fire. It was powdery with decay. This rather pleased him, as proving that, despite all postures, his anxiety had really been his master.

"Oh, we'll soon have a cheerful bitta flare here," said Hollins, kneeling down with difficulty and rather heavily, while Mr. Bruno, in his mind, was providing her with her next words : "There's nothing like a bit of a coal fire to cheer you up."

Hollins took the poker and probed the embers with the delicacy of a surgeon whose scalpel was more in danger of killing than curing. Over the moribund glow she arranged some small coals, like a child building bricks, and then swept the hearth. "There's nothing like a bit of a coal fire to cheer you up," said she ; and, being a heavy woman, got up with as many divided motions as a camel. The window curtains required straightening, so while this was being done, and till she was gone out, Mr. Bruno drew parallel lines on a piece of paper.

The closing of the door suggested that he sought some new occupation for his mind. He rose and walked towards the bookshelves. He was examining his present condition with the detachment of a literary artist; indeed, the whole affair was, to him, an exceedingly familiar literary incident, on which the trite comment was the truest :

"This is one of my great hours."

His eye fell on the fifteen volumes bearing his name. It was always good to see this long chain of Tenter Brunos among the works of immortal essayists. He took down a volume issued from the house of his American publisher, and on a slip inside it read the enthusiastic praise of its contents.

"No one can afford to neglect the writings of Mr. T. Tenter Bruno. With great critical acumen he combines pungent wit, gay humour and a coruscating style. ('Disgusting bit of prose, that,' thought Mr. Bruno.) His reach is ubiquitous; he seems to write with equal scholarship on literature, art, music, history, sociology and political economy."

He replaced the book. Even if one discounted half of the American publisher's cheers, the residue spoke of a triumph. And though Mr. Bruno had enjoyed this fine fame for fifteen years, there were still times when it seemed too good to be true, and he wondered if it were a dream from which he would wake up to find himself an unrecognized aspirant of forty, bombarding publishers but abandoning hope.

But no; he had been successful from the beginning. He had been carried to Harrow on a brilliant scholarship from one of the cheaper preparatory schools; and there his master had said, as he entered his name :

"' T. Tenter Bruno !' Good lord, what a name ! With a name like that you ought to go in for being a literary pundit or something. I mean, it inspires confidence, Bruno; and once heard is not easily forgotten. I mean, it sticks and festers in the memory like a poisoned dart. With a name like that, and a few eccentricities like Byron's curl, and a modicum of natural gifts, which apparently you possess, why, Bruno, you might go far."

The End of the Long Prologue

Young Bruno thought the same. Every talent he possessed he built into the genius of a great critic, essayist and philosopher. A famous university prize brought his name before the world of letters. For a few years he was assistant editor of a critical journal. Every spring he published a volume, and each volume made ripples wider than the last, till he was in a position so secure that he needed not to call any editor master, but could retire to his study and write what books and articles he pleased.

On the whole, then, he was satisfied. Occasionally he would have liked to live with a larger flourish, instead of in a small country house with one old servant and an undermaid. And he could have done so if two tyrant weaknesses had not always quashed the impulse—the one a timidity that dreaded a failing wit and its consequence, a falling revenue, and the other a settled indolence which made him prefer studying in an arm-chair to creating at his desk.

A tray of tea-things clattered outside, and he walked rather quickly back to his chair. Why he did this he hardly knew; perhaps because he wanted Hollins to tell the maid that he had never stirred all the afternoon. And as he sat down, he rebuked himself for the thought; it was contemptible to expose his anxiety for the study of his servants, like an interesting specimen on a pin.

He heard the corner of the tray rested against the jamb of the door, while Hollins freed one hand to turn the knob.

"There you are, sir. I've made it nice and strong."—His brain instantly provided her with her next words: "It *do* put new life in you, a cuppa-tea."—"It *do* put new life in you, as I always say myself," continued Hollins. "And I should be inclined to kind of eat something. I've boiled you an egg in case it should take your fancy."

"Thank you, Hollins, thank you." His manner with his servants and their devotion were a pride with him.

The thought of the egg was appetizing; and he ate and enjoyed it so much that he wished it had been two. The tea raised his optimism and expelled his anxiety.

"Everything'll be all right with little Sheila, of course. It's no use picturing the worst. I'll read."

He pushed the tray to one side, and from a little bookstand on the desk took a new volume. It quickly interested

5

him. Only the tiring of his eyes, as the room darkened with the fall of a February evening, told him how the hours were passing. Outside in the passage an opal-glass lampshade jingled on its stand, and a moving ribbon of light appeared beneath the door. It would be Hollins bringing a light.

As she entered and rested the lamp on his desk, he felt rather guilty to be reading, but refused, this time, to hide the fact. She drew the curtains, and went out, taking the tray with her. Mr. Bruno turned again to his volume. It stimulated him sufficiently to demand pencilled annotations, and he was lost in this task when a bell gongled alarm through the house. His heart jumped; and the bell, repeating itself, jarred his nerves.

Voices in the hall: "Bruno?"

"Yes."

The telegram, beyond a doubt.

Hollins entered, as delighted and funereal as every one is who carries a telegram. With fingers that fumbled, Mr. Bruno opened the envelope.

"Daughter. Wife doing splendidly."

His eyebrows went up. "A daughter. H'm!" But his momentary disappointment was lost in an uprushing, swelling tenderness. In a voice, not under perfect control, he said to Hollins:

"Yes, yes. . . . Oh, an answer? . . . No, no answer. I shall be there as quickly myself."

"Yes, sir." Hollins went out to the messenger, but her excitement was like a stretching elastic that drew her immediately back to her master's study. "Yes, sir, I've told the boy; and is there——"

"Oh, Hollins, Mr. Spencer told me he would lend me his trap, if I needed it. You might go—or send Agnes round and ask for it. Old Eadigo's there, and will bring it."

"Yes, sir. And may I—what I mean to say is—is everything all right?"

"Yes, magnificent, Hollins." Stirred by excitement, Mr. Bruno forgot that he ever postured, or that he had felt a second's disappointment at the sex of his child. "I've got a daughter."

"Well, there now!" said Hollins. "A little daughter. I do congratulate you, sir. The noos has just come, has it?

The End of the Long Prologue

And I shall always be able to remember that I brought you the noos. I shall be able to tell her that. And it's a little baby girl, is it? I like a little girl for the first one."

She moved towards the door, but her master wanted to continue talking.

"Yes, a girl. What shall we call her, Hollins?"

"Well, sir, that'll sort of take some thinking about, won't it? Will you call her after her mother, sir?"

"No, that's shirking trouble. Something original, I think."

"Yes," agreed Hollins vaguely, for the elastic was pulling towards the kitchen now. "I'll just go and—and send Agnes for that trap. I'll be back in a minute."

The kitchen of this country house was only a dozen flag-stones away, and Hollins was soon back.

"What do you think of 'Daphne Deirdre Tenter Bruno,' Hollins?"

Hollins tried to look intelligent and pleased; and Mr. Bruno explained more slowly: "Daphne—Deirdre"; and his smile widened.

"Well, yes, sir, those sound very nice. But I expect the mistress'll have her ideas. . . . I'll get your hat and coat."

Mr. Bruno walked up and down, repeating:

"Daphne Deirdre Tenter Bruno. . . . Daphne Bruno."

He was in the power of that up-swelling tenderness. His mind, ever penetrating and introspective, could examine that tenderness and see that, whether or not it were soiled by time, at the moment it was utterly selfless, and charged with reverence and humility. "She's no one but me"; the thoughts were running; "Good lord, I wish I were better. . . . My influence will be immeasurable. . . . She must be good . . . It's unthinkable that she should be bad. . . ." With a heart filling and filling from the reservoir of these thoughts, he pictured her at every age: one year old and crawling about the floor; three or five, and scrambling over his knees; seven or eight, and playing with a spade on holi-day sands; in her school when he came to visit her; a long slim girl of sixteen, slim like the plait down her back; a bride in white and silver.

7

Daphne Bruno

II

WRAPPED in a thick overcoat, muffler and driving gloves, he walked impatiently up and down the study, now and then clapping his gloved hands. Like all men who could drive well, and yet could not afford a horse, he always felt rather proud when dressed for the box seat and waiting for the reins.

"Curse that old Eadigo! Why can't he hurry? Phlegmatic old fool! Hollins has no doubt told him the news with an indecent exuberance, and if he had the imagination of one of his turnips, he'd guess what I'm feeling."

At the sound of wheels on the drive and of a voice gibbering to a pony, he glanced out of the window and, in the light thrown by the open hall door, saw Eadigo standing near the horse's head. Eadigo was Mr. Spencer's gardener, who came for two days a week to work on Mr. Bruno's much smaller plot. Mr. Bruno, looking out at him with the detached amusement of a critic, saw a large, corpulent man in a blue serge waistcoat and trousers that had once been Mr. Spencer's. These trousers, enabled by some triangular insertions of Mrs. Eadigo's to surround her husband's paunch, stayed there, as the open waistcoat showed, without aid from braces or belt: palpably they needed none, being less likely to fall than to fissure.

Eadigo, who never dreamed of taking an uncovered head into the air—not through fear of catching cold, but simply because the two ideas of open air and a hat were inseparable —was wearing a soiled felt hat discarded and given to him by Mr. Bruno three years before. It was too small; and perhaps to give it an appearance of being larger, the brim was turned down all round. Mr. Bruno could see the sweat-stains round the faded ribbon, and remembered how God had promised such things to Adam in a garden. He heard Hollins bustle out to Eadigo and say:

"Well, you *have* been a time! The master's in a hurry. Naturally."

And the even voice of the gardener returned:

"It's ready for 'e. 'E can have it anywhen now."

Without waiting for Hollins, Mr. Bruno walked out and mounted to the seat and took the reins.

The End of the Long Prologue

"Lamps all right, Eadigo?"

"Yessir."

"Well, get away, Nipper."

The horse, fresh from little use, clattered out of the open gate on to the country road. It was the last moments before the final darkness, and the stars were in possession. On one side of the road the tall beeches, looking more slender and tapering than in the daylight, stretched their bared branches like long tenuous arms towards the sky. On the other side a line of Austrian firs, marking a private park, stood dense and black against a sea-green glow. The road ran along high ground; and as it left these skirting trees, Mr. Bruno overlooked the waving weald of Sussex. The sea-green glow sank in the west, and its answering light in the east; and now the candle-lamps of the trap shone at their prime. The monotonous clatter of Nipper charmed Mr. Bruno into a reverie.

It was picturesque, this driving to find his baby girl. But though the drama of it pleased him, he knew that this was but a small part of his emotion. That tenderness and excitement was crowding into a corner all lesser thoughts. He examined it again, happy about it. "Daphne Bruno." A little girl . . . then a slip of a school-miss, satchelled . . . seventeen years, and a tall, affectionate sapling, with her own concealed emotions . . . a lover in the embrace of some long youth—his heart beat quicker at the thought of this—and then, a bride—from which point he cared not to carry on the pictures. And she was born from him; she was out of him.

By God! he must do his part by her. Humbly, Mr. Bruno, as he flicked the pony, felt that he was being lifted to a moment of nobility. With a grim smile he wondered if it would last.

"*Clop*-clip, *clop*-clip, *clop*-clip." Nipper's hoofs, in the darkness, knocked a spark from a flint. Mr. Bruno, in his waking dream, touched the beast again.

All his books were written from one view-point: that of a detached mocking at convention. They proclaimed the right of the artist to accept nothing on authority, either in religion or in art, but to build his own authority out of his own experience. With the rest of the thinking world (as it appeared to him) in that latter half of the century, he had rejected Christianity; with many artists, though he was proud to be unplaceable in any school, he had questioned the accepted canons of art. This mocking viewpoint he had kept consistent. His readers might believe that behind it was a philosophy of his own. They might believe that he spoke from some sure though hidden ground; that he at least had found a code by which to live, and thus achieved his integrity. And indeed, some of his followers had written articles on "The True Philosophy of Tenter Bruno."

But Mr. Bruno, driving to his daughter, knew that he had achieved no such thing. He felt dissatisfied with his management of life. He was vain, thought he, and indolent and selfish; and when all brilliant theories were puffed away, he knew that he had an unconquerable conviction that vanity, indolence and selfishness were wrong. And there was a corruptive falsity, his keen mind told him, in his whole position; for, while intellectually a revolutionary, he had no courage to be a libertine; he wrote it all from his brain, while his will allowed his life to drift conventionally enough. If only he had really found a sure code, that he might give it to this little girl—or, rather, to that long, slim girl, slim as the plait down her back! . . . She would have brains.

"I should like to vow that henceforth there's to be one good thing in my life : my self-effacing service of her." The shoulders of the sceptic shrugged in distrust of himself.

With tenderness, too, he thought of his wife; and his head shook regretfully. Poor little Sheila, she hadn't had much of a time. He saw her as she was at their first meeting : a little fair-haired thing of twenty, beautifully frail, eighteen years younger than he. He studied how he had come to marry her. All his life he had waited in the hope that he would fall in love with someone, but the monopolizing love of his own books had kept other loves out of doors. Still, the one last sentimentality had persisted in him, this hope that love would arrive and last for ever. Then came this exquisite little creature (as his fancy had seen her), bringing a manifest adoration—and the thought of possessing her had been sweet. How delighted she had been with the attentions of so famous a man ! In her feebleness she had rather thrown herself at him. He had begun to wonder if he was in love with her, and had given answer: "Yes, since I am nearly forty, if this be not love, no other will come." So they had become engaged. And though before marriage he had discovered the poverty of her mind, he had lacked the strength to withdraw—and the cruelty. Chaffingly surrounding her with a haze of adjectives, "frail," "fay," "gossamer," "little Thistledown," he had kept his promise and married her.

"She's mindless . . . little . . . weak . . . cowardly," muttered he to the horse's crupper.

It had hurt his pride that he had given himself to one intellectually so far beneath him. Self-pityingly he would remember the wives of other famous men, whose gifts had largely made their husbands what they were. Poor little Sheila. And now she mooned rather dully about his cottage. Doubtless her illusions had been as short-lived as his. Henceforward all must be different. He, as well as she—hang it all!—had undertaken duties in marriage. . . . And he was the stronger and wiser.

Pity for her filled him.

Pity. The word was the bell-note for all the emotion in him to-night. Perhaps it was the key-word to a philosophy. One could not know much in this dark and candle-lit world, but one could hang on to pity. One could wander at will in search of other secrets about religion and art, but one must keep tight hold of pity.

"What pity ordains is right; what pity condemns is wrong. . . . When all's said and written and done, every-thing in me knows that much to be true. . . ." He saw the long, slim Daphne again. "I shall teach her that, if nothing else."

Relief came to Mr. Tenter Bruno, for this idea had a face as of revelation. And the cynic in him laughed that he should have suddenly seen a newness in anything so old. Old! Ghosts of old philosophers began to do battle in the grey lists of his mind for the principle of man's inherent benevolence—Hobbes and Jeremy Bentham, Hartley and Paley, Shaftesbury and Hutcheson and Hume.

"*Clop*-clip, *clop*-clip, *clop*-clip." He was hearing Nipper's hoofs again.

And then a horrid thought leapt up. Supposing this Daphne were deformed in any way; supposing she were an imbecile; or blind; or deaf and dumb; or had some freakish limb! Supposing the Christian God had punished his sedition like that! The telegram had only said: "Daughter. Wife doing splendidly." Not "Both doing splendidly." Good God, not *"both"*! He pictured the news being broken to him before he was taken to see her.

"Nonsense!" He pulled himself together, and urged the horse to a canter. "She'll be beautiful, because her mother's beautiful; and she'll have brains."

III

WHILE Hollins was bringing tea to her master, before the bell jangled through the house, Sheila Bruno was lying back on her bed suffering her final pains. A nurse watched her as they waited for the doctor. The nurse, seeing many such month by month, was not easily moved, but her patient of to-day seemed like a child who was bearing too early; and, even in her suffering, she held her beauty. Her hair, very fair, was of the fuzzier sort that looked as pleasant when tumbled as when tidy, and her lids were down over childish cheeks in an abandonment to pain that was almost calm.

Sheila Bruno's eyes were closed because she had no interest in the world beyond her racked body. Pain filled her mind, leaving room for no altruistic thought. All that she wanted was to die and be done with pain. She could not care that it left her husband deserted and her baby motherless; she could not think for them. Somewhere in her pain-filled thoughts she felt ashamed that it should be so. Labours! Maternity! Why, she could still only think of herself as a fifteen-year-old schoolgirl, punishable by mistresses; she felt no different in mind or body from what she was at fifteen.

Somewhere lurked shame and despair of herself. From the beginning her thoughts about this baby had caused her secret shame. Instead of being delighted at the prospect of its coming—as were all the good wives she had read about, and as she pretended to be—she had only been frightened, exasperated and rebellious. She had made the futile effort

12

to think of it prettily as her husband's child, and to love it and him the more; but in her months of sickness and disfigurement this thought had actually worked an opposite result. It had encouraged criticism and dislike of him. There had come to the surface of her mind thoughts that hitherto she had kept submerged. He had marred her life by marrying her—that was the unveiled truth of it. Almost she might say he had tricked her. He had seemed so wonderful—with his brilliance, his tall and graceful presence and his courtesy. And she had paid out everything for the prize, her whole future and the right to love again. Then in a few months he had cast off all ceremonial vesture, probably because its wearing was too much of an effort.

Oh, life was a roomful of pain. If only she could die! What matter if it were cowardice? Let her admit her feebleness and die. Once she was blotted out in death, her self-contempt would not worry her.

Oh, this miserable, hard, business-like room in the nursing home! Even her death would be a failure in a white box of a room like this. Why had she come here? It was wrong of Tom to send her. Of course, she had wanted to come, so as to go through an experience that she expected might defeat her courage, away from her husband and servants. But just now she chose to forget her willingness in order that she might keep her grievance against Tom. Why had he sent her here? It was a thing seldom done. Despite all his talk about her greater comfort, the greater facilities available, and their isolation in the country, she suspected that the contemplation of his own ease had not been absent, nor a satisfaction in the unconventionality of such a step.

"I think I hate him."

And since she hated him, she had better die, for there was nothing before her except a long life of dull exasperation. She was a failure. Best admit it, and go upon the scrap-heap.

Oh, this pain! And this underground stream of aching thoughts that kept appearing above the surface! Sometimes sharper agonies made her abandon thinking and only suffer. Voices far away and yet near by reminded her of nursery days.

A crowning, unbelievable agony. . . . And then peace—

lovely liberation and forgetful rest. This was the beginning of death, sweet like drowning. The voices were still about her, and there was a new voice, a crying voice like a baby's. Sheila's heart stirred, as she had always read it would : it must be the voice of her child, the thing dragged from her and now living its own independent life. She who had been *one* a few minutes ago was now two. That other one was she—and alone now, poor lonely little darling. Her consciousness cleared, and, wondering with a thrilled anticipation if it were a boy or a girl, she opened her eyes and saw the nurse by her bed.

"Splendid, dear, you were splendid; and you've got a little daughter."

A disappointment at the word "daughter" was rolled aside by an out-stream of love and excitement. And her relief from agony made her feel gay. She stared up at the nurse with an unintelligent smile, wondering what they did next.

The nurse was leaning a bundle forward to show her something in its cowl-like opening : a tiny model of a human face, complete with smooth brow, eyelashes, nose, and lips and chin. It was placid now, with its eyelids down. She looked at it for a long time, riveted; and at length, without a word, shut her eyes. . . . Oh, the adorable, incredible little thing ! It brought a recurring glow, the recollection of that little face. Sheila felt exultant—perhaps hysterically so, for she was ready to pour out a mixture of crying and laughter. The pain, now that it had receded into memory, seemed nothing so very terrible after all, and she wondered why people made such a fuss about it.

Downstairs the hall door closed. Ah, the matron was sending to Tom. How delightful to have this news to send him ! An hour ago she had thought she hated him, and here was she imagining delight at his excitement ! She began to enwrap him with her tenderness. After all, perhaps he had as much to criticize in her as she had in him. In some ways she had tricked him too. Had she not used every art to appear before him as beautiful? Had she not tried to appear more cultured than she was? Had she not often lied—that was what it amounted to—in representing her education as much finer than it had been, and her circle of friends as much more impressive? After marriage, Tom, with his penetration, must quickly have found her out. She wondered that he had not done so before. Yes, he had claims on her which she had disappointed : henceforth she must always remember that.

She imagined all that was happening in the cottage. Hollins, dear, stout old Hollins, how full she would be of the news ! And Tom, of course, was getting the trap from Mr. Spencer's. In less than half an hour he would be here. She saw him mounting to the driver's seat, and clattering out of the gate along the country road. She saw the trap moving through the daylight, till, noticing that her gas had been lit and curtains drawn, she changed the picture into a night scene. There came the yellow candle-lamps, and Nipper tossing up his head as he trotted over the ringing road. Now Tom had probably reached Shadwell Green and was driving along the mossy, listing wall of The Ballards. That would mean that he would be here in less than ten minutes.

A short, timid ring at the front door set excitement a-tremble. Yes, that was Tom's voice, rather stuttering and nervous. And here was the matron bringing him upstairs. The door opened, and Sheila turned her head towards it.

"Hallo, dear."

"Sheila, darling ! Why, you look rosy. One'd think you were resting after a tennis match."

She parried this with a smile and glanced towards the cot at the fire.

"There it is."

Mr. Bruno carried to the cot his fear that there might be something amiss. The thought, "One second now, and I shall know," accompanied his steps. But no hare-lip or fingerless hand met his eyes : instead he saw the sleeping face, turned on its side, with its perfect little nose and chin, dropped lids and exquisite ear. One hand showed above the blanket, palm downward.

It broke one's breath.

Sheila was speaking. "Isn't she like you. And I'm sure she'll grow up and adore you much more than she will me. Girls always do."

A quick vision of the long, slim Daphne stirred his heart. He bent down to study the features again, trying to imagine them fifteen—nineteen years hence.

Daphne Bruno

IV

WHEN Daphne was brought to her father's door, Hollins received her with the expected magnificat.

"Now let *me* take her, ma'am. The love! You must be tired, and you must go sort of—what I call—easy. Let *me* take her. . . . Well, there's a beauty. O ma'am, she's a cherub! And ain't she the living image of you?"

"Don't be absurd," corrected Mrs. Bruno, as she passed into the cottage. "Why, I'm seeing more and more likeness to her father every day."

"Well, yes." Hollins touched the little face with an ingratiating giggle. "She is like the master, but she favours you too, ma'am. Oh, yes, you favour your mummy, miss, don't you? Oh, what big wondering eyes!"

Mrs. Hollins, being a widow and the mother of an only child who died young, was determined by right of this experience to take a leading part in the management of her mistress's little girl. She felt as if at last she had come into her own. Very deliberately had she taken the purchase of nursery equipment out of the incompetent hands of her master and mistress.

The best of her purchases was the princely perambulator in which young Mrs. Bruno took her daughter for a ride the following day. As she pushed the carriage towards the garden-gate, half nervous of taking this public confession of her motherhood into the highways, and half proud, she saw Eadigo stooping over a flower-bed. His waistcoat, as usual, hung open; and on his crown was the hat, a small and greasy derelict, that she could remember being often raised from her husband's head in the days of their courtship. Her heart absurdly quickened with anticipation of his comment. The sound of the perambulator on the gravel caused him to look up, and he touched his cap and turned to his bed.

Sheila paused. Their gardener was a person she liked to chaff, and it was not to be suffered that he should say no word on such an occasion. No matter if he did think this appearance of a baby in the world as of the same order, and no more interesting than the appearance above ground of one of his onions.

"Well, Eadigo," said she, stopping the perambulator,

and holding it with one hand while she stood sideways and faced the flower-bed. She was conscious, as she naturally assumed this position, that she was pleasurably imitating all her sisters of the perambulator. "Don't you want to see my little girl?"

He glanced up again and straightened himself.

"Yes, mum."

"Well, there she is."

Eadigo looked into the carriage and said:

"Yes, mum, she be there right enough."

"Think she's nice?"

Eadigo turned back to his bed.

"Well, mum, it's early yet."

"I suppose so," agreed Mrs. Bruno, pushing the pram on. "And she'll improve as she gets bigger."

Daphne's improvements, her father used to declare, were chiefly physical. She improved herself out of long clothes into short ones, and out of her wicker cradle into a fine cot, and out of her shoes and socks twenty times a day. She improved her squinting into a straight if rather doubtful stare. She improved her early screaming into gurgling and chuckling, which her father maintained was the greatest improvement of all.

Generally these remarks were made at meal-times when Daphne, or "Duffy," as he now called her, was at play upon the floor. He liked to watch her and to offer a witty and polished commentary; or sometimes just a crudely humorous one, since it was only for the home and not for publication. As Daphne was always busy and restless, and always anxious to do another thing than she happened to be doing at the moment, Mr. Bruno would enter the dining-room and inquire of Sheila, "Is it one of your daughter's busy days to-day?" or express the hope that Mrs. Bruno's daughter had got on well with her work that morning. And Sheila, stirred by the picture of Daphne these words created, would reply no more brightly than to ejaculate, "The darling!"

But this persiflage was a veil for things unspoken. He had not forgotten his desire to introduce *one* self-effacing love into his life. And he gave the love its exercise by forcing himself to be patient when Daphne's restlessness bruised his nerves or shipwrecked his work. He kept, too, his heightened love for his wife. She was a brave little girl. He had kissed her very affectionately when she declared that she would nurse Daphne herself and that Hollins and she would do everything: "Yes, I never meant to do it, daddy, but I've made up my mind to. Hollins says it's the only way to give them a proper start. And she's so adorable." He tried to be a better companion to his wife by coming in to her tea parties and sitting through the insupportably fatuous conversation of the ladies. Oh, *mon Dieu!* it seemed that women spoke never of ideas but only of things and persons; or if they did enunciate an idea, it was always a stock one off the shelf, and he could provide them with the very words they would use.

But in time he decided that too much self-abnegation, if you dealt with weak women, was itself a weakness. They were allowing Daphne to make an infernal noise in any and every room of the cottage. As sure as she cried they stampeded past his study door to save or sympathize with the child. And the more they sympathized with her, the more she sympathized with herself and determined that her present trouble was a case for regular refills of air which must be expelled again in shrieks of temper. The household, in fact, was circling round Daphne instead of round his workroom which (they all seemed to have forgotten) was the mainspring of everything. Yes, when his daughter should reach intelligence, then would be the time for him to consider how he could efface himself for her. Meantime he *must* get on with his work.

He summoned his wife, and explained that he was considering everybody else as much as himself when he stipulated that Daphne should be kept to an upstairs back room. For such brain-work as his he needed silence and freedom from domestic cares. Sheila could see that, could she not? "Rousseau, with more courage than most of us, sent his children to a foundling hospital when they interfered with his work. You remember: *'Comment les soucis domestiques et les tracas des enfants me laisseront-ils la tranquillité d'esprit nécessaire pour faire un travail lucratif?'* "

And Sheila said, "All right, Daddy."

Sometimes in the next weeks, however, the thought of the

The End of the Long Prologue

old lumber-room, which Sheila had cleared and furnished for a nursery, with its two easy chairs, one for herself and one for Hollins, troubled his compassion; and he would leave his books and climb up to it, saying he had come to see Daphne in her bath. Once Hollins had taken over the bathing, and he could see that the good soul was determined to show them how such a business should be performed. Listening, as she rhapsodized over the infant in her wide, aproned lap, he thought many thoughts about the native poetry of all peasants, from the Hebrews of old to the Cockneys or the Hodges of to-day. And he called her runnel of nonsense "The Song of Hollins."

"They didn't give you much hair, did they, darling," she was saying, as the upper frock went over Daphne's head. "No, she said, I'm going to spend all my money on a big pair of eyes. She said, I don't reckon hair is very important, or a nose. As regards them things, I'll just have any fairly decent reach-me-downs out of the cupboard, but I shall spend all my money on a very extra special pair of eyes. She said, eyes are the thing. You can do a lot of damage with a good pair of eyes. You can break the hearts of the handsome young beaus and—keep still, lovey—and, until they come along, you can see all that ought to be seen and most that ought not to be seen, and, she said, you can see every opening for mischief. There now. There's a boo'ful little body. Into tub it goes. *In* she goes. Nice waters. Oh, lovely waters. Oh, such a lovely silky skin. That's right, splash your walkers about. Kickey walkers. Up she comes, all clean and smelling of soap. Such a 'licious feeling! Big, big towel. There's a little, round, hobgoblin face, out of miles and miles of nice soft warm towel. Look at its chin. No, she said, you've got it wrong. I kep' a little of my money back for a really dainty chin. Gr-r-r-r! She said, Oh, I am a cute one, I am. When the time comes, won't I flutter the hearts of the handsome young mashers? I knew a thing or two, I did."

By this time Daphne was in her long flannel nightgown, and stretched out both hands with spread fingers towards her mother, who, captured by such an appeal, picked her up, tossed her towards the ceiling, and then hugged her, murmuring:

"Oh, she says, I like Hollins all right, and I find my daddy quite amusing, but it's mummy I really want. She says, I'd sell 'em all up for my mummy."

But now Mr. Bruno had wearied of these sentimental rhapsodies, and withdrew downstairs.

V

WHEN Daphne was something over a year old, Sheila knew that her second baby was coming. The knowledge was a shock of dismay, and then a sickly, dull acquiescence. Though at the first sight of Daphne all hostility had surrendered, still her picture of the future had shown only this one child playing about her. The picture of herself with two, or perhaps a flock of children, was horrible. Before telling her husband, she went away like a hurt animal into her bedroom and sat by the window, staring out at the garden.

"I don't want it. Oh, all that sickness again and ugliness and shame. And I shall have to begin nursing all over again. Oh, I know all this is selfish, and I ought to be delighted, but I'm not. I *am* selfish. I like my little Daphne, but I don't want another. Daphne was different; she was the first, and strange, and adorable."

Into the despair rose the thoughts that she usually shut underground. It was all wrong, children issuing from a partnership that she knew to be nine parts bankruptcy and disappointment. There was no true intimacy between her and Tom, and never could be. And Tom had quite obviously learnt this, and accepted it as their incommutable sentence. An incommutable sentence! Life stretched dark in front of Sheila, and the word "death" had trancing, sweet overtones again.

"I thought marriage was going to be heaven. . . . And it's—it's this. . . . But no. My Daphne was worth it.

"For Daphne's sake I'll try and bear this new cross." She found a refuge in these suburbs of nobility. "They say it's bad for a child to be an only child. They're much better off, if they have a brother or a sister for a companion. . . . I'll look at it like that. I'm providing something that's really good for my baby—a playmate. I made

20

up my mind to be unselfish where she was concerned. . . . All right, my darling, you shall have your playmate."

Overcome with her own self-sacrifice, she burst into tears.

As the time of her confinement drew nearer, she concealed under a mask of quiet liveliness a premonition of death. How this idea arose she could not remember, nor when; but it was now the unsleeping master of her mind. Perhaps it was born from her languor—a languor that grew till she lived with a sense of physical decline. Once she hinted at her fears to Hollins, who laughed the laugh of common sense.

"Nonsense, ma'am, if you'll excuse me putting it like that. You'll hardly feel it this time. It'll come as natural as natural. And each time it'll seem more and more natural."

"But people *do* die in childbirth," submitted Sheila. "One reads of heaps."

"Not young ones like you, ma'am, if I may say so."

"Isn't it sometimes the young ones who are most likely to die?"

"No, no—you're a bit sort of—what I call—down, ma'am. You put all those ideas out of your head."

"But I never was strong. When I was ill as a child, I was always worse than anyone else."

"And they're always the wiry ones, that sort of anæmic, skinny type," assured Hollins. "Anyone'll tell you that."

Nevertheless the idea stayed, strengthening its hold. In the hours before sleep, when the mind was susceptible to auto-hypnotism, it sent its roots deeper and deeper. In the daytime it haunted the background of all her thoughts and conversations. So fixed was it that she determined to have her confinement in her own house rather than die in a distant, hard, unloving room, with Daphne far away.

She was walking in the garden when this thought wandered into her mind; and she stopped dead as she faced another thought that came behind: Daphne would never remember her.

She shrugged her shoulders and closed the lips that had parted. Her mouth quivered. Old Hollins would have to tell Daphne when she grew up what her mother had been like.

These twilight thoughts she never exposed to Tom's

kindly ridicule. She only told Hollins gaily that this time she was going to stay in her own home. And Hollins heartily approved.

"Of course, ma'am, since you mention it, I may say I never did like the idea of your going away last time. It seemed out of—I mean, sort of unnatural like. If I couldn't have looked after you, who could, I should like to know? You'll enjoy it in your own room."

Merrily Sheila smiled in answer, though to herself the smile felt wan. The conviction that her life had been given its term was in complete occupation.

Complete. She would wander along the garden or the country roads, and any stretching green prospect that troubled her with its beauty stirred also the sad self-pity. The half-heard chirrup of the birds in the deathly slumber of a windless day; the red glow after tea-time behind the fir trees; the sound, one autumn evening, of a crowd of men singing in harmony as they went down the road; the tales in her books of the raptures of first love—it was a wistful matter suddenly to apprehend the beauty of these things and to feel that she had only a few more weeks with the world.

She felt the same faint ache when she patted the sleek neck of the pony, Nipper, or saw on a shelf in her bedroom the books that she had brought from home. They reminded her of a hundred places where as a child she had been merry. Strange if all those scenes had only preceded an early death! And if she chaffed old Eadigo as he laboured in the garden, she felt the ache in her spurious laughter. Once the sight of her own face in the mirror, looking pretty with its fair hair, filled her eyes with tears; but she pulled herself briskly together and forced laughter from herself all that morning. No one but she detected the settled despair in that noisy laughter.

Perhaps the most poignant thing of all was the sight of Daphne's toys upon the floor.

VI

MR. BRUNO this time felt none of the fears that had disorganized him before the birth of Daphne. He remembered with something of contempt the way he had then worked himself up to the proper anxiety. His main trouble now was an annoyance that another child should have come so soon, but this was balanced by a pride in remembering how he had shrugged his shoulders and decided to greet the inevitable with goodwill.

When Sheila took to her bed he kissed her very lovingly and told her everything would be all right. And when the hour came, and the doctor and the nurse were with her, he walked into the garden, taking only an anxiety that poor little Sheila should not suffer too much. Her moans hurt him cruelly.

The year was one month older than when Daphne was born. The primroses were under the hedges, and young grass appearing in many places where it ought not to appear, and the old grass turning to a deep green after humid March days. His tea had just been cleared away, and there was the usual silence of half-light in the garden : a thundery stillness, this evening, and the birds, chirruping on the branches, seemed less to break it than to be part of it. As he walked along the herbaceous border, now and then removing a gravel stone from the turf edge, a sudden cry of pain sounded from the house. He stood up erect and listened. The cry dwindled back into moans again, and above the moans sounded the plaint of a baby. It was not Daphne's voice. He hurried excitedly back to the hall to hear the news. As he expected, Hollins was coming down the stairs as fast as her figure would allow her.

"It's a little boy this time, sir."

"Oh, good—good! How's the mistress?"

"She's low, sir, distinctly low. But that's nothing, sir. They sometimes take it badly like that. I'll nip back and see if you can come in and see her."

Hollins climbed up the stairs, while Mr. Bruno waited in the hall. He heard a man's step, evidently the doctor's, leave his wife's room and come along the passage, so that he met Hollins at the top of the stairs. There was a murmured colloquy, voices pitched very low, as if in reverence for suffering. Then Hollins came more slowly and rather timidly down to her master.

"The doctor says the mistress is very sadly, sir. But I shouldn't worry, or the like of that," faltered Hollins. "They're often sadly."

He did not listen to her, but ran up the stairs. The doctor barred his way. He was an old man, and seemed as perplexed and dismayed as Hollins.

"Just a minute, Mr. Bruno. I—er—can't understand it. Your wife seems—there's no fever—her pains were very bad, of course, but I thought that was due to muscular strength—but she seems to be sinking. It looks like collapse."

Mr. Bruno tried to push past him. A sob was in his throat, and his mind was overborne with self-reproaches— for what he hardly knew.

"The boy's perfect—quite perfect," said the doctor, by way of comfort.

Mr. Bruno had forgotten the child as he rushed into the bedroom and looked down upon his wife. Hollins followed with tear-stained cheeks.

Sheila lay in the last surrender to death. When he touched her hand she lifted her eyelids.

"I knew it would be like this, Daddy," she said.

He dropped on one knee by her side.

"My darling, it's all right. You're only weak and worn out, and feel depressed. To-morrow you'll be feeling splendid again. And such a beautiful boy, they tell me. See, down there by the fire. My darling, I'm so proud of him."

"That's right," smiled Sheila wanly. "But I knew it would happen like this. I knew all along, but I wouldn't tell you. Where's Hollins?"

Hollins, who had been behind, came forward, violently sobbing.

"Bless you, ma'am, don't you worry. You'll be all right. They're often took like this. I ought to know."

"Where's my baby?"

"In his little crib, ma'am, by the fire. Such a beautiful child. He's fallen asleep."

The nurse picked up the little bundle to bring it to her. Sheila lifted again her heavy lids.

"No, I meant Daphne. Bring my baby to me."

"Daphne's in bed. It's after six o'clock," began Hollins; but seeing the dying look on her mistress's face, she moved towards the nursery.

Sheila opened her eyes again.

24

-Is it so late? . . . Don't disturb her. . . . She mustn't
be disturbed. . . . It's bad for her to be disturbed.   She's
always slept an unbroken sleep at night right from the
start. Hasn't she, Hollins? . . . Let her sleep."

"Sheila! Sheila!" cried Mr. Bruno.

Behind he heard Hollins muttering to the doctor :

"She seemed to have sort of made up her mind—been
telling me things to tell the children when they're grown
up." The recollection of this broke up Hollins, and the
hearing of it made Mr. Bruno cry out :

"Sheila! Sheila! Don't go!"

His senses carried inappropriately to his brain the
sibilance of the birds in the branches, and voices over the
evening stillness of the fields, and some laughter of girls.

Sheila's eyes were closed. All the thoughts that had
kept her sad during the past months were in her mind
again, and her bewilderment at the failure of her life. "I
don't understand—I don't understand," she kept thinking.
"I can't understand." Then she remembered Daphne, and
this boy—what was his name? She would never know.
And that neither could have lived if it hadn't been for her.
There was some comfort in the thought—if God gave them
a good life. "O God, give them a good life." . . . "O
God, make them happy. . . ."

VII

MR. BRUNO'S first idea after the loss of his wife was to
leave the children and the house to the management of
Hollins and to retire into the solitude of his study.   Such
an attitude would best suit his grief, and had its picturesqueness. His grief, when he analysed it alone in his room,
seemed a pain of pity for little Sheila, mixed with remorse
for not having made her happier, rather than a sense of
irreparable loss.

But his sister, who had very kindly swept down upon
his cottage the day after Sheila's death, had other views
about the children. Belle Phillimore, the widow of a cavalry
officer, was twelve years older than her brother, and, in
his opinion, an unutterable fool. Her head could hold no ideas

except those provided by her dead colonel and the superannuated clergy and ignorant ladies of her circle.

"No, Tom, it won't do," she pronounced. "This Hollins is a good soul, I'm sure, but what little Daphne and her brother will want is a lady. For instance, look at the way Hollins talks. She misuses grammar like all those sort of people do."

Mr. Bruno nodded. "Yes, grammar is a ticklish business."

"Yes, children are always vulgarized by the society of servants. Besides, she's sure to be full of old superstitions and fill Daphne's head with them. Can Hollins teach the children their Bible and Catechism? Why, she probably doesn't understand them herself."

"You forget, Belle," interrupted Mr. Bruno, "or perhaps I should say that, being a sister and an elder sister, you naturally have never read the few poor books that I have written. . . . Or if you have read them in an idle curiosity, you have naturally not taken them seriously. But, as a matter of fact, I am quite serious in my inability to accept your Christianity."

"But, Tom! You surely wouldn't have a child brought up without religion?"

"I didn't say that. But I don't see why I should have a child brought up in what I believe to be error."

"Oh, but it's different for you. A child always goes to pieces if it isn't given some religion. *You're* a full-grown man with some cleverness."

The description did not please Mr. Bruno, and he told himself, "That's as much as a relative will ever allow." But this self-protecting thought was an intruder among others, and quickly lost. Standing by the window and staring out, he was really thinking of the afternoon Daphne was born and the night Sheila died.

"I should like them to have *some* religion," he said suddenly.

"Exactly. We must get some good Christian gentlewoman to manage the household and the children—that was what I was going to suggest. We'll advertise in a Church paper."

Mr. Bruno brought his eyes away from the window.

"I've just had an idea. Since these children went

through the whole course of evolution when they were in the womb "—Belle moved uncomfortably—"it may do them no harm to go through the Christian period as well. It may keep them fairly straight till they are developed enough to wander alone."

"Exactly. A sort of housekeeper-guardian. Your servants will obey her. They would never obey Hollins, one of their own number who'd been promoted. They never do. My poor Charlie used to say that the ranker officer had precious little control over his men; they preferred a gentleman any day."

"Oh, my God!" thought Mr. Bruno; and his reading chair called to him like a refuge.

"Well, look here, Belle," said he. "Is it too much to ask you to draw up the advertisement, and perhaps to stay here and keep an eye on the place till the proper person is engaged?"

His sister gave a ready nod. She would be only too pleased to do so, she said.

VIII

THESE were years before public libraries and reading-rooms were to be found in every borough. But in a suburb that was developing beyond the green fields of Hammersmith, one of the first of them had appeared, thanks to the munificence of a departed M.P. It was an oblong room with some tall lecterns for such daily newspapers as the *Times* and the *Standard* on one side of the gangway, and on the other long elm-wood tables for the reading of weekly journals which, when not in use, roosted in wire mangers on the walls. On the Friday after Mr. Bruno's conversation with his sister—Friday being the day the best religious papers appeared—a woman entered this reading-room and, walking as one who knew her purpose, glanced immediately at the rack where the *Warden* usually rested. She was tall and thin, and might have been thirty-five or forty years old. Thirty-five probably, the care-lines and the hint of hardness having come prematurely to a face that had once been soft and handsome. Her walk had the rectitude of a woman who defends her title to gentility by her manner, since her dress, though neat, can betray little but poverty. Her black skirt was frayed where it touched the ground, and the first finger of one black kid glove was split at the seam. As proof of her social grade, however, she wore a veil, or "fall," terminating just below her mouth. And she carried a neatly-folded umbrella and a reticule in which were visiting cards with the name (printed, not engraved) "*Miss Durgon.*"

She gave a little "St—! st—!" of annoyance when her glance at the wire shelf showed her that the *Warden* had been removed. She must see who was reading it, and make sure that she got it next. Walking among the tables, she found that it was being read by a middle-aged woman in a brown skirt and coat and a fur, all slightly decayed; and, as this woman had a stunted and bitten pencil in her right hand with which she was tracing down the "Situations Vacant," and in her left a soiled envelope on which she was noting addresses, it seemed probable that she would monopolize the journal for most of the morning. Miss Durgon said "St—! st—!" again. The calm way these people sat, as by right, over papers for which they had paid nothing! The ferrule of her umbrella beat impatiently on the ground, but without results. So, to intimate that she was waiting for the *Warden,* she sat down rather deliberately in the empty chair next the woman, and tapped out a resigned tattoo on the table-top. The woman with the pencil glanced round, and, resenting such a hint, slightly turned her back towards Miss Durgon. Her right to the paper she defended by being a little slower in her perusal and a little more deliberate in her noting of addresses. She thought it most annoying the way these women came and sat rudely beside you, as if they had some claim on a paper for which they had paid nothing.

Minutes passed, and Miss Durgon could only express her impatience by repeating her tattoo on the table-top, and occasionally consulting a large watch at her breast. Once another woman, a fat creature with a basket, came and stood by the person in possession, as if, in spite of Miss Durgon's long wait, she expected to have the paper next. Then Miss Durgon advanced her chair nearer to the *Warden,* rehearsing the words she would utter if the fat creature stepped in before her. But the fat woman, seeing she was forestalled, walked away with just such a "St—! st—!" as Miss Durgon's.

At last Miss Durgon's impatience compelled her to speak.

"You'd oblige me if you'd allow me to see this paper. I've waited fifteen minutes already."

The woman with the pencil turned towards her; and then without answering gave Miss Durgon her back again.

Miss Durgon's blood was up, and her hand went out to take the paper. But its possessor snatched it back and held it tight.

"If I were you, I should learn to speak the truth," said she, and pretended to be lost in the advertisements, though her stumpy pencil was trembling.

"Speak the truth!" snapped Miss Durgon. "What do you mean? . . . Insolence. . . . Perhaps I can find an attendant."

"Saying you've been waiting fifteen minutes when you've not been waiting five. You'll be saying you've been an hour next."

Miss Durgon tossed her head, and adjusted a brooch.

"I've no desire to speak to you. All I ask is that, when you've found your situation——"

"Situation yourself!" hissed the woman, deeply offended at this term. "If you want to do the highty-tighty, I should mend your glove."

And she resumed her perusal of the paper.

Miss Durgon scorned her, and trusted that the creature felt the scorn. The woman, however, finished her study and, to annoy this detestable creature beside her, turned to a column of "News from the Dioceses," and read them. Miss Durgon continued to enfilade her with contempt, and at length the woman got up and walked away.

Miss Durgon slid along to the vacated seat, and, opening her reticule with dignified calm, took out a thin silver pencil, somewhat bitten, and a penny note-book whose leaves were dog-eared. But she had hardly read two advertisements before the fat woman with the basket, who had appeared once before, came back to see if the paper were yet disengaged. Annoyed to find it occupied by a person who, to judge from her pencil and note-book, intended remaining for some time, she sat down in the seat

Miss Durgon had just left. This was too exasperating. Here she had only just secured the paper, and this fat sack of a woman came and seated herself menacingly beside her, as if to make her hasten. She would do nothing of the sort. If anything, she would travel over the advertisements with greater precision and an ostentatious calm. Nor should the fat woman's drummings or "Tut-tuts!" create any panic in her. So she jotted down the possible situations, none of which animated her much, till suddenly she read:

"WANTED, for a Widower's home. Lady Housekeeper, and Guardian to two very young children. Two servants (one as nurse). Governess later. Apply Tenter Bruno, Underwold, Francefield, Sussex."

So exactly did this suit Miss Durgon that she immediately felt confident that Destiny had led her to it this morning, and the post would undoubtedly be given her. She must hurry back and write at once. In her satisfaction she only handed the paper to the fat lady with a pleasant smile that made her think, as she walked away, how much more agreeable her manners were than those of the disgusting creature who had first held the paper. Tenter Bruno? Tenter Bruno? A familiar name. She had seen it in papers, and heard it in conversations. Could it be the well-known writer? She must find out. If it were, it would make the position doubly desirable. She foresaw herself studying the comfort and securing the quiet of a literary man, and becoming quite indispensable to him.

IX

WHEN Mr. Bruno's sister heard from Miss Durgon's lips, in the dining-room of the cottage, that she was the fifth daughter of an officer, she felt satisfied on all points. And with some pride, as though her labours had been extensive and exhausting, she came into her brother's study to announce her complete success.

"I think I've got the very person, Tom, the very person you need. An excellent person. First and foremost, she's a lady, the daughter of an officer. A good-looking woman, too. I've represented to her, Tom, that what she's got to do is to relieve you of all anxiety, whether it be about the children or the *ménage* of the house. She was most interested in your writing."

Mr. Bruno, who like all comfort-loving literary men was sanguine about everything except the sale of his books, was only too pleased to believe all his sister said.

"Excellent, Belle, excellent. I'm sure I'm very grateful to you. It *is* of paramount importance that I am left to the undisturbed pursuit of my writing and reading. The kindest thing I can do for the children is to go into my study and shut the door and work. But that I could never have done—at least, not with the necessary detachment"— Mr. Bruno seemed almost to be trying to reassure himself in a dubious abandonment to comfort—"unless I had your assurance that everything possible was being done for the children."

"Yes, I think you can be comfortable about that," interposed his sister. "She struck me as a lady in every respect."

Mr. Bruno, thinking, as usual, what a fool Belle was, merely replied :

"Well, I'm sure I can trust your judgment on *that* point, Belle. I feel very satisfied and relieved at this stroke of yours."

He was seeing long, quiet, self-sufficient days with his books, varied by an occasional kindly patronage of his children. He felt vaguely that Belle had accepted the responsibility of the choice, and called down any blood upon her own head. His clearer mind told him, in quickly closed moments, that he whose best works had tried to battle through to the secrets of life and art, had, in the matter of his children, been too indolent for thought.

X

THE resentment of Hollins at this promotion of "Miss Skin-and-Grief" to the place she had hoped to fill was given its airing before the young maid in the kitchen :

"I knew she was going to be awful. I went to the door myself, and she says, 'Does Mrs. Phillimore live here?' And I says, 'No, miss,' I said. 'This is Mr.

Bruno's house, but he's got his sister staying with him.'
'Well, can I see her?' she says tartly. I don't think
she liked the 'miss.' And I says, 'I'll see if she can see
you, miss.' I wasn't, so to speak, going to wave flags
in front of her. I said, 'What name, miss?' And she
says, 'Durgon.' So I went up and came down again, and
said, 'Yes, Miss Durgon, Mrs. Phillimore can see you
if you step this way.' She bridled up at the 'Miss Durgon,'
but said nothing, feeling, I suppose, that she hadn't sort
of secured her position. And, well, here she is, for good
and all, if you ask me; and I don't reckon she'll worship
the very ground I walk on."

"'Slike as not she'll get you the sack," suggested the
maid.

"'Slike as not she'll do nothing of the sort! The master
knows as how the mistress lef' me messages to tell the
children when they grow up, and for their sake he'll see
that I'm there when they're old enough to hear. No, Miss
Skin-and-Grief won't be able to come it over me. I'm
not afraid of her, and she needn't think it."

From the first, then, a skirmishing warfare existed between Hollins and Miss Durgon, with eye-darts for bullets
and word-stabs for bayonet thrusts. Hollins's sharpest pin
was to distinguish her from all other ladies to whom she
spoke by changing "Yes, ma'am," and "No, ma'am," into
"Yes, Miss Durgon" and "No, Miss Durgon."

This was exceedingly difficult to parry, and Miss Durgon
spoke to her employer about it.

Mr. Bruno was polite, as always, but inwardly annoyed
at this intrusion of a domestic question into the privacy
Belle had promised him. He h'med over some remark about
"a natural licence to an old servant," and then added,
with the smile of delicacy: "But all this is your sphere,
Miss Durgon; you must do what you think best. All I
ask is to be entirely free from these petty worries. Do
what you think best, only don't offend Hollins. My wife
thought a lot of Hollins."

Miss Durgon, whose sword-arm was always weakened
by her fear of losing the position, realized that she had
made a false step, and never again obtruded a domestic
question on Mr. Bruno.

PART I

LES TRACAS DES ENFANTS

PART I

LES TRACAS DES ENFANTS

CHAPTER I

DAPHNE'S earliest memories were of being awake in her cot while the daylight was still outside the blinds, though flushed with sunset. Downstairs were footsteps and closing doors and women's voices; and sometimes her father's voice, only this was so deep as to be but half heard. In another and smaller cot slept Owen, her baby brother, who often woke and cried for a minute and dropped off to sleep again. He frightened her a little when, after dark, he would suddenly climb through a crescendo from whimpering to crying, and crying to screaming; and she would be glad when Hollins came up and quieted him with a fruity and ingratiating, "Now, go to by-by like a good little boy," or picked him up and sang to him:

> Sonny go round the sun,
> Sonny go round the moon,
> Sonny go round the mulberry bush,
> On a Sunday afternoon——

though Daphne was always faintly worried by this equating of a mulberry bush with the sun and moon. If Miss Durgon came up instead, she was much more prosaic. She put Owen firmly on his other side, and added as she went out, to Daphne, who was sitting up, big-eyed, to watch the rearrangement of Owen:

"Now *you* go to sleep. We don't want nonsense from you too."

With the passing of time Daphne learnt that there were three stable people in her world: Hollins, round, and in a blue cotton uniform, chiefly associated with comfort and friendliness; Miss Durgon, long, black, and chiefly asso-

35

ciated with correction, church and manners; and her father, with a pointed beard. She conceived that fathers and beards went together, and was much surprised the first time she saw someone else's father who had not even a moustache. How he could be old enough to be a father was not clear.

Her father was a jolly person in the early morning before breakfast. At half-past seven she was allowed to go into his bedroom and to climb on to the eiderdown for the playing of a game called "When I say ' kipper.' " It consisted in Daphne's inventing a long story to which her father must listen carefully, because directly she worked in the dangerous word ' kipper ' he was to tickle her violently. Her shrieks of alarm, after uttering the word ' kipper,' always began before the tickling got really started, and her yells of laughter and screams for mercy generally rewarded Mr. Bruno's tickling campaign within thirty seconds of its inception. When Owen was old enough to play this game it was doubly exciting; for sometimes *he* would work in the dangerous word, and she, unprepared for it so soon, was caught and tickled till she rolled, screaming with hysterical laughter, off the bed to the floor.

Some mornings she woke very early, and knew she would not go to sleep again, because it was daylight; and then her games had to be silent, for it was an offence to wake Owen; so she would use her knee or her foot to lift the bedclothes into a tent and sprawl about under them, divided in her mind whether they formed an Indian's wigwam or a Commander-in-Chief's headquarters. Wearying of this, she would lie on her back and with her knees form the white quilt into a range of mountains. There were Alpine pathways up the folds, and if she half-closed her eyes she could see the St. Bernard dogs and the pious monks as they looked for dead men in the snowdrifts.

Hollins was a good person when she told them tales, but her nursery rhymes struck Daphne from the first as rather silly. Cows couldn't jump over moons, nor dishes run away with spoons. And "Old Mother Hubbard," which told of an old woman going to the larder to get a bone for her dog and finding the place empty: vaguely Daphne felt that as a story it led to nothing, and certainly wasn't worth making a song about. Nor could she see that little Jack

Horner's remark, "What a good boy am I!" had any sense or sequence. Though in courtesy she applauded Hollins for her frequent rendering of these poems, she felt uncomfortably that the pleasant old servant was sinking in her estimation by uttering such nonsense. Her father agreed that Jack Horner's exclamation was a *non-sequitur,* and told her that she had a quite exceptional clarity of brain, which would be a curse to her through life. And then he added : "How's this for a nursery rhyme, Duffy?" and recited gently :

> How many miles to Babylon?
> Three-score and ten.
> Can I get there by candlelight?
> Aye. There and back again.

"That's not far from beauty, Duffy, as I hope you'll be able to see one day."

And somehow it *did* sound different. Its measured movement pleased her, and its blue sadness; and these made her feel solemn and dreamy.

Fairy tales weren't nonsense, because they were admittedly stories of people in an imaginary world, and so could be completely, engrossingly satisfying. They were her monopolizing delight when she could read—at least, Grimm's were. Grimm's she read again and again, lolling in a deep arm-chair with her heels beneath her, and the book on the chair's arm. Grimm's stories were real stories, clear and exciting. Hans Andersen's were different : she could not get hold of them, and they were rather terrible. Yet after she had abandoned the annoying book they haunted her strangely : "The Girl who Trod on the Loaf"—ugly, dark, wonderful story; "The Red Shoes," "Ib and little Christina," and "Something." Whole sentences from them hung in her memory : "She flew away, as if she were flying straight into the sun." "They said 'Clink' and were broken." "And that was something."

"You don't understand, Duffy," said Mr. Tenter Bruno, when the annoyingness of Hans Andersen was pointed out to him. "But while Grimm only entertains you with what is agreeable, Hans Andersen *troubles* you with beauty."

When, in Hollins's phrase, she was "rising nine," her father decided to move to town. Earning a much larger income now, he could have lived in considerable style, but for the ever-gnawing fear that either his brain-power or his vogue would dwindle, and the workhouse ensue. This made him resolve that his place in town should not be in one of the expensive districts. But it would have to be fairly big, if it were to accommodate the two children, Miss Durgon, Hollins, and another servant.

Such a house was found at last in Deseret Road, West Kensington. The sanguine Mr. Bruno was quite pleased with it : a tall, red-brick place, with basement and area and four stories above—the sort of place which would both make him very comfortable and allow itself to be called a suburban barbarity The back of the house looked over the grounds of Queen's Club, so that one could watch the Varsity sports and football matches from all the windows that were above the grounds' encircling trees. Opposite the house front, across a good road, was a sunken waste ground waiting for the builder to arrive upon it. In the neighbourhood were many such places, though the long screens of uniform houses were building apace.

So there joined Daphne's more vivid memories the picture of that exciting day when they journeyed up to London and their new house. To her, who had only been told of London, it was a move as exciting as the departure of town children for the sea; the packing in the previous week, the trunks standing in the hall the night before, the arrival of the "fly" from the Ballard Arms, the stacking of the trunks about the carriage, and the drive, thus laden, to the station. Hollins and the maid had gone ahead to prepare the house, so Daphne and Owen secured one pair of corner seats in the railway carriage, and their father and Miss Durgon the other. More people got in, which meant extinction for Owen, Miss Durgon telling him he must keep his seat and not fidget. Daphne, having been wakeful most of the night, was lulled to sleep by the passing of the hedgerows and palings, and by the slow rolling and swinging of the train, till the voices of the strange occupants, and of her father and Miss Durgon, floated in a luminous mist behind her half sleep.

She was awakened by a jolting and slowing of the train and the movements of the people in the compartment. The

November day had darkened, and out of her window she saw more interlacing railway lines than she could have believed possible, all of them wet, as if rain had fallen here, and shining in gas-light. The backs of the houses were dark-grey and gloomy, and the few lit windows frightened her with their suggestiveness. Unconsciously she created stories of misery for the people behind them. The train rolled into the colossal station that bruised and battered her with its noises and smell and hurrying.

"We must get a four-wheeler," said her father importantly.

She wondered what a four-wheeler was, till the porter trundled their luggage alongside a "fly" much more squat than the carriage sent by the Ballard Arms. There was a head-achy smell inside it, and she was glad when her father sat her on his knee, for she received a draught from the window, as well as being able to see the things coming into view. First, there were lighted shops and entangling traffic; then a broad, roomy road of tall houses; then a great highway that seemed all coloured buses and four-wheelers and jingling hansoms. These hansoms, she said, were like sedan chairs drawn by horses. All of it kept her commenting and questioning, till of a sudden she was given a fear—one of those fears that one did not tell to adults for they were not liable to them. There was a man running beside their cab. A man in a cloth cap, with a muffler round his neck. In and out of the pedestrians he padded, sometimes on the roadway, sometimes on the pavement, often glancing at the luggage stacked on the cab's roof. The scenery changed, but the padding man was as unlosable as a shadow. She drew back her face from the window.

They were bowling now down a wide road, on one side of which were rows of tall houses, painted white or cream, or left a cindery grey, and on the other an interminable line of railings with trees and grass beyond. Daphne could only judge that a garden so endless must be the Queen's, and she inquired of her father:

"Is that where the Queen lives, daddy?"

"Yes; she used to live there, or a little farther on—in fact, she was born there, but, like us, she's moved."

"And who lives there now, then?"

Daphne Bruno

Mr. Bruno controlled a smile.

"Oh, the Prince Consort has a seat there."

"Who's the Prince Consort?" She thought foggily of Grimm's princes.

"Well, he's a howling swell in his place in there," assured her father.

Daphne said no more, for, in staring out, she had seen the shadow-man still keeping level with the cab. They had passed into a neighbourhood that, though it had some tall, red-brick houses, was subtly inferior to anything they had come through before. Miss Durgon made the remark: "Dear me, this is all very familiar ground," and Daphne, while envying her this knowledge, thought that somehow the neighbourhood suited Miss Durgon. What she meant she could not have said: probably that it was a dark and well-behaved neighbourhood, a genteel hanger-on of the fine white houses, and a place that would prohibit the noisier games.

Now the cab left the streets where the buses were, and got into quiet roads of residential houses. It seemed to turn round every corner that Daphne gambled it *would* turn round. And always the running man turned with it. It stopped at last before a high house, one of a red-brick row, with many white steps leading up to its front door. There was a lamp-post opposite the area gate, and she could see by its light that the dark-green paint on the hall door was raised into little blisters. Interesting things to prick.

The cab-door opened by itself—or, rather, it was opened by the shadow, who touched his cloth cap. Daphne, whom her father was about to hand out, shrunk back as if she were being handed to some dark, night messenger.

"It's all right," laughed her father. "This gentleman has only come to help us with our luggage."

That moment the hall door of their new home opened, flooding the steps with gas-light; and Daphne, seeing Hollins standing there, rushed hurriedly past the shadow into her arms.

Because of its complete difference from their Sussex home, the house in Deseret Road appealed to Daphne as a place much more romantic and thrilling—especially on foggy falls of their first November, when it could assume an air of the sinister. She and Owen early examined, not without fears, its every room and cupboard and cellar. Owen at first had not seen much reason to be afraid of them—nor, in truth, had Daphne—but, in order to make them more interesting, she had deliberately worked on his imagination and her own with rather disturbing ideas about secret panels and subterranean passages, till Owen was obviously terrified of them, and she herself wondered what exactly her feelings about them were. To explore at night the kitchen and pantries, which were actually below ground and down a stairway like a mine-shaft, was a thrilling adventure when prosecuted with a companion—unthinkable alone.

The long dining-room was a dangerous place because of the huge syphon for making soda-water that stood in the centre of the side-board, before the mirror. This great bulbous, though neat-waisted glass thing, encased in a trellis-work of wire, was as large as a child, and Hollins had told them that the wire casing was to prevent it exploding.

"Dangerous things," she had said. "They have to be all wrapped up in wire like that, being apt to go sort of—what I call—*off.*"

So Daphne, in the first weeks, always went past the sideboard quickly; and she marvelled, with hand at her mouth, when her father lifted the thing carelessly, and even shook it.

The sounds outside the house, too, were so different from those around their Sussex home. There the birds had sung, hardly heeded, in the boughs or under the eaves, or fluttered out of the creeper on the walls; and footsteps were seldom heard unless they were those of Eadigo on the gravel, or some visitor approaching the door. But here in Deseret Road sounded the rattle of two-wheeled tradesmen's carts, almost under the breakfast-room window; the crunching of errand-boys' hand-barrows; the ringing on the pavement of the feet of passers-by; or a loud and continued vibrating as some idle, whistling urchin dragged a stick along the area railings. In the winter came the bell of the muffin-man; and at other times the musical, sad cry of men and women selling lavender:

> Lavender, sweet lavender,
> Sixteen branches a penny.

Daphne Bruno

The errand boys were interesting because they could often be encouraged to put out their tongues or make long noses. And the muffin-man was never to be missed; if Daphne announced his appearance, Owen rushed to the breakfast-room window. He balanced a whole tray of muffins on his head, with nothing of the contortion, nervousness and reaching of one's tongue up to one's nose that Daphne had found inevitable when trying to do it with the butler's tray.

Ever afterwards the muffin bell made her think of a winter Sunday afternoon in Deseret Road. A year had passed. Father was away—tremendously far away. Having decided to treat himself to a holiday in India, he had departed in a cloud of romance, after showing the children his cabin trunks, his tropical hats, and pictures of the huge ship in which he would actually *live* for several weeks. Once he had "dressed up" in his Indian toggery, and beautifully neat and handsome, distinguished and whimsical he had looked in his white drill, smiling above his brown beard. Father's absence brought one advantage: Hollins, instead of Miss Durgon, took them to church. When father was at home, Miss Durgon had always conducted them with great parade to St. Antony's near by. It was a long, unintelligible service, and Daphne's only interest was to hope that someone would faint again, like a young woman who had caused a splendid diversion one warm spring morning. But nobody ever obliged again, and Daphne's detestation of church was suddenly increased to horror by the fixed idea that one day *she* was destined to provide the excitement. This heart-stopping thought would come over her, if the sermon were at all long, so that she would send up an ejaculatory prayer as sincere as that house of prayer had ever known: "O God, make him stop!" Miss Durgon's deportment at church incensed her more than anywhere else; it was so silly the way she opened her Bible, directly the preacher announced the text and its reference. What was the sense in looking them up when she had just been told what they were? Guessing that her father did not approve of church, she one day announced to Miss Durgon that "she didn't think she would go that morning; father didn't go." But Miss Durgon made short work of this: "Your father's a very clever man. When you're as clever as he is, you'll be able to question whether or not you'll go to church"; to which Daphne answered promptly: "Father says I *am* clever."

But now that Mr. Bruno had gone away, Miss Durgon ceased going to church, delegating to Hollins the task of taking the children. And going to Hollins's church was nothing like so detestable as going to Miss Durgon's. Hollins had a church of her own fancy, quite a distance away, to which you went in a bus.

"I do seem to fancy it, I must say," she told the children. "I can't explain it—it sort of *gets* me. Your St. Antony's doesn't get me at all."

She had first taken them there in the morning, telling them they would be pleased with the procession; it was as good as a theatre. This had excited them, and in their pew they eagerly awaited the beginning of the entertainment. When the banners and crucifixes and candles and incense and scarlet-skirted boys and quilted clergymen poured out from behind the high altar, Owen, who had been watching them with a falling mouth, suddenly looked up to Hollins and said:

"Is it all right?"

Hollins murmured "Sh—sh," and nodded "Yes," thereby answering the question that England had essayed to answer for sixty years.

On this particular winter afternoon, the children's service was more than usually entertaining. Glossy coloured pictures were brought round by the stout, smiling gentleman in the linen and lace, and distributed to the children. It was better than the crackers thrown by the clown in the pantomime, for every child seemed (if craning heads saw aright) to receive one, and the stout gentleman had almost as merry a smile as the clown's. When he came alongside Owen, who was at the end of the pew—in fact, almost in the nave, such was his open-mouthed interest—and offered him a picture, Owen looked up at Hollins and asked:

"Is it all right?"

And Hollins said:

"Yes. Sh——! Quite all right. Take it."

So he took it and began to chew one of its corners. Daphne had some difficulty in taking hers for she was struggling with a fit of giggling.

Daphne Bruno

Towards the end of the service, when the church was darkening, another exciting and mirthful thing happened: the verger lit the gas-brackets one after another. Then came a hymn, "All things bright and beautiful," and a procession in which the children fell in, pew by pew, behind the choir, and walked round the church. The little ones, Daphne noticed with a throb of pity that hurt her, held the hands of older brothers and sisters, and ran and stumbled along, dropping their books and weeping bitter tears that were unheeded in the roar of:

> *All* things bright and beautiful,
> All creatures great and small,
> *All* things wise and wonderful,
> The Lord God made them all.

One by one the pews in front of the Brunos emptied, and Daphne got quite exhilarated, as it drew near their moment to turn into the nave. Owen, being on the outside of the pew, had to lead off, and he prefaced so unusual a proceeding by looking up at Hollins with eyebrows that obviously inquired into its correctness. Reassured, he stepped out to join the others, first making certain, however, that Hollins and his sister were coming too.

When, after the blessing and a hymn sung most amusingly on one's knees, they passed out with the crowd into the road, they found it quite dark, though they had not yet had tea. They walked quickly down the road, Daphne talking excitedly and skippingly to Hollins about the service. And then the muffin bell sounded. And even while they were drawing attention to it, a muffin-man swung round a distant corner, and approached them along their very pavement.

"Is there muffins for tea?" asked Owen.

"You shouldn't ought to say, Is there? Where's your grammar? You should say, Are there?"

So Daphne said it.

"Well, are there?"

"No, Miss Inquisitive, there aren't."

"Well, couldn't we take some back with us?"

"Well now, did you ever? Of course not."

"Oh, do let's."

Owen said nothing, being not quite clear whether so abnormal a development were all right.

"Oh, Holly, may we?"

Daphne always gained her point by calling Hollins this endearing name.

"You know you didn't ought to buy anything of a Sunday."

"Yes, you ought. Didn't he tell us that the disciples picked the corn as they walked through the field? Why, I believe Owen's is a picture of them. . . . It is!" She gave a little jump. "Oh, Holly, I believe you're a Pharisee. Look, that's you in the background, looking snitchy."

"You're a clever one," said Hollins. "You say more than your prayers, you do." And, as the muffin-man was now close, she stopped before him.

"Oh, *good!*" muttered Daphne, as Hollins bought.

They were soon at the wide high street, where the buses were. They clambered inside one, Hollins refusing them permission to mount to the top, on the score that the air after dark was treacherous. So, wrapped up in their reefer coats, they sat in the bus, swinging their legs, and staring up at the advertisements of Sapolio, or down at a new one, which was fixed at the bus's end, a picture of a very discontented baby climbing out of a bath to get a piece of soap.

"What does it say beneath?" asked Owen

"It says, 'He won't be happy till he gets it.'"

"What's he want it for?"

"How should I know, silly. Eat it, I expect."

Hollins was always shorter with Owen than with Daphne. She believed she had some special feeling for Daphne, having been beside her father when the news came of her birth.

"Did he get it?" asked Daphne.

"How should I know, silly one? No, I don't think he did. He fell down and hurt his nose."

Owen's hand shot to the bridge of his nose in nervous sympathy. He brought it away quickly with a timid glance, to see if anyone had remarked so absurd a motion. But no one had because the bus had stopped to allow of a lady's entrance. As all the seats were occupied, she would have been obliged to stand if Hollins hadn't nudged Owen and whispered, "Who's a little gentleman now?" Owen was dreading this; not because he minded giving up his seat, but because he so disliked the publicity, and the not knowing what to say to the lady. She, however, saved him from speech by saying, "Well, that *is* kind of you," and Hollins by adding, "Not at all. He's pleased."

When they were home again, they found that Miss Durgon was out, and not likely to be back all the evening. Then it was that Daphne heard Hollins mutter her mysterious words, "I guessed as much. I thought so. . . . Well, come down to my room, and we'll have a jolly tea together there. . . . Ha—I knew it. . . ."

Down in her common little sitting-room, she poked up the fire till it flared with excitement.

"I do like a nice blaze on a winter's afternoon. There's nothing like a bit of a flare to cheer you up. See that blue flame? That means frost. Now you watch that, and if you're very good, I'll bring up something that's even better than muffins."

"Oh, what's that, what's that?" demanded Daphne.

"Ask no questions and you'll hear no lies," teased Hollins as she disappeared. In a few minutes she returned with a paper bag, and, kneeling heavily on the rug before the fire, produced chestnuts, to a shriek of delight from Daphne and a request for further information and explanation from Owen. The chestnuts were placed on the bars of the fire.

After tea they told stories in the glow of the fire, and had a concert, singing with the help of Hollins, "Way down upon the Swanee River," and the hymn, "I love to hear the story," not out of piety but because its tune was so curly. And lastly, Hollins gave her famous solo about the little tailor boy, who went skipping into smoke with a broadcloth under his arm:

> With a broadcloth under his arm,
> With a broadcloth under his arm,
> And the little tailor boy went skipping into smoke
> With a broadcloth under his arm.

Which was always a signal for Hollins to say, "And now you go skipping off to bed."

CHAPTER II

DAPHNE was growing tall. If by mistake she ran into a room of visitors and rushed out again with an "Oh, sorry!" the impression she left was of thin legs seen above the knee, and untidy brown hair. Also of a hot blush, less of shyness than of sudden guilt and consequent laughter. And somebody was sure to say, "She's going to be a tomboy and no mistake." Her high spirits were so high that often when she was alone she felt she could scream with them. This over-plus of vitality, her father used to say hopefully, would run to creative work or a passionate love one day.

Disliking most things that Miss Durgon recommended, Daphne had not decided what sort of character she would like to have. She was a malleable mass. But one ambition was forming. The frequent repetition of the phrase "tomboyish" had pleased her, and she decided to live up to it. She decided to hate dolls, doll's houses and sewing. And she was secretly pleased when people said, "The girl ought to have been the boy, and the boy ought to have been the girl," for she did not doubt that she could dominate Owen any day of the week. This desire to be masculine, introduced from without, was perhaps the earliest principle to strike a root in her.

She imagined that her hatred of repression—or, in other words, her hatred of Miss Durgon—was the natural outcome of her manliness. The obvious fact that Owen was timid of their guardian while *she* could be outspokenly rebellious, and, please God, intended to be more so, gave her a deal of satisfaction.

Once, sitting in the little room below stairs, and talking to Hollins, who was working a sewing-machine, she asked her for an opinion on Miss Durgon.

"Is she a good woman, Hollins?"

Hollins appeared to lift her lips towards her nose.

47

"Well, that's not for me to say. What some of us think we keep to ourselves."

"I say, Hollins, shall I tell you what I think, if you tell me what you think."

"No; I shan't tell you what I think if you tell me what you think."

"Oh, Hollins!"

Hollins turned the wheel monotonously, her head slightly on one side.

"There are some things one thinks that are best thought and left at that."

"But why?"

"Why? Because they ain't pretty, silly one. Now do you know?"

"You mean, you think Miss Durgon a beast?"

"Miss Daphne, I never said nothing of the sort. And I'll thank you not to go putting it about that I did."

Daphne started to be ingratiating.

"No, but you meant it, didn't you, Hollins?"

"I never, so there! All I mean is, some people are made in their own way and can't help it."

"Made what way, Hollins?"

Hollins snapped an entangled thread.

"Made so as they know how to worm themselves into positions, and sort of make themselves indispensable, and get the power into their hands. Oh, it's clever; I'd be the last to say it wasn't."

"She doesn't like you, Hollins."

"She doesn't, doesn't she? Milady doesn't. Well, I wonder now if that'll spoil my appetite. I wonder if I shall lay awake fretting about that. . . . And how, Miss Mischief, may you happen to know whether she likes me or not?"

"Because she often says I oughtn't to hang about you so much."

"She does? Says you shouldn't ought to hang about me so much? Oh! There's where you are. I hold me tongue from speaking against her, but she'll say what she likes about me readily enough. There's the lady. And mind you, I've kep' quiet about more things than one I've noticed.

"I've noticed, f'r instance—however. . . . Common

people like Hollins, you see, haven't got eyes, and what
they think don't matter, as they've no brains worth speaking of. . . ."

The forces moving towards a more overt war between
Daphne and Miss Durgon were not only working in Daphne.
Miss Durgon, who had now been many years with Mr.
Bruno, was no longer nervous of jeopardizing her position
by a false move. She had summed up her employer, and
knew that his love of ease and unworried seclusion would
resist any idea of change. She was still under forty-five,
and very different, of course, from what she appeared to
the eyes of her wards. Naught of her slimness or good
carriage had left her, and now that she was earning a
fair stipend and could supplement it from the housekeeping
money, she dressed remarkably well. To people of her
own generation and class she showed a vivacity and cleverness such as never appeared before those creatures who
could not interest her—children and servants. Of late Miss
Durgon had enjoyed the admiration of some men, though
in each case, unfortunately, they were the husbands of
her friends.

This admiration had increased her self-respect, and, as
a result, her indignation at the rebelliousness of Daphne.
The indignation demanded an early overthrow of the child.
And by the side of this sense that Daphne must be taught
her place sat an unhealthy but growing desire. Though
she knew nothing about suppressed sex, she saw that there
was perversion somewhere in an idea that could so stimulate
her. She wanted to whip Daphne at least once. There was
a sensuous quality about the child that would make the
whipping of her pleasant.

The collision came when Miss Durgon tried to stop
Daphne's game of "Getting up early."

The children had discovered this game in the months
before their father left for India. Those were summer days,
and Daphne would wake up Owen as soon as she herself was
awakened by the sunlight streaming behind the blinds and
the chatter of the birds in Queen's Club Gardens. They
would dress with all the interest of getting up before anyone
else was astir, and then creep down the stairs, a little
nervous of the deserted, blind-dimmed house. Unchaining

and unbolting the hall door, they ran out into the sunny publicity of Deseret Road. In their hands they carried a toy cricket bat (one solid piece of yellow wood without a splice), four stumps and a tennis ball. Their destination was a sunken waste ground at the corner of Goscombe Road, which, though hillocky, weed-grown, and not empty of refuse, required no great imagination to be converted into Queen's Club Gardens. There they would set their stumps and imitate the white-flannelled cricketers whom they had watched from their back windows. Daphne represented Cambridge and Owen Oxford.

The clearest line of division in the human race was that which divided the people who were Oxford from those who were Cambridge. Owen was Oxford, because Oxford always won the Boat-race; Daphne was Cambridge because Cambridge never did. There were other reasons for their choice: Owen was Oxford because his father was, and his name began with an O; Daphne was Cambridge because light blue was a nicer colour than dark blue, and D, her initial, was nearer C than O, and because hardly anyone else she knew was Cambridge, and because Owen was Oxford.

Cambridge batted first, and Owen, for Oxford, opened the bowling. If Owen's ball came near enough, she tried to hit it; and when she missed it, ran after it, picked it up and returned it to him.

"Bowl us something one can hit," she shouted.

Sometimes, after she had hit it, Owen stopped it and gathered it up; and then she would instruct him to hold it while she ran to his stump and back.

"That's what I have to do," she explained.

So Owen examined the stitches of the tennis ball while Daphne ran to where he was standing and back to her wicket.

"Now you bowl again."

"But when can I bat?"

"When you've knocked over these three stumps, silly. Don't you know the game?"

Owen looked a little sulky.

"I can't hit them with you in front."

"Well, when I've made thirty I'll retire."

When Daphne bowled she would only consent to bowl overarm. That was the way they did it at Queen's Club.

Sometimes the milkman would stay his clattering cart to watch her, and call out : "Good old W. G. ! What price Lord 'Awke?" His "That's right! Sling 'em up, miss!" always deepened the colour of her cheeks, already warmed with running; and she would try to impress him by sending down an especially good ball. If it proved, however, to be rather wide she would call out to Owen loud explanations of so unusual a failure, hoping to keep her reputation with the milkman. When the game was over she hurried back to tell her father the result of the match, the number of runs she had scored, and how she had been obliged to retire in order that Owen might have an innings.

But now that Mr. Bruno was abroad Miss Durgon withdrew her consent from the game. At breakfast one morning, when she heard that they had been out, she pronounced, as all rose from the table :

"You're not to do that any more. Do you clearly understand?"

"Why?" asked Daphne, with symptoms of sulkiness.

"Why? Because I say so. You must allow me to know better than you. Ladies' children don't play in the streets."

(In the vocabulary of Miss Durgon there were two kinds of children—"ladies' children" and "district children," the latter being sometimes called "poor people's children.")

"Father used to let us," grumbled Daphne.

"Don't answer back. Your father has entrusted your bringing up to me, and doesn't want to be bothered about it. You're older now, too. Besides, cricket isn't a nice game for a little girl."

"Why?"

"Never mind why. You'll understand these things later on. It's indelicate."

Daphne was a little nervous of her next remark, but as she was more frightened of convicting herself of fear, she hurriedly forced it out.

"I shall ask father when he comes back."

"You excessively rude little girl!" exclaimed Miss Durgon. "You want a good whipping. I've a good mind to give you one. You've been getting quite out of hand lately."

Daphne Bruno

That Miss Durgon was empowered to give her a whipping had not entered Daphne's mind. Hitherto, when it had been a case for such extreme measures, Miss Durgon had spoken to her father. But that was when she had been very young. These words of her guardian momentarily repulsed her. But feeling the ignominy of surrender, and observing that Owen was staring open-mouthed from one to the other as they exchanged these interesting remarks, she persisted. One had to play up before him.

"In the Bible they played in the streets. Father Alderwood said so. They played at funerals in the market-place, and Jesus Christ played with them——"

"Daphne! I never heard such talk. Go out of the room at once. How dare you talk blasphemously like that? Upon my soul—mark my words—if you try on this arguing with me I shall one day take a stick to you. I mean it. Mixing up religion and play like that! Little humbug!"

"I'm not a humbug," said Daphne, walking round the breakfast table to keep it between Miss Durgon and herself.

"You're a little humbug," repeated Miss Durgon, who had so lost her temper as hardly to know what she was talking about. "Parading religion, and at the same time being insolent and disobedient. You're a regular little Pharisee."

To be called what you have called others is always as wounding as it is astonishing.

"I'm not a Pharisee." The tears sprang to Daphne's eyes.

"Yes, you are; and will you keep quiet, I tell you?"

"Well, if I'm a Pharisee, you're a Sadducee."

"Upon my soul! Come here! Don't run away! It's no good; I shall catch you sooner or later." Miss Durgon had paused, feeling the indignity of running after a child. "Insulting a woman who's giving up her life to you like that! Sadducee indeed! You don't know what a Sadducee is."

"Yes, I do. It's someone who doesn't believe in the Resurrection."

"Daphne, come here. I'm going to give you a thorough good whipping. You've earned it richly."

Daphne ran towards the door. Miss Durgon arrived there at the same time. Daphne slipped past her, and, crying loudly, ran out of the room. She heard Miss Durgon call, "Stop that child!" so raced upstairs, and remembering the bolt on the bathroom door, rushed in, slammed the door, and shot home the bolt.

Breathless, she threw herself on the linoleum floor, and sobbed with heaving shoulders. Knocks came to the door, and the voice of Miss Durgon.

"Open at once, Daphne. Bad, naughty little girl! Open the door at once."

"I shan't! I shan't!" sobbed Daphne.

The door shook. Daphne had a wild idea, should the door yield, of leaping out of the window and crashing to her death in the street. She jumped up at a moment when the door seemed likely to give, and flung up the sash.

"What are you doing?" cried the alarmed Miss Durgon, and the door ceased to shake. "Daphne, what are you doing?"

Daphne roared through her tears.

"If you come in, I'm going out of the window. Out of the window."

"You're a bad, evil little girl. I'm sure I don't know what to do with you."

Miss Durgon retired; and Daphne and she were separated by the bathroom door, both a little alarmed at the storm, and rather vague as to how it had arisen.

More than once this bathroom had been the scene of a solitary performance at which Daphne would have been ashamed to be caught, though it gave her a sweet, troubled delight such as no other game could give. It had sprung from the everlasting lilt in her mind of some lines of poetry, found in her history after the story of King Charles's beheading:

> He nothing common did nor mean
> Upon that memorable scene . . .
>
> Nor called the gods, with vulgar spite,
> To vindicate his helpless right;
> But bowed his comely head
> Down, as upon a bed.

Daphne Bruno

The nature of her delight in them she did not analyse; but a kindred delight—an emotion not empty of troubling had used to come to her, in the old home, when she saw a shaft of yellow lamplight thrown on to evening grass; or a wood of dark firs spining a hill in the landscape's blue distance; or those stretches of rusty bracken, with here and there a lonely, blown tree, that were Shadwell Common in autumn; or red firelight on old wood, when sunset had fallen before tea, and the lamps were not yet lit. It was the same haunting something that came out of Hans Andersen : "She flew away as if she were flying straight into the sun." And the old nursery rhyme had it :

> How many miles to Babylon?
> Three score and ten.
> Can I get there by candlelight?
> Aye, there and back again.

"He nothing common did nor mean." A scene in which she died like that, wrongfully condemned but too proud to protest her innocence, was Daphne's shameful game in the bathroom behind a bolted door. At first she used to place the chair for a block, and walk towards it through a street of staring faces. Before its feet she knelt down, so that her hair fell away from the neck. There, without visible tremor, she awaited the blow.

But gradually the drama in this form failed to express fully the movements within her. She wanted the cruelly executed person to be herself, Daphne Bruno, not a character in history. And in these days people were never beheaded. If the game was to satisfy her, it must be brought into the realism of the present. And so it changed into a trial 'for murder, where Daphne stood in the dock (her hands on the woodwork round the bath) and listened in silence to the perjury of witnesses, or turned grave, brave eyes on the judge as he pronounced the sentence. After hearing his words, while the tense solemnity remained in the court, she made a brief speech, proclaiming her faith that her character would one day be cleared, and thanking those friends in the gallery who had never doubted her innocence, and the Q.C. who had defended her as ably as it was in the power of man to do.

Then, having done nothing common, mean or vulgar,

she turned and followed the warder to the condemned cell.

But to-day, in stormy mood, she could play no such game. Picking herself up from the floor, she sat sideways on the chair with her arm along its back. Her sobs were now internal and intermittent. The chair as a permanent seat proved uncomfortably hard, so she sat on the cork mat on the linoleum and picked off chips from its broken corner. When this palled, she stood up and traced her finger along the squares in the tiled wall-paper, reaching at last the hole in the plaster made by the door-key. Here she played "snowstorms," putting a finger in the hole and, by scratching it downwards, sending a tenuous shower of powdered plaster to the floor. But this palled too.

Very quiet was the house, as if her disgrace were like an illness, compelling all the inmates to go about their business with subdued steps. She looked out of the window, and watched the passing of carts and pedestrians. Sometimes she saw children known to her, and drew away her head lest they guessed anything.

If only she had a book to read! If only she could make a silent dash up the next flight of stairs to the nursery, and seize a book, and rush back to her fastness! Guiltily she pulled the bolt, opened the door, and listened. Not a sound anywhere. She tiptoed through an ante-room on to the landing, and then leapt like a chamois from stair to stair. Her heart beat fast as she searched quickly along the shelf that contained her few books. There was hardly anything she had not read several times, except indeed, "Little Women," that Aunt Belle had given her for her birthday, and she had refused to read on account of its feminine title. On the ground floor a door shut. Instantly she seized the book, and hurtled downstairs to her bathroom. She rested her book on the woodwork round the bath, whose varnish had been so spoiled by soap; and with her head on her left palm and her right hand playing with the tap-handles, she began to read. In a few minutes the tap-handles were neglected; she was in America with Joe and Meg and Beth and Amy. Her disgrace withdrew from memory, save in moments when she contrasted Miss Durgon with the lovable Marmee, or saw a likeness between her and the peppery Aunt March. The high sentiments emitted by Joe and Meg and Beth and Amy made her feel rather good herself.

Wearying of the hard seat, she placed the open book upon the floor, and herself on her stomach before it, with her hands supporting her chin, her legs opened, and one foot occasionally rising into the air. By now the Marches were the most fascinating family in the world.

The book must surely be literature of a high order, with all those noble resolutions and elegant little sermons by Marmee. There stirred in Daphne, for the first time, the ambition to write. She stopped reading for a minute, and stared over the book's edge. As pain in the adult artist liberates itself in created work, so Daphne's present misery sought liberation in a dream of great books. Books of this kind, very sad and uplifting and beautiful. The Marches stood cataleptically fixed in the positions in which she had left them, while her thoughts swept forward over a life of successes, and down many side avenues, and beyond death into the long centuries of fame. Yes, she had made a decision; she would be an authoress. It was thrilling. She released the Marches from their trance, and followed their rapid movements again. But the dream had to be returned to. . . . Only after many such breaks did the book win her back to oblivious concentration.

Then, in the enthralling company of Joe and Meg and Beth and Amy, she guessed nothing of the passage of time, till the house filled with a smell of greens and roasting fat; and dinner-things began to clatter in the dining-room. Mingled with her reading was a wonder if anything would be done about her dinner. She was quite determined she was not going to unlock the door and go downstairs. The dinner-bell rang—louder than usual, as though addressed to her—but she did not move. Only now she could no longer read; she could only listen. Evidently, by the silence, they had sat down to the meal, leaving her to come or stay away as she cared. Further clattering of plates; that was the meat-course being taken downstairs—and she was too late now for any. Here was the pudding coming up the stairs and being taken in. And now, to judge by the silence, they were eating it. . . . Ah, footsteps were coming up to her landing, rather slowly, as of a person who found it none too easy to manage all the stairs of these London houses.

A heavy breath heaved on the landing. Hollins, undoubtedly.

"If I had a sovereign every time I climbed these stairs, I should be a wealthy woman. Dearie . . . dearie, are you there?" Daphne answered with a shapeless sound. "Why not come down and have something to eat? I've come myself to ask you. She's given orders that nothing's to be kep' hot for you. Come down, there's a good girl. You can't go starving yourself, you know. Even I should call that naughty of you. Come on, dear, you must eat something. There's no smell in nothing, as the saying is."

"Am I going to be whipped?"

"Well, she says so. She says you're making your punishment worse by this persisting. But I dare say she's only trying it on. She's punishing you in another way, and I do call it nasty." The door was open twelve inches by this time. "She's purposely taking Master Owen to the Zoo this afternoon. Heaven knows I'm the last person to encourage children to be saucy, but if I'd been him, I'duv refused to go. . . ."

Daphne shut the door, but gently, in Hollins' face and slid the bolt home; silently, so that Hollins should not be offended. Hollins' voice pursued through the wood: "Never mind, darling. Never mind. When they've gone you and I'll go for a nice walk together. And now come and eat something. Spite of what she says, I've kep' a plateful in the oven."

Daphne's reply was moaned:

"I'm not coming down to be whipped."

"No, and I'm not sure that I blame you, neither. . . . Well, don't cry, silly one. Let's hope they'll start soon, and then you can come out."

When she was gone, Daphne went to the window, out of which she stared dreamily at the stretch of Deseret Road. Already she had heard the rush of Owen's feet up the stairs, and the preparations of Miss Durgon in her room; and it was not long before the descending steps were heard, and the movements in the hall, and the shutting of the front door. In a second they would be in view. There they were, Miss Durgon walking quickly, and Owen running at her side. Once Owen turned round and, after looking up at the bath-room window, said something to Miss Durgon, but she walked on without impairing her dignity by a look behind. Daphne slipped out of sight—she had not wanted Owen to see her.

Now she opened the door and carried her swollen eyes and red nose down into the dining-room. There was no one there. Too ashamed to show herself to the servants in the basement, she moved heavily about, hoping her feet would be heard by Hollins. A sham fit of coughing was also tried. Then she heard the jingling of a tray, and Hollins coming up the steep stairs.

"There!" said Hollins, as she placed the tray on the table. "I expect you'll enjoy it all the more for being hungry."

Seeing Daphne's eyes she gathered her against her breast, muttering only, "What a shame! What a shame!"

The walk in the afternoon was clouded for Daphne by her memory of the morning's emotion and by the shadow of the evening when Miss Durgon would return. She was subdued as they passed along the shop-windows. One bright interlude came when Hollins stopped in front of a sweet-shop and told her to choose a penn'orth to her fancy. Every jar or dish in the window she examined. "Hundreds of Thousands" were four ounces a penny, but they went so quickly. "Pontefract Cakes" didn't last, either. "Liquorice, Linseed and Chlorodyne Lozenges" were always good, because little bits could be broken off and dissolved slowly in the mouth, flavouring it for hours; but grown-up people forbade these as drugs. A glass jar of gelatine discs at two ounces a penny decided her. These discs, sometimes used for mending broken panes, stayed in the mouth for a wonderful time, and could even be taken out and kept in a handkerchief. It would be lovely to lie on the ground sucking them while she pursued the adventures of Joe and Meg and Beth and Amy. For already the book, whose atmosphere had never quite dissolved, was calling for her return. She persuaded Hollins to take her once past the fire-station on the chance that their arrival might synchronize with a call for the engines. Never yet had she seen the great doors swung open, the horses harnessed like lightning, and the smoking, spark-dropping engines galloped past a gathered crowd. But her despairing conviction that there would be no movement in the station proved correct. Only a faint thrill could be got from the rows of shining helmets on both walls, and the shining brass of the engines.

The walk home was depressing since it led to the moment of Miss Durgon's return; and when they were in the hall Daphne suggested that, now she had had her walk, she should go back to the bathroom and bolt the door.

"No, you're not going to," said Hollins. "She shan't whip you now. If she says she will, I shall take the liberty of telling her that she's punished you once by not taking you to the Zoo. . . . You read your book and we'll see."

So after tea, Daphne read on, sucking the gelatine discs. But the reading was all spoiled by her underthinking, which kept reminding her that Miss Durgon was due. On the sounds of people coming up the front-door steps, her heart leapt in fright. The latch-key turned, the door opened, and an umbrella was put into the hat-stand. Here was Hollins toiling up the basement stairs to her defence. Her voice mingled in the passage with Miss Durgon's. Then she entered.

"She says you're to go to bed. She says she's no wish to see you at all." (In truth, Daphne's stormy revolt had quite frightened away Miss Durgon's desire to whip her.) "She says——"

Just then Owen rushed in to tell his sister all about the Zoo, but he had scarcely uttered a word before Hollins interrupted:

"Well, I took you for a little gentleman, I did."

Owen looked at Hollins with the timid glance of the corrected.

"A little gentleman wouldn't mention anything about where he'd been, a little gentleman wouldn't."

Owen lapsed into a dubious silence, while Daphne declared:

"I didn't want to go to his dirty, beastly old Zoo;" and Hollins hastened to prevent trouble by saying:

"Now, Miss Daphne, that'll do. Suppose you zoo off to bed."

CHAPTER III

In the beginning Miss Durgon had given the children their lessons. But now her dignity, generated in the warm air of leisure and comparative luxury, and sunned by certain other things that lay beyond the walls of Mr. Bruno's home (and beyond the walls of his knowledge), was, if anything, given a sharper outline by Daphne's insolent rebellion. Transformed from an impecunious gentlewoman who sought a housekeeper's situation into a lady of social graciousness, who consented to take over the reins of a distinguished writer's home, she began to think it unreasonable that she should be asked to play nursery governess to a brace of obstreperous children. So, on Mr. Tenter Bruno's return from the East, she laid before him a project that had long been maturing in her mind. He looked up from his easy chair and his book, desirous only of being relieved as quickly as possible from this visit of a domestic problem.

"Yes, by all means, tell me, Miss Durgon. By all means. . . ."

She explained. She felt that the engagement of a daily governess for her charges would be well worth the small outlay entailed. The children were getting older and should have longer time for lessons than she could give them. She was worried by the feeling that she was hardly doing justice to the two departments of her work : the management of his household and the education of his children.

"Forgive me," smiled Mr. Bruno. "The market in governesses is a thing I've so little studied that I've no conception what they cost. Are they quoted these days at two figures or three? . . . H'm," he added, seeing his housekeeper uncomfortably bewildered. "Their salaries, I mean."

"Forty pounds a year, with lunch and tea, should secure us a really good governess."

Les Tracas des Enfants

Mr. Bruno had a restive feeling that if he could purchase the right to continue his present chapter for forty pounds a year, it had best be done.

"Oh, well, we could afford that much," he said.

"Yes," confirmed Miss Durgon, "and then I should be at liberty to devote myself entirely to the management of the house and the moral care of Daphne and Owen—with, of course, the oversight of their studies."

Mr. Bruno's hand turned a page of his book, and Miss Durgon therefore stepped obligingly towards the door. It was as she had foreseen; he would edge away from any long thinking on a theme unrelated to his books.

"Of course, you'll do all the advertising and interviewing necessary," he tendered over the tops of his reading spectacles, now happily replaced. "I cannot possibly be besieged by young governesses."

Miss Durgon assured him that she would certainly undertake all that.

And few undertakings could have given her more pleasure. It was a serene satisfaction to be on the luxurious *employing* side of an advertisement in the *Warden,* after inhabiting the meagre country on the employee's side. She saw herself sitting with some state in the dining-room and giving an audience to nervous applicants. She would be impressively dressed for them.

There were but two replies to her advertisement for a "governess, young, bright, willing," of which she had only ordered one insertion, since it was being paid for out of the housekeeping money. To these two applicants she wrote instructions for them to call at given hours. The first was a lady unmistakably older than Miss Durgon herself, and quite unsuitable, because it would be difficult to order her about, besides the creature was offensively careful to parade the plumes of a fallen gentlewoman. The second, who called an hour later that morning, seemed far more suitable, and her suitability received adventitious increase from the contrast with her predecessor. She was a little, spare sprig of a girl who could be easily planted and trained, and would never, one imagined, dare to be "superior" with such a long-rooted and graceful tree as her lady employer. Her round cheeks, slightly flushed, her simple frock, her hair the tint of a harvest field, and her shy, escaping eyes were the likely efflorescence of a nature ingenuous and pliable.

When Miss Durgon floated into the dining-room, wearing the majesty of a prospective employer, this little Miss Carrell rose respectfully and remained standing; and it was not till Miss Durgon had taken her chair and rested leisured and well-to-do hands on her lap that Miss Carrell, in response to a hint, sat on the edge of an arm-chair, holding her little hand-bag on her knees. And yet she was not nervous, Miss Durgon saw; it was simply good manners.

"I am Miss Durgon, who wrote to you, you know. I am the—er—the guardian of Mr. Tenter Bruno's children; in fact, I've managed everything for him since his dear wife died in giving birth to the younger child." Miss Durgon paused, thinking that perhaps this slip of a girl understood none of these things. "Well, Miss—er——"

"Carrell," breathed the girl.

"Of course, of course. Well, Miss Carrell, I want to do my best for these children—in fact, hitherto I've felt I ought to teach them the elements myself; no one can do it so well as their parent or guardian; but now they're getting bigger and demanding too much of my time, and Mr. Bruno's household is a large and increasing charge, and my social engagements forbid me doing full justice to the children's needs."

"I quite see," was wafted from the easy chair.

"Yes. Well, I imagine you would arrive in the morning, soon after breakfast, and give them lessons till one o'clock, having lunch with them—and then perhaps a walk in the afternoon, and tea. And after that Hollins will take care of them till bedtime. Hollins, I should tell you, is of her kind, an excellent person, whom I retain in the service of the house, though I must say she's not very loyal to me, and I've reason to believe is not above speaking against me; but she's been with the family since before her mistress died, and you know these old servants—they never do take to, or admit any good in a new—er——"

"New régime," supplied the easy chair understandingly. "Yes, I know. They're always like that."

"Yes, admit any good in a new régime. Well, I suppose you've had some experience."

"Oh, yes." Miss Carrell bowed her pale hair over her hand-bag and produced an envelope. "I can show you this testimonial. I have been for three years a mistress at Hemans House."

She said this (unfolding the testimonial) as though she expected any well-informed woman to know Hemans House by repute; and Miss Durgon, in knowing nothing about the place, felt in danger of a social fall.

"Oh, were you? That's interesting. But you hardly look old enough for——"

"I am twenty-two," interrupted Miss Carrell.

"You went as junior mistress, I imagine."

"Yes. But later on Miss Vidella entrusted the elder girls to me quite a lot. You see, I'd been there over two years, which was longer than any of the other mistresses——"

"This Miss—Verdella, did you say?—must have been difficult to get on with."

Miss Carrell shrugged.

"Well, she was rather quaint." A blush rushed over her face, as if she had unthinkingly let some little monkeyish animal, deliberately battened underground, peep out its nose. "I don't think the other mistresses tried to understand her and shape themselves to her ways."

"And why did you leave, if you were so helpful to Miss Verdella?" asked Miss Durgon, who, not having noticed the peep, was thinking, "This girl is just what I want," and imagining herself making of Miss Carrell a pleasant companion, though a properly subservient one.

"Oh, mother was not at all well, and I felt I ought to get daily employment and live at home. Here is Miss Vidella's testimonial."

The sheet of notepaper accepted by Miss Durgon showed, beneath the name "Hemans House" and a crest, a paragraph written in an inordinately neat and punctilious hand:

Miss Vidella has pleasure in testifying that Miss Mary Carrell was an assistant mistress at this school for nine terms, during which she gave every satisfaction, discharging her very responsible duties with propriety and considerable ability.

AMY VIDELLA.

Miss Durgon handed it back.

There was further question and answer, much of which amounted to saying again, in a different shade or with new accompaniments, what had been said before; and then Miss Durgon hinted :

"Well, I shall be interviewing other applicants, so I will let you know my decision later."

Miss Carrell rose obediently.

"Thank you very much indeed. I feel I could do all you want. Though I'm afraid I can't let you know finally till the day after to-morrow, as I am seeing some other parents to-morrow, and one the following day."

It was said so gently that Miss Durgon could suspect neither impertinence nor guile. And directly she heard of these other prospective employers she desired to secure at once this only suitable girl. And really, too, despite her vesture of an employer's ease, she had no experience of engaging governesses.

"Hum. That's a nuisance. I'm particularly anxious to know definitely by this time to-morrow. I think—yes, I think that, for my part, I could definitely say that I should be prepared to offer you the—the post. Is it at all likely that you could decide definitely now? Are the other situations likely to be more attractive than this one?"

"No, I don't think so," said Miss Carrell, her bag in her hand, and prepared to leave. "Only—only one of them is worth fifty pounds a year—and, for mother's sake, I feel I ought to consider it."

"Fifty pounds a year! That seems a large salary for so young a woman. I don't think Mr. Bruno would be prepared to give that."

"No," agreed Miss Carrell, "and I've no doubt you will get somebody equally suitable for a less amount. Thank you so much for considering——"

"Yes, but wait a minute. Mr. Bruno entrusts most of these affairs to me, and I feel I can commit him to fifty pounds a year. I am so anxious to have things settled early. Would you say definitely that you would come if I offered that?"

Miss Carrell smiled brightly and gratefully.

"Yes, I think so. I don't like to force you up in that way—but I have my mother to consider."

By now Miss Durgon could picture the mother in her shabby room, and felt a pity, mixed with inevitable contempt, for the indigent lady.

"Precisely. Then you will come?"

Miss Carrell nodded and smiled.

Daphne was excited about the arrival of a new governess, and Owen pretended to the same enthusiasm, though, to tell the truth, he could not see that it was matter for congratulation. But Daphne had ascertained from Hollins that the approaching Miss Carrell was little and pretty and fair-haired. "Almost a child herself, you might say, and likely to be as much a playfellow, so to put it, as a governess. I don't often take to people first go-off, as the saying is, but there, she fair got me."

"Well, she'll be better than old Durgon," answered Daphne, who liked abusing the housekeeper to Hollins, perceiving that, though the "sauce" was properly condemned, it was not unsavoury.

"Now, then, Miss Daphne, you're getting that rude and bold, I don't know what's coming over you."

"Well, she *is* a beast, and you know you think it."

Owen, who was listening, looked alarmed at such a plain statement of fact.

"I know I never said such a thing in my life," affirmed Hollins. "You know I never."

"Saying's one thing, and thinking's another."

"And saucing's one thing, and getting out of my way when I'm busy's another. So you be gone, miss, or it'll be idling's one thing and bed's another."

It was early evening, before bedtime, and Daphne, hardly knowing why she did it, ran into her father's study. She forgot to knock, and was only checked half-way across the carpet by a mutter of protest from the lips of Mr. Bruno, who, sitting in his easy chair, dropped his book a few inches, but no farther.

"The idea embodied in a closed door, Miss Cataract, is that it should be nervously knocked at—even apologetically knocked at—by mere idle children. Also, should it admit them on sufferance, that they must tread delicately across the privacy beyond."

Since his return from India he had been aware of something in his daughter's large, sparkling eyes and un-restrained naturalness that always compelled him to adopt with her a gnomic tone, highly civilized. He liked to dazzle her with a Roman candle of words, or reduce her to temporary immobility with some massive period. His skill at the game pleased him.

"Well, can I come in?"

"On a rapidly expiring lease—yes."

Daphne stood there and wondered what she had come for.

"We've got a new governess, papa."

"I should have thought a lion-tamer was more what was wanted."

"She's coming on Monday."

"Well, it seems hardly an occasion for turbulent rejoicing. A task-mistress who will (I hope) press your nose firmly on a grindstone is not a new doll or a new dress."

"I hate dolls."

"I forgot. Let us say, then, she's not a new football. Why this strange frenzy?"

"Oh, it'll be fun."

"I haven't gathered from Miss Durgon that you saw much humour in your tasks with her."

"I hate Miss Durgon."

"Hush, maenad! What you hate is restraint and healthy discipline. I hope this new governess swishes you often and soundly."

The subject of whipping always fascinated Daphne. She was accustomed to ask her friends in a lowered voice if their fathers and mothers whipped them, and to read over and over again all stories where such execution was done on refractory boys and girls. It was a subject that gave a curious exaltation similar to that provided by pictures of little black savages disappearing into the maw of a crocodile.

"Were you ever whipped, papa?"

"Most certainly. And by its gracious effect I am what I am."

"Well, why don't you ever whip me and Owen?"

She sat on the table to hear his explanation.

"I am a very busy man, Duffy; and though the task you suggest is important and honourable, and of real service to society—even one to which no artist need be ashamed to

lend a hand—I yet presume to think that the work on which
I am at present engaged"—he significantly replaced his
glasses—"is even more important. Besides, I can remember
past occasions when——"

Daphne changed her position, lying along the table so
that she rested on her elbow and one foot hooked itself over
the table's edge.

"Oh, yes, you've spanked us sometimes, but I don't call
that the real thing."

"Let us hope, then, that this governess will be made of
heavier metal. What did you say her name was?"

"Carrell."

"It doesn't sound promising. I can hardly hear the
swish of a rod in such musical syllables. But we must
hope for the best." He lifted up his book. "Well, are you
sure you have not outstayed your tenancy?"

With a half-sulky "All right!" Daphne departed, but
her father did not immediately continue his book. This
slight change in Daphne, noticeable after a long absence!
It was as if she had crossed a first boundary line. With her
long, narrow limbs, her figure like a boy's, and her unconsciously sinuous movements—yes, already feminine and
alluring—she had a power to ruffle the still pool of his
complacency. It would need, after such a glimpse of her,
to be calmed again. He protruded his under-jaw as he
faced a problem, and his thinking ran along courses such
as these: "What more could I have done for her? While
she was a baby, I could only trust her to these women,
and was surely wise in getting on with my work for her
sake and her brother's. But now—now that her mind is
like a sponge, and a good quality sponge, too, I fancy,
ready to soak up all things—what can I do? I have brains
and ideas, both of which are probably absent in all these
women. Ought I to leave her entirely to them, content that
my love should be nothing more than an expansive emotion?
But what can I do? I must work and read, and talk with
stimulating minds, and her little mind has nothing to give
me in the way of stimulus."

The question what he could do was so difficult to answer
that Mr. Bruno turned again to his book.

But after a line or two he found himself analysing
Daphne's enthusiasm about her governess and diagnosing

it as a child's delight at playing at schools. Well, no better approach to studies could be imagined, and at least he could encourage it. A pleasing resolution occurred to him, and as it eased his conscience, he was able to get on with his book.

The next afternoon there arrived in a van two huge packages, wrapped in straw and sacking, and addressed to Miss D. D. T. Bruno and O. T. Bruno, Esq. To tearing fingers and searching eyes they revealed two school-desks in highly polished yellow wood, with sloping lids that covered deep interiors smelling like school-rooms. In the chair-back was an adjustable boss which could be raised up and down; it fitted the small of the sitter's back, and was designed to prevent stooping. Daphne soon raised hers to the right position, and Owen's to his, hers being several inches higher than her brother's.

Not till the following day could they watch the amusing process of turning the lower end of the nursery upstairs into a schoolroom. The two desks were put with their backs to the fire-place, and opposite them a table for Miss Carrell. An empty book-case was carried to a side wall, its shelves to be used for school-books and the earthenware bottle of ink. Daphne devoted the afternoon to stocking her desk with all the old exercise books, atlases, pencil boxes with sliding lids, freehand drawing books, rulers, sketch blocks and paint boxes she had used in the past. Always it was to be as tidy. Owen joined in the game, echoing her merriment, though he still found the preparations depressing enough.

On the Monday morning Miss Carrell arrived, and was shown by Miss Durgon into the schoolroom where the two children stood, somewhat sheepishly. But, as she removed her hat and patted her hand over her fair hair and smiled merrily at her pupils, Daphne recovered her ease and prepared to like her.

"You see," said Miss Durgon, who was particularly stately during this introduction of an employee to the scene of her labours, "I have prepared everything for you—desks for each pupil—so that your work may be as congenial as possible."

With a child's quick condemnation in elders of the fibs

and brag that children sometimes employ, Daphne thought :
"It wasn't you, it was papa." Mentally she said this to
Miss Durgon's long back as it passed through the door,
which shut rather quietly. They were in school.

Miss Carrell was going to be a great success. That
was proved in the next few days. That was seen of all.
What was not seen was the working of the lively, if somewhat unlettered brain beneath that innocent hair. It was
Miss Carrell's policy just at present to win the enthusiastic
appreciation of her pupils; and the same imagination which
out of and during school hours was occupied with schemes
for getting on could convert lessons, were the effort worth
while, from dull tasks into captivating games. In these
games Daphne was always given the lead, for Daphne, being
manifestly the more important factor, was the one to be
favoured. Sums, then, were done as races. Geography
was a series of imaginary travels and trading expeditions.
History was stories and make-believe, when Daphne would
be Cœur-de-Lion or Warwick or Henry VIII, and Owen
played the second lead, such as Anne Boleyn. "You ought
to have been a boy, and he the girl," said Miss Carrell.
"But then, of course, his mother wasn't quite so well when
he was born."

They had exchanged history for some less interesting
arithmetic when Miss Carrell offered this remark, and
Daphne thought that compound division might well be held
up while they pursued its bearings further.

"Why should that make any difference? " she asked.

The subject was palatable to Miss Carrell, even though
it could only be discussed with children in a pretence of
teaching them propriety.

"Because it does, and there's an end of it."

"But why? "

"You *why* on with your work, as your friend Hollins
would say."

This remark, implying a criticism of Hollins, was
designed to impress her pupil with the governess's intellectual superiority to the servant, and certainly achieved
its end. "You'll understand these things when you are
older."

"How much older must I be? "

Daphne Bruno

"Oh, a lot older."

"Must I be sixteen?"

"Much older than that."

"Twenty?"

"Twenty-one at least."

"Do you understand these things?"

"Certainly I do. Now get on."

"But don't you have to be married before you understand?"

Owen was looking from one to the other as if he doubted whether the conversation were all right.

"Maybe I'm married; maybe I'm not."

"You're *not!*" triumphed Daphne. "You're *Miss* Carrell."

"Well, I understand what I'm talking about, so there!"

"What—how we were born, and all that?"

"Certainly."

"You have to be married, don't you, before you get children?"

"Yes." Her lips trembled a little.

"Can you get them without being married?"

"It has been done, but don't you get talking."

There was a knock at the door, and Mr. Bruno entered. Miss Carrell flushed brilliantly from throat to brow, not in fear of her pupils' father, but in fear lest he had heard their current studies.

Mr. Bruno, misunderstanding the flush, was gratified by it.

"You'll forgive this intrusion," bowed he, "but I thought I should like to see the children in surroundings to which they have so looked forward. . . . Dear, dear, this is real school. It revives memories of many fears and many disgraces. I hope you find them studious, Miss—Miss—er——"

It was Daphne who supplied her father with the missing name.

"Carrell."

"Silence, child. Don't you know you must not talk in school without having first raised your hand. . . . Are they all they ought to be, Miss Carrell?"

"They're progressing very well. Daphne is especially promising."

"Yes, I have always said that it's a relief she has brains, since she has neither beauty nor goodness."

"She would naturally have brains."

Miss Carrell turned away as she offered the compliment; and Mr. Bruno covered his embarrassment by asking, "And what were you studying when I interrupted you?"

Miss Carrell flushed again, and hoping the sharp eyes of Daphne observed no guilt or prevarication, said:

"Let's see. Yes, we were doing multiplication and division."

"Multiplication and division," smiled Mr. Bruno. "Well, that *is* the whole of life. There's scope for you to point a fine moral, Miss Carrell. There's the multiplication and aggregation of gaseous matter to form the solar worlds, and its division again. There's the multiplication in childhood of ideas and impressions for their division later. And the multiplication of pounds, shillings and pence all through life, for their division and disintegration as fast as you can multiply them. It's the whole of life and the whole of knowledge. H'm——" Seeing that he had fogged everybody in the room, Mr. Bruno came to earth. "You will be sure to tell us what you want, will you not? I do not see a birch anywhere."

Daphne tittered delightedly, and Mr. Bruno felt he could depart without loss of reputation.

In the afternoons, the governess and children went walking to Brook Green; or to the towing path by the river, in the hope of seeing the practice of the Oxford and Cambridge crews; or towards the police station near S. Mary Abbott's, Kensington, in the hope of seeing a Black Maria. The conversation was mainly in the management of Miss Carrell and Daphne. Miss Carrell admitted that she was Cambridge, having learned that Daphne was Cambridge. And finding that the child loved to listen to stories, she often told stories all the way out and all the way back; terribly pathetic stories of her own invention, for she had not only written stories, but even sent them to editors, and could tell of one that had been detained fully seven months before the editor had decided that he must regretfully decline it.

In brief, Miss Carrell, by such methods and by subtle endearments and gentle touchings, was striving to insinuate in Daphne's mind the idea that she could love her governess, and love her passionately. And it rooted and blossomed with surprising quickness. Hating Miss Durgon, Daphne was ready to adore Miss Carrell; and adoring, to love the feeling of adoration. Motions came beneath her breast which made her want to hold Miss Carrell's hand, or lean against her on a seat; and she saw at once how ill they partnered with her fancied boyishness. But it was so lovely, the fact of loving, that she decided to suspend her masculinity for a while, trusting that if her demonstrations of affection were not too public, no one but Miss Carrell would observe the temporary change.

The greater tracts of lesson-time now were occupied by the subjects which were popular. Arithmetic and grammar were allotted a grudging half-hour, and then preceptress and students leapt the fence into the broad pleasances of history and literature. History had degenerated into "stories from history," when the picturesque incidents were collected from Dickens' "Child's History of England," or into "history from stories," when Miss Carrell retold such romances as Lytton's "Last of the Barons," or "Harold," or actually read to them some new sensational novel which she felt would entertain herself as much as her charges. Literature, which Miss Carrell, being a craftsman, considered her great subject, consisted in the governess's reading of the more delightful parts— that is, the more sentimental parts—of Dickens (High Literature and Dickens being, in the mind of Miss Carrell, almost synonymous).

The deaths of Little Nell and Paul Dombey and Poor Joe were held up before Daphne as the perfection of beauty. She listened with staring eyes, ambition running fast in her brain: "I should like to write like that. I should like to tell people beautiful things. I should like to create characters that are beautiful, and scenes that make your eyes all hot and your throat lumpy like this. . . ." And even while Miss Carrell was still reading and she listening, ambition had shown her a triumphant career, and a death and burial that a nation mourned, and the people visiting her tomb for generations afterwards. Her wet eyes were Miss Carrell's delightful reward.

At the sound of any words that were called beautiful Daphne fluttered her wings to fly.

Les Tracas des Enfants

Poetry was hardly attempted. "You cannot be expected to develop a taste for poetry yet; it'll come later," explained Miss Carrell, knowing that she herself was still waiting for it. Just a few of the easier poems of Tennyson and Longfellow she had taught them (Great Poetry being almost synonymous with Tennyson and Longfellow): "The Schooner Hesperus," "Break, Break, Break," and "The Legend Beautiful," with its lovely line "Do thy duty, that is best. Leave unto thy Lord the rest." For Miss Carrell, like all completely self-centred women, loved noble thoughts.

At last, in her devotion, Daphne confided as a great secret to the understanding governess that she was resolved to write.

"Oh, well, it's easy in your case," said Miss Carrell. "You've got influence. Your father'll get all your stories published."

Such an idea had never presented itself to Daphne, but now, lingering and growing in her mind, it one day impelled her into Mr. Bruno's study for an examination of its worth.

"Papa," began she, a little shy of revealing her secret, "if I was to write books, would you be able to get publishers to publish them for me?"

"Me? No!" laughed her father. "I'm a critic. My business isn't to persuade publishers to produce the work of a young writer, but to discourage them from ever doing it again."

Daphne, as often when her father bantered her, looked confused and beaten back; and he felt sorry for her.

"Write, my little one. Write, if you feel the urge. I should be proud to think of you as a creative artist. But anything that you write, if it's to be stuff for pride, must have a quality that will get it through the doors, without a helpful kick from your father." He stared at her, standing there. "One day we must talk it all over. I can help you much, I dare say. But you're too young yet."

And he took up his book again.

CHAPTER IV

A GENERAL content, sinister, some might think, in its promise of an early break-up, had settled in the Bruno home.

Mr. Bruno was very contented. His mercury, as he phrased it, was high. The phrase was a new use of his. No other word could so well describe, in his detached and humorous analysis of his own emotions, that abject financial depression which followed a damaging review of his latest book, or that quick rise in spirits induced by a handsome tribute or a publisher's statement showing excellent sales. After a grand morning's work, when his brain had outrun his pen, the mercury, as it were, rose to his head, filling it with visions of an imperial home, with horses in the extensive stabling and forty wines in the cellar, and cattle moving among the trees of the park. After a morning when nothing but the commonplace or the obvious would take sub-stance on his paper, he saw a lower-middle-class jerry-built house, in which, with two children who went out to poorly-paid jobs, lived a writer whom the world had once acclaimed and quickly forgotten. To read about such a person, as one did sometimes in the paper, was to send his mercury to freezing point. He no longer saw the bankruptcy court, however, or the casual ward, for against these disasters he had amassed a capital sum, and if his brain collapsed to-morrow (thought he), his dividends would pay the rent of the jerry-built house and put some bread and cold meat in the larder.

There were reasons just now why his mercury should be high. A year before he had written his first play and secured its production. It had failed most noisily. When a destructive critic produces a play that has obvious weak-nesses, it is to ask for artillery; and Mr. Bruno and his play went down beneath a reverberating bombardment. Concluding that his fame was mortally wounded and a year or so later would see the end, he wondered how he could cut down his style of living, and began to turn off gases that

74

people had left alight on the stairs, or to complain courteously when coke was not mingled with the coal on the fire. "No one ever yet put coke on a fire," thought he, surprised how the worrying thought could make his head ache, "who didn't pay the fuel bill." And to his daughter if she prattled glibly about the pleasure-seeking life she would lead when grown up, he would say, "Nothing of the sort, my child. You'll go into a milliner's shop; and, as for Owen, he'll earn his ten shillings a week sweeping out a solicitor's office." But then, as the mercury crept up, he wrote another play, freeing it from the weaknesses that the crowding critics had pointed out in such detail. It was as lively and noisily successful as its brother had been wilting and moribund. The critics crowded to its jubilees instead of to its funeral. Mr. Tenter Bruno was more than ever *news;* he had long been known to the literary and the vaguely literary world, but now his face and his repartee and his movements and his anecdotes were the property of readers of the halfpenny press. "And you can write him a liar," said Mr. Bruno, "who denies that that pleases him."

He was content about his children, hearing excellent reports of the new governess. Daphne spoke enthusiastically of her, because her motions of love made all talk of Miss Carrell a pleasure; Miss Durgon reported the girl in the highest terms, because she had to justify her move in securing her; and Hollins said, "Why, that little Miss Carrell can do anything with the child, she can. It does me good to see it." So no household or parental cares needed to cross the doormat of Mr. Bruno's room. He began to play with the idea of setting forth on his travels again. And from the moment he welcomed the idea into his lonely study, he knew that he would finally succumb to its charm. And at length he introduced it to Miss Durgon.

"My work, I begin to find, demands that I move—and travel, rather than stagnate. One's imagination is starved by living too long in a London street. So few people realize it. . . . I brought a lot of stimulus out of the East. What I am really longing for is the day when my daughter shall be old enough to be my constant and enthusiastic companion. Then my powers of observation will be doubled, I verily believe, by the delight of revealing to her the romance of other lands and other manners."

Leaving these sentiments behind him, Mr. Bruno departed for a winter in Madeira.

Miss Durgon was contented. Released entirely from the charge of the children, which Miss Carrell and Hollins shared, she needed to do little but reign elegantly over the household. And the encomiums, confidences and frequent absences of her employer made her feel finally secure in the position which she had now held for nearly nine years. Incredible that it could be nine years! Her mind told her that she looked younger, more vivacious, and certainly more fashionable than when first she came knocking at Mr. Bruno's door. Her security made her, perhaps rashly, indifferent to the comments of servants. Her excursions when she was absent a whole day were more frequent than before. And once or twice she entertained Mr. Stokes, or Mr. Antony, in the breakfast-room, which she had now made into her private sitting-room. They came singly, of course, the visits of each being unknown to the other.

Mr. Stokes and Mr. Anthony were gentleman friends who liked her companionship at theatres and suppers, though they conducted these relaxations beyond the regions swept by their wives' eyes. Tacitly it was understood that the wives were not informed. Miss Durgon saw no reason why they should be. There was nothing scandalous in their husbands' change of companionship; and she found herself quite able to meet Mrs. Stokes and Mrs. Anthony at tea-parties, or in their own homes. But it was unlikely they would understand her reasoning—a reasoning learnt from their husbands, which made play with words like Life, and Naturalness and Affinities. So her concealment was the concession of a reasonable woman.

Little Miss Carrell was contented because she lived and slept and woke in the morning with her own schemes. They required that she did all in her power to develop Daphne's adoration, and to secure its publication to Daphne's papa and its concealment from the housekeeper.

"You know what Miss Durgon is, Duffy darling. If she thought you were so fond of me, she would do her best to get rid of me. I'm sure she would. And I don't want to leave you, now that I've grown so attached to you. And I really believe you'd miss me."

To confirm this Daphne put her arms about Miss Carrell —since nobody was by.

"You must pretend sometimes that you don't like the way I make you stick at your work; and that I'm a bit of a tyrant. That'll be a sure way to make the old Durgon think I'm a person to be kept."

And Miss Carrell, for her purposes, had made a friend of Hollins. She set out to be attractive to the good soul, conceiving her to have a heart that could be easily engaged. With Hollins she was always polite, smiling, considerate and talkative, though never losing the slight dignity that lent worth to her condescension. The balance was skilfully kept.

The wisdom of this *entente cordiale* had been shown to her one morning when she was passing the dining-room door, and overheard a conversation between Hollins and a sweeping maid.

"She's ordered the decanter of whisky and the soda water and the sandwiches to be put to-night in what she's pleased to call her room, though when it became her room and stopped being the breakfast-room *I* don't know. And I wonder which it is that's coming to-night. Some people have got a cheek—using the house in that high and mighty way, as if she was its lady."

"High and mighty!" scoffed the maid. "Low, I call it. Who are these Mr. Antonies and Mr. Stokeses? Not that they can be much if they see anything attractive in *her*."

"Ah yes, who are they?" said the voice of Hollins. "That's what many of us'd like to know. I reckon it's laughable being a charmer at her age. And do Mr. Stokes approve of Mr. Anthony, I want to know, and do Mr. Anthony approve of Mr. Stokes? Why are they never here together? That's what wants sort of—what I call—answering."

"There's many things that want answering that don't get it," said the maid sententiously.

"Yes, there are," agreed Hollins, and the listening Miss Carrell could picture the mysterious nod of her head.

Miss Carrell left no openings unguarded, however small.

77

Daphne Bruno

If she were to keep Hollins's good opinion it would be well (she imagined) that Daphne's adoration were none too visible to her old nurse.

"She mustn't be allowed to think, dear, that you are fonder of me than her, though I suppose it *is* natural that there must always be more between people of the same class and of a nearer age than between a young mistress and her ancient servant. But you mustn't hurt the dear, fat old thing. It wouldn't be kind. Also she might get jealous. So you be especially nice to old Hollins. For she *is* a dear, fat old thing. I love her. And let her know (just so that she mayn't dislike me) that I love her, and realize how much she has done for my little Duffy, and that I impress it all upon you."

And after saying this, Miss Carrell was more than ever satisfied with her skilful pilotage; and Daphne was more than ever satisfied with the essential goodness of her governess; and Hollins, when Daphne had done all she was bidden, was more than ever satisfied with the high breeding of Miss Carrell. "A real lady. It's a treat to have dealings with one at last."

With Miss Durgon, Miss Carrell was obliging and considerate, relieving her delicately of one duty after another. She made herself a pleasant companion, always interested, generally agreeing, but disagreeing sufficiently not to become insipid.

"I hope that child's getting on," the elder lady would say. "She's a little girl that wants a lot of control if she's not to run to seed."

"She needs to be kept hard at it, certainly," agreed Miss Carrell. "The boy is much more amenable. He's a really lovable little thing."

"Yes, he is. No trouble at all."

Once when Miss Durgon complained of a headache, Miss Carrell assured her that she needed a holiday. Impossible, declared the martyred Miss Durgon; she would never trust the household to Hollins alone. Then Miss Carrell made her suggestion. Couldn't *she* (Miss Carrell), who had long kept house for her mother, and now knew the ins and outs of Mr. Bruno's home—couldn't she come into residence for a week or so and manage things? Miss Durgon demurred, but finally saw something in the plan.

78

Les Tracas des Enfants

When the plan was tried Miss Carrell had need to hold her wheel with a very delicate hand indeed. Her elevation to deputy housekeeper, even though only for twenty-one days, very nearly lost her the adhesion of Hollins. Hollins could not see why a chit like that should be required when *she* was on the spot. Miss Carrell was fortunate enough to be in the hall when Hollins was discussing the matter with the other servants in the dining-room. "The Durgon's done it on purpose to spite me," Hollins was saying. "Of course she has. It's as plain as the nose on your face. I don't altogether blame the little governess. I don't think she'd hurt anybody if she could avoid it. But what I do say, and what I have always said, is that it was a bad day when that Durgon woman came knocking at our doors. And who is she going away with, is what I should like to know? Is it your Stokes or your Antonio?"

Little Miss Carrell saw her course. By gently refusing to notice any sullenness, and by skilful reductions of work and an increase of privileges and an improvement in the kitchen meals, she gradually persuaded all below stairs that it was a pity she hadn't always had the management of the house.

When Miss Durgon returned the regent stepped down from the throne with all the grace and some recollection (since she had just been reading about him to Daphne) of Cincinnatus returning to his plough.

In time it became quite a custom for Miss Durgon to take a week off now and then, and hand over the reins to her lieutenant.

But not when Mr. Bruno was back from Madeira or elsewhere.

"I feel I ought to be in my place when Mr. Bruno is here. There's really more to do then."

"Of course," said Miss Carrell, wondering if Miss Durgon really supposed she didn't see through her. It was beginning to dawn on her that the lady housekeeper, inside her fine clothes and her dignity, was a very considerable fool.

Probably Mr. Bruno would never have known of these arrangements if Hollins hadn't thought it on her conscience to say, in the course of a conversation with him:

79

"Oh, but that happened when Miss Carrell was doing the housekeeping—when Miss Durgon was away."

Mr. Bruno looked up.

"What did you say, Hollins?"

"I said that happened when Miss Carrell took Miss Durgon's place and ran the house."

"Did she? When was this?"

"Oh, she often does when you're away, sir. I thought you knew, and sort of suggested it."

"I did nothing of the sort," said he, feeling rather important. "I must ask Miss Durgon about it. I can't think Miss Carrell is old enough to manage a household such as this."

"Oh, she's done none so badly, sir," assured Hollins. "And, of course, I was there to help her."

"Of course, Hollins. And she's really a wonderfully capable little person, isn't she?"

Hollins gone, Mr. Bruno sat in his chair for some time thinking. It was perhaps a small thing, this French leave habit of Miss Durgon's, but it seemed to show him traces of falsity in her character which he knew his quick vision could have seen long ago had he given it the order to see. He dreamed out a conversation after dinner that night when he rebuked Miss Durgon. It was a conversation from which he issued with increased dignity. "I cannot think, Miss Durgon, that such a step was within the autonomy with which—— Please don't think I am anything but highly satisfied, but—— Your need of a holiday no one would deny, and I confess to having been remiss in not thinking of it before. Had you so much as mentioned it to me——" But as the meal drew to its close he felt what an exceedingly uncomfortable thing it was to administer rebukes to a person in Miss Durgon's position, and how the contemplation of it was spoiling his appetite and his conversation. Even she might say: "Very well, Mr. Bruno, if you think I am incompetent or neglect my duty, I had best resign my office. With all thanks, I am sure, for your kindness and unvaried courtesy in the past." And he would be reduced to the horrid necessity of begging her to reconsider her decision. No, things were perhaps best left as they were. Doubtless Miss Carrell *was* capable, or Miss Durgon would not have done such a thing. And this even-

ing he especially wanted to work on a play with an un-
agitated mind.

"But I can't help admiring the impudence of that little
Carrell girl seating herself astride my home like that.
There's a lot in her."

Miss Durgon, ignorant of these movements in her employer's mind, had been so pleased to find that the governess
could fill the position of deputy housekeeper that she was
seeing the convenience of having the young woman in permanent residence. Then she would at any moment be free
to go away, if only for a night or so. Miss Carrell, after
some doubts, fell in with the scheme more readily than Miss
Durgon had dared hope. It was a grateful matter that the
difficulty of her mother could be so easily overcome.

Now to approach Mr. Bruno. In his room Miss Durgon
hastened to pour out all the points she had previously
enumerated on her fingers' ends : that she was very satisfied with the governess's remarkable success with the
children; that Daphne was getting too big to be left, in
the evenings when she herself happened to be out, to the
charge of servants; that Miss Carrell would be able to
help the children with their home-work; that it would relieve them all of the sewing and care of the clothes,
which was getting heavy; and that, in a household of so
many persons, it would hardly cost a penny more a week,
since she already had lunch and tea with them.

"Oh, if we can have all that for nothing a week, let's
have it," Mr. Bruno smiled.

But he thought this would be a good opportunity to
mention his knowledge that his household had already been
somewhat frivolously left, for weeks at a time, to the
management of a twenty-three-year-old girl. And his eye,
the eye of a dramatist, saw at once the hidden embarrassment of Miss Durgon.

"Yes," she admitted, "I was feeling so run down while
you were away that I made that arrangement, but only with
a deep sense of responsibility. I would not have suggested
such a thing had I not decided that Miss Carrell was quite
exceptional. Quite exceptional."

"I feel she is," endorsed Mr. Bruno.

"Yes, she is. Quite exceptional," repeated Miss Durgon,
since this was her justification.

Daphne Bruno

So Miss Durgon helped to weave the rope that hanged her.

Miss Carrell hanged her at Christmas time. Quite simply. To be sure, it had been simpler to suggest that Hollins mentioned Mr. Stokes and Mr. Anthony to the master; but it would be rather undignified, this enlisting of servants' aid. And yet simpler had she herself alluded innocently to Miss Durgon's friends; but this savoured of ugly informing, and Mr. Bruno, a clever man, would see through it. And she didn't want Miss Durgon to go to the rope thinking her companion had "sneaked." In their conversations Mr. Anthony and Mr. Stokes had necessarily been spoken of, but always very casually, as if their visits were naturalness itself, and Miss Carrell the sort who could understand : the foolish woman even (so thought Miss Carrell) was not without a pride in hinting at her attractiveness. Besides, the thing, if only told, might not be very effective with Mr. Bruno : preoccupied, he would but half take it in. It must be seen in being.

Conceiving of Miss Durgon, Mr. Anthony, Mr. Stokes and Mr. Bruno as the chess pieces of Miss Carrell—Miss Durgon the queen, Mr. Anthony and Mr. Stokes her knights, and Mr. Bruno the opposing king—obviously the plan was to get the king into a position from which he could capture one or both of the knights. Always a difficult position to contrive, for the moves of knights are crooked. Herein came Daphne. When at last the occasion offered, she was used as pawn to lure out the king.

Christmas time brought the children's parties; exciting entertainments that illuminated not only the day whose evening they would adorn, but many of the days that went before. And the most brilliant of these, throwing a light that reached down weeks, was Lady Montefiore's fancy-dress affair, from four to nine, in the Kensington Town Hall. Costumes had to be resolved upon and made, and sewing became more than tolerable—joyous. Daphne was to go as a Shepherdess, and Owen as a Musketeer, Miss Carrell having just finished Dumas' romance and decided that it was the finest book she had ever read. But she gave far less time to Owen's dress than to Daphne's.

Their father had been told of this party, by Daphne

often, by Owen three times, by Miss Carrell once, but he had hardly heard. And it was soon known that he would be at a dinner in town that evening. Presumably he would be late, since Miss Durgon had ordered a tray of spirits, siphon, sandwiches and cigarettes for the entertainment of one of her guests.

Mr. Bruno had lunched out, but he returned to his study before three o'clock. He had just sat at his desk and taken up his pencil to write down some memoranda, when a timid knock at the door made him use the pencil for a patient tapping on his paper.

The governess entered.

"Excuse me, Mr. Bruno, but just for once I felt I simply must intrude. Would you mind if I showed you Daphne in her fancy dress? She looks so sweet, and I think it'll please her if you like it."

"Fancy dress?" echoed Mr. Bruno. "Oh, yes, of course, she's going to a party of some sort, isn't she? Certainly I'll come."

He laid down the pencil and rose quickly, having assumed the gay cloak of an interested father. He followed the governess upstairs to the schoolroom. Miss Carrell passed in before him and apparently whispered to the children to hide. Her face reappeared. "Now, Mr. Bruno, if you'll come in."

He entered a room that seemed to be empty, and looked around as if interested in such a strange apartment. Then Miss Carrell said: "You can come now, Daphne."

Daphne appeared, half shyly and half merrily, from behind the screen; and Mr. Bruno gasped. He had intended all along to gasp, but when he saw his daughter the gasp was genuine. She stood before him in a straw bonnet, her brown hair curled into ringlets. A black velvet corselet bodice reached to a point below her waist. A fichu was about her neck, frills at her elbows and black velvet ribbons at her wrists. Brocade panniers swelled out on either hip above a quilted satin petticoat. Her stockings were white, and her black shoes had silver buckles. In her right hand she held a crook, necklaced with ribbons. Mr. Bruno gasped, and something caught at his heart.

"Good heavens!" he laughed; "is that my Daphne?" But though he laughed, the word "my" gave him unexpected pleasure. "No, it's a changeling, stepped out of a Watteau canvas. . . . What's all this talk about a party? Why have I not been better informed? And there's Owen, too, all dressed up. What's he? Mephistopheles?"

"I'm a Musketeer."

"Not one of Dumas', I hope." But seeing by everyone's chapfallen silence that Owen was Dumas' hero and none else, he put them at their ease by saying: "Well, please announce to everybody that the dress is founded on your own literary taste and not mine. You must be careful how you tread on the literary grass, Mr. Owen. . . . Where's this rout to be held? Buckingham Palace?"

Miss Carrell explained.

"It's Lady Montefiore's party at Kensington Town Hall. A very big affair. I did tell you about it, but I don't think you quite heard."

"No. I'm afraid I don't sometimes. It must appear very rude. I'm sorry."

"Oh, Mr. Bruno." Miss Carrell looked almost beseechingly into his face. "I hardly like to suggest what's in my mind."

There's no sentence surer to stimulate intere:

"What's that?" asked Mr. Bruno.

"Run away, Duffy darling, and take Owen, and show yourselves to Hollins."

The children gone, Miss Carrell proceeded:

"Oh, don't you think you could look in for a minute at the party? Just before it's over—perhaps to bring the children away. There are to be such a number of famous people there, and reporters, and I do want Duffy to see her name in the paper to-morrow, and a mention of her dress. But in such a huge crowd she's hardly likely to be noticed unless you come too. What a wonderful surprise it'd be for them, if you came and drove them home! But of course, it's impossible . . . it's impossible. You're out to dinner."

"It's not impossible. It's not at all impossible," interrupted Mr. Bruno, to whom the word "reporters" was bait difficult to refuse. Besides, the vision of Daphne had stirred his desire for the envy and admiration of those who should know her for his daughter. "My dinner is only an official monthly business, and I can escape. I shall make a point of getting there. And don't you tell them. What time's it over?"

"Officially at nine o'clock. But I doubt if we shall get away before half-past nine. And I don't suppose the—the celebrities will be there till fairly late. I've promised Miss Durgon to have the children home by ten o'clock."

"I shall be there soon after nine, Miss Carrell. And keep it a surprise from them. . . ."

The governess was such a pleasant little person that he quite enjoyed having a secret with her.

At ten o'clock there were laughter and children's voices on the front steps of 18 Deseret Road, as Mr. Bruno, followed by Miss Carrell, Daphne and Owen (who had been allowed to pay the cabman), ascended to the hall door, searching for his latch-key.

"Shall I ring?" asked Miss Carrell, who may have been tired, for she looked pale and her voice trembled. "The maids will be up."

"No. Here we are. . . . Now then, Owen, open the door and don't keep us all waiting. The ladies are cold in their cloaks. That's right. Open Sesame!" The door opened. "Enter Ali Baba and two of his donkeys."

Miss Carrell passed in first, and Owen was about to go in after her when his father pulled him back, saying: "The lady your sister first, if you're the swashbucklering gallant your dress suggests." Daphne passed in. "That's right. Now the old man, because his great age gives him right of precedence. Then the young D'Artagnan."

He was hanging his hat on a peg when he observed the coat of Mr. Anthony.

"Hallo! A visitor? Who's this?" He lifted the lapel of the coat as if it might answer him.

Just then a maid appeared to see if the master or the children needed anything before retiring. (Or that was her ostensible reason. Actually she was the reporter commissioned by the kitchen, which had heard with surprised delight the master's voice on the steps, to proceed at once to the seat of war. As Hollins had said: "*Now* how's she going to explain her masher in the breakfast-room?")

"Who's the visitor, Alice?" asked Mr. Bruno, glancing at the coat.

Daphne Bruno

"Mr. Anthony, sir."

"Mr. Who?"

"Mr. Anthony."

He turned inquiringly to Miss Carrell.

"You know," she explained; "Mr. and Mrs. Anthony, who live in the new flats near the station."

"Oh, yes. Well, what on earth can he want with me at this time of night?"

"He's with Miss Durgon, sir," said the maid, taking his coat from him.

"Has he been here long?"

"Since eight o'clock," answered the maid innocently. "He often comes."

"The first I've heard of it." He turned again to Miss Carrell. "Does he——" But he stopped, perceiving the indelicacy of discussing Miss Durgon with the governess or the servants. "Well, good night, Duffy. Good night, Owen, old man. I'm sure neither of you'll sleep after all that pastry. Good night, Miss Carrell." And he walked along the passage into the dining-room to be alone.

He was troubled, annoyed; but not quite clear on what to base his annoyance. Why was it that Miss Durgon mustn't entertain a married man from eight to eleven on evenings when he was away? There were passages in his books suggesting the right of any woman to entertain any soul-mate she liked. But none of that could apply to Miss Durgon. She wasn't doing it because she was an intellectual in conscientious rebellion (so sneakily, too, when his back was turned), but because she was a damned hypocrite. That utterly conventional and pietistic fool, Miss Durgon, as a social rebel—pshaw! it was funny! She'd been secretive, too, now he came to remember, over those holidays of hers. . . . No, the whole thing was false and wrong. The children, he had said, must be taught conventional morals, till they were old enough and strong enough (if ever) to venture into deeper waters. Of course. If they were ever to be taught to resist the tyranny of out-worn creeds, they should be taught it as a high philosophy, not as a sneaking truancy. He would like to hear more about these visits of Mr. Anthony, whom, by the by, he remembered as rather an ill-bred cad, material and gross. Should he ask Miss Carrell about them? No, that would be quite out of place. She was too young and—pretty. Hollins? She had been with him a dozen years, a heavy, married creature. He laughed. It would please the old thing enormously to be taken into confidence. He liked to please people. But she'd certainly brag about his confidence to the other servants—he could read her character as well as anyone else's. But there, the servants knew all about it already. A pretty fool that woman had made of him before his servants. God damn it! He rang the bell.

"Is Hollins in bed yet?" he asked the maid.

"No, sir."

"Ask her to come and speak to me, please."

"Yes, sir."

Though there was no quaver in the maid's voice, he knew she was delighted.

Hollins, on being questioned, was completely communicative. It had not been her place before, but since Mr. Bruno asked her . . . there were times, she would admit, when she thought she ought to speak. . . . But then she had said to herself, the master knew what he was about when he appointed Miss Durgon. . . . And doubtless Miss Durgon, who was a lady, knew more about these things than she. . . . She had not been able to bring herself to speak. Besides, what did she know? She had only begun to smell a rat, as the saying was, when that Mr. Stokes——

"*Stokes?*" exclaimed Mr. Bruno.

Yes, Mr. Stokes. Mr. Stokes was an occasional visitor when the master was away.

"But not surely when——" began Mr. Bruno, but he stopped and walked away and stood looking out of the window on to the veranda.

"Thank you, Hollins. Thank you. I'm obliged to you. Please don't mention our conversation in the kitchen. Confidences are confidences."

"No, sir," promised Hollins, and withdrew, quite obviously as happy a woman as any in London.

Standing there with his hands in his pockets and his eyes staring vacantly at the window, Mr. Bruno indulged in a bath of warm self-sympathy. It was a shame of Miss Durgon to have taken this advantage of him, a widower so dependent on his dependants; an author, so necessarily kept busy at his work. It was too bad, considering the children:

if she was that sort they had been probably neglected whenever he wasn't looking. Damn it, it was insufferable to have treated so facilely the privilege of caring for T. Tenter Bruno's children. There must be people all over the country who would regard it as an honour—something to boast about—to be charged with the children of a man of such fame. To do all this, and at the same time to accept the generous salary he had given her, the comfortable home, and the extravagant courtesy with which he had always treated her! It was enough to make a cynic and misanthrope of any man. Had all people to be watched by a foreman lest they scamped their tasks? Was there *no* one who would care for his children without his perpetual supervision, so that he could be free to work for them. He himself needed no such dragooning. He worked hard enough, undriven, to keep the home over everybody's head.

Mr. Bruno dropped into a chair that he might loiter in this bath of warm self-sympathy. But, as with all people in their baths, the pleasure was partly spoiled by the knowledge that at some moment he must achieve the courage to step out of the grateful warmth; and he knew he would leave the enervating self-sympathy for the cold air of self-reproach. . . . As if suiting the action to the thought, he rose from the chair and stood on the floor. Confound it! He was to blame. With his indolent *laissez faire,* his forever choosing of the line of least resistance, he had undoubtedly suffered the weeds to spread. For his children's sake he ought to have been perpetually on the watch, lest they were being moulded by soiled or clumsy hands. Daphne in her shepherdess costume! She was an exquisite thing; he could pick her up and crush her to him in his swelling love. Let one hope that so far no harm had been done. Thank goodness, that little Miss Carrell was an exceptional person; she seemed sane enough, and steady, and a perfect lady, as Belle would say. But who ever would have thought that Miss Durgon would have been anything but a subdued, middle-aged virgin? "Confound it!" thought he, "what a blasted fool I must have looked all this time to this woman and her friends! It's a damned insult to me." Thus Mr. Bruno stepped back into his bath.

He had a mind to go abruptly into the breakfast-room next door, and to break in upon Anthony and Miss Durgon.

to their confusion. But, as he foresaw the awkwardness of a meeting between Anthony and himself, and the discomfort Anthony and Miss Durgon would endure, and his own discomfort in witnessing their discomfort, he decided he could not face the scene. If you discover your butler in the act of drinking your whisky out of its decanter, it is an open question which suffers the more, you or he. Had Mr. Bruno possessed a butler, and chanced upon him in such a pilfering, he would have retired like the guilty party in the hope that his butler had neither seen nor heard him.

He sat again in his chair. In the morning he would take a strong line. The phrase was pleasing. It savoured of a monarch dismissing his prime minister : or of a father performing his stern duty by his children. In the morning he would show Miss Durgon that these quiet and trusting men had, none the less—what was the trite metaphor?—an iron hand beneath the velvet glove.

With this resolve he mounted to his bedroom, that mercy might attend poor Anthony to the door.

At breakfast Miss Durgon appeared with a mien of studied composure, and he rather admired her for not keeping her bedroom and publishing a headache. He talked of everyday subjects ; they could not handle over cold bacon and boiled eggs such an explosive grenade as dismissal. After breakfast it should be. He would send for her to his study. It would be painful having to treat a woman of forty-five like a schoolboy : "Miss Durgon, I feel that, as my daughter will soon be going to school (the first he had thought of it), perhaps. . . ." No, he would not prepare his speech. He would wait on inspiration. "Mr. Bruno, I can only thank you for your unfailing courtesy and consideration. I hope we part with no ill-feeling, for I consider it has been a privilege to share in. . . ." "Not at all, Miss Durgon, not at all." If she had any tact, she would drop such a curtain of gauze over the harder features of the scene.

But when, after breakfast, he was reading his paper, he postponed the event till his pipe should be exhausted ; and, after that, till all the matter in the *Times* necessary for a well-informed mind had been exhausted. Then he dropped the paper on his knees. No, the thing would best be done through a woman : that would be more consistent with the courtesy she had invariably received from him. Belle had engaged her, and Belle should be summoned to conclude the engagement ; he could imagine her enjoying it thoroughly and all the while deceiving herself, like the brainless creature she was, that the duty was unpleasant.

Belle arrived the next afternoon ; and it was delectable to watch her surprise and indignation.

"Extraordinary, Tom. Extraordinary in an officer's daughter. So ridiculous, too. A *passé* creature like that ! I don't know which is the more ridiculous, she or the idiotic *roués* who could flit round such a—such a——"

"Rushlight," suggested he.

"Rushlight ! The creature must go at once."

"Yes. But there's nothing gained by doing it otherwise than gently. Let her have some excuse with which she can withdraw in a haze of dignity. Let her have everything that's owing to her, and let—let crowns for convoy be put into her purse."

Belle seemed hardly less childish than Daphne, and to be similarly bantered and confused.

"But, meantime, we shall have to look out for someone else," pursued Belle, who was indubitably spending a delightful afternoon. "I'll busy myself about that at once. But in the interregnum, what's to be done ? "

"Oh, the little Carrell can carry on. She's done it before."

"Carol who ? "

"Carol no one. Miss Carrell, the children's governess."

"But she can't manage the household."

"Indeed she can ; and the War Office and Admiralty as well, if necessary. With marvellous competence."

"But, Tom, she doesn't look twenty."

"She's twenty-three, I believe. If Pitt was Prime Minister of England at twenty-one, Miss Carrell can be mistress of my household, for a fortnight, at twenty-three."

"Yes, but Pitt was a genius."

"He was not the last of the race." It was always annoying, the way Belle spoke about geniuses. "Perhaps Miss Carrell is one too. In fact, I've been wondering whether she couldn't permanently fill the breach." The idea, to be truthful, had only just struck him.

"What? Become your——"

He enjoyed Belle's dismay.

"Yes. Why not?"

"Oh, no, no. Why, the servants wouldn't obey a child like that. And what about the children?"

"They love her. She's been more successful with them than anyone else."

"And then again—forgive me mentioning it, but you literary people are so unworldly-wise—she's too pretty." Belle smiled rather roguishly. "People would talk. With a man in your position it might do untold harm to have a Mistress of the Household, as you call her, of such youth and beauty."

With contempt Mr. Bruno saw, under the veil of righteousness, his sister's relish for the subject.

"You mean they would say that the Mistress of the Household was also the Lady of the Bedchamber?"

"Tom! I wonder why you artistic people always love to shock."

The altercation continued, with the result that Mr. Bruno saw more and more sense in his idea as he saw more and more foolishness in Belle's arguments against it. She fell back on the personal appeal.

"Oh, Tom, let me beseech you to do nothing of the sort. It would be unwise in the extreme. I will do all in my power to secure you a really worthy and capable housekeeper. You can trust me."

It occurred to him to retort: "Your last effort was no proof of your trustworthiness. And it justifies me in a bold innovation." But he only replied:

"It might, at any rate, be given a trial. The children love her as much as they distrusted Miss Durgon, and I begin to believe they are good judges. The servants unite in praising her. We'd better see Miss Carrell."

He leaned forward and touched the bell. As it rang down below he wondered if he was rashly committing himself to something that wanted longer thought. Was he being driven by the character that was now his tyrant to take again the line of least resistance? No, surely this time the easiest line chanced to be the best.

"Tom, you don't mean to say you have determined?"

He had not meant to say so; indeed, was wondering

how, if necessary, he could avoid saying so; but such a question from Belle was answered as soon as asked.

"Yes, I think I have."

"Well, I wash my hands of the whole business. It's bound to be a failure."

This made him resolve that, if possible, it should be an echoing success.

When, happy to be the purveyor of pleasure, he took Miss Carrell into his confidence, offering her £80 for a start and £100 later "if the arrangement answered," she looked both pleased and frightened. (Frightened, because there is always something uncanny in the success of all one's plans.) And he was charmed with the little creature's ingenuousness.

"I know one person who'll be delighted," said he, to reassure her. "That's my little daughter."

CHAPTER V

VERY carefully did Miss Carrell justify her election. By courteous handling of the kitchen population, by preserving unprofaned her master's private hours, by consolidating the affection of the daughter of the family and the approval of the quieter Owen, she showed how straight was her eye, how cunning and steady her hand. But, like Miss Durgon before her, she had yet to make her metamorphosis complete; it was her policy to slough off for ever the nursery governess and to put on the handsomer scales of the lady housekeeper. "School." The word popped about in her mind. "Boarding-school." The children were getting older. How insinuate into the minds of everyone that they must soon go to school? Then she would enjoy the not unfashionable duties of purchasing their outfits, interviewing their principals, conveying them on the first day of term to the thresholds of their schools, and writing to them afterwards like a conscientious guardian.

She would do it through Daphne. Miss Carrell had read her pupil's character, in so far as a thing still amorphous had features to be read; and what she saw was this: the child's surging vitality, because no one was directing it to a selected field, would run down any channel that might be laid invitingly before it. There was the whole-hearted readiness to be masculine, just because half a dozen people had called her "tomboyish"; there was the whole-hearted readiness to fall in love with her governess, when the governess hinted that the gates were open. She was like a mass of rising water that, insecurely prisoned, had been making its own little channels, and would certainly, did Miss Carrell trench wisely, run down her new-chosen course.

So, on evenings after tea, when the dusk was in the schoolroom, Miss Carrell would read tales of school to the children, Daphne sitting on the floor at her knees, and

93

Daphne Bruno

Owen staring from his chair at the fire. It was difficult to secure enough of these "Stories for Girls." They read "Winifred of Greystones," "The Most Popular Girl in the Fourth Form," "Fanny the Prefect," and "The Tomboy of Tatterden House." And as Daphne's imagination breathed abounding life into Winifred of Greystones, Fanny the Prefect, and, above all, the fascinating Tomboy of Tatterden House, it was only through fear of hurting the love of her governess that she refrained from asking: "Do you think I shall be able to go to school soon?" Miss Carrell read these stories very well, for, to tell the truth, she was as interested in them as her pupils; it was as much as she could do to restrain herself from pursuing the career of Winifred or the Tomboy after the children had gone to bed. Owen, also, though he said little, was more interested in the tales than was proper for one of his sex.

At length, hand-in-hand with assurances of unfailing affection, Daphne introduced the proposition that she went to school soon. She would write every week to Miss Carrell full details of her adventures. And Owen would go to his prep. school, and they would be able to compare notes.

This enthusiasm for going to school was unintelligible to Owen, who secretly dreaded his first visit, but he pretended to be as excited as she.

"You'll have to ask your papa," Miss Carrell replied. "I don't think he'll like it. You're too young. Besides, schools—boarding-schools are expensive."

"Oh, but father's got lots of money."

"His expenses are very heavy."

"Yes, but I shall have to go to school one day. And I'm just on twelve."

"I believe you want to get rid of me. I believe you're tired of me. You're ashamed of being taught by a governess."

Indignantly Daphne protested, but Miss Carrell continued: "Well, well, I suppose it *is* humiliating for a child of eleven to be tied to the strings of a governess." And she knew she had successfully bedded out *that* idea.

The same evening Mr. Bruno's study was entered by his daughter, who, guessing from his position in the armchair, with book and spectacles, that no more than three minutes would be allotted her, came straight to the point.

"Please, daddy, may I go to school?"

"To school? Why, you're not yet out of your cradle."

"Don't be silly. I'm in my twelfth year."

"So? Well, what school are you going to?"

"Oh, I don't know. Some school."

"Well, there's an excellent school, financed by the government, in Star Lane. You could go there, I suppose. I noticed the other day that there was an Infants' Entrance."

"Oh, but father," protested Daphne. "That's only for district children. I mean a proper school—a boarding-school. For *ladies'* children."

"But, gracious lady, art thou the daughter of an earl's castle? I'll tell you what you are. You're just the encumbrance of a public entertainer, who has, so to speak, to drag you round in a box by the side of his barrel organ. Even so, aren't you being taught by an excellent governess?"

"Yes, but no one in double figures has a governess."

"No one in double figures has a governess. Translate, for a dull mind."

"No one eleven years old has a governess. Did you?"

"Ah, did I? 'Twere well, were you brought up as I. The rod, my child, frequently and soundly applied."

Daphne, for a response, smiled delightedly.

"What does the excellent Carrell say?" asked Mr. Bruno.

"Of course, she doesn't want me to go, as she'd lose me——"

"Upon my soul!" began Mr. Bruno.

"But she said I might ask you and "—here Daphne, who had come and leaned forward against the arm of his chair, drooped her head in an acted sulk—"she *said* you wouldn't agree."

"Did she though?"

"She said you couldn't afford it, but I told her that was all my hat."

"All your what?"

"All piffle."

Daphne Bruno

"If there's a school, Miss Billingsgate, where they teach seemliness and decorum, and such a modicum of English as will enable you to get through society without expulsion, I think it had best be looked for immediately."

"Well, when may I go?"

"I don't know. Not to-night, certainly. It's already approaching six o'clock. Which reminds me that 'the clock upbraids me with a waste of time.' You'd better let me get on with my work, especially if I'm to pay all this new money for your education. . . . Good night, Duffy dear. Go and get into your cradle."

The next morning, as he was crossing the first-floor landing to the door of his study, he saw Miss Carrell coming downstairs, and remembered his conversation with Daphne. Keeping hold of his door-handle, as a sort of insurance policy against protracted talk, he asked:

"I suppose you've heard of my daughter's latest freak? School?"

"Yes, she's always harping on it."

"Is she? Good gracious! Why, it was but yesterday that we had to be thinking about getting her a governess." He had almost forgotten that the important little person before him was the governess in question. "Her wedding will be upon us before we've folded up her swaddling clothes. . . . However. . . . School. Do you think she ought to go? At what age do girls go? Of girls I profess to know nothing, except that, speaking generally, they are a great ornament to the world. Do you think she ought to go?"

Miss Carrell shook her head and lifted her shoulders.

"*I* don't want to lose her, but sometimes I think that with her vital nature she ought to have more of the society of girls like herself. My Latin, for instance, is poor."

"*Mensa-mensa-mensam*," began Mr. Bruno helpfully. "But how does one find a really good girls' school, and go and examine it?"

Miss Carrell's head went slightly on one side.

"Of course, I know a good deal about the scholastic world, having been a mistress myself."

"No; is that so? I didn't know that, or I had forgotten it. This is exceedingly useful. Tell me some more about suitable schools."

"Of course, I know best the school where I taught for three years. Hemans House."

"If it's named after Mrs. Hemans, I've no opinion of the poetess—

> The boy, oh! where was he?
> Ask of the winds that far around
> With fragments strewed the sea!

No, we can't send her to a place named after Mrs. Hemans."

"I rather fancy it was. But Miss Vidella is old-fashioned. I expect to your thinking she'd be a very antiquated type. There's nothing the least bit modern about Hemans House. It's a very strict, and I suppose you'd say a very prudish place."

"Not at all, not at all." It is a quality of incisive minds that they must ever brief themselves for the opposite of what has just been said. "I'm more than ever convinced that all children, girls especially, should have a course of old fashions before they begin to be modern. Christian ethics, after all, are an extraordinarily good system on which to run your life, and the modesty of our grandmothers is a necessary base for later liberties. Yes, I've given the subject considerable thought. Childhood should be a time of very vigilant restraint. They must be pruned, so as to make less gay blossoms and more wood. Then, well rooted, they can blossom as they fancy."

Mr. Bruno had paid the exceptional Miss Carrell's intellect the compliment of thinking she understood him; but he was quite wrong—Miss Carrell, by his second sentence, had retired from further understanding, and was allowing her mind to fill with a new scheme. When he had finished. she said, "Yes, of course."

"And where is this Miss Vidella's school?"

"Windsor."

"Then at any rate she has some unimpeachable neighbours. . . . And, from your three years' experience, do you really think it is a good school? A good place for Daphne."

Miss Carrell appeared to deliberate before she replied.

"Of an old-fashioned kind, yes. . . . Yes, I think certainly. It is purposely limited to a few girls, because Miss Vidella, though strict, likes to mother each individual girl."

Daphne Bruno

"I see. Vidella is an extraordinary name. Was she born with it, or is it a *nom de guerre?*"

Miss Carrell said she didn't know.

"I should think it's a trade-mark," suggested Mr. Bruno. "Prima donnas and ballerinas and hat-makers adopt names like that, don't they?"

Miss Carrell said it was just the sort of quaint thing Miss Vidella would do. "She's a personality, if ever there was one."

"Is she? Well, you want a personality at the head of a school. We must think this over. . . ." He turned the handle of his door. "Meantime, work calls. You must think it over, too."

Miss Carrell did think it over. She had started to think it over before his door opened. And now she continued her journey downstairs but slowly, stopping at times to examine the idea again. She unconsciously nodded to herself. Yes, she knew that little stout Miss Vidella through and through. It would be a pretty piece of work, and rather satisfying to one's vanity.

When next Miss Carrell had a day to herself, she dressed in her latest-bought costume for the confounding of her old employer, and took the train to Windsor.

Leaving the station, she passed the castle on her left hand, and, descending the hill, walked to the outskirts of the town. It was wonderfully pleasant to follow these familiar streets, thinking how her position had improved since the days when she used to tread-mill them regularly behind a crocodile of garrulous young girls. A narrow, stringy life, a young mistress's in a school like Hemans House! How she had envied, though vanity had hardly admitted it, the visiting parents to whom Miss Vidella would show such consideration! And now she was approaching the place almost like a parent herself. No suitor for employment, but a prospective employer of the odious little Miss Vidella. There was something very near glee in the thought.

It was a long walk, but at last she saw the high, grey wall, of about eighty foot frontage, that screened from sight the lower floors of Hemans House, seeming always to intervene between the charges of Miss Vidella and the immodesties of the world. At either end were tall carriage doors painted green, but dust-coloured and spattered in their lower halves, where the assoilings of the world's highway beat against the sequestrated school. These carriage doors were termini—as Miss Carrell so well knew and soon saw again—of a bow-shaped drive that encompassed a darkened haunt of trees and shrubs. The gravel, moss-green at the gutters but clean at the crown, suggested that nowadays it knew feet more than wheels—like a lady who has once belonged to the carriage folk but has had losses and must now be content with an occasional cab. The house, before which its arc swept, was wide, flat-fronted, flat-roofed, and, as one suspected after seeing the garden wall, faced with a greying stucco. Its windows were curtained with the simplicity of dormitories and class-rooms. The drive broke from its bow-sweep for a space to touch the bottom of the dead-white hearth-stoned steps. These brought one to a hall door painted the same green as the doors in the garden wall, but scrupulously washed; indeed, at this door, with its brilliant brass knocker, letter-box and bell, one seemed to be in real touch, for the first time, with the niceties of Miss Vidella.

Conscious of her new quality, Miss Carrell ascended the steps. In the past and pitiable years she had always been obliged to enter the house through the pupils' entrance at the side, for only parents or visitors might defile the hearth-stone steps. She rang the bell and knocked a confident ratter-tat-*tat;* and, while waiting, peeped through the two lights of leaded and coloured glass to see the old familiar hall, now in a dull green, now in a sickening blue. Here came a maid. Miss Carrell turned her head and looked towards the shrubbery. The door opening showed the maid in a black dress, neat apron, and cap with streamers—in fact, just as presentable as the brass knocker. Yes, Miss Vidella was at home, and what was the name, please?

"Miss Carrell. She will know me."

Miss Carrell did not say, "I was once a mistress here," because she remembered how the servants had always despised the mistresses. "And how could they do anything else," thought she, as she stepped in, "knowing that the governesses were paid but ten pounds a year more than themselves, and fed no better?"

Daphne Bruno

The old familiar hall! The same well-polished linoleum, narrow mahogany table pushed against the heavy red-and-gold wall-paper; the same two mahogany chairs; the same hat and coat stand, jealously guarded from hats and coats; the same comparative darkness and inalienable odour; the same hum of voices from the class-rooms; and the same sound—which, to be sure, she had forgotten for years, but was a necessary ingredient—of a pupil playing scales in one of the music-rooms on the first floor.

She was imagining the mistresses in class-room or music-room, and feeling sorry for them, as she followed the maid into Miss Vidella's reception room. So familiar! this congregation of mahogany pieces and knick-knacks with a display of antimacassars over the backs of arm-chairs. There was the upright piano which would be used for practice when no guests were in the room. On all the tables, on the top of the piano, and along the mantel-shelf were cabinet portraits, in assorted frames, of girls who had left; and all these photographs stood parallel, but obliquely, as if they had once stood shoulder to shoulder but had heard the command, "Half left turn!" Miss Carrell studied the pictures of girls she had known, many of which bore signatures such as "Grace," or "Your affectionate pupil, Dorothy Brewer," or "To dear Miss Vidella, from her affectionate Violet."

"Miss Vidella says she's engaged for a few minutes, but will not keep you waiting long."

Yes. That would be the message she would send to an ex-mistress. Miss Carrell walked to the window and looked out. She could re-create what had happened when the maid announced "Miss Carrell." "Who? Miss Carrell? Miss Carrell? Dear me. Well, ask her—tell her I will not keep her waiting long." She could hardly be expected to come expeditiously to a person whom once she had employed at a salary of thirty pounds a year. And actually it was a full five minutes before Miss Vidella was heard approaching. Even then she delayed in the hall, while her high-pitched and affected voice whined some instructions to a passing pupil.

The door opened, and unsmiling and deliberate, Miss Vidella sailed towards her late governess. Miss Vidella was short and very stout, and her dress was black, from the

100

collar at her ears to the end of the skirt, which seemed lifted
by the dome of her hips some irregular inches off the ground.
Her hair was as black as her dress, and mercilessly parted
in its middle, probably to complete the resemblance to an
ancestral portrait; but the fat face, with its steel spectacles
on a nose that did not appear to have developed much since
infancy, hardly matched the dignity of her walk or the
queenly attitude she assumed in her chair.

"Ah, Miss Carrell." Not for twenty years, one
imagined, had the inflexions of Miss Vidella's voice been
true and natural; they were always taken from a cupboard
to suit her pose of the moment; she had a favourite one of
injured surprise, which she supposed was very effective with
her pupils and staff; another of quiet indomitability; and
another of mirthless sarcasm. Her present voice was the
voice of a patron conceding an audience. "I'm sure it's
very kind of you to come. And where do you teach now?"

"I am no longer teaching. I—I manage a gentleman's
household for him."

That a governess could rise out of her caste to something
higher was not easily conceived by Miss Vidella.

"What? A housekeeper? Isn't that a pity? Surely
the training of youth was a higher calling."

"I did not say 'housekeeper,' Miss Vidella. What I
mean is, I manage a widower's household for him, and act
as guardian of his children."

"But surely that means he's making you combine
governess and housekeeper in one? I hope he is not taking
advantage of you, and that you are not being overworked."

("Fat little beast," thought Miss Carrell. "You
naturally don't want to think that I bettered myself by
leaving you.") But while thinking this she said pleasantly:

"You don't quite understand the post, Miss Vidella. I
must confess I consider myself very lucky, and I thought it
would please you too. Mr. Tenter Bruno is a widower, and
he has appointed me to the sole charge of his servants and
his children. He gives me, in addition to a luxurious home,
a hundred pounds a year."

As a tadpole might legitimately be called a frog, so her
present eighty pounds, by virtue of its promise, might be
called a hundred.

"A hundred pounds a year resident!" Miss Vidella's

101

little black eyes at last showed amazement. "But surely that's an enormous salary for so young a woman, is it not? "

"It is very good, certainly."

"He must be a very wealthy man, this Mr.—Mr.——"

"Mr. Tenter Bruno."

"There is a writer of that name, is there not? Though I confess I have little acquaintance with any of these modern writers. They are so revolutionary, and their writings have a distinctly immoral tone. Shelley and Keats, of course, I am passionately fond of. Is your Mr. Tenter Bruno of the same family as the writer? "

"He is *the* Mr. Tenter Bruno."

"*Indeed?* "

It was clear that Miss Vidella was giving some thought to this information, for she had looked again, and with a new expression, at the fine plumage of her late governess. If you brought together such notions as a loose modern writer, a pretty dependent, and the ridiculous remuneration of a hundred pounds a year——

"Indeed ! " she said. "It's a curious appointment."

Miss Carrell smiled. She did not trouble to repudiate the suspicion, even feeling a humour to encourage it. Raising her shoulders, she replied :

"Perhaps all artists are unconventional."

There was a rustle in her hostess's chair.

"Unconventional theories, in my experience of the world, Miss Carrell, often end in—er—in all sorts of things." She began to enjoy playing the mentor on such a subject to the young woman. "Are you sure that you are quite wise in accepting such an equivocal position? Artists are so often loose-lived. You must forgive me, but this is the warning of an old woman."

A merry laugh was Miss Carrell's reply.

"Oh, I can look after myself all right. Why, I've been there over two years."

(Not, of course, on her present throne, but it was unnecessary to explain that.)

Miss Vidella bridled and shrugged. Obviously she was thinking that, if such were the position, the worst had probably happened. And in the face of this probability, Miss Carrell was no person to encourage in Hemans House.

"Well, I happened to be in the neighbourhood," said

Les Tracas des Enfants

Miss Carrell, "and I couldn't resist inquiring after the old school. I hope it's prospering."

"Certainly," said Miss Vidella, slightly ruffled. "My school has never been more prosperous."

"The numbers keep up?"

"I do not desire too great numbers, for then each individual child receives greater attention from myself and my staff."

("Fiddlesticks!" thought her listener. "That stuff may go down with the parents, but what's the good of palming it off on me?")

"I would have asked you to stay to tea," said Miss Vidella, after a pause, "only I have hardly a minute to spare. I am really very busy indeed. I am afraid I shall have to ask you to excuse me."

Miss Carrell rose and picked up her umbrella from a chair. It was rather fun angling for this plump trout.

"All right—yes—I mustn't keep you. I don't think I'd better stay to tea, as I want to get to town early. There's just one thing I wanted to ask you, and it was this. The elder of my two charges is a girl, Daphne Bruno. She is about to go to school, and Mr. Bruno has commissioned me to find a suitable place for her. I thought you knew so much more about the scholastic world than I did, so as I was in the town it occurred to me to look in and ask you to advise us. Mr. Bruno would want a really first-class school, of course, and I don't suppose money would be a very great object."

"This is very interesting. Please sit down again, Miss Carrell." Miss Vidella sat down herself. "This is very interesting. Tell me about the little girl. The mention of her alone interests me, my life having been spent in the service of such as she. How old is she, and what is her name?"

"She's eleven, and her name is Daphne Deirdre."

"Such strange names!"

Miss Vidella said it in a voice she kept for parents, or for the girls when they used slang: it had a faint savour of mittens and quiet-handed surprise at anything less strictly regulated than herself.

"Yes," Miss Carrell agreed. "As you said, these people are unconventional. What school do you really think would suit the daughter of such a man? Of course, to modern parents the very possession of his daughter would be an advertisement for the school."

"Miss Carrell, why should she not come here? I am fairly full, as I intimated, but I could make an exception for such a child, in the hope, of course, that she would inherit her father's talents and bring great credit to the school. And for your sake, too, as an old member of the staff."

It was a demurring answer that Miss Carrell gave to this.

"I had hardly thought of that. Of course, she'd do credit to any school. She has a clear, inquisitive brain and a tremendous vitality that she gets from her father, and at the same time a soft and adoring side that I suppose comes from the mother, who seems to have been a frail, affectionate creature. Altogether a charming child. But I don't think it would do. I expect that Mr. Bruno contemplates paying much higher fees than you ask."

"We can always arrange our fees," began Miss Vidella, luckily seeing nothing of the laugh that trembled through her visitor. "I mean mine has always been a sliding scale suited to the pockets of the parents. By which I have been able to help a lot of children of less well-to-do people."

"As far as I can remember, quite a lot of them came at reduced fees," said Miss Carrell in obliging agreement.

"Yes, I have made many sacrifices. It has been my work in life."

"Mr. Bruno is particularly anxious about the social status of the girls his daughter will meet."

"Of course. Naturally. Well, we shall satisfy him there. You know I make a point of receiving only the daughters of officers, clergy and professional men."

"Yes, I remember it says so in the prospectus." This reply particularly pleased Miss Carrell, for it would leave Miss Vidella wondering what exactly she meant. "I must admit the idea had not occurred to me, and frankly I don't think it would quite answer. Still, I'm grateful for your suggestion." She rose. "I must be hurrying, or I shall miss my train, and we have some guests to-night," which last statement was a fiction provided for atmospheric effect.

"Of course, you understand," said Miss Vidella hurriedly,

and smiling to repudiate any false construction that might be put on her words, "that in the event of your sending me a good pupil I should save an agent's fee. I don't know if it——"

A laugh rippled from Miss Carrell.

"What an idea! Were you going to suggest that I received it instead? Oh, yes, I remember you used to offer it to us. I shouldn't mind taking it at all, if by chance Daphne came to you. I have no false pride and make no bones of the fact that I earn my living. What fee do you usually give the agents? "

"Oh, they vary. But I really shouldn't mind offering you, in this case, if Mr. Bruno paid, say—say, a hundred a year, a commission of ten pounds. I should regard it as only fair."

"Well, that would be a pleasant little windfall, supposing Daphne did come here. Though you understand, of course, I must put the little girl's interest before all things."

"Naturally. Naturally. I would be the last person to suggest anything else. But, of course, I have such faith in my own methods that I don't think she would do better elsewhere. I feel I should like to have your little ward here. And it's only because you're an old friend of mine, and I knew your position, that I offered what I did."

"Oh, I think it was exceedingly sweet of you, Miss Vidella. And if Mr. Bruno decides to send his daughter here I shan't at all mind taking it. Well, we must see. It's quite a new idea to me. Good-bye."

If Miss Carrell, as she passed into the street, was faintly reminded of the sons of Jacob selling young Joseph to the Midianites for a few pieces of silver, she quickly forgot so silly a thought.

PART II

DAPHNE'S SCHOOLDAYS

PART II

DAPHNE'S SCHOOLDAYS

CHAPTER VI

DAPHNE, her governess, and a new trunk marked D. D. T. B., were all in the Windsor train as it moved out of Paddington. A sense of well-being accompanied Miss Carrell too. So often had she seen parents bringing their children to Hemans House, and envied them the position in which they stood to the school and to the mistresses. It was the difference between the paying and the paid, between the clients of a firm and its servants. Not so much those whose children came for notoriously reduced fees; them she had rather pitied. And now here was she, wearing gracefully the clothes of the leisured classes, and bringing to Miss Vidella a best-paying child. Under a manner of graciousness and charm she would talk to the junior mistresses.

She could congratulate herself on the skill with which she had played for Mr. Bruno's decision. She had used Daphne first, hanging before her gaze pictures of life at Hemans House as it lived in her memory—its fun and mischief, its quaint customs, and its tales of friendship between girl and girl or between governess and pupil, till the child's imagination was possessed by Miss Vidella and her establishment, and she would pester her father to be sent to that school and no other. With the father Miss Carrell had kept her recommendation free from over-emphasis, though unmistakably strong. She made capital with the idea that Daphne would probably do best at a school on which she was keen. And Mr. Bruno had agreed.

Daphne was less happy than Miss Carrell. After all

109

her noisy enthusiasm for school, she did not like to admit
a present anxiety that was almost a dread. Even from
herself she pushed away a wish that she and Owen and
Miss Carrell could have gone on for ever in the schoolroom
upstairs with the two desks. As the train hurried towards
Windsor she gazed out of the window and affected, for
her previous attitude demanded nothing less, a great excitement about the journey and its destination.

"You'll soon see Windsor Castle," said Miss Carrell.

"Shall we? How ripping!" But she felt that the
moment of seeing Windsor Castle, where it towered above
the distant trees, would be a moment of something like
fright; and one could wish that the train would roll on
and on, so that the moment never came. The hunched carters
whose wagons rumbled on the country roads were people
to be envied for their age and freedom; so were the porters
on the platforms, who would be doing to-morrow what
they were doing this afternoon; and the engine driver,
alone in his engine day after day, with no head mistress
or big girls to overawe him. Something was wrong with
her breathing; she kept wanting to rearrange it with a
short, quick inhalation or a downward sigh or yawn. But
when Miss Carrell, looking out of the window, began to
search the skyline for the Round Tower of Windsor Castle,
that she might point it out with an exhibitor's pride, and
at last exclaimed : "There it is—there between the trees!"
Daphne jumped up and stared out of the door-window in
an imitation of effervescing delight. A sickish business,
because her heart was not in the effervescence; it was lying
somewhere lower than usual and beating too fast.

"Is Hemans House far from the station?" she asked,
and though her voice was meant to suggest impatience, the
words were really an appeal for delay.

"Yes, it's a mile or more, but we'll take a fly."

Usually taking a fly was a treat, but now, as the train
slowed into Windsor station, the cab seemed little better
than a Black Maria or a tumbrel. But life bustles you on
regardless of your desire to go slow, or even to stop still,
and Miss Carrell bustled her on to the platform. There as
she waited, trembling in the cold wind, she sank herself
deeper in that despairing envy of all the other persons who
were getting out of the carriages : the young people whose

schooldays were behind them, the middle-aged who must have forgotten all about school, and the old men who were near death.

Miss Carrell pushed her into the fly, and said "Hemans House" to the cabman, who nodded "Yes'm," and flicked at his horse, starting it up the hill.

Daphne watched out of the window. "Now we're almost there!" she exclaimed, to keep up the fiction of excited happiness.

The high garden wall of Hemans House was not likely to diminish her anxiety; nor the depressing tangle of trees on the other side of the wall, the moss-greened gravel, and the stucco house. There was more cheer about the white hearthstoned steps and the green hall door. But the clang of the bell in the basement had a ring of irreparability, as if it had snapped off the past; and the waiting for the door to open was unlike any other waiting she had ever known. Fears seemed to have vivified her thinking and heightened her imagination above the normal. White hearthstoned steps, hollowed where the feet trod, were no longer steps and nothing more. Steps? Steps were romantic things. What one-time tenants of this old house had come up these steps and gone down them, and with what emotions! And now they were in their graves. Perhaps some daughter of the house had eloped down these steps with her lover, like Dorothy Vernon of Haddon Hall. A fraction of those hollows was made by their flying feet. School girls, converging from all parts, had come up these steps, and wondered what years lay before them. And after a time they had taken their farewell journey down them. Stirring, sweet thought, that last walk down them! Long after Miss Vidella had died—one could be selfishly happy if she died this afternoon—other tenants, not yet born perhaps, would come up these steps. A crowd would stand here to watch a wedding pair descend to their carriage on the drive. And the bodies of people would one day be carried in coffins, feet foremost, down the steps. That time they would make no impression on the hollows. . . .

The door was opening, and a maid, who recognized Miss Carrell, was inviting them to come in. They were walking through a rather dark hall to the reception-room. Now they were waiting in the reception-room. This was like an interval between two parts of one's life, an empty, silent pause, like the place where the coupling was, between two coaches of a railway train.

Daphne here began to fill the interval, and thus to contract to commonplace thinking again, by a study of the framed portraits of former pupils. All of them seemed to have written, something like, "To dear Miss Vidella, from her affectionate Violet," and she was cheered by these proofs of lovableness in her head-mistress. How pleasant, when she should have left school for ever, to send a photograph, signed, "To my dear mistress, from her loving Daphne Deirdre Tenter Bruno!" She was startled away from the frames by the sound of a high-pitched voice outside; and the door opened, and Miss Vidella made a dignified entry. Daphne had heard from Miss Carrell that her future principal was "short, stout and very quaint," but the words had suggested no such caricature as this. With a moment's homesickness she knew that, had Owen and she in their former freedom seen such a figure in the street, they would have giggled and hurried out of sight.

"So this is little Daphne Bruno!" said Miss Vidella, stretching out a cold hand which Daphne took. The hand seemed to share none of the affection of the high-pitched voice, but to be a sort of perfunctory companion who did what was expected of it without enthusiasm.

"We generally call her Duffy at home," said Miss Carrell.

"Duffy! What a strange name! I don't think we can call her that here. Sounds too much like Duffer—and we have none of them here." Daphne wondered if this were supposed to be funny. "Besides, being her father's daughter, she'll be anything but a dunce. No, we shall only call her Daphne."

Daphne had a sense of seeing Duffy dismissed from the room.

"And how is your dear father?"

"Very-well-thank-you."

"And is he writing another of his splendid books?"

"Yes-I-think-so."

"That's right."

"He's always at work," interjected Miss Carrell.

"Dear me. You must be a proud little girl to be the daughter of so celebrated a parent. Are you?"

Daphne had never thought of it like that—one hardly did about one's father—but she dutifully mumbled "Yes."

"Well, Daphne dear, you must be happy with us. Your father was most careful to choose a school where you would be happy, and you mustn't disappoint him, but tell him how happy you are here." She turned to Miss Carrell. "I am hoping he will consent to act as a reference for us. . . . And I tell you what would be nice for you, Daphne, and make you feel more at home, if you could persuade some other dear little girl friends to come to school with you here. Will you?"

"Yes."

"And to think that Miss Carrell, whom I know so well, should have been helping you with your studies for the last few years! Have you learnt a lot from her?"

"Yes."

"That's right. Well, you're a little shy now, aren't you? Very natural, I am sure. Perhaps you'd like to go downstairs to the dining-room, and see some of your school-fellows. Would you like to do that?"

"Yes—thank—you."

"That's right." Miss Vidella struck a bell on the table beside her. "You'll stay here, won't you, Miss Carrell? I am expecting some more of the dear children's parents, and we shall have a cup of tea up here." The maid entered in response to the bell, and her mistress said: "Knight" (she achieved added dignity by calling all her maids by their surnames), "please take Miss Daphne Tenter Bruno and show her her dormitory—she's sleeping in the Eliza Cook room—and then show her to where the other young ladies are assembled in the dining-room. Miss Sims is looking after them."

"Yes, madam."

"Thank you. . . . Now do you go with Knight, dear, who will show you the way. . . . Ah, yes, yes, Miss Carrell will come and see you before she goes."

Daphne passed out of the door behind the maid, Knight. As the door closed, the thought of Miss Carrell partaking of an exalted tea with the parents made it seem as if she had been assumed into a heaven, leaving Daphne to work out her salvation in loneliness below.

"Come on, your Shyness," the maid surprised her by saying as, not without kindness, she took her by the hand. "You'll soon get used to us. There's worse places than school when all's said and done, and worse schools than this, I daresay. Come and see your bedroom. Up this way. . . . Just the next floor. . . . Now in here. . . . There. . . . That's where you'll sleep, and I wish I had half as good a room."

Daphne was in a large, bright room, with six beds whose top blankets were scarlet and their linen well laundered. On the floor at the foot of the nearest she recognized her trunk. The five other beds started more nervousness.

Knight helped her to remove her coat and hat, brush her hair and prepare for the dining-room. Then she led her downstairs to a big, bare room in the basement. Here were three long tables laid for tea, a vase of flowers at every four feet giving an air of gaiety suitable to the day when the girls returned. Round the walls were hung Maud Goodman's pictures: "Taller Than You, Mother," "When the Heart is Young," and "They Lived Happily ever Afterwards." In the bay window, whose panes looked out upon a shallow area, sat a young mistress, evidently Miss Sims. She was a short woman with a colourless face, not ill-featured, and dull, fair hair. Her popularity was shown by the girls who were dancing around her, or sitting with dangling legs on a table at her side.

All heads turned as the maid entered with Daphne.

"Here's one of the new girls, Miss Sims. She's Miss Daphne Brunner, or some name like that."

"Oh, yes. We've heard all about her—Daphne Bruno."

Miss Sims, in her relations with her pupils, was the complete sentimentalist. She lived with emotions she would have been ashamed to reveal. And yet, to herself, she liked to call these emotions the noblest thing in her. It was just this, she *had* to have somebody to love passionately. The six years of her teaching had been a chain of such hungry, largely concealed loves for some fair-featured pupil. And at the moment when Daphne first saw her, though she was laughing gaily with the girls, for all of whom she felt affection, her mind was really full of treasured regrets and self-pity, because an older pupil, Audrey Stanton, who had held her heart and filled her dreams, had left the school the previous term. "Doubtless," Miss Sims had thought during the holidays, "she will write me a few affectionate letters, and then forget all about me." The pathos of this had evoked a few verses, one of which ran :

Upon the threshold of a broader view,
    Where lay revealed what girlhood sees,
I left my little pupil standing, and withdrew
    To fondle memories.

And another, supposed to be written in ten years' time when all the girl-children on whom she had expended her love should be dispersed :

O Time, reverse the glass, and let flow back the sands !
Within a stucco house once more a figure stands,
And smiles on upturned faces, grasping outstretched hands.

Revive the past? Ah no ! Nor yet retie the knot,
For time must move, and early-formed attachments rot,
And so the tale is told, a girlhood friend forgot.

The melancholy of her return this term to familiar walls empty of Audrey Stanton had been relieved (though in loyalty she hardly admitted it) by the hope that some new pupil would win her heart. When she had been told about the great Mr. Tenter Bruno's daughter, she had wondered whether this interesting child would be able to succeed to Audrey, and to give her all the exquisite delights and sufferings that *that* gracious girl had had the power to bestow.

And now she saw Daphne. She saw an eleven-year-old child whose brown hair had not yet been tied back with a ribbon. The eyes were brown, large and inquiring; the nose straight and small; the mouth at the moment, unmoving and sad—though the sadness, perhaps, was reflected from a timidity in the eyes. The narrow figure, with its early promise of long, thin limbs, was indistinguishable from a boy's. . . . The child looked lost.

Miss Sims's heart moved out to her aid, swelling with hope.

Daphne, quite unaware that there was a person in the room who was wondering whether she would be able to love her better than anyone else in the world, was introduced to all the girls, none of whom made any impression on her except a certain Gertrude Wayne. This girl, who was perhaps a year older than Daphne, but no taller, had deliberately come and sat beside her, and studied to be pleasant.

(The hidden fact was that Gertrude Wayne had just finished reading a boys' school story, "The Best House at Whitefriars," whose hero, a Godfrey Baldwin, had always been very kind and protecting to new boys, and thereby earned their worship; and her behaviour just now was modelled on Godfrey's. She had even a hope that the bigger girls would be unkind to this new kid, so that she could stand up for her. It must be splendid to have the admiration that Godfrey inspired.)

"What did they say your name was?"

"Daphne Bruno."

"Any other names?"

"Yes; Daphne Deirdre Tenter Bruno."

"Oh, I think Deirdre is a ripping name. Which are you called by at home?"

"I'm generally called Duffy at home, but Miss Vidella says I'm not to be called by that here."

"She would. Nicknames are the same as slang to her, the old—— But really she's not so bad." (Gertrude had suddenly remembered that Godfrey never spoke unkindly of anyone.) "She did the same with me. I'm always called Trudy at home, but she said, ' My dear, what a strange name! It's too much like Judy,' and she made me be called Gertrude. I shall call you Duffy, if you'll call me Trudy. Will you?"

"Yes."

"Where are you sleeping?"

"In the Eliza Cook room I think it was called."

"Oh, blow! I'm in the Frances Burney room. Never mind. If there's anything I can do for you, let me know. I remember how rotten it was when I was new. I've been here two years now——"

The conversation was stopped by the sound of Miss Vidella's voice outside, and when she entered with some parents, all the girls stood up and kept silence. Some older ones giggled, though their lips were compressed.

"This is the dining-room," sang Miss Vidella, and the parents, male and female, gazed helpfully round. "Such a nice, cheerful room. South aspect, and gets the whole day's sun. . . . Sit down, dears. . . . You won't mind them sitting down, will you? Yes, they have all their meals here—not luxuries, I'm afraid, but good, plain, wholesome food." (She pronounced this word to rhyme with "good.") "Where's little Daphne Bruno? Ah, there she is. Getting quite at home already. . . . Come to me, dear, and let me introduce you. This is the great Mr. Tenter Bruno's only daughter."

"Tenter Bruno was an old Harrovian," said one corpulent father, interested for the first time. "He was at Harrow with me."

"There. Now isn't that interesting? Here's someone who was at school with your father. How small the world is! . . . Now do you run away, dear."

She soon took out the parents again, who bowed graciously to Miss Sims before withdrawing. Then tea was brought in, the first day of term being celebrated by such extras as blanc-mange and jelly and bananas. The girls, now increased in numbers, were chatteringly occupied with the meal, under the supervision of Miss Sims and another mistress who had appeared, when all were compelled to stand again with full and giggling mouths by the entrance of Miss Vidella and a second little shift of parents.

"Ah, they've started, I see. . . . Miss Sims and Miss Stevens." The parents bowed. "Yes, I don't pretend we give them luxuries, but we study always to have good, plain, nourishing food. . . . Well, sit down, dears, and get on with your meal. I am sure you will be excused. This is one of my new girls this term." Daphne stood up, blushing because her mouth was full, and she was overborne by this semicircle of parents about her. "She's Mr. Tenter Bruno's daughter."

"Really?" exclaimed one lady.

"Yes, he's just sent her. . . . Sit down, dear. . . . It's a fine, cheery room, isn't it? Perhaps you'd like to see the dormitories."

They filed out, and the frost-bound chattering violently thawed.

After tea, Daphne was left quite alone and unspoken to,

Daphne Bruno

Trudy Wayne having gone away, and Miss Sims been relieved by Miss Stevens. She sat on the edge of a table, and passed the time looking up and round at the Maud Goodman pictures, or watching some big girl whose voice was commanding a moment's attention. Quite half an hour must have gone before Miss Carrell came into the room to kiss her good-bye.

"Good-bye, Duffy, dear. I've got to be off to my train. Try to be very happy."

"I think it's lovely," said Daphne.

CHAPTER VII

ON awaking next morning in the Eliza Cook Room and looking round upon its iron bedsteads, beneath whose tumbled red blankets the hips and shoulders of five strange girls made miniature mountain ranges, Daphne yielded to a dull resignation. Owen, whose attractions she had too much overlooked, was now seen to be a friend whose absence left a damping blank. How good the holidays would be when once again Hollins would come in, pull up the blinds, and wake them! All these five schoolfellows were still asleep, and she coveted the ease and familiarity which enabled them to hunch up and sleep like that. Herself felt perfectly awake. She would have liked to get up, but dared not move till some of the others, by rising and dressing, showed her what to do. There were six basins on a long trestle table, with a clean, white cloth and four new pieces of brown carbolic soap. To look at these squares of soap was to catch their smell. Which of those basins ought she to use, and which piece of soap? And how much of herself ought she to wash? Always at home Hollins had taught her that when she didn't have a bath she must wash, like all ladies and gentlemen, right down to her waist, and never be guilty of the "cat-lick." But she knew, as she lay there, that if the majority of these girls made use of the "cat-lick," she would follow their example. Moral courage, of course, demanded the opposite (like Tom Browne saying his prayers), but she had no desire to show moral courage. All she wanted was to do nothing remarkable.

When at last, one by one, and with unembarrassed talking, the girls got up, after a loud bell had rung downstairs, they soon solved for her the problem of washing. All of them seemed to dress as far as their princess petticoats before approaching the basin, and then gave a hasty polish to their faces and necks with the damp end of a towel. One girl, even, who had lain in bed long after the bell had gone, did not wash at all, but dashed downstairs with her dress undone, plaiting her hair as she went.

Into the stream of girls which, fed by tributary rivulets from other rooms, was cascading downstairs, Daphne slipped, so as to flow along with it and see in what pool it finally settled. It settled in the dining-room, where all the girls were taking up places behind the chairs they had occupied at yesterday's tea. Only whispered talk was passing across the breakfast things, as 'f even that were contraband. Daphne slipped to the chair that had known her yesterday, and in the absence of Owen, Hollins, and Miss Carrell, the chair seemed a friend. She saw Trudy Wayne, and Trudy saw her, and smiled and looked dreamily ahead. Daphne wondered at the wistful self-sufficiency in her eyes—not knowing that Trudy was posturing for her admiration as Godfrey Baldwin of White-friars. The whispers evaporated into empty silence as Miss Vidella walked into the room. When Miss Vidella walked, everything from her head to her waist was as stationary as the bust of a stout lady carried on a tray, but everything from her waist to her skirt-hem moved, and this motion gave her passage across the room the character of a slow, dignified flounce. It also shook and jingled the silver chatelaine, which, now that her school was really in session, she had hung at her belt, much as a mayor hangs his chain about his neck.

She went and stood in the window-bay, and immediately Miss Mitchell, the music mistress, walked to the piano and sat down. Daphne guessed. It was to be Prayers.

They sang, apparently by heart, the hymn :

> " New every morning is the love
> Our wakening and uprising prove."

and Miss Vidella in her high voice read a chapter of the Bible. Then all knelt down behind their chairs for the collects and prayers. Some who could not be seen of mistresses sat on their heels. Daphne held on to the upright bars of the back of her chair like a caged monkey, and stared through its tracery at the bare seat and the drooping table-cloth. She tried to say *Amen* when the others did, but the word would not come quick enough, and was even once in danger of saying itself after the next prayer had started; and this dreadful moment decided her to leave the word alone. The public and common worship over, all knelt in silence, till the head mistress, who had been standing, began to move away, and then all finished their private prayers at the same moment, jumped up, pulled out their chairs, sat on them, and released the first trickles of chatter. The door closed on Miss Vidella, who had retired to a more dignified breakfast in her private room, and the trickles of chatter swelled into a spate.

But throughout the meal Daphne employed only one word, "Thank-you." She used it several times, to maids who brought her food, and to the neighbours who passed the plate of bread and butter. She ate her porridge without sugar, being afraid to ask anyone to pass it, and her bread and butter without any marmalade, because the dish was so far away. There was much talk of someone called "Petsy," whom she gradually identified as Miss Vidella, and of someone called "Chutney," who was apparently a man. Once or twice she thought she would start a conversation and feign the ease she did not feel, beginning "Who is Chutney?" but the words never got past her throat. She hardly knew herself. At home she had always been a dominant note, and now she was completely overawed, and in the tightening grip of a horrid desire to cry. The moisture, indeed, was near her eyes, and the nearer it came the nearer her vexation drew it, till at last she was in an agony for the meal to be over, so that she could escape from the crowd. Trudy Wayne had been at too great a distance to speak to her. Only one other person had come out clearly from the noisy background. Shortly after her arrival in the room she had noticed Miss Sims seeking along the faces of the girls for a particular one, and had felt a telepathic certainty it was hers she sought. So she was not surprised when the mistress's eyes encountered hers, and smiled a sympathy. Daphne smiled confusedly back. After that she caught Miss Sims looking at her frequently.

In the half-hour between breakfast and classes the girls went to their various Form Rooms, which they were allowed to use as Common Rooms. Daphne, being as yet placed in no form, wondered where to go, and found herself left in the long hall or corridor that ran behind the form-room doors. Here she delayed, and when people passed, pretended to be doing something definite lest she appeared lost and ridiculous.

Suddenly from a small door at the corridor's end Miss Sims appeared, bearing a load of stiff-covered and glossy exercise books ready for dealing out to the members of the form, and directly she saw Daphne she stopped, and then advanced towards her.

"Are you looking for someone, dear?"

Daphne looked up at her, and seeing the kindness in her eyes, determined to be frank.

"Please where do I go to now?"

"My poor child, have you been out here all alone, wondering where to go? I'll show you. Come with me."

She had intended to lead her to the girls in her own class-room, but changed her direction. Here was the soft-featured child whom last night she had chosen as first favourite for the throne of Audrey Stanton, and it would be rather sweet to have her alone for a few minutes in an empty room, and to talk kindly to her there. Perhaps the child would cry, and she would comfort her, stroking her head, and from that moment the desired adoration would kindle in Daphne.

So Miss Sims walked towards the corner, where the corridor made a right-angled turn and led to a back wing of the house. The first door on her right was a music-room, a cell-like place, containing a piano, two chairs, a table, and a music-rack. With Daphne behind her she entered, and pushed the door so that it closed but did not latch.

"Just come in here a minute where I have one or two things to do."

She pretended to be engaged in sorting some music, but soon stopped. Seating herself on one of the chairs, she said :

"Now come, Daphne dear, I want you to tell me all about yourself."

Daphne came two or three steps nearer.

"Come dear, don't be afraid of me. Don't think of me as a mistress, but just as a friend."

Daphne came up close against her knee, and Miss Sims put her arm about her waist.

"There. You look sad and homesick. I want you to

tell me all your troubles. Always, will you? Anything that's on your mind, no matter what it is. If any girl's unkind, or any mistress doesn't understand you. Always tell me, for already I feel so fond of you."

Perceiving that her pupil's head had dropped a little, as though to hide a moisture, she pulled her closer by the waist, and let her pressure speak silently of sympathy and understanding. For quite a while she held her like that, till Daphne, though grateful and beginning to reciprocate the affection, was not without an embarrassment at its rapid progress.

"Promise me you'll let me do all I can for you. I want to do a great deal. Will you promise me?"

"Yes," muttered Daphne.

Miss Sims pulled her close again; and it would have been difficult to see how the conversation was to be continued or closured, had not a high-pitched voice in the passage outside caused Miss Sims to release the child abruptly.

"There," said she. "We must be getting to the classrooms." A disturbance was in her voice. "You help me to carry these exercise books."

"Miss Sims! Miss Sims!" cried the voice without.

Miss Sims immediately issued from the music room with Daphne following.

"Here I am, Miss Vidella. Little Daphne Bruno is helping me with these exercise books. I thought perhaps I had better give her something to do, lest she should be inclined to mope at all this first morning."

Miss Vidella was apparently angry about something, and eager to vent it.

"What a strange idea, Miss Sims! I think there can be no reason why a child should mope in a school such as mine, where everything is done to contribute to their happiness. I think it's a strange idea to put in a child's head. Very unwise. But that's neither here nor there at the moment. I must ask you to communicate to Miss Mitchell my exceeding displeasure at what I saw just now." She made suitable play with her fat hands. "There was Mr. Pulteney calling to hear if the same pupils were taking the violoncello, as indeed was very proper of him, and there was Miss Mitchell talking to him in the hall. I dislike

Daphne Bruno

intensely to come down the stairs, and see in the entrance hall of my school a young man and a young woman talking together like that. I wish you would convey that impression to Miss Mitchell. Supposing someone had called at that moment. If she as music mistress has any communication to make to the visiting music master, she must make it at the proper time and place. I think I left that impression on them, however. I gave them one look, and they went their several ways. . . . Well, Daphne dear, I hope you are happy. . . . Do you like very much your new school?"

"Awfully."

"Awfully! What strange terms these dear children do use! Well, dear, I think you had better start in Miss Sims's form, the Fourth. We can examine you, and if you know much more than the others of your age, we can move you up. . . . Dear, dear, it is already half-past nine o'clock. Why doesn't someone ring the bell for First Hour?"

In spite of Daphne's distinguished father, the verdict, after an examination of her attainments in Miss Sims's class-room, pronounced that she had but little scholarship, and her intelligence was apparently unremarkable. In truth, she had but few goods to display in her window. Her governess, Miss Carrell, had directed her instruction to achieving popularity with her pupil, and not to her future academic success. Daphne's knowledge, therefore, was below the standard of her age, and, more serious consequence, her capacity for concentration on subjects she disliked was enervated and flabby.

Her failure this morning, while drawing from Miss Sims the becoming sounds of disappointment, really relieved and delighted the mistress. Now there was no chance of her favourite being promoted to the form above. And with Miss Sims, though the thought of cruelty could only sit under aliases and disguises in her mind, it was always sweeter to see her favourites in disgrace and hurt than successful and rejoicing. So she did not minimize Daphne's ignorance when Miss Vidella came in to hear the report, and to examine such papers as the new girl had written.

"Strange!" whined the head mistress, as she took off the steel spectacles with which she had scanned the work.

"Strange indeed that a father of such eminence should have so backward a child. But it is often the way. Ordinary parents have extraordinary children, and *vice versa*. Were your grandparents utterly simple, child? Well, perhaps you don't know. Perhaps one day you will have a little daughter who will redress the balance. Meantime we must see what we can make of you, and you must apply yourself studiously. Now do you return to your seat, dear. You will remain in Miss Sims's form."

With that decision Miss Vidella carried out her stationary bust and back on her swinging hips; and Miss Sims tapped Daphne on the shoulder—it was a pleasure to touch the child even thus far—and murmured, "Never mind. Never mind."

Which rather surprised Daphne, since she had not greatly minded, being dimly aware that Miss Vidella was acting up to a part, and that it was a rather pompous and foolish one.

At dinner only French might be spoken. Of French (Daphne was to learn) Miss Vidella made an enormous feature. She took all the French classes herself, and gave long lectures on French literature, with special attention to Victor Hugo. They were like perpetual masses, with Miss Vidella as priestess, in honour of Victor Hugo. On the strength of having once when eight years of age (so Daphne was told) sat on Victor Hugo's knee, she considered that her French accent was perfect and everyone else's egregious, and her knowledge of French literature vast, and everyone else's insular and limited. "I wish to goodness," the elder girls would say before, during, or after a memorial mass, "that she'd never met the man."

In the afternoon there was talk of a walk. It was the Lent term, and a walk was the normal recreation. Hockey was in the very first stages of its adoption by girls' schools, and to hockey Miss Vidella could never be resigned. Tennis she allowed in the summer term, on the stipulation that the girls kept their legs well-disciplined. But in the Christmas and Lent terms, apart from a walk in crocodile formation, the only athletic pastimes were gymnasium and riding; and riding was limited to those whose parents paid for it. Riding she probably allowed because it gave a school such a *tone;* but she fluttered around it with much care for its propriety. It was not easy to see the riding master, on his chestnut horse, riding away with a score of her girls. Had she been able to sit a horse herself, she would have cantered among them as a chaperon; but she could not, and none of her governesses were ever likely to be familiar with a saddle, even if they could be trusted with a riding master, so she was reduced to being sternly present at the mounting and departure, to instructing the elder girls to look after one another and their younger school-fellows, and to watching the cavalcade as far as the bend in the road.

With gymnasium it was different; one of her mistresses, or herself on days of condescension, could accompany the girls and sit in the spectators' gallery, and ensure that only the seemlier exercises were performed. Definitely she forbade the "spread-eagle" on the rings, and the "circle" or the "hock-swing-off" on the horizontal bar, and the "short-arm-balance" or "long-arm-balance" on the parallel bars. These circles and balances were only so many gilded somersaults. When Hemans House had first gone to the Royal Gymnasium in the Cambridge Road, and Miss Vidella, at first sight of these exercises, had interdicted them for ever, the instructor had declared :

"The other schools allow them, madam."

And Miss Vidella, from her seat in the gallery, had replied :

"I dare say they do, instructor. In fact, I feel very confident they do. But the aims of my school are probably different from theirs. My aim is to turn out little well-bred ladies rather than acrobats and harlequins."

"Quite so, madam."

And Miss Vidella, conceiving that she had made a good point, dulled it by making it again.

"None of my children, instructor, are likely to earn their living in the circus ring."

"No, madam," admitted the instructor, muttering for the amusement of the nearest girls, "not a dog's chance o' that."

So gymnastics were confined to swinging on the travelling rings or the bridge-ladder, gentle vaulting over the parallel bars and the horse (though in this matter there would be a cry of disapproval if the upward swing of any

126

girl's legs was more unladylike than was inevitable), and to Indian clubs and dumb-bells, which Miss Vidella considered most rhythmic and refined.

This first afternoon, since neither gymnasium nor riding had begun, the girls could only go for a crocodile walk, and at the pointed invitation of Trudy Wayne Daphne paired with her.

On this walk Daphne awoke to the idea that men could be important before you were grown up. The conversation of the girls in front danced around the prospects of meeting such and such a man. They spoke of "The Dandy Fifth," who, Trudy explained, was a young coach at an army crammer's, and earned his nickname from the waist-line in his coat, his fawn vest, and his patent-leather boots. And there was Arthur Belsize, the famous young novelist, whose three books, "The Homes of Mogador," "The Purple Orchis," and "Dust on the Scaffold," had made him a local celebrity second only to the lady in the Castle. And there was the Holy Innocent, a curate at Holy Innocents Church, where Hemans House went on Sundays. These gentlemen, Trudy garrulously explained, were often to be passed in the park, the novelist, Arthur Belsize, especially, who had a habit of strolling every afternoon down the Long Walk. "I expect he hopes it'll one day be called the Belsize Walk," suggested Trudy, "like Addison's Walk at Oxford." Here, then, was the explanation why the senior girls whenever possible led the Hemans House column through the gates into the Great Park.

Daphne was excited about the chance of seeing Arthur Belsize, not because he was a young man, but because he was a famous story-writer. His tale, "The Purple Orchis," since it was based on history, had been read to Owen and herself by Miss Carrell. It did not occur to Daphne that, being the daughter of a writer, she had no reason to be excited about them as a class, because she hardly thought of her father as an author in this true story-telling sense.

Neither the dandy nor the curate appeared, and the twitter and chattering of the girls was passing to other subjects, when one of them discerned the novelist, Arthur Belsize, walking slowly towards them. A tremor ran down the crocodile from its head girls to the smaller ones in the neighbourhood of Trudy and Daphne. Daphne put her head outside the column to see the approaching celebrity, and was very disappointed. He looked exactly the same as any other young man who might be seen in a third-class railway carriage.

A silence dropped on the girls. It appeared they had a custom of readjusting their conversation to the novelist's ear. As soon as he came within hearing distance they would discuss only (and this rather loudly) his novels. He was now alongside the column, and the discussion began.

"I liked 'The Homes of Mogador' best, didn't you?"

"I sent 'The Purple Orchis' to my cousin for her birthday."

"'The Homes of Mogador' wasn't a patch on 'The Purple Orchis.'"

"'The Homes of Mogador' was rot."

"I didn't like 'The Purple Orchis' much, but 'Dust on the Scaffold' was ripping."

"That's Arthur Belsize."

He passed by, affecting to have heard nothing, though Daphne suspected that his lips trembled.

To her, who had played with hardly any girl friends in Deseret Road, this interest in men while your hair was still down your back was an idea entirely new. That a lover might come to her after she was eighteen or twenty had, of course, often been in her mind, especially when she read or listened to the love scenes of a romance. But that men as a genus, apart from the individual lover, were interesting she had not grasped, nor that her earlier love stories might be looked for at once.

When the crocodile had returned from its walk it disintegrated into its classes for afternoon school. In Miss Sims's room, darkening behind its Japanese bead curtains, the subject was Latin, a language of which Daphne knew very little and pronounced that little wrong. Her quantities were false, Miss Carrell having learned the grammar after she left Hemans House, and learned it from a book without help from the spoken word. When Miss Sims arranged her girls in a row that they might "go up" and "take each other down," she told Daphne that as a new girl she should be given a start and might go to the top. Doing even this little for her favourite gave her a mild pleasure.

"Now, we'll see what you know of Latin grammar. 'I shall love.' Let us have the future of *Amo, I love.*"

The question pleased Daphne because she knew the answer.

"*Ammer-bo,* I shall love, *Ammer-bis, Ammer-bit, Ammer-byemus, Ammer-bightus——*"

The remaining word was lost in a roar of laughter.

"No, no, no, no," smiled Miss Sims, which amazed Daphne, since she knew she was right; she could see in her mind's eye the whole page of the Latin Grammar, and there was the future, "*Amabo, amabis, amabit.*"

"No, no, no. It's *Amābo,* not *Ammer-bo; Amābimus,* not *Ammer-byemus.*"

At this word the class laughed again, and a sudden unreasonable burst of temper inflamed Daphne. It was the break-through of all her resentment at the failure of school to satisfy her picture of it; she felt ready and anxious for some violent rebellion, as once before she had felt with Miss Durgon. The tears started to her eyes, and this exposure made her angrier and more defiant.

"Say it again now—properly," ordered Miss Sims.

"*Ammer-bo, Ammer-bis——*"

"Next!" The mistress turned her head to the next girl.

"*Amābo.*"

"Go above her." And Daphne went down one place.

Miss Sims had seen the symptoms in her favourite's eyes, and they produced a curious mixture of pleasure and love. After caressing and fondling, she enjoyed most (though it disturbed her to think so) punishing the thing she loved.

"Say it again, and properly, and don't be sulky."

To be told she was sulky was enough to fix Daphne in her obstinacy.

"*Ammer-bo, Ammer-bis——*"

"Next!"

Down went Daphne another place, and the class began to enjoy the game.

"Now say it properly at once."

"*Ammer-bo, Ammer-bis——*"

"Next!"

And a little girl who had been breathlessly rising on her toes said "*Amābo,*" and went up.

Daphne Bruno

There were eleven girls in the class, and Daphne said "*Ammer-bo*" ten times till she reached the buffers of the bottom place.

"You're a very naughty little girl," denounced Miss Sims. "You're the oldest girl in the class, and you're content to be taken down by those much younger than you. And just to gratify sullenness and rebellion. You will write out fifty times, 'The second *a* in *Amabo* is long.' And don't let me see anything of you till that is done."

She had visions of herself being cold and haughty with the child, and of Daphne, whose advances would thus be repelled and bruised, suffering the tortures of a loved mistress's scorn and finally breaking in humility at her feet.

After the classes and tea there was an hour before Preparation. Silent at her desk in Miss Sims's room, now a chattery Common Room, Daphne wrote twenty times, 'The second *a* in *Amabo* is long,' and decided that she had done enough for to-night. Feeling so lonely she wanted to write to Miss Carrell—even to Owen. She got some of the note-paper that had been given her to take to school, and began her letter.

"DEAR MISS CARRELL,

"I hope you got back safely. . . ."
(The picture of Miss Carrell getting back to her home and entering the old rooms made her lip shake.)
"We have been for a lovely walk this afternoon in the park. It was lovely. We passed Arthur Belsize. I sleep in a room called Eliza Cook. There is another room called the Frances Burney room. This afternoon we did Latin. I am going to have my first riding lesson to-morrow, and I am looking forward to gymnasium. I like school awfully. What fun it will be when the holidays begin in three months' time. I must not write much more as I am going to write to Owen.

"Much love

"From

"Ever your loving

"P.S.—Love to Hollins." "DUFFY."

130

CHAPTER VIII

DAPHNE soon became used to Hemans House, its population and its practices, and could look back with wonder at the first days of fear. More than that, the life, for a particular reason, had become flushed with colour and richness. The one thing needed to lift her hatred from the school-rooms and the Windsor streets and to throw a glamour over them had happened: she was possessed by a romantic attachment for someone whose background they were. Before half-term had signalized to the girls that the top of the slope had been reached, and they could now go quickly down hill to the holidays, she knew that she adored Miss Sims. It had taken some five weeks of the alternate caresses and punishments, warm intimacy and stern aloofness, to betray their meaning to Daphne; but once it had broken on her that she was the object of a popular mistress's favouritism, she was flattered into reciprocation. The slide from fondness to love was easy and quick. As with her affection for Miss Carrell, so now with her adoration of Miss Sims: she loved to think that she loved. But the later attachment was as much stronger than the earlier, as Daphne was older, warmer, and more conscious of her sex. It was an emotion too strong for reticence—except in words; on walks she fought to be at Miss Sims's side; sometimes she threaded her arm into the mistress's; and once, when they were right behind all the others, she rested her head against her shoulder. At gymnasium every exercise she performed on parallel bars, horizontal bar, or bridge ladder was done with an eye on the gallery in the hope of impressing Miss Sims. She suffered the pains of jealousy when Miss Sims (deliberately) made much of another girl. And her letters home to Miss Carrell were enthusiastically full of her form mistress. There was pleasure in writing about her.

But her pains and pleasures were weak compared with those hidden behind Miss Sims's indulgent smile. As Miss Sims assured herself: "The child is fond of me—very fond—

really devoted, I think. But it must inevitably be a small return for what I am giving to her. It is always so with children. . . . Still, it is happiness to give." She made a resolution that her influence must be a power for good. She must be associated in the memory of Daphne Bruno, when that beloved girl should have grown tall and given herself to a man, with all that was best in her childhood. She must be the person of whom Daphne would say: "I really owe everything to her."

And a salient truth of Daphne's schooldays was this, that Miss Sims—Miss Sims, with her thirty pounds a year and her cubicle with an iron bed and tin wash-stand; Miss Sims with her high-coloured make-believes, of which she was half ashamed; Miss Sims with her thirst for emotion and her squeezing of pupils like sponges for its sating—*was* the most of what she resolved to be. Everyone is an expert in the hobby that fills his dreams, and Miss Sims had seen exactly how her influence could be this "power for good." Her little worshipper would most surely model herself on her idol, and so Miss Sims must appear to embody in her own nature all the noble qualities she would give to Daphne. She created a character in her imagination, and always acted it before the eyes of her pupil. And this was the Character: great gentleness masking concealed strength; a perfect feminine sympathy mingled with a capacity to be stern; remarkable sensibility to beauty wherever it was to be found, and thus a passionate love for all the arts, with a predilection for literature; a taste in dress, and a beautiful serenity in manner.

As a background to the Character, she hinted in her talks with Daphne at a collateral relationship to a very old family; at reasonable private means, her present work being done for the love of it, there being no nobler task; at holidays in romantic places abroad; and, of course, at a love story of which one did not speak.

In her first holidays Daphne returned home, full of the importance of a schoolgirl, and talked incessantly of the customs at Hemans House to Owen, who was not interested, and to her father, who was quite amused—at least, till he took up his book again. It was his daughter's tales and imitations of the head mistress that pleased him—"By

Jove! she can *see,* that child." Miss Vidella appealed to
the dramatist in him, both as a picturesque character and as
a type.

"She belongs to a type that is doomed to pass, Duffy
mia. There is pathos as well as humour in her posing and
her prudery. I always think it's rather sad the way such
people imagine they are being applauded, while all the time
they are being laughed at by modern minds. . . . However,
you'll understand these things later."

One result of this ridicule was that his daughter saw how
much better it was to be on the laughing, rather than the
laughable, side of a dividing line, and that she must therefore join the moderns who always did the laughing. She
was modern. She saw Miss Vidella from a new angle, and
much more clearly, and she determined to carry this interesting view-point back to Hemans House. As a view-point it had
much to recommend it : it meant that when Miss Vidella pro-
hibited this and that—circling over the horizontal bar, or
any display of the feminine leg above the lower calf—she
was probably out of date, and the best way to express one's
advance from such rulings was to glory in their breach.

The only conflict in her mind was how far this healthy insurgence, imitated from her father, clashed with the obedience
and serenity imitated from Miss Sims. And when she was
again under the roof of Hemans House and the influence of
Miss Sims, a settlement of the conflict was found to be very
necessary. So on a walk to the tennis fields, when the mistress and her favourite had dropped behind the girls, she
sidled up to the subject.

"Father says Miss Vidella is out of date, and so are all
her ideas."

"H'm. Your father is doubtless a representative of
extremely modern minds."

"So'm I."

Miss Sims laughed, provoking Daphne to defend herself.
"Well, she *is* rather absurd."

"Hush, dear," said Miss Sims, for the Character was
nothing if not loyal. "Miss Vidella's aims are of the
highest, and there's a lot to be said for the kind of woman
she tries to produce—modest, controlled, and quiet. . . .
But I do think that perhaps she doesn't make sufficient
allowance for the heyday in the blood of youth. Probably

the animal spirits ought to express themselves sometimes in a little wildness and tomboyishness—so long as these things go with affectionateness—and with high ideals. Later, when one has experienced the disillusions of life, it will be time to acquire a tranquil resignation."

This was an excellent verdict. For sympathy and sense there had been no one before quite like Miss Sims. Everything had now fallen into place. Daphne saw that she could postpone the final serenity till she had grown up and passed through the fire. She was thus at liberty to express the modernity of her intellect, as compared with Miss Vidella's, by flagrant breaches of Miss Vidella's rules.

The first time she displayed it was at the gymnasium. She hung it out, so to speak, on the horizontal bar.

It was a morning when the head mistress herself was in the gallery watching carefully through her spectacles. The girls had been vaulting backwards over the parallel bars, and Daphne, when her turn came, had swung herself with such ardour that the oblique line of her body was rather from her legs down to her head than from her head down to her legs—a position which Miss Vidella stipulated must be guarded against in this dangerous exercise. Her legs had just swung down again on to the mat when she heard the high-pitched voice coming from the gallery top like the voice of a bird from a tree. All eyes had turned towards it.

"Instructor! Instructor!"

The instructor made a grimace, seen only of the girls, and called back: "Yes, madam."

Miss Vidella made her favourite point.

"Instructor, I take it this is a place for teaching young ladies a becoming deportment, and not for training circus clowns."

"Yes, madam," agreed the instructor.

"Well, will you kindly correct them when they forget it? . . . Daphne dear, come here." Daphne approached a little way, and Miss Vidella, leaning forward with her hands on the balustrade, like some preacher who must deliver his sermon sitting, explained to her: "You must remember, dear, that it is the glory of human beings that their head is usually above their feet. With cows, and ruminant animals generally, the head is often on the same level as the hoofs. But it is only serpents and apes in the trees, I take it, which have a tendency to progress with their heads in a lower sphere than their other members. Now go back and remember that. All right, dears, you can resume your exercises."

The public rebuke rankled in Daphne; so the minute the lesson was over, and the girls were trooping to the dressing-room to change their rubber shoes, and Miss Vidella was managing with some difficulty the little hidden staircase from the gallery to the ground, she ran to the horizontal bar and circled it four or five times. Having thus liberated her resentment and proclaimed her faith before the other girls, she ran, very red and breathless, to the dressing-room.

It was uncommonly pleasant, this feeling of emancipation and this expressing of it before her schoolfellows. Her riding lesson gave her another opportunity. One day when their horses were gathered outside the gates of Hemans House, and the girls were mounting, she tried for a second to sit astride her horse, that she might see what it felt like and appear daring. But it was surprisingly difficult, with her skirt, to change from the side-saddle position to the astride. As she got her leg over the horse's withers the skirt went right above her knees, and she was in these difficulties when Miss Vidella came out on to the pavement to review the parade.

"Daphne! What *are* you doing?"

"Mounting, Miss Vidella," stuttered Daphne, who had struggled back to the correct position.

"Do you generally climb over the horse to mount it? Or are you up to some of your monkey tricks again? Riding master, have you observed that Miss Bruno is mountaineering on her horse in the public street? But, of course, I know you cannot have done so, for you are always so careful with your pupils. Please keep Miss Bruno in front of you all the way, or there's no knowing what strange contortions she may not attempt."

The riding master, annoyed, said nothing, but examined the riders, touched his horse and led the cavalcade away. Daphne was just in front of him, and immediately they were out of the head mistress's view she pretended to scream with laughter, thinking this would divert the riding master, who, like all the outside instructors, was inclined to make fun of Miss Vidella. But, to her surprise, he called out :

"Come on, Miss Bruno! Sit properly at once. You've been foolish enough already to-day. I'm not taking out a chain of Margate donkeys; and I shall report you to Miss Vidella. Come here and ride beside me."

Daphne felt foolish at the failure of her jest, and, very flushed, came and rode by the master's side with a beating heart. With all her fancied insurgence she was still a little afraid of Miss Vidella and her black-rimmed spectacles and whining sarcasm. When the horses arrived back at the Hemans House gates she watched the movements of the riding master, whether he would go in and see Miss Vidella or wait for her to emerge from the garden wall. But he only turned towards herself, and, as though softened by her long silence, smiled.

"All right, kiddy, I shan't report you. And one of these days you'll be able to ride astride. In my opinion they'll all be doing it one day. But at present we must do what we're told."

"Yes," murmured Daphne. "Thank you very much."

It became quite a custom for her to entertain the gymnasium girls with three or four guilty circles on the horizontal bar while Miss Vidella was descending the gallery stairs. Sometimes she managed six or seven of the forbidden things before rushing, red as a beet-root, to the dressing-room. Here she looked serene and innocent when the head mistress appeared and sounded some variant of "Come along, dears. I feel sure your healthy exercises have engendered an appetite for your dinners."

But one morning, by some failure in her swing, she did not complete her fifth backward circle, and was left hanging over the bar like a bolster thrown over a rail. Time was short; Miss Vidella's feet must be on the last few stairs; so she straightened her body on the bar, and was just about to drop behind it to her feet, when she saw Miss Vidella standing at the dressing-room door and watching her through her spectacles, chin slightly uptilted. The sight so unnerved her that instead of swinging backwards she swung forwards, her head falling like the clapper of a bell, and the weight of her body flinging her legs in an arc through the air. Her hands retained a panicky hold of the bar, but her feet struck the mattress and its coco-fibre mat with a jarring impact. A little giddily she stood on the mat and wondered what to do. If only Miss Vidella had not stood across the dressing-room door she would have flown through it and drowned her confusion in the business of unlacing her shoes. But now she could only stand on the mat beneath the bar and stare at the head mistress, while the head mistress stood in front of the dressing-room and stared at her. Girls peeped behind.

"What are you doing, Daphne?"

"Nothing."

"What were you doing on that bar?"

"I only just did a circle or two."

"And do you call that nothing?"

Clearly "Yes" was not the right answer, and "No" was incriminating, so Daphne stood on the mat and gave no answer at all.

"Come here."

She approached.

"Did you"—seemingly Miss Vidella could not bring herself to name the offence—"do that thing because it was against my express orders?"

The true answer, "Yes," was somewhat too dangerous to be employed, so Daphne said "No." Politeness required no less.

"Then why did you do that thing?"

In Daphne's head was a foggy conception of modern minds enfranchising themselves, and a phantasmagoria of related ideas, out of which came nothing more remarkable than :

"I thought I should like to."

(It *was,* perhaps, modernism in its simplest expression.)

"And why should you like to do it?"

"I don't know."

"I will tell you. It can only have been out of a spirit of deliberate evil-minded rebellion, or it was because you have a natural liking for the buffoonery of the uncivilized which you are too weak to suppress." It was humiliating to hear one's strength called weakness, and Daphne wished she had the courage to plead loudly that hers had been the evil-minded rebellion through and through. "You are one who must be trained, not by liberty and encouragement, but by restraint and correction. Get on your shoes. You shall not visit the gymnasium or the tennis field for a fortnight. Both places are too beset with opportunities for the outlandish contortions that so appeal to you. A walk each afternoon instead will perhaps teach you that it is perfectly possible to exercise every muscle of the body in the upright position, and all other contortions can be left to the jungle and——" Here Miss Vidella's sarcasm ran out. "Get changed. I fail to see why these dear girls here should be kept waiting for their lunches by you."

Daphne passed sullenly to her shoes and pulled them on viciously. She was being persecuted and enjoying it. And as she walked home with Trudy Wayne she was so ostentatiously noisy (this being her indirect claim to the "deliberate rebellion") that Miss Vidella called:

"Daphne, come back and walk alone behind me. You hardly seem to understand that you are in disgrace. Gertrude dear, I wonder at your encouraging her."

By this time, in Miss Vidella's mind, there was both a flabby dislike and a faint fear of the Bruno child. Recently she had acquainted herself with some of the father's books, and while wondering what much of them meant, grasped enough to feel uncomfortably that the great man probably ridiculed her ideas and her methods. And now, gnawed by the fear that Daphne Bruno might have heard and believed this ridicule, she determined to humiliate the child into a sense of her own simplicity and foolishness. The backwardness shown in Daphne's work on paper provided plenty of opportunities, though the child's quickness in *viva voce* work, and her skill and rushing imagination when anything had to be *made*—a poem, or a map, or a clay model— sometimes reminded Miss Vidella that her genuine opinion was very different. But for the good of all, and lest she spread her doctrines, Daphne Bruno must be discredited and kept down. She often came, therefore, into Miss Sims's class-room, and on examining the pupils' exercises, deplored the poverty of Daphne Bruno's.

"And this is the girl who thinks she knows better than any of us, and is so sure of her right judgment that she allows herself to do things just *because she likes to*. Go to your seat, child. When you can construe a simple piece of Latin we shall perhaps consider whether or not we will revise the rules of this school to suit your little fancies."

Daphne rather liked this bullying. It gave her the pleasure of mildly hating Miss Vidella as once she had hated Miss Durgon; and it enabled her to act in front of Miss Sims the tranquil resignation of a martyr, or in front of her class-fellows the fine, furious flash of a tragedienne. Also it justified and increased her love of the sympathetic governess; and she was keen on making a good thing of this.

Mr. Tenter Bruno, in these days, was prospering; and his mercury, though never free from fluctuations, was generally high. He was very satisfied, and something of radiance could be seen in his face and manner. In this, his fifty-third year, his brown beard was turning grey, and his hair receding from his fine forehead, but his figure in its grey suit was as neat as it had been at twenty. For some time he had considered that the house in Deseret Road lacked the necessary picturesqueness. It was a moot point whether one's books and fame were not injured by an address in the suburbs. His readers ought to be able to imagine him in some quaint old habitation, set down in green and lonely places. Besides, such a move from London into the quiet was always good copy for the paragraphists. And, to the delight of Daphne and Owen, when they returned from their schools, he suddenly announced, as a complete surprise, his purchase of Old Hall House, between Wivelsfield and Ditchling Common in Sussex. It was not far from their former cottage, and their old gardener, Eadigo, still hearty, was coming into permanent residence.

"When shall we go? When shall we go?" demanded his daughter.

"These very holidays, of course," smiled Mr. Bruno, delighted at the success of his surprise.

And in August when they moved there, he was happy in watching Daphne as, excited to see what the house was like (though she had declared she could remember it), she hung out of the carriage that was rattling them to its gates. When the carriage stopped, he saw the house anew through her eyes: a rectangular place of two stories, roofed in

J   139

Daphne Bruno

Horsham stone, with a new wing jutting out at right angles towards the road. The whole place was perhaps disappointingly near the road, and the low railing that separated the lawns and drive from the travellers to Ditchling was a little —finicking. But this weakness could be forgiven, when you looked at Old Hall House itself, with its mossed roof, its disorderly outbuildings, and its setting of silent country, closed in the diminishing distance by blue and shadowed downs.

Within doors, round about a square hall, rather dark, were three large, low-ceiled sitting-rooms, and a red kitchen with an undulating floor. Above these, up an oak staircase, were seven or eight bedrooms; and in the new wing, a room for Daphne, and a room for Owen, with a great chamber underneath that should be their privy playground. The servants had a staircase of their own leading to bedrooms in the back parts.

This segregation of children in the north and servants in the east Mr. Bruno had imagined would secure for him that ideal silence which he had yet to find in this plane of existence. In the sitting-room to the left of the entrance-hall he arranged his study furniture and his unnumbered books. But it was a grievous blow, and one that shook his household for weeks, when he learned that there was not one of the sitting-rooms but heard every sound in the house. The movements in the hall came through the walls, the staircase squeaking like an animal when anybody walked on it; the noises in the kitchen came through the shrunk oak doors; and if the maids were cleaning the bedroom above, their sweepings and voices, even their actual words, came through the low-pitched ceiling to Mr. Bruno, and his groans and exclamations (he imagined and hoped) went up to them. It was damnable.

He didn't know what to do. The paying of the mountainous bills created by the purchase, the alterations and the move had resolved him to live quietly for some time, and save money on postage stamps and tobacco. He *would not*—though his own mind saw clearly and humorously the weak logic—he simply *would not*—spend another halfpenny in making his study sound-proof. Instead, if there was a clatter in the kitchen, or a step, unmuted, on the vile staircase, he got up, opened his door, and put out his head with a diffident and over-courteous request that whatever was being done might be postponed till the afternoon; if the noise was in the bedroom above, he pushed back his chair that he might knock on the ceiling with a stick; till, at last (much to his amusement in the midst of his irritation), he would hear the scurry of the maids, or the guilty silence in the kitchen, directly his chair was pushed back. That push-back of his chair, if done viciously enough, could turn the house into a sepulchre.

After several weeks of encouraging economies, however, he decided that the young maids (who rather appealed to him) had a right to laugh and be noisy and even sing at their sweeping; and he spent fifty pounds on sound-proofing his room.

For Daphne the memorable thrill of this first summer holiday in Old Hall House was something quite independent of its fascinating rooms and the undiscovered country around. Or perhaps not so independent of their romance as she thought. In Owen's bedroom she learned that he had developed a taste for "penny dreadfuls." She saw a pile of the things, with their vivid picture-covers, on the top of his chest-of-drawers. The first of them, whose cover showed a gay highwayman in scarlet cape, three-cornered hat, and lace neckwear, firing a bell-mouthed pistol into the face of a black and bulbous Bow Street Runner, she read in her own room. From that day her imagination, like a city that had thrown open its gates, was yielded to Dick Turpin. Eagerly she selected all the rest that dealt with the handsome blade, and found twenty-three. She spent the best week of her life, up to that point, reading these twenty-three stories one after another.

She took all twenty-three and her inflated enthusiasm back to Hemans House, and introduced the enthusiasm and one of the books to Trudy Wayne. Trudy, having read one tale, borrowed the whole twenty-three, and succumbed to the highwayman.

This common interest strengthened the friendship of the two girls, and marked the moment when Daphne, though a year younger, began to dominate the partnership. From her imagination came the idea that, on their walks, they should be Dick Turpin and Jack Sheppard. Miss Vidella, with her black clothes and her corpulence and her piggish ways was obviously the head of the Bow Street Runners—or a Bloody Assize judge. It was incumbent on Trudy and herself to organize into an Outlaw Society. This was to have been called a "Hate Society," but memories of Miss Sims's gentleness limited the name to "The Dislike Society." During riding lessons, Daphne on her mild bay pony trotting or cantering beside the troop of girls, was really galloping Black Bess, with the Runners hard behind. In gymnasium, when she ran and vaulted over the horse, she was really Dick Turpin leaping a hedge or a toll-gate to escape his pursuers. If she was kept in, the class-room became a Newgate cell anterior to Tyburn, and her dismissal after half an hour's detention was a dashing escape amid the cheers of her followers who were waiting at the prison gates. Beneath her sheet and blankets in the Eliza Cook room, she had really taken to the heather and was sleeping in a cloak under the stars.

"Wouldn't it be ripping," she exclaimed to Trudy one day, "if we could spend a holiday together, and play Dick Turpin on some real lonely road?"

And as she said that, there flashed into her mind the very scene where such a drama could be staged. Good heavens! It was perfect! Ditchling Common. Strangely, it spread itself before her, not as she had just left it, under summer, but as she had seen it in May one morning of her earliest childhood, when it must have hit her imagination far more vividly than she had known; Ditchling Common with a mauve haze of bluebells over its coarse grass, shot here and there with the yellow of buttercups; the ribbon of road switchbacking over the successive brows to the humpy bridge above the railway line; the wavy horizon of downs, bare save for two windmills on the west; a hawk—how well she remembered watching it!—hovering above the common. There were dwarfed gorse bushes, like black patches on the stretching grass, and taller shrubs of entangled blackberry. And, most wonderful of all, at the entrance to the common was a white gate like a toll-gate, and just beyond it Jacob's Post. Jacob's Post was a real gibbet, with a cock at its top bearing the date 1734 to tell when last a man had hanged there.

"*Coo*, what a fool I am! Trudy, you should see Ditchling Common near me. It's absolutely the spot. Oh, you must come and stay with us next summer. I'm sure father'll agree, and we'll make Owen play too."

This plan, thenceforward, was a never-failing spring of conversation. For Trudy there was no taste of doubt in the merry cup. Daphne was just aware of a lurking anxiety lest, ten months hence, they would have forgotten all about Dick Turpin, or, alternatively, their undying friendship would have died.

CHAPTER IX

DAPHNE was right in fearing that the influence of the high-wayman would abate with the months, but wrong in doubting the endurance of her friendship with Trudy Wayne. This didn't expire, for the simple reason that she set herself to keep it at a sufficient heat. And when the next summer term drew towards the golden August that was to bring Trudy to Old Hall House, she as deliberately exhumed Dick Turpin, guessing that, did they but read the old romances once more, their imaginations would be snatched up again by the inspiring highwayman.

A mellow evening, the fourth of August, she climbed into a trap, driven by Eadigo, and was taken to meet Trudy at Hayward's Heath station. Why her eager anticipations should make her a little afraid of meeting Trudy she didn't know, but it was a disturbing fact, as the train rolled in, that her heart was faintly answering its noise and speed. Only a few passengers alighted here, the most being travellers to Brighton; so Trudy was quickly seen. Daphne ran towards her, followed without enthusiasm by Eadigo. Trudy, too, one could see, was rather shy of the strange station and all her circumstances, but she cloaked it with an ostentatious self-possession, talking much as she mounted the trap. Eadigo drove off silently, and Daphne felt a pity for the old man because the six weeks in front of him were the same as the six weeks before. His silence and phlegm made her look at Trudy, after which they both had fits of giggling.

Miss Carrell welcomed the visitor in the dining-room.

"Well, I hope, Trudy—may I call you that?—you'll have a very happy holiday with us. I'm sorry Mr. Bruno is away. . . . It's very nice for Duffy to have you with her, I'm sure. Owen, come here and say how-do-you-do to Duffy's friend."

Owen these holidays had brought back from his pre-paratory school a new and (one would have thought) quite

144

uncharacteristic tendency to laborious humour. It involved his addressing of Hollins as "Herbert," and his sister as "Casabianca." And now he bowed till his head was aligned with his waist, and extended a hand. Trudy took it, and inquired :

"How do you do?"

"I don't," answered Owen.

This strange new growth in her brother was in the process of being discouraged by Daphne.

"It's not funny," she said.

"Sorry. Heaps of ajoppolies," answered Owen.

"Daphne wanted you to share her bedroom," interrupted Miss Carrell, "so I've arranged it for you both."

"Oh, how ripping!" exclaimed Trudy.

"That'll be monstrous fine," said Owen.

In their beds that night the two girls arranged plans for the next day till the clock on the stairs sounded midnight.

"*Coo,* you wait till I show you Ditchling Common," Daphne rattled on. "The road lies like a white ribbon, all up and down, from the Toll-gate to Ditchling. There's one big clump of blackberry that I call the Observation Post, because it's at the top of a brow, and you can see all the way to the next brow and beyond that to the railway bridge. So you could see anyone approaching half a mile away, and give warning to your confederates hidden lower down the road."

The clock struck midnight, and the conversation swung suitably to the age of the house in which they slept, and whether it was haunted. It had not occurred to Daphne that it was till this moment, but now she romanced about eerie noises and panels that rang hollow.

Immediately after breakfast the next day all three hurried to the common. Daphne as guide, walked importantly ahead, leading the others through the white gate, and longing for the moment when Trudy should see the gibbet. The common lay before them in summer dress : the thistles high by the flying road, the grass tall and bearded where it mingled with bracken and rushes, and over the dusty highway and the disorderly herbage the sunlight quivering in a diaphanous haze. A few slow cows pastured in a hollow, and cocks and hens picked the green about Jacob's Post.

Daphne Bruno

Trudy's interest in this gibbet was even more than one desired; in fact, there was some difficulty in getting her away till she had properly fixed upon her imagination the picture of a felon suspended there. It was already nine o'clock.

"Come on," said Owen. "We dine at half-past one."

The games were conducted just as Daphne had planned them. Owen was sent away to reappear as a traveller a quarter of a mile up the road; the girls put on black masks and held sixpenny pistols; and Daphne went and lay behind the tall clump of blackberry called the Observation Post, while Trudy threw herself under some gorse lower down the highway. It was for Daphne to signal Owen's appearance in the distance. While she waited for him she selected any blackberries that showed a trace of ripeness, and ate the trace. Also she sucked and chewed grass, for Owen did not appear for a long time; there was nothing but a cart coming from Ditchling. She did not guess that Owen had been seized by the ingenious idea of approaching under the lee of the cart—such a thing was against the whole spirit of the game. Nevertheless, when the cart had passed in front of her he emerged from his cover with a shriek of triumph and raced down the hill towards Trudy. Leaping up angrily, she gave the pre-arranged signal, which meant that Owen had been spotted in the distance—and followed him as he ran past Trudy.

"Oh, the fool!" she grumbled, and called after him: "It's not funny, if you think it is." And to Trudy, before whom she stopped with this news of Owen's appearance: "He always must show off."

Owen turned round and came back with a victor's smile.

"You'll spoil it all if you want to be cocky," she grumbled. "Why can't you ever play sensibly?"

Having treated himself to one whimsical effort, Owen promised to play sensibly, and for the rest of the morning the games unrolled as they should. The walk home was a-clatter with tongues.

By early afternoon they were standing again on the road by the Observation Post, and deliberating how to vary the play, when Owen said: "Hist! Wait!" He had seen two specks coming with a curious velocity over the crown of

146

the railway bridge. Two men—or two boys, since they were probably racing, and men didn't do such things.

"Hist! Hist! Sister Anne, sister Anne, I see someone coming."

"It's not funny. . . . Who are they?"

"I see two men running, and a cloud of dust."

With imaginations pleasantly troubled the girls looked towards the far-off but quickly approaching figures.

"Let's stop 'em, whoever they are," suggested Owen.

"Don't be an ass. We can't if we don't know them."

"Why not? If they're boys they won't mind. And we're three to their two."

"It would be rather ripping," reflected Daphne, while the others watched for her to give the last word. "I tell you what. You wait here behind the Observation Post, Owen, and as soon as they come near enough for you to see if they're boys and attackable, you signal ' Yes '—make a Y with your arms—and then come and join us lower down behind the gorse. Then we really will hold them up."

Daphne and Trudy ran to the gorse and fell prone behind it. This real holding up of unknown wayfarers on the high road was a completer thrill than any of the mock adventures. It affected Daphne with an emptying sensation below the waist, and shook the hand with which she was hurrying on her mask and cocking her pistol. And when Owen made a Y of his body and arms, and she knew that they were committed to the deed, and that the moments before its accomplishment were fast escaping, her heart began to pound with a delicious fear. Breathlessly Owen joined them, falling to his stomach with the announcement: "Two boys. One rather big." All watched the brow for the first of the boys to appear.

"I'll leap out," whispered Owen, who seemed to have none of that faint anxiety to be quit of the business that was troubling Daphne, "and you'd better follow me. . . . Look alive! Here's Number One."

Daphne looked up from her ground level and saw a figure on the brow outlined against the glazed sky. As he came down the slope she saw with surprise that he was in just such running attire as the competitors wore in the University Sports at Queen's Club: white vest with coloured ribbon edging the sleevelets and the button-opening; very

short white shorts edged with the same ribbon; white socks
and black rubber shoes. His fists were at his breast, and his
dark hair blowing untidily. The figure, while clearly a
young boy's, was tall and beautifully shaped—from the
shoulder-line to the rounded thighs with their muscles astir.
In the few seconds of his coming Daphne felt that vague
agitation which beauty gave; it was but the germ of the
pleasure felt by adults in the presence of a Praxitelean statue,
and as unmindful of sex, and it was not only the lines of
his body that had disturbed her, but the way he had come
over the brow in the sun's light.

"Now!" cried Owen.

All three leapt out and stood across the road. The tall
boy was so startled at this apparition of three masked
bravoes in his path that he stopped suddenly, and, slipping
on one foot, nearly fell.

"Damn and blast!" he muttered. "What the deuce
are you playing at?"

"Your money or your life," said Daphne.

He was looking at her; first at her mouth and chin, then
at the eyes that were staring at him through the mask;
then at her disarrayed hair; then up and down her body.
He smiled grimly, and as if it were impossible to insult a
girl, turned towards Owen and said:

"Look here, I'm going to give you a lamming."

A younger boy, also in running clothes, had now come
up and stopped.

Owen retreated a step or two, but the bigger boy seized
his wrist and twisted it right round.

"Don't!" commanded Daphne, pleased with this opportunity of being heroic.

Taking no notice of her orders, the boy twisted her
brother's arm again, and Daphne promptly hit him a heavy
blow with the butt of her pistol on the bone of his wrist.

"God——!" he began, but controlled the curse, and out
of respect for the girl dropped Owen.

"It's a game," explained Daphne. "We thought you'd
see the joke."

"That bally thing of yours hurts. I don't see why you
should hit me with it just because, being a girl, you know I
shan't give you a lamming. Others would."

This angered Daphne. It was the unfairest accusation

that she had taken cover behind her sex. The thought had not been in her mind at all, and the suggestion of it made her pluck look like cowardice.

"Oh, I never thought of that at all," she protested. "You can have a shot at giving me a lamming if you like."

With his grim smile the boy seized her wrist and turned it strongly—but not too strongly. Daphne set her teeth and deliberately looked defiance into his eyes. He stared commandingly into hers. And holding her thus captive, though still with a hint of gentleness, he suddenly whipped off her mask and put it behind his back.

"Don't!" she shouted. "Give that back to me. It's mine."

"No, I shan't!"

With her spare arm she reached round him to recover her property. Her arm was now about his waist, but the feel of his body, thinly covered by the vest, neither raised a blush nor intruded diffidence. She only fumbled for her mask while the boy looked down upon her, grinning confidently and enigmatically.

"Rescue!" shouted Owen, and he and Trudy rushed for his sister.

"Get away, you little worm!" said the tall boy, letting go of his captive—while Owen got away. The boy seemed to give himself to thought, looking now at Daphne and now at the mask, which he drew away as she tried to snatch it. Then he turned to his companion. "I say, Cyril, we might get these kids to join us. . . . We were training when you barged in. But we've an idea to start paper-chasing or something." He looked at Owen. "I say, Face-ache, what are you called, and what are your sisters' names? You do look a guy in that mask."

"They're not my sisters," answered Owen, a thought overawed, and removing his mask. "At least, only one of them."

"Well, which one, fool? Introduce us properly."

"This one."

The tall boy looked a little shyly at the girl whose wrist he had twisted and whose arm had held him tight about the waist.

"And what's her name?"

"Duffy—or Daphne—Daphne Bruno."

"Comic names. Still "—he bowed gallantly though yet shyly—"very happy to make your acquaintance. . . . Now the other one, Fifth of November."

"Trudy Wayne, who's staying with Duffy for the hols."

"That's like Cyril. . . . Where's Cyril? Come here, man. This is Cyril Evans. He's my cousin, and he's coming up to Sillborough next term. . . . Now we all know where we are."

"But you haven't told us *your* name yet," pointed out Daphne, not the least shyly, and sucking the wrist he had twisted.

"Nor I have. It's Muirhead—Roger Muirhead. . . . However, that'll do for that. Let's get on with this game you're playing. . . . Cyril, look here, man, we'll pick sides, and as I'm the biggest, I'll only have one of these people, and you can have the other two. And, as I'm only to have one, I'll pick first."

He went through an elaborate pantomime of indecision, looking each of them up and down, as if appraising their adroitness or speed. And, rather casually, he smiled his decision at Daphne.

"I'll have this one. I forget your name—Duffy Something, wasn't it?"

"Bruno."

"Of course. . . . Righto! The Bruno-Muirhead Combine against the world. Cyril, you take your crowd a half a mile or so back along the road, and I bet none of you get through us two. If a single one of you gets as far as Jacob's Post, your side's won. D'you see?"

"Yes, man."

"Well, nip off your way, and we'll go ours. Come on—Duffy." He coloured as he used the name.

Roger and she stepped off the roadway on to the grass, and they were about to cross a stretch made dirty with the large droppings of kine, when Cyril called out: "Mind the cowslips!"

Trudy giggled; Owen too, for it was humour after his heart, if a trifle daring; but Roger, to everyone's surprise, swung round and, running after Cyril, who immediately began to escape, tried to give him a punitive kick.

"You know you don't talk like that in front of girls," he muttered breathlessly.

150

"It was nothing much," Cyril grumbled.

"Well, much or not, don't say that sort of thing in front of girls unless you want your behind kicked. Now clear out. . . . Come on, Duffy." And he led her away with the silence of a man who has just shown his chivalry and his power. No heed gave he, though undoubtedly hearing Cyril's "Sidey swine!" and Daphne felt she must suggest, "But supposing your cousin won't play now?"

"He'll play if he's told to," said Roger.

Roger, now that he was alone in a wilderness with his partner, appeared a little awkward. He had difficulty in finding anything to say; and Daphne, to ease him, ran merrily to the gorse screen and flung herself prone upon the ground behind it. Roger stood for a minute and looked down upon her.

"You're longer than I thought when you lie like that. . . . How old are you?"

He sat down.

"Thirteen!"

"Is that all? I should have thought you were fourteen at least. I'm—I'm fifteen. We're both on the long side, aren't we?"

"You look quite sixteen."

"Do I? Yes, people generally think I'm older than I am." He lay down on his arm beside her. "Do you live near here?"

Daphne answered this and several other questions, while Roger listened, masticating one blade of grass after another and throwing them away as they were drained of their pleasure. He seemed given to thinking long on all he heard. In his turn he explained that he was the only son of Sir Roger Muirhead, "of the Muirhead Traders, you know," and that they had just bought the Downway House on the Plumpton side of the common, "partly for holidays, and partly as a spec." When Daphne asked if he would one day be "Sir Roger," he replied vaguely, "I daresay."

"And did you say Sillborough was your school? I think Owen's supposed to be going there."

"Yes, I've been there over a year." And rather pretentiously he added, "I must show your brother round when he comes, and look after him a bit."

The talk failing here, Daphne pretended to look for signs

of Cyril and his party, but Roger, apparently anxious that she should not elude his conversation, said : "Oh, they won't be in sight for some time yet. . . . Look here, here's your mask. I'm sorry I took it."

"No, you can have it," demurred Daphne, touched by his apology. "I can easily make another."

"Oh, well. Perhaps I'll keep it, then. . . . I hope I didn't hurt you when I twisted your arm like that, but you dared me to, didn't you? "

"Oh, not a bit."

When the words had left her she knew, somehow, that she had said them wrong; with too much contempt, or with insufficient appreciation of his courtesy. She had very slightly bruised his self-esteem. There was no doubt that, if he was very chivalrous, he was also rather conceited and pompous.

"I could have done so, of course," he explained, "but I didn't want to. I was only shamming."

By now his manner had stirred the suspicion, and it was accompanied by just such a pleasant emptying sensation as she had experienced when awaiting the adventure, that he was attracted by her. She looked for a swift second at his face, hoping he would not trap the glance, but his eyes were towards her, and she swept hers past his. His were brown eyes, rather small, perhaps, but when the enigmatic grin was at his lips, they twinkled mischievously. This moment, as she took them in her sweep, they were thoughtful. She continued the motion of her head, pretending that it had all been done to ease her neck. Her eyes fell upon his extended legs, of which the left was crossed over the right. They were bare—bare and very shapely. With a laugh she turned her face back to his and asked : "Aren't you awfully cold? "

"No, I never feel the cold much. I've purposely inured myself to it, like the Spartans, you know. . . . I'm awfully keen on the Greeks, and their ideas about athletics, and so on. . . . Look here, we'd better arrange our plan of campaign. You'll catch your school-friend and I'll have young Cyril in two twos, and then I'll chase after your kiddy brother."

"Oh, you'll catch Owen all right——"

"By Jove, here they are ! "

He slipped into a position ready to run.

"Now!" commanded he.

Out he shot, and with his fine strides soon ran Cyril down. Daphne took longer to secure Trudy. Owen rushed past and ran delightedly towards the gibbet. Roger set off in pursuit with a long, unworrying, relentless pace that was probably intended for the gaze of Daphne. Daphne watched him with that partiality which comes from the prospect of seeing the humiliation of a relative, especially one who tries to be clever. It was quickly over. Roger brought back his prey after the fashion of a policeman, one hand holding his collar, the other his wrist.

In all the games that filled that afternoon save one, Roger contrived to secure Daphne for his partner. The exception was when Daphne said, "*No*, I'm going with Cyril now," and Roger looking nonplussed—even hurt, as at the shattering of a dream—refused, of his courtesy, to force Daphne against her will. Of his courtesy, too, he was gracious and gay with his new partner, Trudy. At the afternoon's close, they agreed to meet early the following morning. The last game was spread all over the western side of the common, for Daphne, with Roger to chivy everyone off, had to reach Jacob's Post without being so much as touched by Cyril, Trudy or Owen. She ran diagonally and ziz-zag, and Roger with his long legs ran all round her, intercepting any who threatened her. They could not pass him and abandoned hope.

Throughout the evening, when they were playing table-games in the great play-room at Old Hall House, she was as noisy and skilful as Owen or Trudy, but she had moments of wool-gathering when she wondered about many things. She would have liked to escape to an empty room, there to walk up and down with her friendly questions. The once or twice that they played a guessing game and she was outside the closed door, she let her thoughts run to the subject that called them. Yes, for a little while he *had* been—he *was*—— But why? She felt like a child —of a different order, almost, from him. He was so mature and majestic (these were not Daphne's words, who had less words than blindfolded thoughts), and strong and proficient. But he *was*, for a little. She could not doubt it. Incredible.

Nothing would come of it, nothing *could* come of it. It had only been a momentary attraction. Still, she *could*—oh, yes, it gave her that curious, delightful emptying when she imagined it—she *could* love him very much. He was, of course, the very perfection of her idea of a lover; not faultless, but exactly what *she* would like. Everyone else she could think of seemed less than he. But it wouldn't be . . . it wouldn't be . . . She would hold herself in and wait on the future.

Soon after nine the next morning they were waiting by the Observation Post and looking down the Plumpton Road for Roger and Cyril. A hooded cart rumbled towards them, and when it passed their gathering, dropped from its tailboard, as it might have been two bundles, Roger and Cyril. They were very differently dressed from yesterday. Roger wore a suit of grey flannel, apparently new-bought for the holidays, royal blue socks and brown shoes, a plum-coloured tie, and his dark hair plastered down. Though still a comely boy, he looked rather more ordinary than he had done in his running kit.

"We'll toss for partners to-day," said he hurriedly, lest anyone suggested something else. "Cyril and I being the two eldest males had better pick." Tossing up a coin he turned to Cyril. "You call, man."

Cyril won, and chose Trudy. And throughout the day it so fell that, whenever they tossed, Daphne always fell to Roger's share. The first time he won he paraded doubt before choosing her, and the second time said casually: "Ah, well, best stick to the old firm." They played all the morning and all the afternoon, having tea as guests of a rather lordly Roger at the Royal Oak, and when the glamour of evening was over the common, and their ravenous appetites cried to them that it must be supper-time, Roger said mysteriously:

"Look here. Gather round, all. An idea's been festering in my mind all the afternoon. Sit down. In a ring. This is a bally conspiracy. . . . The first fine night we'll all meet on the common at midnight. Don't be alarmed. It'll be topping."

"Oh, *let's*," agreed Cyril.

"We'll meet at Jacob's Post at half-past midnight, and bring food."

"Oh, ratner," suddenly said Daphne.

"Well, when shall it be?"

"To-night," said all.

"No, father isn't back yet. And it'll be no fun escaping if there's no one dangerous to escape from."

"Is your father dangerous?" inquired Daphne.

"Oh, he's all right, only he thinks he's a deuce of a disciplinarian."

"Would he whack you if he caught you?"

"Well, hardly," Roger grinned. "However, to-morrow night's the night, if fine. Especially as we shan't have many more nights——"

"*What?*" exclaimed Trudy.

Daphne, who had been fiddling with something on the ground, looked up quickly and caught Roger's eye watching for her.

"Oh, are you going away, then?" she grumbled.

"Yes. Father joins us to-morrow, and in a few days we all go off to Cornwall. Cyril and I were keen on it, but I'm not so keen now. However, there it is." There was a fine Roman note in his acceptance of adversity. "We won't meet at all to-morrow afternoon, so as to be fresh for the night. If it's fine, which it will be, and Cyril and I decide we can do it, we'll come outside your house some time between six and eight o'clock, and fire two shots in rapid succession."

"I say!" ejaculated Trudy, and an alarmed thumb-nail shot to her teeth.

"No, it'll be all right, I promise you. Everything the whole night. I'll guarantee no harm of any kind comes to you. I shall regard it as my personal responsibility."

In imitation of this grandiloquence Owen drawled: "Wow-wow-wow."

Roger turned sharply on him. If he were elaborately courteous to girls that was no reason why he should stand any lip from prep. schoolboys.

"What did you say, Stinkpot?"

"Nothing," answered Owen, subdued by so sudden an approach.

"Well, don't say it again. If you can't keep your mouth shut, put a sock in it. Well, now we all know the programme. . . ."

Daphne Bruno

When Daphne, Trudy and Owen were littering the walk home with their chatter, it gradually emerged that every one of Trudy's remarks held a sly under-meaning. Daphne refused to perceive it, though a rising colour betrayed her pleasure; Trudy shaded off her remarks into the less and less equivocal, but still Daphne saw them only as innocent, and at last Trudy was forced to say outright:

"Of course, it's perfectly obvious that Roger's gone cracked on you."

"What?"

"Of course, it is perfectly obvious that Roger has gone cracked on you."

"'Course it's perfectly obvious he hasn't!" protested Daphne, the blood now flooding her face.

Hearing the words spoken aloud and deliberately like that had set her heart beating quickly and irregularly.

"Well, at any rate, you're blushing."

"At any rate, I'm *not!*"

"All right. If you say you can't see that Roger's silly about you, you must be either a fool or a liar."

"I don't think it's obvious at all."

Here Owen unadvisedly stepped into the discussion.

"It's obvious to the meanest intelligence."

"Lot you know about it, copy-cat."

"Thank you. I do know a lot. My experience is extensive."

"It's not at all funny. . . . Besides, I was talking to Trudy. What makes you think so?"

"I can always tell," Trudy explained.

When they entered the house, Daphne, whose cheeks were still flushed and her heart still delightfully irregular, wanted to get away alone, far more urgently than last night, so as to think about it all. But supper detained her, and then Trudy would keep her talking; and what was annoying about Trudy's talk was that she had apparently forgotten the one interesting topic, as if, after all, it were nothing very impressive. Daphne answered her frequently enough to maintain a show of interest, though really she missed large chunks of what Trudy was saying. And as soon as possible she invented an excuse and ran away to some place where she might be private. An old habit sent her to the bathroom, where there was a bolt on the door. There she leapt on to the mahogany framework of the bath, and, sitting sideways, stared out at the dark orchard and the brick walk that ran by the kitchen door.

Then he *did*. He, so much older (somehow), so much more important, did love her. She saw him again—tall, dark, wide-breasted, his eyes sparkling when excited with plans; twinkling mischievously—almost possessively—when she struggled with him; frowning angrily when he insulted Cyril or Owen. He had twisted her wrist sharply, and to remember it was delicious, and she, struggling for her mask, had had her arm tight about his waist. The thought disturbed her internally, and she moved a little as she sat on the side of the bath. She liked the disturbance, and sought it by returning to the memory again and again.

In her bed that night, when Trudy had talked herself to sleep, she turned on her side and directed her will to thinking only of Roger, in the hope that this would bring him into her dreams and carry her into his. She struggled to keep her erratic mind's-eye playing on the figure of Roger; Roger coming over the brow in white running kit, wrestling with her for her mask (her body straightened in bed as she remembered it), choosing her for his partner, running about her and fighting her battle. Surely this hard thinking would propel her soul over the dark common to the Downway House where Roger slept.

But this sunlight in the room, and the white and twisty singing of birds! It was morning, and she hadn't dreamt at all. She stared at the clock on the mantelpiece. Only twenty past five. A dead silence in the house, and a perfect stillness in the garden, except for the birds. Twenty past five. . . . Let her spend the next hour thinking of Roger. To enjoy the thinking, she pulled the clothes warmly about her.

When, after breakfast, the two parties met again on the common, Roger was still shy and awkwardly imperious, and Daphne studied to be natural and lively as if unaware that love was in anyone's mind. Now and then, when Roger and she, in hiding from the others, lolled under the gorse, she languished a little before him, but it was more unconscious than deliberate. Her face she kept averted, giving him only an occasional glance, which she hoped he

would not see. If they had long to wait, she lay backward
so that her head rested on her interlaced fingers and her
eyes dreamed at the sky. The glare tiring them, she let
her lids fall, after which a hundred noises of the common
seemed to become audible : birds, a cow's bell, a dog bark-
ing far away, the breeze in the tree-branches, and the distant
suggestion of a cart with a trotting horse. Roger would
be extraordinarily silent at her side.

During the morning his nearness, though so desired,
became almost oppressive. She could scarcely answer him
now, if he spoke to her, and her part in the games was
formal and remote—she carried too pleasing a burden of
thoughts. When they returned to lunch, she carried them
with her in silence. As companions they were easier than
Roger ; and she was not unhappy that the afternoon and
evening were to be spent at home, before the adventure of
midnight. Trudy spent the afternoon reading; Owen drawing. In Daphne the emotion that was causing her heart
to flutter or her voice to shake funnily, began to press on her
old vent—the desire to write. This brought direction to her
thoughts, and a rest in moving with them. She dreamed
out a story, in which two people met while children, as
Roger and she had done, and after being parted for many
years, both remaining faithful and both imagining themselves forgotten, met again in middle age, to pass the
evening of their lives in a sheltered and fragrant calm.
"Coo, it'd make a beautiful story," thought Daphne, a
contemplative thumb arrested at her lips. Her imagination,
playing on it, teemed with ideas; and as, one after another,
they came to her, the story that should contain them all
seemed so good that its early publication was placed beyond
doubt. Already she saw it in book form. By tea-time she
had completed a scenario on a sheet of foolscap, and was
writing the first paragraphs. But the actual writing was
a laborious exercise, and a drag on her impatient thoughts ;
only dreaming could keep pace with thoughts. No, by her
fine afternoon's work on the scenario she had earned the
right to sit and think about it. And she spent an enchanted
evening in this service of her compulsion to write—wonderfully oblivious of the outside world, and at rest. Always its
service was perfect freedom.

They were sitting at supper, with Miss Carrell at the

table's head, when suddenly a loud report was heard in the road.

"Good heavens! What's that?" exclaimed Miss Carrell. There was another shot, but farther away.

Daphne felt that everybody in the cottages round must be rushing into the road to see if murder had been done.

"Oh, it's someone killing rabbits, I expect," said Owen. She found herself admiring her brother's composure. Owen was not an easy mixture to analyse. Though often timid, he showed flashes of daring, and would be quite undisturbed by circumstances that started uncomfortable fears in her. To-night, for instance, in this period between the half-light and bed-time, when both girls had begun to be afraid of the secret conspiracy, Owen had assumed an ascendancy.

"I'll come and collect you two as soon as the clock strikes midnight," said he.

Trudy yawned. Her enthusiasm was at its lowest.

"But suppose we all drop off to sleep, and wake to find it's morning."

"We must divide the night into three watches," Owen decided. "We can go to bed at nine. There'll be three watches of one hour. Trudy can take the first as she's tired, then Duffy, then me. . . . I think I shall turn in soon, as we have a long and dirty night's work in front of us."

In their bedroom Trudy lightened her watch by talking with Daphne, and at ten o'clock said: "Now it's you on duty," and, turning over, was soon asleep. Daphne lay awake, staring into the darkness and listening to the last sounds in the household below. In an hour she would see Roger again. But what then? They would only be awkward with each other. They found it so difficult to talk. The only perfect satisfaction—and this was an impossible dream—would be to hold each other close and long and in silence. . . .

Thinking thus was such a restful happiness that she could only keep awake by forcing open her eyes and staring at the light on the blind or trying to distinguish the outlines of the fire-place. A few times she did doze and was obliged to pull herself back to watchfulness. Suddenly she heard a step outside her door, and a creaking board. Her heart stopped. There was a tickling knock, which nearly drove her under the sheets.

Daphne Bruno

"Duffy!   Duffy!"

"Yes?"

"It's eleven o'clock.   You should have called me."

"Oh, you might have given me time."

"I'll take on now."

"All right. . . ."

She turned over and remembered nothing more till she awoke with another heart-leap at the sound of someone moving outside her door.

"I say. . . . I say. . . . It's just on twelve."

Daphne sat up in bed.   The memory that in half an hour she would be with Roger had strengthened her to overcome sleepiness.

"Trudy!   Trudy!"

Something about the darkness forbade more than a strong whisper.

But Trudy was heartily asleep.

"Trudy!"

She said it aloud, and coughed when she heard how loud it sounded.

Getting up quickly, for she was half-afraid of the whole room, she crossed to Trudy's bed and shook her shoulder.

"Trudy, it's midnight."

Trudy turned over resentfully.

"No, get up.   Don't spoil it all.   Owen and I are up."
Trudy threw off the clothes.

"Ooo! it's cold!   I didn't think it'd be as cold as this."

A whisper came through the door.

"Aren't you two nearly ready.   I've been ready for a long time."

"Well, don't show off about it," enjoined Daphne.

In five minutes the two girls and Owen were creeping down the stairs, stopping whenever they heard a distant door shaking or a stair squeaking under their feet.   On the road, the air freshened them and the quick walking awakened them, and they began really to enjoy themselves.   The blind houses that looked at them through the darkness, the sleeping Royal Oak Hotel, the closed cattle gate at the entrance to the common, by increasing their sense of guilt, gave a pungency to the adventure.   The empty common was, perhaps, almost too like a desert; and all were feeling the eeriness of Jacob's Post, seen through the night, when two figures leapt into their path, their arms shooting to the sky in a demoniac gesture.

"Sorry," apologized Roger. "Cyril insisted on us doing that."

But this lively item barely concealed that they were all rather shy of one another; and Roger, determining, as the originator of the conspiracy, to save it from awkwardness, said cheerily:

"We'll grub first. I want you all to come right to the centre of the common. . . . So come along. Squad, march."

They followed him to the heart of the common, where he led them to a stretch of low gorse, and unshouldered his haversack, bidding Cyril do the same. From these they produced five bottles of ginger beer, some buns and bananas, and a lantern.

"Strike a light, my son," said Roger, addressing himself. "See, it's a dark lantern. . . . Now we sit down and gorge."

None of them was hungry, and the buns were hardly a success, but bananas were things you could eat at any time of the day, or with a stomach in any state. And when the last of them had been finished, Roger issued orders:

"This is the game. As there are five of us we divide into two sides of two each. The fifth person must hide on the common. Whichever of the two sides finds him first wins. It'll have to be Cyril or me who hides, as Owen is too young and foolish."

"I *beg* your pardon," said Owen

"What?" asked Roger.

"I beg your pardon, I said."

"Oh, well, that's granted. . . . So Cyril——"

"But I mean I didn't gather the full purport of your last remark."

"Well, wash your ears out next time. . . . Here, Cyril, we'll toss who hides."

They tossed, and Cyril won.

"Oh, I'll take the lantern and do the hiding, you bet," said he.

"All right," permitted Roger; "and as I lost the toss, I'll have first pick. . . . Well, may as well stick to the old firm. Duffy and I will be on one side, and Trudy and Owen the other."

Daphne Bruno

"But we'll never find Cyril in the darkness," said Trudy.

"You haven't heard all yet. Cyril takes the lantern, and if we're nowhere near him, he shows its light on the common. He may then darken it and move away. If he's slick, he'll move in the opposite direction to the one you're expecting. (I half wish I had the lantern.) But as sure as he finds you're going all wrong, he's got to show a light again."

"Oh, how topping!" agreed Trudy.

"Right! Streak away, Cyril. Take to the heather, my bonnie lad. Any direction you like. We'll count a hundred before we raise the highlands and pour down after you."

Aloud, monotonously, automatically, Roger counted one hundred.

"——ninety-eight, ninety-nine, a hundred! Now, you and your party, Owen, had better trickle southward towards Brighton, and I and Duffy'll prospect the common northward towards York."

A few uncomfortable seconds, and Daphne and Roger were walking alone through the night. Her heart began to race. She walked unspeaking beside him, aware of his equal discomfort. They struck across the grass, sometimes tripped by the branching bracken or a rush-crowned tussock, when Roger would extend to her help a gentle hand. His talk about the search for Cyril was so empty of conviction that she guessed he was summing up courage to say something else. They reached a clump of bramble, and Daphne, after stupidly looking behind it, moved on.

"No, don't go on," stuttered Roger. "I've something to say to you. Let's sit down." She obeyed him without speaking. "When do you and Trudy go back to school?"

"September 14th."

"There! I knew it. I guessed it. Fate's against us. We shan't return from Cornwall till two days after that. Heaven knows if I shall ever meet you again. We were destined to see each other in a flash and no more."

These words, so picturesque and sad, amounted to an avowal of tenderness; wherefore Daphne could only keep silence, pulling up blades of grass.

"Duffy, let me kiss you, may I?"

The words had, beyond doubt, come out of the darkness.

"Of course not."

"Duffy, don't be a rotter. Can't you see that any other fellow'd have taken you, now he'd got you here, and kissed you whether you let him or not. But I've never been rude to you, have I? I have my own ideas about how you ought to treat women. I reverence them. Duffy, I'm madly in love with you—I am, really. You're—you're like a magnet to me." He took her hand gently. "All this business to-night, and all its beastly expense, I've engineered simply because I was determined to have you for half an hour to myself, and in complete privacy—out of the beastly daylight. Those kids are just being used to serve our ends." He was obviously proud of his manœuvring. "Duffy, I'm not a flirt. I've never flirted with a girl in my life, not because I thought it wrong—that wouldn't have worried me, for I'm afraid I generally do what I like—but just because they've never interested me. I didn't want to fall in love with you. But from the moment you jumped out of that hedge at me you diverted the course of my life." She guessed this had been rehearsed, for a similar sentence had presented itself to her. "You may not remember, but you flung yourself down on your face at my feet."

"Oh, I didn't."

"Well, behind a hedge, I mean. Let me finish. And the minute you did that I was metaphorically at *your* feet. . . . Duffy, do you love me, too?"

To this she preferred to give no direct answer, and he repeated:

"Do you love me, too?"

"I like you."

"Well, let me kiss you. I shan't if you won't let me. But if you don't I vow I'll never see you again. And I don't go back on a vow. . . . And hang it, Duffy, I'm going in less than a week."

"Oh, can't you get out of going?"

"No. Father's one of those who never changes his mind. We're exactly like each other in that way, so I can't complain. Duffy, are you sorry I'm going?"

"Yes, of course I am."

"Well, does that mean you do more than like me?"

The "Yes" would not leave her lips.

"Duffy, I believe you love me, do you?"

No answer.

"Do you?"

After a long silence she answered by resting her body against his.

"Duffy!" He had immediately drawn her closer. "You—you lovely wild flower on the heath."

And he kissed her—awkwardly rather than rapturously, as if uncertain how such things were done, and the kiss was only in the full of her cheek. The taking of her lips was an impertinence that chivalry did not sanction.

But he kept her long in his pressure, and under the silence she was trying to realize that these were Roger's arms. It was so wonderful a thought that she feared lest her imagination missed its fullness. And in the effort to keep her imagination up to pitch, she probably did fall short of any complete rapture. Roger seemed lost in his happiness, and it was she who first drew away.

"I say, we're forgetting the others. They may be near."

Roger laughed significantly, and jumped up.

"I don't think so. Come this way, and I'll show you something."

He led her to the nearest rise, where, after sweeping the whole common to the south, he suddenly pointed and said : "Look!"

A tiny light twinkled—it seemed miles away—and went out, leaving nothing but darkness on the common. Then again it pricked the night, and one could imagine voices.

"Coo!" exclaimed Daphne in admiration.

Roger gave a grim, self-satisfied laugh.

"Cyril has his orders. Jove! he's a faithful henchman. Rather a nice piece of generalship, that! I don't fancy he'll let himself be caught by that wretched little brother of yours or that girl. He has his orders where to hold them, and for how long."

"Does he then what—what you were going to to me?"

"I told him I jolly well wanted you to myself, and intended having you. It's nothing new to have a squire in these matters."

"But he may tell someone."

"Not he. He knows what he'd get if he did."

They were walking unthinkingly back to the clump.

"I'm awfully tired," she said.

He sat down and patted the grass.

"Lie there, then, and rest against me."

She obeyed, putting an arm about his waist and laying her head on his coat. He patted it lovingly, and occasionally kissed her hair, to which she would respond with a little hug. Once he said : "Are you sure you're not cold? " and later, after a long kiss on her forehead upturned : "My God, I'm glad I was born."

CHAPTER X

In the morning she told Trudy. This had been Roger's advice, and she was not at all averse to acting on it. "Cyril knows, and Trudy and the young brother must know," he had said. "Otherwise we shan't be able to escape away alone." And Trudy, after an annoying "What did I say?" was magnificent, showing a deep interest in the romance, and out-talking Daphne with plans for the next few days. Owen said, "I protest it shocks me," and did what he could to help.

There were three days before Roger left. The first two, as was right for lovers, they wandered together along country roads or up on to the downs. Often they were at a loss for conversation, but always Roger embraced happiness, and Daphne lost herself in it, when the time came for her to sink into his arms. She discovered, too, that he could always be given conversational facility, and the desirable mental ease, if he were encouraged to talk about himself. She learned then that unless he did something big he would not really be *Sir* Roger Muirhead, because his father was only a knight, but that he intended to do some very big things, and preferably in the field of politics. Herself talked little; she did not want to talk; the love affair was a dream—a dream like that one in which she was tried for murder before a watching world and unjustly condemned— but a dream that had solidified. Here in undeniable fact at her side was Roger, splendid to look at, clever, dominant, strangely older than she, and yet so deferential to her, so chivalrous. She was immensely proud of him; no grown-up girl with a lover had more than she, and of girls her own age who had such a one as this?

The third day, being the last before Roger's departure, a great scheme of his was carried through. Under cover of a few fabrications he and she escaped to Brighton, as other illicit lovers have done before and since. They lay on the shingle, each very proud of the other. They bathed, and

166

afterwards stretched white, firm limbs to dry in the sun. They were photographed by a beach photographer that Roger might have her image in his breast pocket; but so revolting was the likeness that she begged him to smash it, and had a presentiment of disaster when it went with a strong man's finality into his breast. There were also in his pocket a big supply of envelopes addressed to her in Owen's handwriting, by means of which he intended to get his letters through the protective barriers at Hemans House. A brilliant stratagem! They had lunch on a restaurant balcony overlooking the sea, and tea at the end of the pier. With the falling of the sun the melancholy that had been with them all day took on a likeness of pain. He told her the train that they were taking to-morrow, and reminded her that it would run along the side of Ditchling Common.

"You must be on the common and wave to me, and I will see you the whole length of that bit. You must stand on one of the higher parts and I'll see you as long as I can. After that—well, I simply don't care to think what'll happen after that."

She said nothing in reply, so he repeated:

"Will you be there, Duffy?"

Her face turned towards him, and her eyes sought his. As if he didn't know she'd be there!

"Roger, I believe you think you love me more than I love you."

"Well, you never say much."

"I don't want you to go."

"Say, ' I love you better than all the world, *darling.*' "

"I love you better than all the world, darling."

That little sceptic who always crouched in a corner of Daphne's mind—that little sceptic who had enabled her to question Hollins's nursery rhymes, to see that Miss Vidella acted up to a part, or to suspect the ephemeral quality of the friendship with Trudy—had not been unheard during these rose-flushed days. It had whispered to her what grown-ups would say of the whole affair: that it was the veriest calf-love and the breath of a moment, and if there were pain in parting, three weeks would heal the wound. It had whispered that, of course the grown-ups were right. And yet the fact remained that she had so worked on her imagination, so lost herself in her dream, that now she suffered, and in her suffering, these thoughts could only peep and run.

She cried when she left Roger that night, and the cries became sobs, and her dreams when at last she slept were troubled with his presence. "I shan't see him any more," was her first thought on waking. "I know I shan't." As soon as possible she fled. Half an hour too early she was standing on the highest ridge of the undulating common, waiting for the distant smoke of Roger's train. Except for a cart trundling to Ditchling the ribbon of highway on which he had first appeared was deserted. A few cows cropped the grass near the western hedges. The cocks and hens, like the care-free creatures they were, pecked at the ground by Jacob's Post. As she waited she fiddled with her fingers, or nibbled at unripe blackberries, or looked around in search of the gorse bushes under which they had lain together. The action of her heart had sickly moments. She dreaded the coming of the train, and yet longed for it. Would it never come? Surely she had been waiting a long time. It would be better if it came soon and got its sharp moment over.

It was a relief when she caught her first glimpse of it— but a shock as well, for she had been in a brown study. It rushed on and past. She thought she distinguished Roger at a window, but could not be sure. But he at least must have seen her, for she had stood on her hill and waved her handkerchief in the same arc again and again, till the train was out of sight and there was nothing left but a broken puff of smoke in the sky.

Not three weeks, but three months were required for her cure. And even after that—for long after that—the memory of Roger, so handsome and so courteous, could give her a pleasant melancholy.

At first, however, she had been surprised to find that the rest of the holiday was anything but empty and dull. She was able to enjoy herself with Trudy and Owen, melancholy only adding a charm. Laughter came as easily as before, though sometimes she arrested it. She and Trudy would stare out of the window at old Eadigo in the garden, watching him as he bent low in his too-tight trousers, and hoping for the best. "Now—this time!" she would say, as he stooped to remove a weed—"it must happen soon," and she would wonder if such humour were consonant with Roger's absence. But he had written to her, and though his letters were infrequent, they were couched in the correctest language of a lover.

This was more than she had hoped, and she was very proud. When she went back to school, and Miss Vidella came fussing into the dining-room to welcome back her dear girls, Daphne felt sorry for her as an old maid who had never known the sensation of being loved. In her pride she felt the other girls ought to know about her romance, and in order that they might at least suspect, she encouraged their chaff when they found her in a deserted class-room writing to a secret correspondent. She liked to have this privacy disturbed by some inquisitive girl and to snatch her letter guiltily away. She was even tempted by the shameful idea of losing a letter of Roger's that it might be found and read.

But she was saved from this by the failing character of Roger's letters. Only the first two or three had been really passionate. And only two had come to Hemans House in the carefully prepared envelopes, and they had been little more than a resumé of his doings.

"He won't write again now. He'll never write again."

And he didn't. All the rest of those envelopes must have been destroyed.

After two months without a letter, she grew used to the pain, and gradually lost it. She no longer, when lying in bed, projected herself to Roger, but imagined instead their meeting one day when he would plead for forgiveness, and she would be too indifferent to cut or punish him; or, as a variant of this, the announcement in a paper which he would see : "A marriage has been arranged between Miss Daphne Deirdre Tenter Bruno, the celebrated daughter of an equally celebrated parent, and Lord Montagu of Beaulieu"—for this title had always fascinated her.

The next summer, when the meeting might just possibly happen, she learned towards the term's end that they were to be whipped away to Devonshire for a long holiday by the sea. This was excellent. Roger, if he came to the common, would learn that the Brunos were away, on dignified travels in the west. The day before they left Sussex she dared to walk past the Muirheads' house. As she hurried along its frontage, expedited by the sight of people in the garden, the side of her eye perceived that they were strange children with a nurse in uniform. This made her halt round a bend. After a moment of deliberation, she walked back towards the house, and asked of a gardener who was trimming a hedge of thuja : "Can you tell me, does a Lady Muirhead live here?"

"No, miss," said the gardener. "Least, it's their house, I believe, but it's let now to my boss, Mr. Bradlaugh."

"Oh!" exclaimed Daphne, conscious of a sharp disappointment. "Have you been here long?"

"We come here last spring, miss?"

"And how—how long will you be staying?"

"I don't know, miss. Two or three years, I reckon."

"Oh—well, thank you. Thanks awfully."

She walked back. The blow had been to learn that Roger wouldn't after all be humiliated and saddened by the sight of Old Hall House empty and frowning, nor by the gorse and brambles on Ditchling Common.

CHAPTER XI

DAPHNE'S sixteenth and seventeenth years might have been called the years of the giggle. In the main they poured over shallows. No successor to Roger Muirhead came troubling her with a like emotion; and except for one short period she had no religion to make depths in the stream-bed. There was but one clear motive in her life that waxed stronger with the months, and brought a pattern to the welter; and this was her ambition to write. Of the rest of her nature the lawless high spirits took possession.

She grew like a blade of newly-sown grass. As her father said, you could almost see her growing; nay more, on a still night, if you listened very carefully, you could hear her growing. Her features lost some of their roundness and softness, and her body became a thought too narrow for its height. It worried her rather, so that she began to take very seriously her physical culture—her gymnasium, riding and tennis.

She laboured at this time on the manufacture of a distinguished signature, "Daphne D. T. Bruno," giving it a tail like an unwinding lasso, till her father, seeing the flourish, expressed acute distress and shame: "Duffy, this is awful—awful. You must have the soul of a tea-shop girl."

The ambition to write increased with every novel she read, and every discussion she heard on other people's novels. In a small part its driving force was the true compulsion of the artist; but the most of it was a mixture of crude ambition and sheer imitation. She wanted no less than a thundering fame, and she wanted to imitate the style and methods of the authors she read. After reading Dickens, she wanted to be a great humanitarian and a master of comic caricature; after Thackeray, an urbane and tolerant satirist; after George Eliot, William Black, or Bulwer Lytton—well, she re-modelled her style on whichever of them was the last read.

Daphne Bruno

She had no idea of working hard to equip herself for greatness; her reading was lazy, and limited to such fiction as pleased her; it could only be compassed lolling in a comfortable chair, and any hard parts she read through without troubling to know if she understood them.

Since she had no sincere religion or stable code of morals, nothing but an antiseptic, compounded of humour, innocence and the herding instinct, saved her from the grosser evils. This, and the two steadying influences of Hollins and Miss Sims. There had to be a show of religion at Hemans House, of course, but except in panicky moments when she sent up ejaculatory S. O. S.'s to God, it made no settlement in her secret life. Already the sceptic in the corner of her mind issued hints that she was probably the only girl in the school who knew that she didn't believe anything. This struck her as rather original, and she would sometimes give it an airing before Hollins. She did it with intent to shock, till one day the old servant, now very grey, discomfited her by interrupting :

"I'm very sorry, Miss Duffy, but I must ask you once and f'r'all, not to do your laughing at these things with me. I don't like it, I tell you I don't. It makes me think you'll be struck leprous, or the like of that. And though you're only a child, it—it sort of upsets my faith. And then I don't know where I am. . . . It's for your pa to say, of course, but to my idea it's a dreadful thing for children to be brought up without any religion. No good'll come of it, I dare swear."

She had a similar experience with Miss Sims.

Miss Sims had kept her favourite's affection, if not the earlier adoration. And on Sundays, when the crocodile went tail-first to church, Daphne would inflate the governess's heart by coming to chatter at her side, and in church by pushing to sit next to her.

It was when walking to church one Sunday that Daphne deliberately shocked Miss Sims by a frank statement of her atheism, with this corollary : that she didn't think she would marry because it would interfere with her writing, but she saw no reason, believing in love as she did, why she shouldn't have intermittent love affairs like other famous women. Here was opportunity for Miss Sims to play the saviour, and she filled the part at once. She hurt her

172

favourite with a swift lash, refusing to be amused and suggesting that Daphne walked elsewhere; and when the girl, who had been silent for the rest of the walk, was sitting beside her in church, Miss Sims acted her own devotion and faith. It distinctly impressed Daphne, who glimpsed a beauty and peace in holiness.

But it was Winnie Chatterton who really led her on a short excursion into holiness. Winnie Chatterton was the only notable successor to Trudy Wayne. The friendship with Trudy had wilted. They had not quarrelled, but just drifted apart. They were friendly, but not friends. After a chain of minor intimacies Daphne discovered Winnie Chatterton, and Winnie Chatterton discovered Daphne Bruno. Both wondered how they could have been three and four years at the school without an earlier gravitation each to the other. In figure and colouring they were much the same, which was delightful, and there was the most wonderful community of taste. And now on walks through Windsor Park these two tall girls went hand in hand. Their place was near the head of the crocodile, and of the many treble voices that made up that peripatetic parliament, one, as likely as not, was Daphne's as she told to Winnie the whole story of the last novel that had affected her. "Vanity Fair" she serialized, telling it in three instalments on three successive walks. And Winnie, whose art was music, talked enthusiastically about that, or about the High Churchmanship that had lately won her. In the end Daphne tried both the music and the religion.

Old though she was, she insisted on taking up the 'cello with Mr. Pulteney, the music master (the "Chutney" of the girls). And after her first lesson, which was disastrous, she rushed to Winnie to give humorous report of it.

She had walked towards the music-room, explained Daphne hurriedly, and seen Petsy (Miss Vidella) waiting for her outside. Together they had entered the room where Chutney was tuning her shining new instrument. Petsy had seated herself on a chair to act as chaperon, for music lessons and the music master, as all literature showed, were the points at which foolishness and sin were most likely to break through. So Petsy had sat in a chair to strengthen the defences. Daphne, on taking the huge instrument, had most unfortunately felt a sudden desire to giggle. It

173

Daphne Bruno

was awful, and when Chutney placed the music-stand before her and asked: "Where's your music, Miss Bruno?" she had only been able to reply, with the giggle trembling through her words: "I've forgotten it. It's up in my bedroom." At that Petsy had rustled in her chair, probably rendered ill at ease by this mention of bedroom to a music master. "Really, my dear child," she had whined, "you are slatternly in many things. Can she not, Mr. Pulteney, use some of the music of the other dear children?" Chutney had said he was afraid not, because she needed the most elementary book, and he had no other girl beginning at the beginning. So Petsy had creaked out of her chair into a standing position, and said: "Well, we must go and get it, dear. It's really very thoughtless of you. Come. Trip ahead of me."

"Why we were both obliged to go out Heaven only knows," commented Daphne. "I suppose because if Petsy had gone for the music, I should have been left alone with a music master, and if I had gone, she'd have been left alone with a music master. And Chutney couldn't go, of course, because of the intimate nature of the room where the music was. So we tripped out together."

When they were in the hall Daphne had run upstairs, two and three steps at a time, while Petsy waited at the bottom in all the safety of that public place. She must needs call after Daphne: "Don't go up the stairs like that, dear child. Supposing anyone had been passing and seen you. So impetuous you dear children are!" Daphne had got her music and come down again decorously. She had re-entered the music-room behind her principal, and sat in the pupil's chair while Chutney placed the 'cello in the correct position, and Petsy watched carefully through her spectacles to make sure that in touching the 'cello he didn't also touch the 'cellist.

Then the 'cellist had commenced. Her first notes had been as horrible as an amateur's first notes on a bugle, and the desire to giggle had got much worse, with the result that her hands trembled, and the next notes were too awful for words. Unfortunately, Chutney, who was a perfect dear, had caught the infection of her giggle. Presumably he had never before had so old a pupil at the clumsy stage of 'celling. At last, after a dreadful prolonged note on the lowest string, her giggle had burst out, and Chutney had only saved himself from disgrace by swinging round, so that his back was turned to Miss Vidella. Miss Vidella had asked : " Has something humorous happened? " and Daphne had apologized, saying : " I'm sorry, Miss Vidella. I can't help it." Then Petsy had begun to rustle a lot, thinking no doubt that this conjunction of a music master, music, and a giggle promised the worst results. She had shut her eyes behind her spectacles for a second, and asked : " Can you approach anything, Daphne dear, without unsuitable levity? If you are not disposed to bring seriousness to these music lessons, which your dear father has secured for you at considerable cost "—Chutney had grimaced at that—" and from the best instructors "—that had set him grinning sheepishly out of the window—" I shall have to recommend him to discontinue them. Now please proceed."

Then there had been a lot of trouble with her fingering. Time and again Chutney had moved to adjust her fingers with his own, only stopping when he saw that Petsy's spectacles ruled out so indecorous a thing. Absurd, because Chutney was really such a pure little man. He had been obliged to demonstrate the correct method by holding another instrument before her, and asking her to copy exactly the movement of his fingers; which she had done, but her sounds had been quite different from his, and induced Petsy to poke in with some advice. "Try to do what Mr. Pulteney says, dear." Not a helpful remark ; and Daphne, getting annoyed, had pulled her bow rather savagely along the string, producing the most painful sound of the morning. This had changed her temper into humour, and for some torturing seconds she had been much more occupied in controlling her laughter than in catching what Chutney was saying. Her wrist work and her holding of the bow had been just as troublesome, and Chutney had kept coming towards her with the obvious desire of putting her hand and wrist into the correct position, but had tripped, as you might say, over the protective ray from Petsy's eyes. And Petsy had most stupidly tried to bridge the difficulty by some more advice : " Do try and remember, dear, that it is a bow that you are holding and not a clothes brush " ; which had made Daphne want to mutter : " Oh, *you* shut up. for the Lord's sake ! "

175

Daphne Bruno

"From somewhere about this time," explained she to Winnie, "the row began to begin. I can hardly remember how it started—I never can—and I had a beastly feeling when it was all over that I had made a fool of myself, but you know what Petsy is—she's such an old fool, posing so pompously and thinking it's funny."

"Oh, what happened, what happened?" asked Winnie.

"Well, I think Chutney said, as a sort of excuse for me, that the exact position was a little difficult to get right at first. And Petsy was sarcastic and said : ' Not, I take it, to intelligence.' And I lost my temper and said : ' But I'm not intelligent.' Chutney stared, and Petsy was rather taken aback, but when she had recovered herself, she opened fire, I can tell you. She said : ' Precisely, my dear. And the less intelligent girls have to make up for their deficiencies by a becoming willingness and humility. They do not boast of their stupidity.' And I snapped back : ' I wasn't boasting. I was deploring the fact.' Then Petsy stood up. I think she was simply beaten by such cold-blooded impudence, and could not for the life of her decide how to deal with it. But she had to do something in front of Chutney, so she began : ' My dear Daphne, I do not like that tone at all. I do not like it at all. I really have not been insulted in a music lesson before. I think you will go to your classroom, where you will wait to hear from me.' Then she apologized at great length to Chutney for taking up his valuable time with a perverse and ill-mannered child, and Chutney was perfectly sweet, saying I was only confused and awkward at first, and would be all right next time. And Petsy interrupted : ' I really do not know whether there will be a next time. I am not at all sure that I shall allow her to continue her lessons.' And of course I said : ' I've no particular desire to,' and went haughtily out of the room. She's said nothing so far, but I suppose I'm in for an interview, and a heart-to-heart talk."

Her conversion to High Churchmanship was a mixture of sincerity and posturing, as the sceptic in the corner would hint through his gags. It was sincere in this : that she secretly disliked much of her character and wanted to improve it; she had depressed moments when she thought herself vain, lazy, much too selfish, and without a decent

control of her temper; and while she couldn't believe that
her own strength would ever pull out these tough-rooting
faults, she was quite sure that a stern religion would do it.
And her lack of any stable morality could trouble her sometimes; she remembered how it had enabled her to suggest
in flippancy things that earned disgust from people like
Miss Sims.   At such times, aided by the placid demeanour
of Miss Sims and her occasional homilies, and by the graver,
brow-furrowing chats of Winnie, and the tales of the saints
that she had read, her imagination would show her the religious life as one of self-respect, happiness in worship, and
peace in believing.

The element of posture lay in her eagerness to perform
the picturesque rites of High Churchmanship; in her instant
response to its spirit of gay rebellion; and in her desire to
do something that would startle her family.

In the beginning sincerity occupied most of the ground.
Her first weeks, after her acceptance of the faith and her
prayer in which she surrendered to God and asked forgiveness for her long neglect, were very happy; and she was
perfectly conscious of a softening and ennobling of her
character.   She went ahead of Winnie, and silently wondered
how her friend could keep certain things in her life as
fellow-tenants with her religion.   These were perhaps the
sweetest days of Daphne's childhood.   But it could not last.
The soil was too unbroken, and there were too many older
roots in the tilth; the little sceptic spread his gangrene : "Do
you *really* believe all this?   You know you don't *really?*
Not if you once thought it out "; and a series of little shocks,
as she realized some of the things that the religion implied,
helped to wither the sincerity and bring in the element of
posture.   That every good Catholic was morally obliged to
go to Confession she had not foreseen, and she knew she
could never go; other duties such as fasting, hearing Mass,
being confirmed, and preparing long and earnestly for her
communions she was prepared to accept, but not this—not
confession to any living creature of some of the things that
hurt her conscience.   And that every really Catholic priest
ought to be a celibate—good heavens, did Anglo-Catholics
say that?

Winnie, who considered that she had to be as extreme
as possible now she was instructing a neophyte, declared

that such of course was the truth. In fact, she made much of this question of celibacy, deploring its widespread disregard. Her first vicar had been married, she said, but had had the decency not to have children. His successor, however, was not only married, but had a boy at Cambridge. "I don't think he ought to have married at all," expounded Winnie, "but if he did, he shouldn't have borne a son."

When Daphne went home for the holidays, the posturing was so far in possession that she was chiefly eager to offend everybody by insisting that she must go into Brighton on Sundays to hear Mass at a respectable church. And her first Sunday she found herself in St. Paul's, West Street, which had the reputation of being as high as was possible. It certainly seemed very high indeed; and disappointment took her when she knew herself shocked, bewildered, and traitorously sure that she could have worshipped more easily in the service to which she was accustomed. But it was only a matter of getting used to it, she supposed, and therewith struggled up to certain points of spiritual exaltation. All the holidays she talked Catholicity to the household; and when her father ridiculed her, saying: "Yes, run and worship in your strange groves, Daphne," she was not displeased at this prick of persecution. Hollins's acceptance of the news was rather disturbing, for, after Daphne had been chattering some time about the joys of religion, the old servant suddenly dropped her sewing, blew her nose, and carried the handkerchief to her eyes before returning it to her lap. "Well, there, miss," she said, pretending to believe that Daphne had not observed anything, "I *am* glad. It's kind of done me a lot of good, and strengthened my faith that prayers, if you stick to 'em, are often answered."

By the time she went back to school, the sceptic had nearly worked himself free of his gags, and she knew that she was only longing to shock the other girls with her advanced Catholicity, and to see what would happen when she exhibited it on the first Sunday of the term to Miss Vidella.

The movements of Daphne and Winnie that first Sunday were the creations of Daphne's brain. She justified them on the ground that it was a duty to reveal to old-fashioned

and prejudiced minds the strength of Catholic thought.
Winnie and she, as elder girls, walked to the church, one
on each side of Miss Vidella; and when they reached the
Lady Chapel, in which were the seats allotted to Hemans
House, they still managed to keep her between them. This
was designed to surround Miss Vidella with Catholicity.
Kneeling down, they made augmented signs of the cross,
prayed for a suitable time, and made second signs of the
cross; and then resumed their chairs and read advanced
manuals. The vestry opened on to the side chapel, and
when the vicar and the curate passed them at the tail of the
choir, the two girls bowed in reverence for the priestly office.
The vicar noticed it and looked surprised.

They made the sign of the cross at the Absolution and
at the close of the creed. They bowed at every *Gloria*.
And in the Ante-Communion Service, at the *Incarnatus*
clause, they genuflected. The genuflexion left Miss Vidella
standing as a sort of indignant Protestant lighthouse in
these undulating waters of Catholicity. Some girls in front
turned round to see what had happened.

All the way home Miss Vidella was menacingly reserved;
and they were soon summoned to her room. This prospect
of imperial persecution was excellent. They had done
nothing, absolutely nothing (Daphne assured her partner as
they walked to judgment) but what they were perfectly
entitled to do—what indeed it was their duty to do. Petsy
wouldn't have a leg to stand on.

Miss Vidella began mildly.

"I could not but notice, Daphne dear and dear Winifred,
that in church this morning you indulged in practices which
are usually associated with Roman Catholicism. You are
not, I believe, Catholics."

"Yes, we are," said Winnie.

"Yes, Catholics," Daphne explained, "but not *Roman*
Catholics."

"Oh, you are, are you?" The imperial power was clearly
annoyed by their bearing. "But not *Roman* Catholics. And
may I inquire how you can be Catholics without being Roman
Catholics?"

To explain to the uninstructed the answer to this question has always been a long and laborious business; so
Winnie turned to Daphne as spokesman.

Daphne Bruno

"All Church of England people are Catholics if they only knew it," said Daphne.

"Oh, I see. Then am I a Catholic?"

This made Daphne want to giggle; and at first she thought she had better leave the query without a reply; but, deciding not to go back upon her church, she said awkwardly:

"Yes, I—I'm afraid so."

It seemed rather a press-gang method of getting Miss Vidella on board the Ark, and it was not surprising that her annoyance was increased.

"I see. But I fear I am not so good a Catholic as to tolerate in my school such ridiculous practices as those with which you embarrassed the greater part of the congregation this morning. You will kindly behave as others do and keep your gymnastic exercises for Tuesdays and Fridays, when I think you go to the Royal Gymnasium for Instruction. Have you anything more to say?"

Daphne knew that what she ought to say now was a modern paraphrase of "O King, live for ever. Be it known unto thee that we will not worship as you wish, nor do anything that you suggest"; but on being asked so abruptly she couldn't shape a single sentence.

"Then that will do, my dears, you may go."

They decided in a mysterious council of war that, having done this much they could henceforth, with the early Christians for a precedent, veil their gestures and reverences.

At the end of that term Winnie left to be "finished" in a French convent, and Daphne, who had been ashamed to backslide before her friend, tried her religion on a charge of personation, and convicted it.

Now she received occasional news of Roger Muirhead. Owen was at Sillborough and would mention him in his letters or on his holidays. Not often though, for Daphne never asked for information, and Owen apparently detested his senior. It looked as if Owen also had a secret desire to be an author, for he affected a very personal and precious style. "At this Academy," wrote he in his first letter from Sillborough, "we have one R. Muirhead, with whose name you will not be wholly unfamiliar. He is, I think, the most conceited ass I have ever known. He's a prefect, and fancies himself hugely as a disciplinarian. ' My word is law and changeth not ' sort of business—as our inimitable Herbert Hollins would say. ' Woe to anyone who crosses my path or thwarts *me!* I am severe but just. Oh, yes. I am not easily angered, but if some groundling does raise my ire, he must expect no quarter. Oh, no.' Funny that these pompous blokes never credit anyone with the brains to see through them. Of course the boys suck up to him, because he's hot stuff at games, which he certainly is, though not as good as he thinks. No one ever was as good as that. And this sucking up makes him ten times worse. I can tell you R. Muirhead is no small panjandrum. Dammy, no."

CHAPTER XII

In the summer of her seventeenth year she read for the first time one of her father's books, and was surprised to find it exceedingly interesting. Here was a book that wasn't even fiction, and yet, with its wit and gaiety and its big, far-sweeping ideas, gave her thrills as pleasant as any story she could remember. She sat on and read devouringly. The grander words danced quadrilles in her head: "Intelligentsia," for example, and "Reactionary." The book was a survey of modern history written from the viewpoint of a doctrinaire rebel, and Daphne's sympathy was always, as the writer intended, for the Revolutionaries and the Intelligentsia, who appeared to be the same. She longed to be accounted one of the Intelligentsia. It was a new ambition, and her heart went wholly to it. She crept into her father's empty study and abstracted another of his books. And then another. Many of their allusions and quoted names she did not understand, but their wit and some of their matter she did—far more than she had dared to hope. But the final result of her reading, thanks to her habit of bolting what she could not masticate, was to increase the confusion of her mind; she retained only phrases and names and a muddled idea that revolutionaries were always right and reactionaries always wrong.

Why it was necessary to abstract the books surreptitiously she could hardly say; probably because she would be utterly ashamed to be caught by Miss Carrell or Owen reading a book by her father. It was Mr. Bruno, however, who surprised her at it. One wet afternoon she was alone in the great play-room at Old Hall House, gathered sideways in a tattered lounge-chair with her legs under her and the book on the chair's arm. Its sparkling survey of a century's literature had her in such thrill that she did not hear his entry. At the moment she was annoyed to have allowed years to pass in idleness instead of in reading all these authors here written of; brain-hot with resolves to read them

182

all immediately, and flattered by her own delight, since it proved that by nature she was one of the Intelligentsia.

Mr. Bruno stood and looked at her. An unconscious grace in her attitude pleased him and stirred as usual the desire to banter her.

"Relaxed and idle creature," he began. "Yes, you may well jump guiltily. Have you no holiday task, or are there no household duties waiting to be done, that you loll there —for all the world like a statue of Indolence—reading some cheap and nasty trash?"

She rolled on to her back, putting the book between her body and the arm of the chair.

"On the contrary, it's quite a decent book, darling."

(She had taken to calling him "darling" ever since on a holiday visit she had heard Winnie Chatterton doing as much by her parent.)

"Decent? My dear, if it were a serious book on logic you would learn that the epithet ' decent ' (which is a disgusting misuse of words, by the way) is what is known as a Petitio Principii, or Begging of the Question. It probably *does* appear decent to one without any literary palate, but that doesn't make it so."

"I don't say it's anything much, but the man who wrote it, I should think, is not without intelligence."

"What's the idle tale called?"

"Wouldn't you like to know?"

"I should not only like to know, but in thirty seconds I *shall* know."

And he thrust out his hand towards the book, while she rolled over to cover the secret with her body.

"No, you shan't! You shan't. Go away."

"Ah, would she?" smiled he. "Would she? Since she forgets she's a full-sized woman and adopts the tactics of a little child, she shall be treated as such." And, putting one arm behind her back and the other under her knees, he lifted her off the chair and laid her on the carpet.

"How dare you, darling? . . . Good night! I didn't know you were so strong . . ."

Leaping up, she threw her arms about his elbows, trying to pin them to his sides and hold him back from the book. "No, daddy, don't be a cad," she begged; but he took a pace forward, wrenched an arm free, stooped down and picked up the book. She released him, saying : "Well, I think it's a dirty shame."

He turned the book so as to see its title on the back, and read "The Decay of Romanticism, by T. Tenter Bruno."

It moved him, and almost unwittingly he placed an arm about her shoulders and pressed her to his side. Then he tossed the book back on to the chair.

"No, Duffy dear. Read your tales, not stuff like that. It's a dull and heavy work, as are all its fellows—stale, flat and unprofitable."

"It isn't," denied Daphne. "It's fine. I'd no idea your books were as decent as that. They're so slick and witty. I've been screaming with laughter. Daddy, how do you write so wittily as that?"

"Rudeness, my dear—that's all—just rudeness. The rudeness is all. All wit, from the highest to the lowest, can be shown to have its bottom in abuse, whether it's the neatest definition of Voltaire or Johnson or just the low comedian saying : ' Your mother must have been fond of children to bring *you* up.' "

"But it isn't only their humour—they're so—they've got such ideas——"

He brought her in front of him, holding her there with a hand at each shoulder, that he might look at her. Flitting in his mind was the memory of that February evening when she was born and he had wondered into what long girl she would grow. And here she was—in his hands and before his eyes. *"Elle est mon rêve."* Strange that one could tell oneself in French, and be pleased with the phrase, what one would condemn in English as sentimental ! *"Elle est mon rêve."*

"You speak, Duffy, as if you'd been wasting your time skimming some of the others."

"I've read two, and this is my third, and I'm going to read all of them."

"No, no, dear. Let them alone." He moved his hands and picked up the book. "I have read them all, and I am a great critic, and think them small beer. I'll get you something that'll really interest you, and be improving at the same time. 'Sandford and Merton,' have you read that? And 'The Swiss Family Robinson.' . . . Or since you were doubtless made for pleasure rather than profit, I'll

get you 'The Worst Girl in the Fourth Form.' Only name
your choice, so that you don't read unedifying stuff like
his."

She snatched back the book.

"My choice is all the other books of T. Tenter Bruno.
They're ripping."

"Oh, they seem more to enthusiasm and—yes, to your
youthful mixture of generosity and ignorance—than they
really are. They will serve their purpose—amuse a few
people and be deservedly forgotten."

"You know they won't. You know you think they're
splendid. You'd be a fool if you didn't. I don't want to
flatter you, but whatever else you are, you're not a fool.
I've never read anything like them. I never thought books
on subjects like that could be interesting like that. Daddy,
I'm awfully proud of you."

Mr. Bruno smiled, and once more pressed her to his side.

"*Pride?* You don't know one-tenth of what the word
means. Pride, Duffy. When *you* have a daughter who not
only speaks well of your books but even reads them, you'll
begin to probe the depths of the word." He kissed her
forehead. "And when you look her up and down and
realize that there's a chance of her—well, a chance of her—
let us say, a chance of her being not without beauty——"

"Oh, no, I'm not," interrupted Daphne. "I can't see it
at all."

"You have tried hard?"

"Of course I have. And I think I'm like a filleted
hatpin."

"Oh, no. No, you're not at all like a filleted hatpin.
But you stoop a little, dear. However, that'll be overcome
as the sap comes up the stalk; the droop will disappear
then, and the whole contraption become less—less green.
It's funny, but Nature sometimes completes her sculpturing
of a woman in seventeen years, and sometimes she dawdles
much longer over the work. If she's anything like me,
she dawdles over those she wants to make best. We'll wait
till you're twenty, Duffy, and see what you're like then."

The mind that she took back to Hemans House was like
a shop whose stock has been largely altered. New goods
were stored where the religion had been. They were goods

of which she knew the labels and the pictured covers better than the contents. The labels were ever pleasant to handle : "More advanced schools of thought," "In advance of the age in which he lived," "A Leader of the Left," "The School of William Morris"; and the pictures and designs showed Cobden and Bright on their platforms hypnotizing great audiences; Ruskin worrying Utilitarianism with the rumble of his thunderous periods; Swinburne singing melodious blasphemies to the dishonour of God and the glory of Man; and Friedrich Nietzsche (succulent mouthful) coming up like a wind from Germany.

She wanted to be a Leader of the Left. And why not? Quite obviously Miss Vidella was the very type of a reactionary, and equally obviously Daphne had always led a more advanced school. The—the school of Daphne Bruno. She was in advance of the system in which she moved.

Take the question of hockey, which she had been playing in holidays with most flattering success. Miss Vidella's absurd prohibition of the game was a piece of tyranny that ought to be resisted. Hemans House awaited a Liberator. A Risorgimento.

Remembering Cobden and Bright on their rostrums, she decided, after a discussion with the elder girls, that they must have a political meeting. Who would speak? Well, anyone who had anything to say; she, if they liked, would mount the platform first. Only the elder girls would be regarded as possessing the full rights of citizens and allowed to attend. It sounded a jolly game, and these elder girls assembled eagerly in an empty class-room at the advertised hour and pushed themselves into desks or along the form that stretched in front of the desks under the mistress's low platform. In the middle of this form sat Daphne with her legs crossed.

"We ought to have a chairman," said she, when nobody seemed to know what was going to happen next.

"Oh, yes, let's have a chairman," said a very lanky girl, Viola Rance, and she instanced her neighbour: "Queenie Dutroit'll be chairman."

"No, I shan't," snapped Queenie, horrified at the suggestion that she should do anything more public than sitting where she was.

"I vote old Viola's chairman herself," called a girl who,

being at the back and rather small, was in no danger of being thrust into the position.

"Yes, yes," endorsed several; and Queenie added, "Yes, she's so ready to suggest others, let her do the chairmaning herself."

Daphne, to push matters on, started a clapping of her hands, with the result, as she expected, that every girl did the same; and Viola, not displeased, though very red and inclined to giggle, slid flexuously on to the platform and into the mistress's chair behind the writing-table. The applause stopped, and the chairman looked down at Daphne in the front row and asked:

"But what do I do?"

"You introduce me."

Viola got up, giggled, and sat down in red confusion.

"Don't be an ass, Vi," grumbled Daphne. "If you'd any gumption you'd have entered into the spirit of the thing and said, ' Ladies and gentlemen, I have much pleasure in introducing our first speaker for this evening, Miss Daphne Bruno.' "

Viola immediately got up and raced through this sentence, though the last words were drowned in the rising tide of the giggle.

Then Daphne stepped on to the platform. No one had the wit or the courage to start the conventional applause; and when she turned and faced the audience she saw only a roomful of girls, some of whom were gaping at her and some sniggering as if they thought she looked rather a fool. She felt disappointed and sad. Why was it that, whether you were creating books or organizing picturesque demonstrations, it was so much easier to see them in dreams than to give them form. The ideas for a speech that had foggily filled her head thinned into nothing. She picked up something off the writing-table, put it back again, and began without heart:

"Well, it's like this. It's—I mean, I think we ought to have hockey. All the other decent schools are."

Not another word could she think of. She saw nothing but a horrid hiatus before her. If only some of those staring girls would say "Hear, hear!" But though it had probably occurred to many of them, all were too nervous of making fools of themselves. And indeed there was nothing more to say. Not being practised in political oratory, Daphne had expressed the origin and the business of the meeting, the reason of her speaking and the views which the audience had brought with them and which they would take away, in twenty words and ten seconds. But it seemed to her a sickly failure, and with a big effort she threw some more words into the awful lacuna.

"It's a topping game. Other schools are playing hockey, and I think we ought to have hockey too."

Someone giggled at the back, and fortunately this stirred temper, and temper stirred speech.

"I don't see anything funny in it. Giggling never did anything yet. It's perfectly piffling to go for a walk when we might be playing hockey. What I vote is that we all go in a sort of deputation and ask Miss Vidella to let us play hockey this term. If she gives in—which isn't likely—she'll probably only treat us to some of her celebrated queenly sarcasm; and if she refuses we shall have to organize a sort of secret intrigue to force her hand—a Liberationist Society, if you like. Like the National Assembly in France. Or the Risorgimento. I've got a plan of action in the event of it coming to that. I think we could all write to our parents asking them to support the general desire for hockey, and simply get her flooded with letters. I've got her absolutely weighed up, and I'm dead certain that she'd never say ' No ' to the majority of the parents. It's always the same; these thing only want the courage and—and someone to make a start. Just you see. If we have the grit to hold out we shall win."

It was not at all a bad speech, thought Daphne, and for its crown needed only a burst of applause. But nothing followed it except an embarrassed silence, and when that was getting too uncomfortable, an upward glance from the chairman, with the question :

"What do I do now, Dafs?"

"Oh, you can ask if anybody has any comment to make on what they have heard."

Viola stood slightly.

"Has anybody any comment to make on——" But it sounded to her so silly that the rest of the sentence was lost in the giggle with which, blushingly, she resumed her chair.

Nobody had anything to say; most were laughing at Viola.

Daphne stepped off the platform and sat again on the form in front, crossing her legs and grasping her knee.

"Is that all?" inquired the chairman, when she saw the principal speaker disappearing like that.

"Oh, I suppose so."

"Well, what happens now?"

"Oh, you can ask them if they agree to what I have said, to show it by holding up their hands."

Daphne knew that when the question was put all would want to hold up their hands and all would wait for someone else to do it first, so she flung up her own, and looking round, saw a forest of arms, many of which were waving about and trying to be funny.

"Ask if anyone disagrees."

"Anyone disagree?"

Not a soul. No one was likely to make herself so conspicuous.

"Well, what happens now?"

Daphne shrugged. Her imagination was vividly showing her what a good chairman might have made of this triumph. "Oh, tell them the meeting's adjourned. "

"The meeting's adjourned," said Viola, and, giggling, she jumped off the platform.

The minute the meeting was adjourned everybody had an undelivered speech to deliver. They stood in a group round Daphne and argued the question. It ended in her plan being adopted and a deputation formed to wait on the headmistress.

Daphne was at once proud and nervous as she led her deputation the next day, just before lunch, into Miss Vidella's room.

Miss Vidella was sitting at a little writing-table. She watched this entry of half a dozen girls with lifted eyebrows.

"What is it you want, dears? I am very busy."

"We want to know—we wanted to ask you," began Daphne, "on behalf of all the girls, if you would let us play hockey this term?"

Miss Vidella stared at the speaker. She removed her spectacles and held them in her fat hand on the table. That she was angry there could be no doubt, and that she was thinking out some sarcasms like a dentist selecting his sharp little tools.

"Have you ever played hockey in the Christmas term?"

Daphne was obliged to answer "No."

"Have you ever played hockey in any term?"

"No."

"Then why should you play hockey this term? I am not clear on the point, Daphne dear."

"We thought perhaps if we petitioned you, you would let us."

Miss Vidella replaced her spectacles on her nose as if the point could now be studied more closely. The point, it appeared, was in the middle of Daphne's face.

"Have I ever, on being petitioned, allowed you to do anything unladylike?"

Daphne couldn't very well point out to her that the epithet "unladylike" was a *Petitio Principii,* or Begging of the Question, so she murmured, "No."

"If you were to come to me, one by one, and say: ' Dear Miss Vidella, may I do something which you consider un-ladylike? ' would not my answer be: ' No, my dear, not at Hemans House '? "

She had acted the "No, my dear," with its inclination of the head, to an imaginary girl at her side, and now turned to Daphne for her reply.

"Yes—I suppose so."

"Well, would not the answer that I give to you severally be the answer that I give to you all together?"

Daphne was confused, and said again: "I suppose so."

"Then I am not at all clear as to what is the idea of your coming in such a funny little group as this. Run away, my dears, and get ready for your dinners. I am very busy, and have no time just now to play with you in your strange little games."

As the deputation moved out, Daphne felt furious. It was the only thing to feel if you were not to feel foolish.

"I told you nothing would come of that," she said hastily, to forestall any criticism of her leadership, "nothing except a performance by Petsy. But I never expected anything to. That was only a flourish. It's the next step that matters. I'm perfectly determined to beat her on this matter. And I should think you would be after she's tried to make fools of you like that."

The letter to the parents, outlined by Daphne, she thought exceedingly well done. As a politician she saw the skilfulness of the phrase, "give your *support* to the request of *many other* parents"; and as an authoress with some idea of emotional effect, she was particularly satisfied with the postscript, "*Please* do." No kindly parent would resist that.

When Miss Vidella watched the flooding in of requests from fathers and mothers that, if possible, hockey might be taught to their girls, she was more than flustered—she was frightened. To be queenly with a deputation of tongue-tied pupils was one thing, but to resist a concerted movement by parents was quite another. It could not be done. The difficulty was how to yield to the parents without seeming to eat the sarcasms she had offered to the deputation. She squeezed through this awkward pass by saying to the assembled school, one day before lunch:

"I understand now that when some of the elder girls waited on me last week with a request for the institution of hockey, they did so at the suggestion of their parents. If the girls had been wiser they would have made this clear. I think it very right and proper of your parents to trust you to come and tell me all that they consider desirable for your welfare, and to know that I shall always give every attention to their wishes. I may in this case doubt the wisdom of their opinion, but I understand that it must take precedence over mine. The request will therefore be conceded. I understand that Miss Bellamy has a knowledge of the game, and that, according to her, our present field will be large enough. I will therefore order an adequate supply of the necessary implements, and hope you will be able to try your hands at this new recreation in a day or two. I shall, of course, be there to supervise your play at so dangerous a game."

She moved away to a chorus of "Thank you, Miss Vidella."

Daphne knew that every girl had thrown at her a swift glance, and she tried to cover her feelings with a mask of unconcern. The smile that broke through her control, and fought with her lips, was rather one of nervousness at being looked at than of exultation in a triumph. Her glow was mixed with a knowledge not wholly pleasant that she had never so completely despised her head mistress. In such contempt, as in the deeps of a pool, lay possibilities of which she could feel herself afraid.

Miss Bellamy was now dressed in an unexpected importance, and very conscious of it. A stout, bustling woman of thirty-five, she fussed about, equipping the two teams which were to make the first venture into the new game, marking the field with their aid, and explaining on a blackboard the principles of hockey to those who had everything to learn. And the day of the first trial, a golden afternoon in St. Luke's Summer, she led the girls to their field as excitedly as any of them. Miss Vidella followed less easily and happily. And Daphne, who throughout the preparations had been as officious and explanatory as Miss Bellamy, declared that Petsy had come simply and solely to make herself a nuisance. She would probably stand on the touch line and worry the game like a fat puppy who was feeling rather sick.

It was an accurate prophecy. When all the girls were in their places, and Miss Bellamy had done pushing them there, or pointing all over the field with her whistle, Daphne shouted :

"Shall I bully off with Viola?"

And Miss Vidella at once raised her voice.

"'Bully off.' I do wish you wouldn't talk slang, Daphne dear. You know I have never tolerated it. 'Bully off' is a phrase I have never heard, and do not wish to hear again."

"But it's the correct term, Miss Vidella."

"It really is," endorsed Miss Bellamy, who had rushed up to bring an expert's advice to the solution of a difficulty.

"Dear me"—Miss Vidella lifted her shoulders resignedly—"what unpleasant terms these rough games do employ ! "

They bullied off, and the game swung into noisy life. Its two most conspicuous performers were Daphne and Miss Bellamy. Daphne was early captured by it, mind and body. She was nearly always in possession of the ball, and the repeated running had damped her forehead and shortened her breathing; she felt the rises of her breast, and a delightful dryness and thirst stabbing her low down in the throat. There was a breeze that would not have been perceptible but for the dampness on her brow, and when it touched that, it strangely heightened her pleasure. It carried fugitive thoughts of long drinks, the spray of the sea, or immersion in bath or lake. Once she had fallen heavily, and the smell of dried earth on her palm toned exactly with the thirst, the quick breathing, the sting of gathering blisters, and the coldness on her temples. Health and optimism had become sensuous things. And how was it that these sensations, though within her, were at one with remembered things without—with firelight on old wood, mellow evenings, birds and squirrels, and sentences in Hans Andersen : "She flew away as if she were flying straight into the sun "—with all those things that she must capture and put into books?

Miss Bellamy rushed about, with her whistle at her teeth or in her hand. When she wasn't blowing the whistle, she was shouting : "Keep your places ! Pass the ball—oh, for goodness' sake pass it sometimes. Now then, Evelyn ! Played ! Oh, played indeed ! " Probably she wanted to impress the pupils and the principal. And certainly she impressed Miss Vidella—but very unfavourably. There was an abnormal second when she was standing at rest to watch a scramble near Miss Vidella, and Miss Vidella took the opportunity to begin, "I can't think, Miss Bellamy, that it's necessary to shout at the children so "; but just then Miss Bellamy saw a crass error in the play, shot out a pointing forefinger, and blew her whistle imperiously.

"Sticks ! Sticks ! Sticks ! " she cried. "Madeleine, you mustn't lift your stick above your shoulder."

"Come on—that's a free hit," shouted Daphne. "Chuck us the pill."

It was useless wishing she hadn't said it, for Miss Vidella was already calling.

"Daphne dear. Come here. What was that you said ? "

"I said, ' Chuck us the pill.' "

Miss Vidella nodded.

"I thought those were the words. Well, I am **so**

ignorant of this game that I do not know if that is the prescribed expression. Is it?"

"Well—no."

"You mean, it was slang?"

"Yes, I suppose so."

"Precisely. And I cannot allow the elder girls to set such an example to the younger ones. Besides, it is great disrespect to Miss Bellamy to use language like that in a game of which she is in charge. Let me hear you apologize to her."

Daphne's first impulse was to throw down her stick and walk off, but she remembered the delight of the game, and determined not to be robbed of it by any pomposity of Miss Vidella. And she so far obeyed her head mistress as to turn to Miss Bellamy and mutter: "Miss Vidella says I'm to apologize to you." Miss Bellamy smiled an acknowledgment, and a bow from the head mistress indicated that she was satisfied, and the game might proceed.

Daphne had no wish to offend a second time, and for the rest of the game, except for the very last minute, managed to play and shout without being called to order. She had, in fact, forgotten her anger with the head mistress, so exciting was the struggle. The two goals won by her side, in defiant answer to two won by their opponents, had been scored by herself, and the girls were saying: "No wonder you wanted to play hockey so as to show off." Her face and neck were streaming, and her body seemed to have been fitted with a new and different breathing system. Frequently she wiped her forehead with her sleeve, or tossed the wet hair-wisps out of her eyes. If she was not driving the ball herself she was shouting encouragement and praise to the others. "Oh, *played!* . . . I say, well played! . . . Look out!. . . *Billow!*" Her will and every faculty was set upon securing the third goal before the shrieking and perspiring Miss Bellamy should sound her whistle for the last time. The low slant of the sunlight and the stretching of the shadows told her that time was very short. Any second now might end the game. The matter was desperate; there was a look of evening over the field. Her stick perpetually reached the ball and forced it through a jumble of confused amateurs, while Miss Bellamy shouted: "Keep your places! Keep your places, all of you!" and Miss Vidella could be heard muttering a dislike of the worser scrimmages. At last Daphne won through with the ball, and came down the side-line with irresistible impetus, confident that now on the very sound of the whistle she was going to score her third goal. She had a faint impression of Miss Vidella stepping back from the touch-line so as to be out of danger. So fierce was her rush that the opposing full-back, frenzied with ignorance and dismay, hit her with great force on the shin. In the moment of sharp pain, Daphne flung her stick anywhere, and muttered : "Oh, damn ! damn ! "

All around her heard, and cast quick glances at the head mistress. All were probably feeling the satisfaction of being present when something really serious had happened. The head mistress, no doubt, was the most satisfied of all, because there are few happinesses so great as the first enjoyment of indignation.

"Miss Bellamy. Miss Bellamy," she shrieked to the referee, who, from her distance, was shouting encouragement to this waning corner of the game. "Miss Bellamy, stop the game."

"Play on, you girls," shouted Miss Bellamy. "Don't stand there as if you were afraid of the ball. Keep the ball moving for goodness' sake."

"Do nothing of the sort," commanded Miss Vidella. "Don't touch the ball. Miss Bellamy "—Miss Bellamy was running, whistle in mouth, to solve the problem that was hindering the game—"I have instructed the girls to stop. They are very rightly too shocked to continue. I wish them to stop. Please blow that whistle, if that is the way such a game is brought to an end."

Miss Bellamy, bewildered, sounded her whistle and stood near to witness a public censuring.

Daphne, after rubbing her shin, walked to her hockey stick, slightly exaggerating her limp, picked it up and examined its binding.

"Daphne. . . . I hardly know how to speak to you. For fifteen years I have given my life to the education and guidance of my schoolgirls, but never till this day have I heard one of them—I cannot bring myself to say it—heard one of them use such a word as passed your lips just now. I pray I shall never be asked to live through that moment again. I—and all these dear girls, I believe—are humiliated and shamed. You, too, I dare believe, are also deeply ashamed."

"Well, I don't see why I should have been hit on the shins for nothing. It'd have been a goal if——"

"Go back to the school. I confess I know not how to deal with you. I confess to being beaten by you. Fortunately there is no precedent in my experience which enables me to deal adequately on the spur of the moment with your offence. You are a girl whom it seems impossible to influence or guide. If all the affection and sympathy and gentle correction of the last few years "—Daphne made an obvious "Pooh!" with her lips—"has been unavailing to soften your nature, I know no other methods. They have always been those of Hemans House. Go back to the school and wait in your bedroom. I shall have to consider how to deal with you. I feel I shall have to write to your dear father——" Daphne was disposed to reply : "I should. It'll amuse him frightfully." "And do not attempt to see any other girls. I cannot have them taught your dock-yard oaths. . . . This evening I will . . ."

But Daphne had not waited for the rest.

CHAPTER XIII

MISS VIDELLA frightened herself more than her pupil when she announced that she would write to Mr. Tenter Bruno. The whole school had heard her say she would do a thing which she particularly did not want to do. The Bruno girl had still, presumably, another year to spend at her school and to bring in good fees, and it would be unwise to give her father the impression that she was getting too big and obstreperous for the place. There must be no quarrel with Mr. Bruno, for she wanted his name as a reference. Besides, she was thoroughly afraid of his brilliant modern mind. And somewhere behind her indignation peeped the thought that the offence was not really as bad as her posing required her to treat it. After a tea-time spent in deliberation she decided that discretion must masquerade as mercy. She climbed the stair to the little single bedroom which Daphne, as one of the elder girls, now enjoyed. She was primed with words of austere forgiveness, but when she saw that the criminal was lolling on the bed and reading a book, anger made her command :

"Get off that bed at once."

Daphne got off slowly.

"Now put it straight."

Daphne did so.

"You are indeed, Daphne, a difficult child. I came upstairs disposed to limit my chastisement of you to words of kindness and advice, and I find you apparently insensible to the gravity of your offence. I intended to say that I would not hurt your dear father by a report of your behaviour, but——"

"I don't mind if you write to him or not."

This was dreadful. The girl was pushing her into the stream of events she desired to escape.

"You don't care? Have you no affection for him? "

"Yes, heaps ; but I don't think he'll die of anything you can tell him."

Daphne Bruno

"Are you being impudent, Daphne?"

"I don't know."

"I do."

"Then why do you ask?"

Miss Vidella stared at her, flounced to the door, said: "I shall most certainly write to your father. I shall do it this moment," and thus made her exit. Yes, she would write that letter at once. Its phrasing shaped in her mind. Like all weak people she was easily made apprehensive lest someone was questioning her strength. A strong gesture was pleasing. Now that her hand had been forced she was proud that she was going to write to Mr. Bruno. The school should know that she had written to Mr. Bruno, and realize that when she said she'd do a thing she did it.

One person was thrilled by the news of Daphne Bruno's disgrace and confinement. Miss Sims, always curiously exultant when her favourite was punished, saw herself coming to her in her prison with sympathy and undiminished faith. Her heart beat quickly as she approached the bedroom where Daphne was isolated. Opening the door with a "May I come in?" she saw the girl sitting on the bed with one heel beneath her, writing something. This was disappointing. Miss Sims had encouraged the idea that she would be crying. "She's been made hard and callous," thought Miss Sims. "She will be better softened. Gentleness will soften her."

"Hallo," said Daphne, looking up. She folded over the letter she had been writing.

"Duffy dear. What *has* been happening? I could not bear to think of you up here."

"Oh, Miss Vidella has been doing a little acting. She thinks she's being very fine and strong. *I'm* enjoying myself immensely."

A pity she adopted this defiant attitude. Miss Sims liked to minister to soft and broken things. And the Character never listened to disloyalty.

"Hush, dear. You know I never listen to rebellious muttering." . . . She sat down beside the girl. "Why did you utter such a word? After all, you are a girl who will always exercise a great influence over those younger than yourself, and you have them to consider."

Daphne looked away, and Miss Sims knew that this veiled flattery was the way to conquer her. She spent a very happy few minutes, giving counsel to the girl, with her heart going out to her as she did so; she pointed out how much it behoved one who was plainly a nature of strong passions to learn control in small things, and she saw that Daphne liked being called a nature of strong passions, and was thinking of Miss Sims as the one person who understood her.

"I know, Miss Sims. But why couldn't Miss Vidella talk to me properly—like you do—instead of making an Aunt Sally of me before half the school. She said I was difficult to influence. I am not, am I? *You* know."

It was a sweet moment for Miss Sims

"I have never found you so, dear."

"Of course not, because you're always so understanding. But she always tries to humiliate me before the whole school, and now she declares she's going to write a lot of lies to father."

"Hush, dear. I think she may be unduly severe, but I can see her point of view."

"She hasn't got a point of view, except the one that goes with her part. I'm writing to father too. . . . Oh, Miss Sims, would you—would you post it for me?"

Miss Sims smiled tolerantly, but really the request gave her much pleasure. It was picturesque, this taking of a missive from an offender in prison.

"I will certainly, dear. There can be no harm in your father hearing what you have to say."

"Oh, that's topping of you."

Daphne added something to her letter, and folded it up and gave it to Miss Sims.

"Thank you, dear," said the governess. "And if there is anything else you need, or I can do for you—bring you books or anything——" Her guilty ear detected a step on the landing outside, and she rose. It was not done hastily, for her desire to impress Daphne with her serenity and fearlessness was stronger than her fear of being caught by Miss Vidella. But her heart, which fortunately could not be seen, was beating faster.

Daphne Bruno

"I will take it for you now. Good-bye for the time being, dear."

She stooped and kissed her favourite.

The next morning over his breakfast Mr. Bruno read of Miss Vidella's pain at being obliged to report that she had had occasion to deal severely with his daughter, and of her desire that he also would write a word of reproof. Daphne had employed on the hockey field language which could not be set on paper, and Miss Vidella wrote in the sure knowledge that her father's rebuke would carry very great weight with dear Daphne, and that, since this outbreak suggested that she had met with unsuitable companions in her vacations, he would doubtless wish to be informed of the matter.

"Gracious goodness!" smiled Mr. Bruno, at the ponderous and lumbering phrases. "What on earth can the depraved child have said?"

And all the contraband language that he could think of seemed beautifully funny as passing from one of her pupils to Miss Vidella.

Then he picked up an envelope written in the schoolgirl hand of his daughter.

"Ah, now perhaps we shall know. Duffy will doubtless strengthen herself to write the obscene word."

His butter-knife sliced the flap, and he read:

"DARLING FATHER,—Miss Vidella says she is going to write to you about the crimes of your daughter. I don't know if the old pig really meant it, but in case she does, I thought I'd get in first. Her only accusation is that I have used slang and one swear word. I don't think the slang business will upset you much because you say in ' The Decay of Romanticism ' that slang is often the natural, urgent poetry of a vital people." ("Good heavens!" thought Mr. Bruno, "she must have copied the sentence straight out of the book.") "And you give examples that you say are Shakespearean in their aptness, energy and high compression, and you say further on that those who use slang brilliantly are often more vivacious and dynamic minds than those who stagnate in a mould of stilted phraseology like Miss Vidella. I quite agree with you, as I do with most that you have written. And I am not saying this just

because I want you to side with me, but because I really
do. Old Petsy could no more think of that about slang
than she could fly. That is really rather witty about her
flying, as you would understand if you could see her. But
the swear word will probably not please you so well. What
happened was this. I felt that Miss Vidella was reactionary
in her ban on hockey, and that it was time Hemans House
advanced a little, so as to be abreast of modern ideas, and I
accordingly led a successful agitation for reform in the
matter. That, of course, stuck in her gizzard, and I'm
sure she came on to the hockey field determined to spoil
the game. What I blame myself for is not swearing so
much "—(Mr. Bruno read this sentence again before murmuring : "Duffy, Duffy, you're getting dangerously am-
biguous ")—"as giving the old cat an opening. Annie
Hurst, silly little ass, caught me an awful whack on the
shin, and before I knew what had happened, I said ' O
damn ! ' which you often say when the soup-plate is hot.
That was all, and it's really painful, a whack on the shin-
bone with a hockey stick, and I've got a huge bruise and
what looks like a little dent in the bone. That side of it
doesn't seem to have struck Miss Vidella.

"Daddy, I have got a suggestion. If you think it wise
to come down and rebuke me, couldn't we do it at a tea-shop
and have a jolly afternoon together.

"Daddy, I'm reading ' Park and Pavement,' and I like
it awfully. It's your best book, I think, in my humble
opinion. But then I think that of each one as I read it.
I'm in disgrace in my bedroom, and enjoying myself awfully.
It's been fun writing to you.—Yours awfully,

)   "DUFFY."

"P.S.—I have been wondering how I was going to post this,
        but an awfully decent mistress is going to post it
        for me.—D. D. T. B."

The effect of Daphne's letter on her father was similar
to that which she unconsciously used to work when she burst
uninvited into his gaze. There was an immediate quickening
of his love, a flavour of self-reproach that he passed so
much time away from her, and, as he pictured her sitting on
her bed and writing to him, a stirring of the heart that was
almost painful.

Daphne Bruno

"Oh, damn! That prehistoric old fool shan't persecute her. She shall swear if she likes. That is to say, she shall do nothing of the sort, for it would spoil her charm. But she's my daughter, and beginning to stand, I fancy, in much the same relation to that slow-going vehicle, her school, as I do to society to-day. I like to think it. With all her ignorance and immaturity she's too dynamic for her surroundings. I must write, I suppose. No, damn it, I'll go and see her, and the absurd place as well. If it's as I imagine, we must do something better for her."

It was impossible for him to be other than courteous, and he wrote to Miss Vidella thanking her for her thoughtfulness, telling her that he would like to come and see her the next afternoon, and requesting her to be so good as to inform Daphne of his intentions. His kindest regards concluded the letter.

Miss Vidella was delighted. Her strong action was justified. Evidently Mr. Tenter Bruno, since he was coming in person, shared her distress and approved her discretion. She began to phrase the high commendation he would give when sought as a reference for Hemans House. "I shall ever be grateful for Miss Vidella's watchful care of my own daughter." And after prayers that mornings she announced to the assembled school:

"I have just received a letter from Mr. Tenter Bruno, who will visit the school this afternoon." She left that to sink in. The children would instantly guess why he was coming, and be impressed with the seriousness of a recent incident and the strong hand of their principal. "And, girls, I hope he will come and see you at your work. Mr. Tenter Bruno, as you all know, is a writer with an international reputation, and you will like to remember that he visited you at your school. It will also interest your parents."

Mr. Bruno arrived about three o'clock; and after an interview in the reception room which was chiefly used by Miss Vidella to explain how fond she was of dear Daphne and hoped to make a great success of her, and by Mr. Bruno in mental generalizations suggested by such a type as this head-mistress, he was left alone in a saddle-bag chair to await his daughter. She burst in, most obviously dressed to receive him. And because she was tall, and he unused to such an interview, he rose like an embarrassed

guest to greet her. After the fat, black, pompous figure of
the head-mistress, she came with something like a shock
of contrast; he saw the roundness of her head under its
brown hair newly brushed, the freshness of her eyes and
cheeks, the smallness of her neck, and the fast-refining outline of her body and her limbs. The critic in him, as well
as the father, approved it all. Wonderful how she could
move him sometimes! In the chamber of his anti-senti-
mental brain, moving without guilt among the censors there,
was the thought: "You are mine . . . you came from
me . . . Daphne."

"Hallo, daddy!"

She rose on her toes to kiss him, and he gave her waist
a hug.

"So you've been using the language of the tap-room
to that strange old woman."

"I haven't," denied Daphne; "I told you exactly what
I said."

"Good heavens, miss! And wasn't that outrageous in
a slender girl?"   "

"No, not considering the hefty blow I got on my leg.
I often say ' Oh, damn! ' to myself, as I'm sure everybody
does, and that time it came out aloud. And with good
reason, too. Just look here." And she made as if to remove
her stocking.

"No, no, no. Don't show me anything unpleasant.
Besides, you've got it all wrong, Duffy. The idea of the
strange old lady isn't so much that you should show me
some trifling bruise on your shin, as that I should talk to
you about the really serious bruise on my heart. That a
daughter of mine should say—such words! You mustn't,
Duffy; for you're in danger of becoming a—a beautiful
creature, and it's out of harmony for one of that pattern to
use squalid words. The whole product is not homogeneous.
It's bad art."

"Well," said his daughter. "That's the most sensible
way I've ever heard it put."

"Yes, and—— However. . . . How old are you, Duffy?"

"Seventeen for all practical purposes."

"Well, I have a practical purpose. Let us sit down
and talk it over. Are *you* allowed to sit in this room?"

They seated themselves, and he told her of a scheme that

Daphne Bruno

he had been pondering in the train. And because it was one
that he knew she would love, he could only approach it
through a cloud of raillery. Publicity, he said, was a very
subtle question, and if in the past he had been seen in public
with so ordinary a daughter as she, the sale of his books
would doubtless have suffered. But now she had changed
and every year she would become of greater and greater
publicity value. He felt he would like to have her with him
as much as possible. He didn't believe this droll school had
anything more to give her, and she could probably do much
better, since the taste for less frivolous reading seemed to
have come, enjoying the free run of his library and having
some music lessons at home. Not that there would be much
time for that, because he had long wanted to spend a year
in Paris, and proposed taking her there next year. In Paris
he would put her on her honour to study the French language
and squeeze all the knowledge that was to be squeezed
out of picture galleries, historic buildings, the *Opera* and
the *Comédie Française*. In the summer they would wander
in Switzerland and down into Italy, and as the weather
cooled make tracks for Rome.

"Daddy!" interrupted Daphne. "Oh, do you mean it?
Lord, I'm glad I swore. What an awful suck for Petsy!"

He smiled as he watched her enthusiasm.

"But mark you, the first time you swear, you'll be sent
back to Windsor, and doubtless to your bedroom there."

"And may I go home with you to-day?"

"Don't be so heady, my dear. Or I shall decide that
you are still very immature, and leave you to your pothooks
for another year. You can finish at the end of this term."

"Oh, well, I can stick that out. . . . Daddy, how
glorious!"

She jumped up and kissed him in gratitude.

"But you must promise to stay with me a little while,"
stipulated he, "and not marry the first lout that comes
lopping up the drive. Say a couple of years at least. . . .
Yes, and now come and be reprimanded at this pastry
shop."

"Oh, but first you've got to go round and see the girls
at their lessons. I think Miss Vidella wants to show you
off, but whether she wants to or not, I do."

"Oh d——. Yes, I was about to use your favourite oath.

Yes, the singular old woman did mention something of the sort. But is it really necessary?"

"Absolutely. Several of the elder girls are reading your books, and, though they don't understand them as well as I do, they are anxious to see what you look like. Besides, I want them to see that you are not angry or anything, and that Miss Vidella's sneaking has hopelessly failed."

They passed into the passage. And the opening of their door was the signal for another to open and emit the head-mistress. Mr. Bruno felt his daughter immediately take hold of his arm.

"Oh, before you go," said the head-mistress, "you promised to visit my dear girls. They will appreciate a visit from you so much."

"Well, so long as I'm not expected to address them," he began.

"Oh no, certainly not," assured Miss Vidella. . . . "Daphne dear, you had better go to your class-room."

Mr. Bruno felt the hold on his arm tightened.

"But father's taking me out to tea."

It was a moment of strain. Clearly the head mistress was at a loss what to say, though the words behind her eyes said: "I think such a reward to the child *most* unsuitable." Mr. Bruno hastened to ease the atmosphere by turning to his daughter with a reproof: "If Miss Vidella is kind enough to consent, you mean." . . . And then to Miss Vidella, with the request: "Having come so far, I trust you will allow me to keep her for the afternoon."

The head mistress bowed austerely, and led the way to the schoolrooms, while Daphne whispered:

"Tell her I'm leaving at the end of the term, do."

"My dear, I couldn't possibly tell her to her face. I never could say anything that was the least unpleasant. I'll write it to her."

"Oh, stuff! She's much more afraid of you than you are of her."

"It's impossible."

All the voyage through the class-rooms she was hanging ostentatiously on his arm.

The first hour of their companionship in the town was very happy, but then supervened a thing that worried and saddened him; his daughter's prattle over the tea-cups palled, and he became a-fidget to get home to his books. Hardly hearing what she said, he began to deplore his intolerance of immature minds that had no ideas or stimulation to give him—whether they were adult minds or children's. Love ought to enable him to come out of himself and listen. But he had lost the power. Only with intellects of his own order, or with books, could he establish correspondence. . . . Still, she would improve, and be his most valuable companion one day.

He looked at his watch and began to discuss his train.

All that evening and the next day Daphne was covertly bragging: "Father's taking me away. . . . I'm to travel with him instead of coming back to school. We're going to Paris for a year, and then to Switzerland and Italy and Rome. . . . I shall probably keep house for him." To her more intimate friends she added: "You must come and stay with us sometimes." The news, told in confidence to the girls, created interest, but no dismay—she was not popular enough for that.

Each day she scanned Miss Vidella's face for some evidence that her father's letter had come. And when a whole week had passed with no trace of a nasty shock behind the steel spectacles, a dread seized her lest his glorious plan, now that she was remote, had been shelved. In suspense she wrote to inquire if he had sent his letter, and, if not, to urge him to do so. "Daddy darling, Have you written about that business? If you haven't, I don't think you should delay. Oh, I do want to do all you said, and travel with you . . ."

His reply was a confession that, owing to pressure of work, he had neglected to write. "But I've just written the letter, and it will be posted with this one. Sorry you've been worrying, but it was my fault. *Peccavi, peccavi, peccavissimi,* as the monk said whose penitence was in excess of his Latin."

Then Miss Vidella had taken the knock this very morning. Daphne studied her to see how she looked after it. There was no visible difference in her. And the morning and the evening passed. None of her words or looks could be twisted into evidence that she knew Daphne

Bruno was leaving. This was Wednesday. Thursday provided no sign. Friday was equally barren, and by the evening of that day Daphne was in despair, tears very close to her eyes. "Oh, he said he had written and posted it. He said he posted it on Tuesday night. He can't have done. I *won't* come back next term. I couldn't, now I've once heard I wasn't going to. If I have to come back next term I shall do something desperate."

But on Saturday morning her impatient eyes did detect a new haughtiness in the carriage of the head mistress when the black figure swept past her. And after breakfast her waking hopes were confirmed by Miss Vidella's request: "Daphne, I wish you would accompany me to the reception-room. I desire to speak to you."

Oh, this meant everything. She felt exhilarated, triumphant, free, as she walked behind Miss Vidella. The moment compensated her for the many times she had walked there in disgrace. The little, stout, waddling black figure led the way into the room, and, sitting down, put on spectacles, and took a letter from the writing-table.

"I am surprised, very much surprised, to receive this morning a letter from your father saying that he proposes taking you away at the end of the term."

She looked up from the letter at her pupil who answered with a sentence she had been longing to use.

"Yes, he told me he was going to the other day when he was down here."

"Oh, indeed?" Miss Vidella's eyebrows went up and hovered a second over the top of her spectacles. "A most unusual proceeding altogether, I think. . . . Er, did you ask him to do this thing?"

"No, he suggested it first."

"And why? Is he dissatisfied with the school in any way? It would be strange if he were, after being content with it for nearly five years."

"I don't think he ever thought much about it," suggested Daphne as a solution.

"And what precisely do you desire to convey by that?"

Daphne shrugged her shoulders.

"Is he dissatisfied—now that he has troubled to think about it?"

She shrugged again. It was so difficult to be outspokenly rude and say: "Of course he is," and she couldn't think of any innuendo that would express the same idea.

"Answer me, please. I am anxious to know if you have—if this school has suffered from any misrepresentation."

"I think he wants me to travel with him. To Paris and Switzerland and Rome."

"Dear, dear," protested Miss Vidella. "I always find you dear girls think I am a fool. Such is surely an obvious excuse. One doesn't decide to go travelling to Paris and Switzerland and Rome during an afternoon's visit, thus foregoing a term's fees. Why do you prevaricate, Daphne? Speak the truth."

"Well, I think he does think the school is old-fashioned and that I'm not doing much good."

"Excellent! Excellent!" nodded Miss Vidella, getting off her seat. "Well, now we know. Yes, from my humble and obsolete standpoint, he is right on both scores. It *is* an old fashion to object with all the strength one can command to the use of foul oaths by one's girls—and as you have never shown any affection or loyalty to your school it cannot be said that you are doing much good."

"I suppose not."

The rebellious note caused the mistress to stare at her. In the pause Daphne knew what Miss Vidella was thinking: that, since there was now no possibility of keeping the Bruno girl, she could afford to be very strong.

"H'm, I think I see." She nodded meaningly. "I begin to see. Yes, of course. Your dear father thought that your position here, after having so disgraced yourself, would be uncomfortable in the extreme. Your surroundings would always fill you with shame, and your school-fellows would to a certain extent reprobate you."

"I don't think they're very concerned about it," fired Daphne, "and if they were, it wouldn't worry me."

Miss Vidella paid no heed.

"And yes, I see. Your dear father conceived that, after much thought, I should feel I could not in the interest of my dear girls keep you here, so he has written *first* to suggest your removal, and thus saved me the painful duty of asking him to take you away."

Daphne's Schooldays

The blood poured over Daphne's face. She loathed her head mistress, and seeing through her weakness to its dregs, cared not what she said.

"You know he doesn't think anything like that. You know you've only just this moment thought of that. You know you really want me to stay so that you won't lose a year of my father's fees. And—and you don't really think it's frightfully serious if someone says ' damn '; but that it's enormously fetching to pretend that you do. I dare say you say it to yourself sometimes. You know you're awfully sick at the idea of my going, and it's only when you've realized that there's no ghostly chance of my stopping that you think you had best appear frightfully strong and get the credit of having expelled me. And if that—and if you give out that that was the reason of my going, I shall get my father to write to the papers about this school and ruin you. They'll any of them publish anything he writes, and only too glad . . ."

Miss Vidella had walked to the bell-push, very likely with some idea that a maid could remove Daphne like a tea-tray. But Daphne didn't stay. Trembling with fear at what she had said and with pleasure in it—a heat tingling her cheek-bones, and her heart thumping—she hurried out, ready to justify herself to the world.

Miss Vidella was trembling too, and her heart going irregularly. Never before—not like that—good heavens, no !—the girl was mad, dangerous—such a thing was un-believable—not in all the years—she should go—go at once —people should see—it made one feel quite sick and faint. What the girl wanted was to be locked up and thrashed. Thrashed !

The maid knocked, entered, and was pettishly dismissed.

Miss Vidella, recovering, tried to think collectedly. Mr. Tenter Bruno's reference being irrevocably lost, there was but one enjoyment left—that of being strong. She would write at once to the man and demand that he removed his daughter. No relief could come to her till the words were in ink—till the letter was posted. With a shaking hand she took note-paper and pen. "I regret—I regret to have to inform you that your daughter has again been intolerably insolent, and, as I am quite unaccustomed to this sort of treatment, I should—I should esteem it a favour if you would allow her to return to her home at once.   Yours truly. . . ."

That anyone should write in that tone to *him* incensed Mr. Bruno   "Hell take the woman," he began, and reached for the bell with a view to dispatching a servant and a wire.   But he stopped as he saw a letter in his daughter's hand.   "Poor kid," thought he.   Impatiently opening it, he read her story of the headmistress's "nasty suggestion," and her urgent request that he would write to her some words which she could show to her friends as proof that she had not been expelled.

"Poor darling !   I won't have her worried like a rabbit by that fat little poodle-bitch.   Thank goodness, I can easily supply her need."

And the following morning Daphne fled with his letter, still sealed, to a deserted room, and there opened it in suspense.

"My dearest Daphne."   (She guessed that he had avoided her nickname lest she were ashamed to show it to her schoolfellows.)

"I think that on the whole the sooner I have you back with me the better, so that we may prepare for our travels. I wrote a few days ago to Miss Vidella, telling her that you would not return after next term—it was last Tuesday I wrote, as I think I told you in a contemporary letter— and she wrote in reply begging me to reconsider my decision and not to deprive you of your last year at Hemans House, which she said was the most important of all.   But I could not agree, and wrote to that effect.   I fear from a letter I received to-day that she is unreasonably annoyed at my refusal to let you stay, though it was quite within my rights ; so lest she should vent her displeasure on you, I have written asking that you may return to-morrow.

"No more at present, for I am very busy.

"Your loving

"Father."

"Oh, he's a dear !" exclaimed she.   "How wonderfully he's phrased it !   He *is* clever !"

She could hardly believe she was to go at once.   Excite-

ment jumped her up and led her to the window. As was
fitting, the room to which she had fled looked out upon
the drive and the exit gates in the garden wall. The wall
appeared grey and green, and the sunlight glorious beyond.
It was too wonderful to be true. Suddenly had come to
her very feet that free country, wide and pleasurable, which
ten days ago she had hazily thought of as many troublesome miles ahead. The goal of the long march of childhood
had not waited for her to reach it, but had come to meet
her. And it shone everywhere with promises : long, indolent
reading; hours when one dreamed out books (the hours best
worth living); travels with her father in places whose names
were romances—Paris, Switzerland, Italy, Rome—*Rome!*
Sooner or later there would be love. Someone in Paris,
perhaps, or in Rome. Among the imperial ruins, as her
imagination created them, she saw his figure moving—
featureless (for one could not decide on his features) and
of vague form (for was he tall or broad or slender?)—just
the grey figure of a youth. Now she was in his arms, and
the thought of it gave her that emptying delight that had
accompanied thoughts of Roger's love. And fame. Fame
was in the distance. It was all incredible. This morning,
before breakfast, a schoolgirl. To-morrow, about ten
o'clock, after running down those hearthstoned steps and
bowling in a carriage through those gates, a free, independent, pleasure-seeking, fame-seeking woman of the
world !

To only one person was the news of Daphne's departure
a stunning blow—Miss Sims. To her it came like an unexpected death sentence.

She had not cared to think what would happen
when Daphne passed out of her life; sufficient that
the dread hour was a year or more away. But ten
days ago, without warning, she had been told that
it was only eight weeks away. And Daphne's excitement and enthusiasm had pained her cruelly. As she
listened to the girl's gaiety she had resolved to suffer without
complaint. That self-pity at least she could enjoy. She
took her pain away to her bedroom, with its tin wash-
hand-stand and its hospital bed. There she dwelt upon it.
"Never to see you again. Never to feel that I am mould-

ing you to a noble shape." Well, perhaps it was better thus. It was better that the beloved girl should pass out of her life before she discovered her governess to be something much smaller and less wonderful than she had thought. And there was still eight weeks more to enjoy her.

And now they told her that Daphne Bruno was going to-morrow morning. Daphne going to-morrow? And as there had been trouble between her people and the headmistress, impossible that she should ever come near the school again! The blow left an ache and confusion that Miss Sims hid all day behind her teaching and her smiles and her small-talk with the girls. Something of the serenity that she had acted before Daphne struggled now to be real, and it did give itself birth.

The next morning, when the carriage came up the drive, she purposely waited in a little narrow music-room that she might torture herself, did Daphne go off without seeking her; or might have her alone, did the girl come.

Daphne burst in, saying she had been looking for her everywhere.

"Good-bye, dear," said Miss Sims.

"Good-bye, Miss Sims. I don't know how to thank you for all your kindness."

Kindness! The commonplace word wounded the governess.

"Good-bye, dear. And God bless you—always."

Daphne hesitated, and then stuttered :

"I wanted to say I owe everything to you. That's the absolute truth. You've been the best thing about my school life. I mean—oh, but I think I'll try and write it to you."

"Good-bye, Duffy. The memory of you will always be sweet to me."

She had resolved to say that much to her and no more. A little more was conveyed in the pressure of her hand and the kiss she placed on the girl's forehead. Then Daphne had gone, and Miss Sims's hand had fallen to her side. She stayed in the music-room till she heard the carriage wheels crunch over the gravel on to the road. She was racked by the half-knowledge that, despite Daphne's words, no passionate love or throbbing pain could be read in her leave-taking. "Thank you for all your kindness." Cruel mediocrity! "But she will write the broken-hearted words she could not say." No. It was all over. A few dwindling letters would come, and they would be no more than echoes.

She walked out of the narrow music-room into the dark main passage of the ground floor. Five doors opened on to it, and a staircase came down from the bedrooms above. It was, so to think, the centre of Hemans House. One could hear the murmurous class-rooms, and the halting scales from another music-room, and the buried clatter in the kitchen. The headmistress passed from the reception-room, where she had been taking some sort of farewell of Daphne, to her teaching in the Fifth Form room. Her voice started, high-pitched and whining.

It was Hemans House, monotonously there, with Miss Sims in its centre. She had a curious, rather unpleasant thought : for ever and ever in Daphne's mind Hemans House would have nothing but a subjective, dreamlike existence, and then only when she willed to create it in memory. And yet here it was. Almost one could think of it, and herself moving in it, as something in an occasional dream of Daphne's.

PART III

DAPHNE'S ROMANCE

CHAPTER XIV

DAPHNE was happy in her new life of freedom at Old Hall House, though it was less than it had promised to be when seen from a schoolroom window. Its worst failure was her father's postponement for a whole year of their residence in Paris, and a lingering doubt lest the day of packing and travelling never arrived. Another was her periods of dulness. Nobody ever seemed to come to Old Hall House; her father kept himself shut up in his study; and Owen for nine months of the year was at school. There were mornings and afternoons when she wandered about the passages and looked aimlessly out of windows, or strolled in the garden humming the fragmentary tunes of the lonely.

But she determined to believe in its delights; and indeed much of it was glorious. It was glorious to shut the door of the great playroom and loll in the tattered chair and read just what she wanted to. Her first plan of reading had been much more ambitious: she was going to work through all her father's critical books, and at the end of each volume study every masterpiece he had mentioned within its covers. But she could not do this. Nothing that required effort could she study for more than half an hour. She boggled at these Sir Thomas Brownes and Donnes and Emersons and Carlyles, many of whose sentences had to be enunciated twice or even three times before one glimpsed a meaning. And poetry wearied her as quickly, though every now and then a perfect phrase or a line of tragic emotion gave her a spasm of delight. But her love of these moments was not strong enough to overcome her indolence; and she decided that she would profit most by reading only those things that came easy to her—fiction, and the lighter essayists, such as Lamb and Stevenson, and the jollier parts of Shakespeare. With her reading of these people surged higher and higher the longing to do as they had done, and the confidence that she could do it. Sometimes she put books aside and got her ink and paper with a view to starting; but nothing at present would come: the swelling *something* in her stayed in its darkness and refused to filter through a pen. So she resolved —as she preferred to resolve, for the deep chair was cosy, and reading was so much easier than creation—that she must go on stocking her mind.

"Besides, I must have experiences, of which at present I have nil."

And then she would look out of her window over the road that ran southward to the downs and the sea, and northward to the cities, and wonder what her experiences would be and where they lay.

Now she discovered the hollowness of Miss Carrell. Full of the excitement of her reading, she would want to pour it all out to her frequent companion, but quickly found that Miss Carrell was unable to understand, and consequently uninterested. She shammed an interest, certainly, but it was at first patronizing, and always astonishingly uninformed. Daphne gradually arrived at the difficult conclusion that she knew more and understood better than her former governess.

Miss Carrell, in fact, was far from contented. Her gradual supplanting by Daphne was painfully proved by the invitations that at last began to arrive from neighbouring society. There had been none of these before Daphne appeared, Mr. Bruno having the reputation of a recluse. But now a few fluttered in like stray birds, and generally they were for "Mr. Tenter Bruno and Miss Bruno." Seldom Miss Carrell. She was not sure that with all her scheming she had not ruined herself. Here was she, thirty, and only a waning manageress in a country house. She had reached her highest point, five years ago, when she had sent Daphne to school, and entered upon her reign. At her age, this had been distinctly good. But now——? There was little chance of marrying, with so few people coming to Old Hall House. And yet nowhere else could she get so well paid a post. She was caught in a prison she had built for herself.

Hazily Daphne saw all of this; but she was too happy to desire the entrance of anything unpleasant, so strove to be affable and even humble with the apprehensive Miss Carrell.

Too good to be yet believed—Daphne had the regular loan of a saddle horse, a tall chestnut of sixteen hands. On frosty afternoons, just before sunset, or summer evenings before the dinner hour, she would ride it on Ditchling Common—*astride*. The whole neighbourhood, she suspected, was impressed, and talked about "new women." She pictured herself as she appeared to them : her hair still down her back and tied by a black bow; her costume consisting of riding breeches, overhung by a divided skirt; her seat good but not yet perfect. She would trot through the "toll-gate" on to Ditchling Common, still with the childish make-believe that she was a highwayman. When off the hard road and on the grass of the common, she would set the horse cantering; and, being a spirited creature, it would soon break into a stretch gallop. As a dance can be the rhythmic medium of urgent emotion, so this straight-flying, body-poising, breath-speeding gallop was the most satisfying art-form for her present feelings; it was the expression of her glorying in freedom and adulthood. The wind rushed through her hair, and the blood tingled in her veins. Her face heated and cooled in the air. She could have shouted. Had she not everything she wished for? Where had Time swept that schoolgirl of a few months back, who was punished in bedrooms? She checked the horse and reined him in, bumping slightly as he slowed down. Now he was walking, and she hollowed her back for relief; and, slackening the bridle, replaced a disordered hair.

Of her few friends Mrs. Montague Jevons, of Wildean Manor, was the best. Mrs. Montague Jevons was a large-boned, vivacious lady, who, as an intelligent admirer of the Tenter Bruno books, had shown a great interest in their author's daughter. A short acquaintance with Daphne had developed this interest into something like a sane favouritism. She called Daphne "her little friend" and treated her mind, not as a child's, but as the equal of her own. She would invite her to tea and a discussion on books, and would declare with sincerity that the daughter would one day be as famous as the father It was she who daily sent the chestnut horse alongside o a groom.

In January of the second year, when Mr. Bruno really was making a move about the *pied-à-terre* in Paris, Mrs Montague Jevons gave a ball at Wildean Manor. It would be the biggest that Daphne had gone to. She was excited And since Mrs. Montague Jevons had been careful to invite Miss Carrell, she could discuss to her heart's content the ball, her dress and the tiring of her hair. Many experiments she tried with her hair, till she decided to keep it exactly the same as it was every day, only tidier. Any trace of effort was a flaw—as one learnt in literary criticism. It wasn't Greek. And her frock was Greek enough in its simplicity—an unornamented thing in a silk of that shining green that suited so well her brown hair and her colouring. As she turned before her cheval glass, to appraise her completed toilet, something childish and (as it were) breakable in the figure she saw there seemed to make foolish the dream of powerful books and world-wide fame. She provided sentences for the reporters who should one day interview her : "No one who has read the works of Miss Daphne Bruno, so masculine in their character, would conceive of her as a shy, slim, and exceedingly feminine girl. But there it is ! Genius alights where it will. Miss Bruno clothes in all the grace and charm of her sex her exceptionally virile intellect."

Soon the carriage was at the door, and apprehensively Miss Carrell and she insinuated themselves under its roof. and were conveyed along the dark, country roads. Wildean Manor was a big, square, stone house to the east of Ditchling, and it was some time before their carriage wheels crunched its half-mile of drive. When the house, brilliantly alight, came into view, both Daphne and Miss Carrell were disturbed by the certainty that they were too early. Miss Carrell, Daphne could see, was pretending to be very much in her element, if only because she was feeling completely out of it ; exactly as Daphne herself was trying to appear old and self-possessed, if only because she was feeling very young and ill at ease.

The sight of other guests in the Ladies' Room, and the

glimpse as they stood in the big entrance hall of quite a few people in the drawing-room where Mr. and Mrs. Montague Jevons were receiving the guests, reassured them.

Daphne pushed Miss Carrell in front of her towards the loud-voiced gentleman in evening dress who was presenting the guests.

"Miss Carrell and Miss Tenter Bruno."

There was a flattering rustle and a silence as the famous name was bellowed out, and she longed for the day when the name of Miss Daphne Bruno could produce a silence and turn all heads. With her companion, after a few exchanges with the host and hostess, which included a whisper from Mrs. Montague Jevons, "My dear, you're looking beautiful," she walked across the floor to some chairs against the farther wall. Here they sat down, and, since they saw no one whom they knew, passed the time in watching the people as they were announced. The lofty rectangular drawing-room in which they were seated opened into a library of exactly the same dimensions, and as both rooms were to be used for dancing, the band had been placed on a platform in the farthest corner of the library. From Daphne's chair she could see both the band in the library and the people forming in the hall.

Among these a group of three suddenly made her crane her neck. A blush began to warm her cheeks, and it spread over her face as the group came through the doors into the drawing-room. The father was a short, big-hewn man of sixty and more, whose grim mouth was apiece with the thick chest and the heavy, competent hands; the mother was a slim, tired woman whose timidity might have been explained by her husband's mouth; and the third was a tall, dark youth who, if his features were not perfect (though indeed they were quite good), had surely a figure of unsurpassable beauty. It was the very measure of manhood: height, width, symmetry and grace. Daphne looked down hoping she would not be recognized behind all these people. Fancy! Was *that* what he had grown into?

"Sir Roger and Lady Muirhead, and Mr. Roger Muirhead."

No resuscitation of an old love troubled Daphne; only rose the eagerness, since a recognition sooner or later was inevitable, to impress him as the possessor of unlimited friends and one of the most sought-after belles of the ball. Her programme must quickly be filled. She stared at the profiles and the occiputs of people she knew to induce them to turn round and perceive her. Gradually they did so, and brought their men up and introduced them. The names dropped into one place after another on her dance card: waltzes, lancers, polkas, barn-dances. It was like a game when one sought to fill vacant places against the clock. She must have a "House Full" before Roger recognized her and begged a place. But there were still some vacant numbers when the band struck up the first waltz. It seemed certain that he must see her as she danced among the other couples. But he did not; as she swung round, talking idly to her partner, she saw him dancing with a feathery girl and conceding to her chatter the familiar twinkle with its incomplete, tolerant smile. It would not have been Roger, nor that youth of the supreme shape, had anyone in the room danced more gracefully than he.

After the first waltz, to her delight, more men were brought up and introduced. There was now but one place on her card. That would fill after the next dance—and then her single desire was to be discovered by Roger. But the next dance showed her to him. She had passed quite close and felt his quick surprised look and thenceforward his ever-returning glances. Not once did she look his way, but talked with vivacity to her partner. Urged on by some of the younger men, the band was prolonging the music, and soon she was aware that Roger and his partner had sat down, Roger pretending to keep up a conversation, but really watching Daphne. Once he seemed to have mentioned her to the feathery girl.

"Would you like to sit down?" asked her partner.

"No, no," she smiled brightly. "Let's last out as long as anyone else. I'm loving it."

On they danced among the thinning couples, Daphne hoping that her high colour would be attributed to the lengthened waltz. The few times her eyes were in danger of meeting Roger's he avoided them. He was evidently in doubt what to do. The band finished at last, and Daphne was escorted to a chair by her partner, who was gossiping gaily. She, too, made a pretence of gay talk, but was really keeping a watch on Roger. And in a little while

Roger made an excuse to his feathery girl and came across the floor.

"Miss Bruno, isn't it?" he said with a smile.

At once Daphne suspected the course of action on which he had decided: he was going to make no mention of his boyish dropping of her, in the hope that she would have expected nothing else from a little fool. *Her* course had been planned for years past: a mixture of friendliness and indifference suggesting that his lordly shake-off had been a negligible incident, without power to hurt.

"Yes," said she. "I saw you before, and wondered if you would recognize me. I should hardly have recognized you, only I heard your name called out."

"Well, at any rate," said Roger, "you're going to dance with me."

The genial command was characteristic; Roger was priding himself on his imperiousness.

"I don't think I can. There's only one I've got free. . . ."

"Well, let's see."

He compared his card with hers.

"Yes, I'm dancing with some wretched girl on your only vacant date."

"Oh, what a pity." She took back the card.

"Well, there'll have to be an extra extra, that's all. If there's an extra extra may I have the privilege——" He bowed.

"Oh, but there won't be one. There are three already."

"Oh, but there *will* be one. I shall see to it."

"All right, then. . . . Yes, thank you very much."

"Splendid. I'll go and tell the conductor fellow at once that there's got to be one. . . . I say, wait a minute. . . ."

Rather self-consciously he walked across the floor, and she watched him speaking to the conductor who smiled. Then he returned.

"That's settled all right. . . . Do you know what I said to the man?"

"No, how should I?"

"Well, perhaps you'd better not."

"All right."

"Perhaps I'll tell you what I said when we're dancing together."

"I don't particularly want to know."

"I didn't ask that. It may be good for you to know. . . .
It's rather taken my breath away seeing you here. I half
fancied I saw you the other day on horseback, riding a
strapping chestnut. I only came down here three days ago.
But then, I suppose it couldn't be."

"Why not?"

"I don't know. I can't picture you quite like that.
How's your young brother?"

"He's just gone back to school."

"Oh, yes. I'm afraid I didn't see much of him at Sillborough."

"You've left, I suppose."

It was meant to humiliate and didn't fail of its
mark.

"Left? Glory, yes. I've been at Oxford a year."

"Of course. I'*d* forgotten how old you were. Where
was it you saw me the other day? I didn't see you."

"Then it *was* you. It must have been by the—just near
the—no, I forget where it was now."

"Probably on Ditchling Common."

"Yes, of course, that's where it was. . . . Well, I must
be getting back now."

The evening was old when he claimed her for his partner.
An old evening with a glittering record. It would have been
an exaggeration to say that she was the belle of the ball,
but none had been more remarked, none more sought after,
none more waited on, none more excited and vivacious than
she. And all the while she had been conscious of his staring
at her—staring in rather a dazed way. That was good.
Good if he fell rapturously in love with her again, while she
felt no stirring of love for him. When he besought her
hand, she would reply: "It's no good, Roger. I can't help
it, but I feel no love for you at all." She could wish that
she were already engaged to someone that she might mention
it carelessly to him.

"Now, Miss Bruno," said he, as he claimed her.

The band had begun. They were playing a little languish-
ing waltz rather slowly. Both felt the wistfulness of the
air and for a long time said nothing. Daphne had a sense
of having lost several inches of her height and some years
of her age now that she was in Roger's arm. He was the

first to emerge from the abstraction into which the tune had sunk them.

"Ye gods, what a tune!"

"Yes, isn't it divine? Do you know what it is? I do."

"Why"—he smiled his patronizing smile—"are you a great musician these days?"

"No; but I learnt the 'cello at school, and one of the girls used to play this on her violin. But I didn't know then it could be so—so troubling as this."

"Troubling—that's the very word. What is it?"

She told him its name, but he didn't acknowledge the information, and when she looked up at him she saw that his eyes had been waiting to twinkle into hers.

"From henceforth I shall always call it the Daphne Bruno waltz."

"Don't be silly."

"Don't be rude, Miss Bruno."

"Do you know, I've just been thinking I've never been properly introduced to you."

"On the contrary, madam, you introduced yourself to me with something approaching boldness from behind a blackberry bush on the King's highway."

"What silly kids we were!"

"I wasn't so silly as I thought——" The unfortunate sentence broke abruptly.

They danced through the door of the drawing-room into the library, and the sight of the conductor suffering (as Roger said) all the pains of the artistic temperament prompted him to ask:

"Shall I tell you what I said to yon fiddler?"

"If it's interesting."

Excitement and supper had heightened his natural temerity.

"I said, 'Look here, Sousa, unless you put on an extra extra, I shan't be able to dance with the only girl worth calling a girl in the room.' And he said—he seems a humorous fellow—he said, 'Well, sir, in that case there'll have to be an extra extra for an extra extra young lady.' And, of course, he got impertinent and said, 'May I ask which one she is?' I said, 'No, certainly not. Besides, it's perfectly obvious to anyone with any eyes.'"

Daphne looked towards the conductor, and saw that

over his violin he was watching Roger and her. She could not feel displeased with the man, since he had been told that she was the only girl in the room. But she chose to turn colder with Roger, and did not speak till he asked :

"What sort of life are you living now?"

She gave him an attenuated answer and deliberately refrained from asking him anything about himself. He was obliged to proffer the story unsought. As soon as he had finished with Oxford he was to travel, and then go in for politics. Possibly he would stand for their Cornish constituency.

"Cornish?" queried Daphne.

"Yes. Didn't you know? That holiday we went to Cornwall "—he blushed as he recalled which holiday it was —"father fell in love with a little smuggler's cove, and swore he'd buy it up and build a house there right on the rocks. And on his principle of 'What I've once determined on, that I do,' he went and did it. I wish you could see the place. It's rather exciting. And what are you going to do in the future? "

"Stay with father, I suppose."

The whimsical sparkle had come again into his eyes, she saw, as she looked up for an explanation of his silence; and the trembling, incomplete smile was at his lips.

"Not for long," said he. "You'll marry."

"No, I shan't."

"Of course you'll marry."

"And why ' of course '? "

"Because—because you're the sort."

"I've just told you I'm not."

"You've just told me you don't want to be the sort, but you'd no say in the matter."

"I wish you'd explain."

He hummed the waltz to the accompaniment of the band. Then in a muted way he whistled it.

"I can't very well. But it's a theory of mine that you can always tell the girls who will marry—bar tragedies. I don't know what it is about them. It's not beauty."

"Thank you very much."

"Don't mention it. I'm speaking generally. It's some other quality—a sort of sensuous attraction "—he stuttered, probably not clear as to the meaning of sensuous—"though the quality is rarely absent from beauty."

"I don't know what you are talking about."

"Well, I suppose you can't understand. . . . If your looking-glass doesn't tell you, it's quite impossible for a man to."

They danced on, and she noticed that once or twice his lips moved as though he were trying to force words through the inhibitions of pride. And at a moment when the band was likely to dwindle to a finale, he jerked out:

"Miss Bruno, I'd like to see you sometimes. Now that the Downway House is vacant, we're——"

She had been waiting for this advance, and quickly replied:

"It's no good. I'm going abroad, and——"

His look drove the rest from her head. His mouth had set like his father's, and she guessed that he was enjoying the strong man's huff. She decided to hurt him further.

"What a long time the band's playing for."

"Is it?"

"Well, isn't it?"

"Why?" he muttered. "Do you want to stop?"

"Yes, I do. I'm tired. I've been dancing all the evening."

"All right."

He guided her quickly towards the chairs, and released her. It was done with the courtesy that never failed him and yet with suddenness, that she might feel he was not used to being snubbed. His features had tightened—"gone tight"—she invented the phrase that moment to express what Roger looked like when thwarted or misunderstood. Triumph trembled through her. The conductor, seeing that the two for whom he had played the waltz had deserted, brought it to an end.

"Well, good-bye, Miss Bruno. It's been quite nice to see you again and dance once with you."

"Good-bye. There's Miss Carrell, I must run and speak to her.

She ran off, unconsciously humming the waltz; and Roger strode as best he could towards his people.

CHAPTER XV

FOR quite satisfying reasons she thought frequently about Roger during the next few weeks; there was no one else much to think of; the only person who had ever leapt your breastworks and kissed you behind a bush must always have a romantic interest; and still more, a man who was patently in love with you, when you couldn't feel the slightest stir of emotion for *him,* was someone to be rather proud of. She wondered if his passion would overcome his pride and force him to write to her; and was already phrasing her friendly but discouraging answer. But no letter appeared, so she indulged herself in pictures of Roger with love gnawing at his heart and pride denying him a cry. Once when cantering on Ditchling Common she passed him, and, answering his raised hat with a friendly bow, galloped away. At a safe distance she swung her horse round to get a covert glimpse of him, and saw him staring after her. He was standing not far from Jacob's Post. One evening she was certain he passed her house and gave it a quick glance.

She determined to learn more about him from Mrs. Montague Jevons. The subject was not easy to open till an afternoon, when, calling at Wildean Manor after the dance, she found Lady Muirhead among other ladies in the drawing-room. Lady Muirhead, she discerned, was a woman of one subject—her son. When other subjects were being bandied across the carpet she was silent, but her interest immediately quickened if someone asked, "And what is Roger doing now?" or remarked, "How handsome your boy is getting!" Daphne moved to sit beside her.

"You've met Roger then," said Lady Muirhead, in response to a casual allusion.

"Oh yes, I danced with him here the other day."

"Did you?" She glanced round the drawing-room, and through the door into the library. "I didn't really catch your name just now."

"Daphne Bruno."

"Oh, *you're* Mr. Tenter Bruno's daughter. I've heard about you."

Daphne coloured. "Have you?"

"Oh yes. Your father's quite a famous man, isn't he?"

"Well, he's written a lot of books," acknowledged Daphne, with a deprecating smile.

"Yes. I'm afraid I don't read much. I never had much time when Roger was young, and you get out of the habit when they go to school."

"You've only one son, haven't you?"

"Yes, only one, though Roger was equal to a dozen in trouble."

"Was he really? Not in health, surely?"

"In health, good gracious, no! I suppose his bounding health was the source of all his masterfulness and mischief."

"Oh, was he mischievous?" exclaimed Daphne. "How ripping!"

"He's essentially a dominating character, I think, and I suppose as they can't help themselves, it's not fair to call it mischief."

Daphne nodded.

And Lady Muirhead, encouraged by such a listener, rattled on with a record of Roger's domestic tyrannies, of which she seemed very proud.

When she had gone and the other visitors were departing, Mrs. Montague Jevons begged Daphne to stay a little longer.

"There, sit down," said she, after the door had closed on the last lady. "And let me sit here. . . . Ah, for this relief much thanks. . . . A particularly boring afternoon. And I was so sorry for you, cooped up with the Muirhead Dowager. I suppose she carried on insufferably about her boy?"

"Yes, it was chiefly about him."

"Pity she goes on like that."

"But it isn't all praise," suggested Daphne. "She spent much of the time deploring his tyrannies."

"Bless you, that's indirect praise. She's as proud as a peacock of them."

"But is it all true?"

"Well, I like Roger. He and I get on splendidly. He's got the most courtly manners with women. I think it's a sort of feudal pose and unconsciously based on conceit, but as it's spiced with a *soupçon* of humour and cheek it makes him a pleasant companion."

Daphne pursued her adverse criticism.

"I should think he's now irreparably spoiled by his mother."

"He's not been spoiled in the usual sense—old Sir Roger's seen to that—but what's happened is this." Mrs. Montague Jevons crumpled her brow so as to find a description worthy of her keen analysis. "She's created a legend about the masterfulness of the Muirhead men, and especially about the last specimen of them, and the wretched boy's heard nothing else all his life. The damage is probably final—he'll live up to the amiable legend till the end of his days. You'll find the characters he likes in history and books are the honourable but merciless Cavalier over-lords—Strafford, or people like the Earl of Warwick, the King Maker. I try to chaff him about it, but every man's sense of humour fails when it comes to himself. Probably my chaffing only makes matters worse. He likes to be chaffed about his ' indomitable will,' and all the rest of the trash. No man ever didn't."

Daphne's head nodded, implying that her experience was the same.

"I tell him," pursued Mrs. Montague Jevons, "that it's a popular type beloved of housemaids, but the obsession's too strong for chaff to expel it. . . . That's Roger."

The cost of a furnished flat in Paris, capable of housing himself, his daughter, Miss Carrell, Hollins, and Owen in vacations, was high enough to drive Mr. Bruno's mercury very low. A new idea shaped in his mind, and the infernal noise of the Gay City, as he walked its pavements seeking his *pied-à-terre,* gave it stronger outline; he would find within a dozen miles of Paris some inexpensive villa, from which Daphne and Miss Carrell might descend as often as they liked on the Gare du Nord, while he stayed with his manuscripts and his books in a countryside peace.

He found the place, and returned to England, not a little eager to tell his daughter all about it. It was a Tuesday evening, just after dark, when he arrived at Old Hall House, flung himself into an easy chair, and cried for tea. That his daughter had met him with a hail of questions, and hurried after him into his study, and was now sitting on the edge of his writing-table demanding information, he affected to have hardly perceived.

"What have you decided, daddy—what have you decided? "

"It's not her father that she welcomes," said he to his boot-laces, "but the things he may have brought for her. A selfish girl, and one without natural affection."

"Oh, daddy, what have you decided? "

"Slippers, dear. If you like, you can get me my slippers. It would have already occurred to a more beautiful nature."

"If I get them for you, will you tell me what you have decided? "

"I have decided to say nothing about anything till I have been fed, and fed very satisfyingly."

"Oh, father, don't be a cad. I've been waiting weeks to know."

"And I've been waiting weeks for a cup of tea. . . . I spent a very enjoyable time in Paris, thank you. It's a city eternally romantic, classic, realistic. You can imagine me entering the Louvre with a worshipper's feet, and lighting my poor candle at the shrines of Leonardo, Titian, Veronese, Rubens. . . ."

"Oh, blow them! I'm screwed up to hear everything. I made sure you'd tell me at once."

"The music of English tea-things! It's unmistakable—and it's music that Paris, in spite of its singular imitations, has never learned."

"Well, you shan't have any till you have told me. I shall hold it back."

"Ah, it's Hollins. Put it here, Hollins. . . . Thank you very much."

Hollins laid the tea-tray on a little table by the side of his easy chair; and Mr. Bruno, with a running commentary on Paris and its wickedness and English tea, poured out a cup and folded over a thin slice of bread and butter. Daphne sat on the writing-table. And over his bread and butter, despite his jesting manner, his mind was asking the usual questions : why, though the sight of her and the nearness of her could inflate his love, he could never

Daphne Bruno

really get close to her, but must always protect himself, as he approached, with a cloud of persiflage; whether now at sixty it was too late to learn the art of emptying himself and becoming like unto her; whether he had exchanged life for books? "This man chose not to live but read." Disproportion. Disproportion. Books should be an elixir to heighten one's awareness to life, not a drug in which to escape from it.

"There." He pushed the tea-things away, and signalled to her to come and sit on the *pouffe* which was his footstool.

"Come here. I have a tale to tell you."

And he lit a cigarette and began.

"Some ten or a dozen miles nor'-nor'-west of Paris there's a little cocksure village that calls itself St. Leu Taverny. It straggles at the very feet of the Montmorency Forest. A few days ago I climbed a cobbled street to the outer verge of the forest trees, among which rose the turrets, not unpicturesque, of the plaster châteaux, or villas, of wealthy Parisians. Grocers, for the most part, I expect. In a little new-made avenue, that finished in nothing, as if it had forgotten that it had ever started, I found a very modest little villa in the centre of a tiny garden of firs. Its windows had shutters thrown back against the bricks, and on the sills those flamboyant iron-work railings that so delight the French. Strange how the French think themselves classical, and are the most flamboyant people in Europe! In many ways the absurd little villa reminded me of you. It was tall and narrow—and pretentious."

"Are you being funny?" submitted Daphne.

"Pretentious, with its turret up one corner for the staircase. At the top of the turret—and this completes the simile—was a cone-shaped roof, like a dunce's hat."

Daphne only continued to watch the fire. She was getting used to this sort of thing from her men-folk.

"No," pursued Mr. Bruno, after thought. "The resemblance can be carried farther, for I found the furniture within to be adequate to its purposes and inoffensive, but quite uninspired and quite without distinction."

"But the outlook was beautiful," interrupted Daphne.

"The outlook was good. Yes, the outlook was good, stretching over the garden of firs to the high ground and the trees of Montmorency. Here and there, however, was a château such as the vulgar dream of. One could wish for an earthquake to remove them. I walked among the rooms, peopling them to my fancy with a certain girl, and the excellent Miss Carrell, and the entirely fundamental Hollins. Also perhaps a French slut for the meaner tasks. I have taken the place for a year."

Daphne leapt up.

"Daddy, let's go to-morrow."

"'Some having no root sprang up.' . . . We shall not go to-morrow nor the next day, but possibly the day after that. The *épicier's* wife was recommended to me as a person who would light a fire and dress a dish to welcome us. She'll have to be communicated with. But you can think about packing."

Packing! The word was galvanizing. Packing to go anywhere was among the liveliest excitements, but packing to go abroad was in a class by itself. In what a cloud of romance had her father, when she was a child, set off abroad! Refusing to hearken to her brain, which assured her there was nothing remarkable in a visit to Paris, she told everyone she met in the next few days that they were leaving for Paris on Friday. Once over there she would really start writing. Foreign scenes would be a spring of inspiration. Against this expected seizure by inspiration she pushed into her trunks pens, pencils, scribbling paper and manuscript books, having vague ideas that French pencils and paper would not be the same thing at all.

Miss Carrell and Hollins, never having travelled before, were equally if more secretly excited. Miss Carrell's inward pleasure was slightly marred by the reflection that her meagre knowledge of French, in which she had once instructed Daphne, would be horridly exposed. Hollins, though pretending to be "put about" by it all and to wonder how she would be able to manage with a fast French kitchen girl, was really much pleased, and inclined to emphasize to the other servants that in this accompanying of the family, she was as usual a privileged person.

Friday, seen from Daphne's bedroom window at six-thirty in the morning, was overcast, but windless and dry. It stayed so. Throughout the day she had a sense that the excitement of continental travel could be measured, as

Daphne Bruno

in a graph, by a rising and falling line. The line began at a high point when the carriage came to the door; it shot higher at the London terminus where the words "Boat Train" flashed at you, and French beards and French tongues wagged among the encumbered people; it dropped and ran straight during the rumble through Kentish meadows and hop-fields; it rose again, very high, when they saw the boat with its twin funnels; it stayed high, as they mingled in the bustle on the quay, and walked a trembling gangway, and were confused by the voices, the loaded porters, the luggage swung in upper air by the crane, the bell from the bridge, and the throbbing of the engines; it was kept high by the rush of wind and the repeated booming of the siren as the boat moved out, and the hand-waving of less fortunate friends ashore. Then it dropped and ran in a straight line as they spent two hours in the grey channel; only to rise to its highest at the first sight of French hills and the gradual delineation of domes and roofs and lighthouses of Boulogne. Through the greyness, France boomed a welcome.

Miss Carrell, though rendered ill at ease by this rapid approach to France and exposure, pretended to all the interest, loudly voiced by Daphne. Hollins, too, smiled pleasantly at her young mistress's happiness. "It's folks as young as them that gets the full enjoyment out of this," said she to Miss Carrell, and a few minutes later was sick.

Dark had almost fallen before they were safely against the quay; and they saw nothing of the place except the hideous Customs and the ill-lit station with its comfortable Paris train. Once the train had started and run into the complete darkness outside the town, the glamour departed from the journey, factitiously recovered sometimes by translating the *Avis aux Voyageurs* printed round the alarm bell. Miss Carrell had a bad moment when Daphne sought her aid, but luckily Mr. Bruno's desire to display his knowledge was as great as her desire to hide her ignorance. He did the translating, and she prepared them for the worst by saying:

"Really, I have rusted so. I can scarcely remember anything. I used to be able to speak quite well."

She need not have worried; both Mr. Bruno and her old pupil had forgotten that she had ever been paid to teach the language.

All were tired, and Hollins after her sickness slept. The excitement only reached its former heights when they ran through the lighted suburbs into the Gare du Nord, Paris.

"Here we are. Out you get. Tumble out."

Daphne descended from the train into a confusion that bruised all her senses at once : voices, pushing people, hiss of steam, smell of smoke and soot, rumble of porters' trucks, and cries of "*Attention là!*" The sounds and the smell—the smell especially—raised into memory the day when first they had trained into a London station, and she but eight years old. Overtones of pleasant melancholy hung round the recollection. "I am in Paris," she told herself. "I am now standing in Paris."

Alone in that overhanging noise and buffeting stream of people Mr. Bruno seemed—or affected to seem—majestically unperturbed. Conscious of the respect of his women, he talked fluently to the porters, and led the way to the *Banlieue* booking office. He chaffed his daughter, telling her to exercise her French by ordering the tickets for St. Leu; but when she tried she could only giggle into the little window. Miss Carrell kept well in the background. Hollins, in spite of her weight and difficulty in walking, often ran to keep in close touch with the master, lest she were lost in this wilderness of unintelligible people.

Soon they were in a far less comfortable train. After travelling first-class all the way, Mr. Bruno, alarmed by the expenses on the journey, had decided that they could do this last little bit in the *troisième classe*. The seats were distressingly upright and wooden. Nor did they have the compartment to themselves. Two Frenchmen, unaware of Daphne's wrinkled nose, got in; one an enormously fat gentleman, with a black square beard which made Hollins stare and Daphne giggle at Miss Carrell, and the other a younger man who never stopped talking and gesticulating to his companion. He struck Daphne as equally funny. The fat man expressed his real interest by nodding and picking his teeth through his black beard; and Daphne whispered that he was perfectly sweet. She maintained this view, even when he spat one of his diggings out of the window, causing Miss Carrell to retire further into her corner.

Sitting in that train, after viewing the crowds in the

Daphne Bruno

Gare du Nord, Daphne discovered afresh the *distingué* appearance of her father. She felt proud that all should recognize him as an Englishman. Tall and slender as an athletic youth, with his pointed beard now grey, and his hair whitening over the ears—in his faultless grey suit and grey overcoat—he had been splendid among the English people on the boat, and was a lesson to all Frenchmen in France.

The train slowed into a badly-lit station, and voices called "*St. Leu . . . St. Leu.*" Daphne, with some idea of having won a five hundred mile race, determined to step out first. She threw open the door, saw a yawning blackness where the platform should have been, and, stepping on to it, fell heavily to the pavement—only saving herself from going on to her hands and knees by her slippery hold on the carriage door.

"There!" said her father. "The daughter arrives. Credulous child to expect such advantages as platforms in a country which calls itself *à la tête de la civilization!* Are you hurt?"

"No, it's lovely," said Daphne, though she could scarcely put her right foot to the ground. She was not going to be disloyal to her vision of this as one of the perfect days of her life.

The luggage was left on the station, no carriages being visible outside its doors; and Mr. Bruno led his party into the darkness of a street lit only by occasional private windows. Daphne could receive no impression of St. Leu as they climbed the hill-road towards their house, except that they were often walking on cobbles which sometimes stirred in that airy emptiness of her ankle the strange, sweet pain.

The little house, as they passed through the double gate into its garden, showed a bright light at the hall door, and the *épicier's* wife standing above the steps, smiling amiably and rattling French. Everything was ready for them, said she, but would monsieur like a glass of wine? Mr. Bruno accepted this in the little dining-room. "*Et pour madame? . . . Madame Bruno, n'est-ce-pas?*" queried the woman, with a look at Miss Carrell. That Miss Carrell should be taken for his wife was an error that amused Mr.

Bruno, and, pointing to his whitening hairs, he laughed, "*Non, non, madame. Regardez mes neiges.*"

"*Oui, monsieur,*" said she, her head dropping knowingly, "*mais souvent sous les neiges on trouve des volcans.*"

And Mr. Bruno roared with laughter.

"What did she say—what did she say?" demanded his daughter.

"Didn't you understand? Well, perhaps you'd better not. A sad people, the French."

In a few minutes Daphne had been all over the house, delighted with everything, though marvelling that it could so fit her father's description, and yet be so different from what she had pictured.

"Oh, I'd like to live here always. Why can't they build places like this in England?"

"Because the French are always faintly fantastic," explained her father.

He then led her to a bedroom at the top and in the front, whose windows, as he threw them open, gave on to the stars above the Forest of Montmorency.

"This is undeniably the best room, Duffy, and it is to be yours. Miss Carrell and Hollins can have the two smaller rooms on this floor."

"But, father——" began she. Having always kept her schoolgirl room at home, she was diffident of taking a room superior to Miss Carrell.

"No, no," interrupted Mr. Bruno. "You are the mistress of this house."

CHAPTER XVI

SHE slept that night with the resolve beneath her pillow to be up and out before breakfast, but her weariness after long travelling and the February darkness of the early morning kept her sleeping till eight o'clock. Awakening and remembering where she was, she jumped up and looked out of the window. She saw the beginnings of the forest hardly a field's distance from their little garden of firs. The fresh air brushed her cheek and throat. Oh, she must be out—out to examine France by daylight. So after quick dressing and a hurried breakfast, she put on a warm coat and hastened through the garden gate.

The road on to which their little avenue ran was called, as she observed after walking a little distance in the direction from which they had come last night, the Rue du Château. All the French history and French literature she had ever read seemed touched to life by the three words. The château, her father had told her, had been inhabited by the Duc d'Orléans, Madame de Genlis, Queen Hortense and the Duc de Bourbon; and she imagined these people walking down the cobbles where she was walking. Madame de Genlis, as a writer of a hundred books and a famous figure in a stirring age, interested her most. She surely was Daphne's spiritual ancestor.

But not only these romantic names of the past thrilled her; the words over the shops, *épicier, charcuterie, estaminet* and the advertisements of *apéritifs* were exotic and quickening. At the Place de la Forge the Rue du Château ran into a wider thoroughfare called the Rue de Paris. Could any name be more suggestive? Could anything be more typical than the tiny statue of the Virgin and Child in a little niche at the corner house, looking down on the road to Paris? In the middle of the Place was a large fountain, from whose centre rose a painted metal statue of a worker with his scythe, stripped to the waist and drinking from a gourd as

238

he paused in his labour. Big-hipped women with shawls about their shoulders and their heads *en cheveux* were filling their buckets there. Little girls passed, carrying loaves as long as children. Boys with socks and bare calves, wearing little capes and porters' caps, walked over the cobbles to school. And the French language in the treble voices of children first came alive to Daphne.

She turned to her right towards a plastery church, and on its walls saw the words, *Liberté, Egalité, Fraternité;* and the whole Revolution with a crowd of ghosts hovered about her consciousness. She walked on till she came to a dusty square, and from here she decided to climb through the side streets to the forest again. As she approached its skied arras of trees, a horn sounded from a café in its fringe, and awoke with its notes Henry IV and Marguerite de Valois and the whole pageant of Dumas.

But a few minutes more and she was in the forest, walking on a rutty and mossed road between untidy trees. On her right she saw traces of a decayed and tumbled wall overrushed by the tangled boscage. Farther, and she came to a ruined gateway with tumbled brick pillars on either side. Within was nothing but the confusion of trees and the interwoven riot of underbrush. One could hardly trace what had been the stately carriage-way. Still affixed to a tree was the weather-worn notice of some haughty castellan, *"Propriété Privée. Défense d'entrer. Pièges à feu."* She strolled on, trying to follow the line of tumbled wall, and thinking of that gate and the words, "Forbidden to enter"; and suddenly she saw, as she looked over it, woodcutters stacking faggots, and hatless, aproned women gathering twigs.

Though impressed by the futility of ambition, she felt the very melancholy an urge to write. "Broken gates of ruined châteaux," she murmured to herself. "Broken gates . . ." Tinkling bells disturbed her dreaming, and round a curve in the trees came a bareheaded girl with a flock of white goats.

That afternoon she took a pencil and some scribbling paper, and walked in the winter sunshine round and round the narrow house, wondering what to write about. She had bad moments when she felt that in all her life there was no emotion on which she could draw, and that her invention, when put to the test, was completely sterile. Still, it was pleasant to moon about the garden thus, striving to see in the populous regions of the past a tale worth telling.

But the next day she was secretly glad that the brain-tiring subject could be put aside in favour of the first exciting visit to Paris. And during the next few weeks she persuaded herself that she might legitimately neglect her actual writing, since she would be completing her preparation for the great work by all the education to be sucked out of intelligent visits to Paris. . . . No, it was not an excuse to escape from effort, but real hard work.

And February passed into March, and the spring came peeping in the trees of Montmorency, and still there was nothing on the scribbling paper—except scribbles.

But if she had not written much, she and Miss Carrell had learned Paris like a loved book. They talked proudly of the Palais Royal, the Louvre, the Boulevard des Italiens, the Palais de Justice and the Panthéon. Sometimes Mr. Bruno joined them in the evening and they dined on the boulevards, watching the crowds and the traffic hurry by, to the music of the paper women shrieking, "La Presse ! La Presse ! " They had been to the Opera, and Daphne, lifted to the roof by the singing of the soprano in the finale of the first act, and by the storm of applause at the curtain's fall, began to wonder whether her own genius might not really find its issue in great singing or great acting. She felt no longer sure of being a great writer. She was sure only that she was a genius.

April, May and June passed in an alternation of gay sight-seeing in Paris and lonely fancy-gathering in the Montmorency Forest. Both were forms of delight, but there was a distinction. Visiting the city was entertainment and stimulation, but the solitary saunter a-dream among the burgeoning trees was that serene happiness that could only be called blessedness. She did not believe a more perfect serenity could be attained. And it could only be compassed alone. Had she had companions who could understand, it might have been very good to talk over her aspirations sometimes ; but there were none. Her father was either too busy, or his knowledge too overawing, to be told of his

ridiculous daughter's pretentious schemes. No, she would
surprise him one day. So she wandered alone with her
thoughts like the girl with the white goats. Bliss it was :
and there hardly emerged the fear, though it moved to birth
at times, that this was the bliss of a drug—that the long,
luxurious brooding on what she would one day do was daily
unfitting her for doing it.

In July, when they should have go to Switzerland, Mr.
Bruno decided that his work would not allow him to gratify
this desire till next year. Nor should Owen, who had now
joined them, take Daphne to the mountains, for himself had
fixed his heart on doing that. So he sent both children to
the Belgian coast, where they spent delightful days in
Ostend and Middelkerke and Westende. This was to be
every minute a holiday, decided Daphne, and writing was
abandoned for bathing and sailing, and mild gambling at
casinos and dancing at hotels. To recline on and finger the
fine shingle, or watch the little rills running down their
channels in the corrugated sand, or to sit up and hurl flat
stones so that they leapt and ricochetted on the smooth sea
was to live with childish memories. This holiday she discovered Owen : that he was a tall, presentable boy with the
graceful figure of his father; and astonishingly efficient,
managing all their money affairs and so leaving her to lax
enjoyment. The fact was, each for the first time was proud
of the other.

In September, when they returned to St. Leu, she
realized that her holiday was over and she must now start
again on her work. But as she and her brother pushed open
the gate of the little garden of firs she was dismayed to find
herself dreading the task and the repetition of the long,
worrying hours that ended in a few scribbled lines and
unmeasurable discouragement. The shock was like a
moment of overthrow. Was she one who had the creative
temperament without the power to create? No, no; that
would be too awful a disappointment. She was indolent,
that was all. When she was supposed to be unpacking
upstairs she was really facing a revelation. *She was mentally and physically slothful.* And why? Why, when she
knew she was charged with a vitality of body and mind? It
was habit. It was the legacy of her childhood. She walked
to the window and looked out upon the forest. Loth to do

it, she was yet angrily blaming her father and all the careless people about the steps of her childhood who had allowed her to learn indolence and practise it to perfection.

Once the chaos stirred and the spirit of creation moved above it. She had been drifting about the forest glades, strewn with old leaves and broken twigs, and after descending a flexuous lane, happened upon a white church. It was Taverney Church, and five hundred years old, from the evidence of its clerestory windows, which were as lovely as those of an Early English cathedral. Beyond it thronged the houses of Taverney. She walked into its walled cemetery, a strangely silent place bounded on three sides by the forest trees and on the fourth by the high wall of the church. Epitaphs were always interesting, so she wandered among the graves, moved to sadness by the tawdry wreaths of wire and beads and the china flowers. One grave, because it had many such offerings and a border of pansies, stayed her to examine it closer. On the stone slab she read:

"Ici Repose
Geneviève Rollier,"

and in silver lettering on one cross of beads, "*A Notre Mère*"; on another, "*A Notre Amie*"; and on a wreath that seemed by right the largest, "*A Mon Epouse.*" There was a scroll across some dirty china flowers with the words, "*Nous ne t'oublierons jamais.*" She stared at it, unconscious of a drooping mouth. She was wondering what Geneviève had achieved before her husband and her children laid her there; whether their loving offerings had outlasted their sadness; whether Geneviève's life had been worth while.

Suddenly she looked up. She knew that never before had she been so conscious of her response to all the pain in life. It pleased her that she could sense it thus and be troubled by it. Here was the secret of how to write. You must really *feel* with men—and what had she felt so far? How completely self-centred her life had been! And as long as it was self-centred you could not really feel with others. . . . She would like to begin being unselfish—a saint perhaps; the peer of St. Theresa as well as of Madame de Genlis.

Out of her pity for this woman, why should she not write an imaginary life? Yes, she would do it. They would be here many months, and how she would enjoy studying local colour, local history and local temperaments! . . . It was so much easier to study conditions and jot down notes in a book than to grind at a table. . . . She caught that thought as it flitted through her mind, and wrung its neck. "Madame Rolland" should be a masterpiece, and she would spare no labour on it.

Throughout that autumn and winter she did struggle on odd days to get something on paper. But oh, it was difficult! How often was she tempted to throw down her pencil and dream again! And that inspiration in Taverney Churchyard—where was it? She had to bully and shake her memory to find out what the emotion had been. And it would be a great relief sometimes to decide she must walk back to the cemetery and find out.

With the spring came all the excitement of thinking about their summer visit to Switzerland and Italy. But April brought moments of dismay. The Uitlanders of the Transvaal, some dusty country thousands of miles away in South Africa, had sent a petition to the Queen for protection from strange Dutchmen called Boers. And Mr. Bruno, pleased with the drama of it and with his own keen vision and understanding, talked of an inevitable war.

"Of course there'll be war. Anyone with twopence worth of imagination and knowledge of Englishmen can see how the tale will write itself. . . . So what about your continental trotting now, Duffy?"

She hardly knew whether to think him teasing or to be alarmed.

"But what on earth has it got to do with us going to Switzerland?"

"Everything. You've never seen a real war, have you? Small things like authors' incomes are apt to disappear. And now you're going to see a war, when English people won't be able to show their faces on the Continent for fear of being spat on."

"Oh, daddy, it won't happen. It can't. At least, not till we've been and come back."

So Mr. Bruno hoped, too indolent, really, to believe

otherwise.   And when the Dutchmen of Cape Colony moved
to mediate between England and the Transvaal Boers he
affected a great relief.

"Yes, Duffy, I think you might pack—with a heart full
of thanks to these godly old men of the Africander Bond.
They've been your good fairies.   At any rate nothing'll
happen for some months yet."

CHAPTER XVII

WHEN, one early July afternoon, Daphne and her father arrived at the Hotel Frohnalstock, at Brunnen, on the Lake of Lucerne, she learned that the news of their coming was already abroad among the guests, and looked forward to her descent that evening into the lounge or one to the terrace where these interested people would be waiting for their dinner. There was the pleasing memory, too, of six very simple but very new dresses in her trunks. She selected in her bedroom the one of pale cinnamon, and had completed her dressing by seven o'clock, which was half an hour too soon. Much too soon, for she had determined that her father and she should not enter the lounge till five minutes before the meal, so that as many people as possible might be congregated there. Twenty-five minutes to wait.

The french windows of her bedroom opened on to a private loggia; and stepping out into an air of Egyptian warmth, she purposed to kill time by staring at the lake. To her this view from her bedroom balcony seemed the most wonderful on which she had ever gazed. From the gardens at the hotel's base, four stories below, the lake spread a width of tranquil water, brilliant in the evening sun, till it lost itself in the dark reflections of the pine-clad mountains opposite. To the left—for Brunnen was almost at the lake's end—the water appeared to finish in a dark corner, shut from light by the wooded slopes. Above the pines before her rose the white peaks of the Urirotstock. At their foot, where the mountains formed a headland, a white rock, not unlike a coarse obelisk, stood alone in the water. Somewhere in the trees was the Rutli meadow where, many hundred years ago, the representatives of Uri, Schwyz and Untervalden swore their forest cantons into an eternal alliance—and Switzerland was born.

It was her father who had decided that they must come first to Brunnen. Was not all its surrounding country— Schwyz, and Einsiedeln, and the Rutli meadow, and Tells-

Daphne Bruno

kapelle—the cradle of Swiss history and the holy ground of Swiss legends? Never would she forget her approach to it by steamboat from Lucerne. The grandeur of the mountains and the serenity of the water had raised in her, as she sat staring over the rail, a longing for intenser emotions than she had yet known—love, she supposed, no matter whether it brought joy or tragedy. She felt that she was ripe for something like that. Her mind was not superstitious; she had no belief in destiny or that she had been brought to this incomparable place for a pre-ordained experience. She just wondered whether, since something must happen some day, it might not happen here. She was now nineteen.

Five past seven. And dinner was at seven-thirty. During the next twenty minutes she kept looking at her watch, like an actor before the calls, "House-lights," and "Curtain." At twenty-five past she walked into her father's room next door.

"Come along quickly," she said. "They all know you're here, and I want to show you off."

They descended the wide, soft-carpeted stairs, Daphne with that unusual quiet and dignity which the consciousness of evening dress can throw about those unaccustomed to wearing it. As they entered the lounge and she pretended to be looking for some chairs the flutter of interest among the people made her more self-conscious than ever. She knew that all were glancing at her father and herself over newspapers, liqueurs or pince-nez. This feeling of notoriety threw her into an over-acted naturalness, and she said rather loudly :

"Oh, there we are, daddy; there's a table and two chairs. I'll bag them."

And she almost ran towards them. Then she sat down, and, picking up a French journal, tried to appear at ease. Sometimes, however, she swept her eyes around the guests. There was still in her mind the wonder if, by faint chance, he, the lover, was there. No, she didn't think so. Once she did encounter the eyes of a young man who immediately avoided hers and became lost in a book—proof that he had been staring at her. Not liking to look his way again, she kept her quick impression of fair hair, none too tidy and inclined to fall towards one eyebrow, a clear forehead, and a very ordinary, rather childish but rather "sweet" face. His dress seemed slightly different from an Englishman's. Later she snatched another glance at him, just as a draught from the open windows blew that falling hair right across his forehead, and she thought that Shelley—at least in brow and hair—must have been like that.

A gong sounded in some remote passage, and its din grew louder as it was brought towards the lounge. The young man rose, and she saw that his figure was other than she had expected : he was tall, stooped a little, and, though probably twenty-five years old, had not yet lost the grace-lessness of seventeen. A girl, almost certainly his sister, joined him, and they walked together into the spacious white restaurant.

During dinner Daphne was more than once aware that he had resumed his study of her, though pretending to chat with his sister. It was always her, rather than her father that he watched, so she began to doubt if it was the Bruno name that engaged him. It looked very like instant admiration. One could not but return an interest.

After dinner, on the broad terrace that overlooked the lake, she sat with her father listening to a string quartette and watching other people walk up and down. The youth was among them, walking with his sister and an older man, who was conceivably her admirer, and every time he passed Daphne he pretended to know nothing of her nearness, talking gaily to his companion.

Soon her father yawned and spoke about early bed after his disgusting night in a train, but she begged for per-mission to stay up at least till ten, and presently he left her there. She got up from her chair, and, going to the balus-trade of the terrace, watched the changing light on the water. A primordial darkness possessed the Rutli trees, and a night that was almost frightening filled the corner where the lake ended.

Next morning she was very late in getting up, and breakfasted alone between half-past nine and ten. Hurry-ing over the coffee and rolls, she passed out of the restaurant's doors on to the terrace to see if her father were sitting there with a book. She saw him twenty yards away in interested conversation with the youth who was seated, with obvious reverence, at his side. Hastily she withdrew into the restaurant and walked into the lounge through its communicating doors. There in an easy-chair she browsed the pictures in some English magazines till her father, entering from the terrace, stared about the room as if seeking his daughter. She whistled a long, fluttering note with a curve at its end, and Mr. Bruno perceived her.

"Duffy," said he. "Do you want to play tennis?"

"Oh, yes!"

"Well"—he sat beside her—"there's an American boy here who came up to me this morning——"

"You mean Shelley."

"Shelley? No, Detmould he calls himself. He came up to me with a most becoming modesty and asked if he might make himself known as he was a great admirer of your father's books—and tried to write himself. We've been having a most stimulating talk. He's got brains; indeed, a remarkable mind, I fancy. I should think he'll do something one day." Daphne exhibited interest, though disappointed that it had been the Bruno name, after all, which attracted him. "But now he's just asked if I and my daughter play tennis. I told him my age, which I am glad to say surprised him, and then said I'd ask you if you'd like to play."

"Oh, rather!"

"Then I think if you'll whistle to him as you did to me just now he'll come to heel."

"*You* whistle to him," suggested she.

"Personally, I make a distinction between dogs and men," said Mr. Bruno, getting up and walking towards the terrace. "To men I generally cough." He coughed and h'med, and drew the American boy into the room.

"This is my daughter, Mr. Detmould." Daphne jumped up, incurably thinking of herself as a child. "She ought to play well, since she's fresh from school."

"I'm *not* fresh from school. I left over two years ago."

"She was more or less expelled two years ago, since when I've had her on my hands. Duffy, this is Mr. Detmould, who kindly says you may play with him and his sister."

"Oh, thanks. I should love to. . . . Shall I go and change?"

She asked this of the young Detmould, who seemed
rather embarrassed, and stuttered :

"Sure ; if you will, thanks ; and I'll go and get Elsie and
Clarkson."

His American accent pleased her.

When she returned in a white tennis coat to the lounge
she saw the young Detmould in flannels, and talking
deferentially to her father. With his white shirt open at
the throat, his hair already blown and his rather childish
features, he would have looked a growing schoolboy, had
it not been for a set—almost pained—thoughtfulness in his
eyes and mouth. He rose as she entered, said : "Well,
good-bye, sir," to Mr. Bruno, and led the way to the tennis-
court.

The tennis-court was of dried earth, and had been cut out
of a wooded slope. On three of the banks, therefore, were
trees : horse-chestnuts and figs, with firs behind, and under
the branches a few old and blistered garden-seats. A beaten
track climbed from the gate in the surrounding network to
the garden-seats. At the minute, on the pale, slate-coloured
earth, Elsie Detmould was playing a single with Mr. Clarkson, their companion of the previous night. They stopped
as Daphne appeared.

"It's awfully nice of you to come," said Elsie with her
pleasant American drawl. "I'm afraid none of us are any
good except Henry "—she nodded towards her brother—
"and he's terrible."

Then Henry was his name—Henry Detmould—and he
didn't fit either.

In the first set Daphne was partnered with Henry, and
whether it was that she was excited by the all-conquering
play of her partner, or aided by the weakness of Mr. Clarkson and Elsie, she knew not, but she played as she never
remembered playing before. The set went to her and Henry
at 6—o.

"Goodness ! " exclaimed Elsie. "I guess you're a
player. What's wrong with a change of partners? "

Flushed with her success, Daphne determined to play
her hardest against Henry, and she and Mr. Clarkson fought
a fine losing battle. The points were contested with
such obstinacy that each time they were won or lost she
threw up both her arms and shrieked with excitement.

And at the set's close she said over the net to Henry Detmould :

"You've no business to play at all, playing as well as that."

He blushed, and his sister endorsed : "He *is* horrible, isn't he ? "

Tired, they were moving towards the seats, Elsie Detmould and Mr. Clarkson in front, and Daphne and Henry following with the net between them.

"But you'll make a wonderful player yourself," said Henry.

"Oh, I'm no good," protested Daphne. "I didn't play all last year."

"You're a born player. All you want is a spell of singles with someone a little stronger than yourself."

"Do you think so ? "

"Yes. Will you—will you play at least one set of singles with me every day. I should love to—to bring you out."

"Oh, may I ? But won't it be horribly dull for you ? "

"Not at all. I——" There he stopped, unable to phrase exactly what he was thinking. They were on the beaten path now, she leading, and when they reached the seat he picked up her white coat and silently helped her on with it.

After a rest they decided on a return set, and Daphne in her keenness ran first down the track on to the court. When all were placed for play, she frowned through the strings of her racket at Henry saying : "Now, don't you be too much of a beast this time," and he looked awkwardly away, but smiled. In this set she did not play so well, being anxious to justify his invitation, and when it was over, felt compelled to say : "You can withdraw your invitation if you like."

"No," smiled he. "I've no desire to. In fact, if you play badly I shall put you through a longer course."

She answered nothing, but again walked ahead up the beaten path. That Henry Detmould, even as Roger six years before, had been attracted to her from the first glance, was plain enough, and that her own response was already troubling her. It was a different response. This American boy had not Roger's good looks to quicken her admiration and pride ; she knew nothing whatever about him, and yet—

Heaven only knew why—she fancied her heart was beating a little quicker for him.

Having returned to the hotel, she ran up all those stairs, dismissing the last of her breath, and, before preparing for lunch, entered in her diary: "Played tennis 10.30 to 12.30 with Miss Detmould, Mr. Clarkson, and Shelley."

She did not see him again till after dinner on the terrace. Then when the quartet was again playing they found themselves sitting side by side and watching the evening as it fell over the water or lit up behind the mountains.

The talk had begun with perfunctory remarks about their tennis, but it only became really interesting when the falling darkness inspired them to discuss themselves.

"Do you know," said Henry suddenly, "I'm really bowled over by meeting your father and you here. I've so long been a student of his books. In fact, I think they decided the course of my life."

Next to hearing praise of oneself the most uncomfortable thing is to hear praise of one's parents, and Daphne replied awkwardly:

"They are quite good, aren't they?"

"I think they're magnificent."

"Have you published any books?"

"Lord, no!" muttered he. "And I've very little hope of anyone ever publishing my stuff; but I'm always writing, and always shall do. Do you write, too?"

"I want to."

"Oh, you will, then. You're sure to."

"I don't know." Daphne's head shook. "I'm losing hope. I seem to have no powers of invention at all. I can't invent any plot that hasn't been done before."

"Invention! What do you want with invention? Invention's the opposite of true art."

Her face swung to his.

"How do you mean?"

"Invention, inasmuch as it *is* invention, must be insincere. Art isn't the invention of entertaining stuff, it's—it's—oh, it's the liberation, for your own relief, of all the emotion stirred in you by the spectacle of life. It's the transmuting into some art form of your reaction, as we say in America—your reaction to life."

Daphne Bruno

"Regardless of whether anyone will read it, or publish it?" queried Daphne.

"Absolutely. . . . Or no. . . . No, you do hope, when you've given a created form to your emotion, that there'll be those one day who will recognize it as akin to their own, and care to contemplate it, and even thrill to it. . . . But that mustn't be the thought that drives you to write."

This was the beginning. Henry poured out his views on art. Art wasn't entertainment. . . . The true artist gave but little thought to the spectator. . . . All he sought was expression—escape—release. . . . And these ideas, coming on a living voice, driven forward by a personality that attracted her, stood clear before Daphne. Never from her confused reading had they come out like this. She'd been wrong—she'd been all along wrong; half of her desire to write had been hunger for fame, and the other half imitation. Her reaction to life? She hadn't got one. . . . And yet there had been moments. . . . Yes, perhaps one-tenth of her desire had been the true impulse.

The talk became a confession where Daphne, as a penitent, sought counsel from her director. She confessed that, so far from having emotions and a view-point of her own, she was never thrilled by a noble passage in an author without wanting to write like him and from his view-point.

"Exactly," said Henry. "Your reaction has been to literature and not to life."

"And yet I don't know," demurred she. "There have been times——" And she told him the story of Taverney Churchyard. Henry listened, sometimes wrinkling his brow at the lake as he thought out answers, sometimes turning to watch her as she spoke. His reply lingered, and when it came was strange.

"Forgive me asking it, but have you suffered at all in your life?"

She smiled over the inevitable reply.

"Not much, I suppose."

"Because I've a fancy that it's not till we've suffered a great deal that our hearts, when they are moved like that, will be so charged with sympathy that it gives us much—*everything* to write."

And ambition. What was to be done about her ambition? Must she believe, then, that she was a sham—for

she was sure, whatever he said, she would never expel it?
"I do want to do all you say, but I *do* want to be famous
too, and soon, while all my friends are alive."

Henry thought long, and once ran his fingers into the
hair that the breeze on the terrace was blowing across
his forehead. "No, it must go," he said; and at that
moment he threw the end of his cigarette over the balustrade as if it were Daphne's ambition. It must go. It was
a corruptive principle. All that could remain of it was her
hope to please the few who would understand.

"I am convinced that many true artists start from those
two points of ambition and imitation, and work through,
dropping the false values, one by one, till they discover
their real selves."

Silence, till Daphne asked:

"But if you never get anything published at all?"

Henry looked along the emptying terrace. They must
have been talking for hours.

"A really big thing, I fancy, always gets through—
sooner or later. But, at any rate, people like you and
me, if we're never able to produce anything big enough,
at least can join the few who understand."

When she smiled "Good night" at him at the lift door
and walked along the corridor to her bedroom, she had a
sense that she had enjoyed the most wonderful conversation
in her life. With no one else had she been able to talk
like that. In such an intimacy was a serenity as delightful,
as blissful—there was no other word—as when she walked
with her thoughts in the glades of Montmorency.

CHAPTER XVIII

But these intimate conversations belonged, as by right, to the darkness of after dinner. The sunny mornings—and in the summer of 1899 the days were monotonously, illustriously sunny—would see them on the tennis court, playing their practice singles. Enthusiasm more and more possessed Daphne as she found her strokes getting stronger, her eyes surer, and her feet swifter. She still ran shrieking from side to side of the court as he placed the ball now in one corner and now in another; and when she shrieked she apologized, promising "she would not do that again." If he beat her with a malicious and impossible ball she looked angrily at him through the strings of her racket, and even threw out her tongue.

When the games were over, and he declared that he was thirsty, she would say, "So'm I. Let's go and get some fizzy." And they would walk back to the terrace, where she poured out the drink for him. Always she remarked that when she was close to him, pouring out his drink, he would be silent and almost painfully abstracted. That she was encouraging him she knew, but could not cease from it; something compelled her to show that she was happy in this fellowship and ready to think of herself and him as a separated pair.

Soon her father took to coming and watching them at tennis. He must learn, he said, whether there was anything in this noisy rumour of his daughter's skill. As an outcome of his survey he was struck by his daughter's exceedingly good form in the matter of tennis and her exceedingly bad form in the matter of manners—shrieking and leaping as she did whenever there was occasion for triumph or reprobation, shouting "Oo!" and "Lordy!" and "Coo!" and even staring impudently at the young man through the grill-window of her racket. The second time he watched, an early evening after tea, he was strongly impressed by the unconscious or subtly concealed way in which she was throwing herself at this American boy. He pulled his moustaches over it, sitting under the chestnut trees above the play. The thing interested him as a philosopher and a student of human nature, and he ruminated, detached from it, as though the girl were not his daughter. In watching this attraction between a man and a maid, thought he, he was very near to the acme of things. If to a vitalist philosophy love was life at its greatest intensity, here was he watching it break through and bud vividly. An unconscious youth and girl didn't realize that this was the explanation of their genius for love. Yes, life touched no higher point than this; and nuptials, therefore, to those who could see were a coronation ceremony of life.

These thoughts were interrupted by the game's early close. Young Detmould had promised to meet his sister returning on the steamboat from Treib; and Mr. Bruno was slightly disturbed to hear his daughter call out: "Oh, must you go? What a shame! I'll come with you to the gate."

"*Bon Dieu!*" thought Mr. Bruno. "That's going rather far."

The gate she meant was at the end of a narrow serpentine path that threaded downward through the crowding firs. He allowed her five minutes before following her; and then, lighting a cigar to fortify him in a difficult interview, strolled along the path. She was leaning, as he saw on turning the last bend, against the post of the little swing gate, and sucking a large and ungovernable sweetmeat. The American boy must have just disappeared, and Daphne be indulging a reverie. This sight of his daughter resting against a gate and symbolizing the acme of things touched him. He called:

"Duffy."

She looked up, startled.

"Come back with me and be lectured."

She replied nothing, but sucked the abominable lollipop (thus treating his promised lecture with scanty reverence), and taking her elbow from the gate-post came to him. And it was as they were walking back that he said:

"You're obviously throwing yourself at the head of that American youth."

"Oh, I'm not!" she exclaimed.

"You said that like a Cockney serving-girl. I tell you

you are deliberately—whether in the body or out of it I can't say—throwing yourself at the besotted young man, who's quite palpably in love with you."

The sentence was music in Daphne's ears. She liked her father to think that Henry Detmould was in love with her, and so said nothing for fear of damaging the thought.

"Tell me, Duffy, what would you think of a bookseller who was so unable to recognize a first edition that would one day be of some value that he flung it into the twopenny box for the first loiterer to buy?"

She provided the answer expected from her.

"I should think him a silly fool, I suppose."

"Well, but thou art the man—the creature, I mean."

"Daddy, I'm not. You're imagining it all. Besides, you might go on saying that for ever. I must like someone one day."

"Yes; but, Duffy, go slow, go slow. What you may think is love is often self-hypnotism. You've always had a fairly clear brain, so make sure first."

"But how does one make sure?"

"How? I don't know. I think time alone will test it for you. What do you know of young Detmould? You've only met him for a week or two. All I can say for him is that he has the grace to be much shyer of encouraging you than you are of him."

"I've never encouraged him one bit."

"Not deliberately and vulgarly. But whether you know it or not, my dear, you hang out teasing flags."

She ran upstairs to dress for dinner, and closed her bedroom door, as if to add more privacy to her thoughts. She stood behind her window and looked out.

How did one make sure?

What did she really feel? Certainly she wanted to keep her lure for Henry, and her long thoughts about him. With this new interest life had dyed itself very bright; and if a wand could wave it away so that it had never been, everything would drop into paleness again. Up till their arrival at Brunnen her book-thoughts had crowded her mind, but now Henry had sent them below and occupied their room. In his talks on the terrace at night he had given her more than anyone else in the world. Not only had he unveiled the wrongness in her approach to art, but his wide-thrown learning had indirectly shamed her into disturbing realizations. He talked of philosophy—and what did she know of philosophy? Wrinkling his forehead, or pressing a hand on his hair, he spoke of painters, sculptors, musicians, architects, declaring that he who would be master of one art must be jack of them all—and she knew hardly anything of the names he mentioned! Greatness, she realized, as she listened in a humiliated silence, was not born from dreaming on it, nor was it attained by the slothful who read only what was easy. If you were to express your reaction to life, you must aim at little else than all knowledge, so should it be the reaction of a fine mind. All this he had given her. Was she in love with him? She created a very private picture of herself lying in Henry's arms, pressed against his heart. It sent a tremor of joy through her.

But what did *he* feel? There was that first night's staring at her. There was his pointed choice of her to play tennis with, though really she could be nothing more than a wild pupil. And sometimes when he caught her eyes he swung his own away uncomfortably. But was it only a passing attraction—a holiday flirtation? No, it didn't seem like that. That strange agitation of his hands, when she stood very close to him and poured out his drink—it didn't look like flirting.

She stepped forward and stood on her loggia, staring over the lake at the fir-woods climbing the opposite mountain. The evening was close, and the water filmed and inert. A little boat with two people in it was coming home to Brunnen from the Schillerstein. After watching it for a while, she quickly turned her head leftward and upward to the floor above—where Henry's window was. He was standing on his balcony, looking down at her loggia. And he had seen her glance, and awkwardly waved his hand, as if to show he was unembarrassed. She pretended not to have recognized him, and retreated into her room.

That night there was dancing in the lounge. Daphne, with a Spanish embroidered shawl about her shoulders, sat next her father, watching the first waltz, and hoping Henry would soon come and ask her to dance, that her father might be further persuaded of his love. But not once did he come near her. He danced two or three dances with his sister, and some more with a very pretty girl, whom Daphne had often noticed. But she was not jealous of her, for Henry as he waltzed seemed abstracted and mechanical.

Daphne was not left without partners. The most persistent suitor was a tall, moustached Swiss, who, having once found her, was beyond question lost in admiration of his discovery. She talked gaily to him in French, but was thinking all the while : "Why doesn't Henry come? Is he hurt about something? Did he think I snubbed him by not answering his wave? I didn't mean to snub him—I was only shy. . . ." She tried a happier thought. "Perhaps he doesn't want to compromise me by being seen so much with me, and this is so public. Yes, it's that. It's a good sign, rather than a bad one." But when they passed each other dancing, and he smiled a merry recognition, as if there were nothing remarkable in their not dancing together, she doubted again. "I shall know to-morrow morning, if he asks me to play tennis with him as usual."

In the morning she dawdled on the terrace in the hope of his invitation, but he passed her gaily, calling that he was going to climb the Selisberg with his sister and Clarkson. Almost it appeared as if he had made up his mind to avoid her. And in the evening, after dinner, he, Elsie and Clarkson sat with her father and her, and all discussed with perfect naturalness their adventures during the day. Never did he attempt to escape from the shelter of a crowd. At ten o'clock she retired to her bedroom with her wound. "Time is so short. We shan't have more than a month here, and we are wasting precious days. Henry, you know you want to be with me. You know you do."

One day succeeded another without bringing back the former intercourse. It was a mystery. Only when other people were with them did they meet. And yet she knew all the while that he was longing to have her alone. She would leave herself in places where he was likely to arrive, and then, shy of appearing to have done it on purpose, stroll away as soon as she saw him in the distance. Sometimes when she was thus set for him, the moustached Swiss would appear, and, though courteous to him, she would be thinking : "I don't want *you*. I don't want *you*. I'm awfully sorry if you're in love with me, because I know what it is to love without return. I'm sorry." And as soon as possible she would escape.

Her father took her on carriage excursions to Tellsplatte and the Einsiedeln Monastery, and Altdorf, and up the Furka Pass to the Rhone Glacier; and on the same days Henry went climbing with Elsie and their friend. A week of this mere friendliness heightened her doubt to misery, and her love to passion. Not now did she bring it to trial. She would not so insult it. She was madly in love with Henry. She wanted Henry with his boyish features and shape and his rich mind—his mind that blent with hers and fertilized it. She wanted him for her exclusive possession, to imprison him in herself. She was unable to read, unable to talk to people, and annoyed with her father when he came to chat. Always she wished to be worrying out the problem, "Does he love me?" sometimes answering it, "Yes, I know he does, in spite of all," and at other times, "He did for a few days, he really did, but not now." Or she refused herself so much comfort as that, declaring, "No, he was never more than just interested." And she would review every look she had seen in him, and every sentence he had uttered, in quest of proofs that he had loved her; and with a sunken heart decide that there was nothing that she could twist into more than a transient interest. She played an old childish game, "If I pass that post before someone speaks to me, then he does love me," and if it went against her, refused to believe in it. The terrace and the tennis court and its seat under the chestnuts, and all the places where they had been together, clothed themselves with pain. And if people in their innocence spoke to her about Mr. Detmould, or "that young American," she felt she had a proprietary interest in him, and gave information as one who spoke with authority.

Her fist had clenched over the vow: "You shall come back to me first. I won't go to you. Time may be short, but you shall come to me first."

In the end, however, she went to him.

He was sitting quite alone in a dark corner of the long terrace, as far as possible from the people round the string quartet. Pretending not to see him, she wandered past.

"You look tired," came his voice from the obscurity.

Daphne Bruno

"Oh . . . hallo!"

He extended the chair that was next to him, leaving his arm along its back.

"Why not sit down?"

After some meaningless hesitation she accepted the chair.

"I will—for a little," stuttered she, as he withdrew his arm. "But it's cold, isn't it?"

"I don't think so."

It was a preamble to nothing; neither found more words. She looked at the Spanish shawl, lying on her lap, and fiddled with its embroidery. Something told her that Henry was agitated and trembling internally, though nothing in his posture or movements suggested it; only the foot of his crossed leg swung gently. At one moment she knew that he was looking at her arms, and she scanned them herself. Hard tennis had made them slenderer than usual, and exposure had browned them; they were trembling.

"If you're cold," said Henry at last, "you'd better put your shawl on. Let me put it round you."

He took it off her lap and, as she bent forward without looking at him, placed it about her shoulders, careful not to touch her. She leaned back in her chair.

"Do you think you've been playing too much tennis?" asked he.

"Oh, no. Why?"

"You look tired—and frailer."

"Then I certainly shan't play much more. It's my ambition to get fatter."

"Oh, no!"

"Oh, yes!"

"No," he repeated. "You're all right as you are. I like your narrow shoulders—and your slimness—and your childish clothes. I wouldn't have you different."

As with such words they seemed to have fluttered very near to something, both withdrew into silence.

"Elsie and I and Clarkson are going to climb the Mythen to-morrow." Thus he deliberately broke the pause.

"Are you?"

"Yes. . . . Or I'm supposed to be going too. I'm not sure that I want to. I feel I'd rather laze about here. We go away so soon."

"Do you?"

"In a fortnight's time."

She showed no feeling, though the shadow of a future pain fell near.

"We're going on a walking tour," he continued—"over the Furka Pass and down into Brigue. I *was* tremendously keen on it, but the prospect bores me now. However. . . ."

"I wish you weren't going. It'll be rotten here without your sister and you."

Henry uncrossed his legs and lit a cigarette.

"Have you ever thought," said he, "that one never discovers the truth of how to live until it's too late to live?"

"What do you mean?"

"Well, I am twenty-five, and I've found no code by which one lives a full life and yet hurts nobody. When I've read enough and thought enough and got the brains to think out a philosophy of living, I shall probably be too old to live."

Daphne nodded as if she partly understood.

After a silence that often moved with undelivered words, he proceeded, gaining time between sentences by tending his cigarette:

"Take a hypothetical case. An artist of some sort—let us say a man seeking to be a great, and above all, a *true* musician—wants to be loyal to life as it calls him—knows that he *ought* to be loyal to it. . . . And it suddenly calls with a voice so sacred that it seems almost like a religious call—through some love, I mean—it—it calls him to the wilful snapping of all the world's inhibitions. He is not in the happy position of possessing a religion to tell him that these inhibitions are the laws of God. If he were, the problem would be solved at once, and his duty plain. . . . But instead, he suspects that they are things improperly thought out, and enforced by those who have forgotten what it was like to love. . . . Well, a vision has haunted all artists that their road to beauty is through lawlessness and danger. . . . They have seen that Art is a sort of Mysticism, because you will never attain to its highest places unless you are ready to leave all and follow life . . . . And it isn't pure selfishness, as people say, for timidity and selfishness and security often pull on the other side. . . . Oh, but this is old stuff—much of it is in your father's books—but it comes

261

alive for one, when one is going through what thousands have gone through before. . . ."

"I don't think I understand," said Daphne.

With that he stopped like a train against the buffers.

Between ten and eleven that night she stood near her window—or out on her loggia, laying hands on the balustrade and looking over the lake tranced by the darkness.

"He *does* love me. I'm sure of it. Just now he does. And I do love him. I love him madly."

But why? Of his past or his full character she knew nothing; she had only looked on his outward appearance, and into his mind with its enthusiasm. But whether, to those who knew him in the deep, he was good or bad she didn't care. She would almost like to be told of sins he had committed, that she might assure him they were nothing to her.

But what would come of it all?

"What do I really believe will happen? I suppose I really believe we shall be separated when he goes, and perhaps come together in the future, or perhaps not. But, of course, we shall part without telling each other anything. . . . He couldn't very well speak, after only knowing me a few weeks."

Strange that, too sunk in the joy of loving, she was not made miserable by this sense of shortness. It had not yet got through her exultation, or the little of it that flushed her feelings, by adding poignance, sweetened them.

But what did he mean by that talk of the world's inhibitions, and of timidity and selfishness and security pulling you back, and of not hurting others? She could make nothing of this. If he yielded to his love for her, how would he injure anybody or affront the world? Was he perhaps engaged to a girl? Or—quick, heart-gripping fear !—had he meant someone other than herself—some married woman, perhaps—when he spoke of a love that called him? Was he only using her as a friendly person to whom he could pour out his trouble?

"No, he meant *me*." Her heart steadied. "He meant me. I'm sure of it. I can't tell why, but I know it."

Resolved to keep this certainty and to take it into her dreams, she turned into the light of her bedroom, leaving the window wide open, for the night was close, undressed, and got into bed. With a mind studiously emptied, like a room for Henry to walk about in, she fell asleep. Her dreams, as often happened, had nothing to do with him whom she had tried to will into them. She dreamt that she was back in the months before they came to Switzerland, wandering along the roads of the Montmorency Forest, and watching the men quarrying the yellow stone for the local villas, or the woodcutters stacking their faggots. Once she was in a gloomy avenue of huge fir trees that approached the gates of a château, and down the avenue came the girl of her own age, herding her white goats. Of such places as Brunnen, or of such people as she would meet there, she had as yet no knowledge. . . . Now she was walking along a sun-spotted glade towards St. Prix, where Miss Sims's class and Miss Vidella's spectacled stare were awaiting her; and abruptly without break in the sunlight, and without wetting her in the least, the rain began to tear through the branches. It was magnificent. Any second the thunder would come. The first crash, with its rolling echoes, woke her.

She saw through her open window that it was early morning, and the rain was rushing down in lines so perpendicular, so visible, and so close as to seem like the warp of unmade linen. A flash of lightning introduced another clap of thunder which repeated itself, for interminable seconds, among the mountains and in the great basin of the lake. There were rhythmical pauses in the rain, and when its curtain was removed, the peaks, framed by her window, stood folded round with clouds. She jumped up to watch. The storm's rhythm was wonderful. For a few moments the clouds would dissipate, revealing the snowfields rosy with sunrise, and then condense again, and there would be thunder and the shattering curtain of rain.

The immediate message of the storm was one of hope. Henry was to have gone climbing the Mythen to-day, and now, perhaps, he wouldn't go. In mid-morning the weather would clear and they would play tennis, or it would stay wet and they would find some sheltered place to talk. Her watch said five o'clock; if only she could keep the storm over Brunnen till Elsie and Henry had finally abandoned their early start for the Mythen! But it began to pass, and in fifteen

Daphne Bruno

minutes might never have been. Stepping on to the loggia she gave a quick glance towards Henry's room; its sunblinds were up and its french windows thrown open. Possibly he was getting ready—but, no, surely he wouldn't go—he would make excuses to remain behind, and after breakfast she would find him lingering on the terrace waiting for her to appear. Free of his sister and Clarkson, he would suggest their game of tennis, and when that was over they would walk together with feigned naturalness along the winding path between the firs, and he would abruptly ask her to let him row her over to the Rutli, and once on the water they would glide to solitary places under the farther bank.

Such would be their morning, and she dressed suitably for it. But in the restaurant there was no Henry dawdling at his breakfast-table, where she had hoped to see him, nor was he on the terrace or in the lounge, when she wandered through them.

He had gone, then. He had gone with his sister to climb the Mythen.

She was stabbed by it. It meant worrying out all over again the problem whether or not he was in love with her. "He must have made *any* excuse to stay if he felt for me what I feel for him. Then he *doesn't*." Seated on a chair on the terrace, she passed in review, one, two, and three times, every symptom of love or every hint of indifference he had shown the first day. And the evidence, after this crowning incident of the Mythen, seemed to show that he liked her a little, but knew none of the doubting, hungry, monopolizing love that was hers. It was a terrible verdict—and she didn't believe it. "He *does* love me, I know it. But why then did he go?" Her father came and sat beside her, and she wished he would go away. He went; but other people strolled up and started to be pleasant. Some of them, deceived by her blithe answers, kept her in conversation for long quarters of an hour, while her problem waited where it was hidden, crying to her to return. At last, for fear of being spoken to, she left the hotel and walked along the streets of Brunnen.

In these streets, if she walked away from the lake, she could see the twin points of the Mythen rising high above the broken sky-line. How exactly like the two humps of a sitting camel they were! No, they were too pointed—a

264

little too conical for that. Sometimes they looked like two pyramids, joined together as Siamese twins were joined. Trees mantled them for a great way up, and then the points rose naked. Through those trees, though they were miles away, one could almost see the paths where he was climbing.

When she entered the restaurant for dinner that evening, a rapid, careless, over-shoulder glance showed him talking gaily to his sister. In that glance his profile had appeared to be almost ugly; and, though surprised, she was pleased, half hoping that, by seeing his plainness, she could be cured of her love and given relief from its pains. But the thought was dead as soon as born.

Waiters cleared the lounge for dancing, but she did not want to dance. And when the tall, moustached Swiss came seeking her for his partner, she declared that she had resolved not to dance to-night. Escaping from her father's side, she went and sat alone in the comparative darkness of the terrace. It was deserted except for a couple in the distance who were sitting out a dance. She left the Spanish shawl on her lap, and, stretching her legs before her, crossed one ankle over the other. There was an iron table beside her, and she rested her elbow upon it. Her mood made her wish she could light a cigarette like a man, and send up her thoughts in puffs or rings of smoke.

She might have sat there fifteen minutes when Henry appeared and walked towards her.

"You've deserted us," smiled he.

"Yes, I'm tired."

"So am I."

"Did you climb the Mythen?"

"Yes, to the very top. That's why I'm done for. So's Elsie. She's danced two dances and gone to bed."

He sat on a chair the other side of the iron table. Taking a loose silver matchbox from his waistcoat pocket, he lit a Swiss cigar and laid the matchbox on the table.

"I thought possibly you wouldn't go," ventured Daphne, "when I saw the storm this morning."

"I shouldn't have minded much if it had stayed a bit longer and prevented our going. I was never very eager about it."

This led them into the accustomed silence; he was en-

Daphne Bruno

grossed in watching his smoke, and she, happy because he had sought her out, picked up his matchbox and twisted it in her fingers, with her face averted. Once, lest the silence became too noticeable, he said :

"I danced three dances with Miss Storry, and they were three too many for anyone so exhausted."

And Daphne, resolved to be generous, answered:

"I think she's such an awfully pretty girl."

"Yes. I suppose she is."

After that he returned to his smoke and Daphne to her playing with his matchbox. The silence was next broken by Mr. Bruno, who walked up behind a cigar.

"Ah, you, Mr. Detmould, being American, can afford to take your holiday slowly, but my daughter and I, being English Imperialists, will have to quicken the *tempo* of ours, I'm afraid."

"What *are* you talking about, daddy?" asked Daphne languidly, as he drew up a chair.

He was talking about the privileges of belonging to an Imperialist nation, he explained, and the chances it offered of conscientiously shooting Dutchmen in their own country. Didn't she realize that, as a loyal Englishwoman, she would soon be at war with the Transvaal?

"I'm not going to war with anyone," she grumbled; and Henry, turning towards her father, said that he had thought the news was better.

Her father then spread himself to be interesting, as, indeed, he could be in such a matter as this. The French and German papers in the lounge, said he, were so much more feminine and indiscreet than the ponderous English journals. And they showed that the Transvaal was arming to the eyebrows, and that trainloads of suspicious packing-cases, labelled as farming implements, were pouring from France and Germany—through Capetown, if you please—and up to Pretoria. And the Boers were buying horses in every market, and Europe's soldiers-of-fortune appearing in the Boer streets. And the English, in their usual humorous way, had answered all this by sending out two companies of engineers.

Henry inquired when the fighting would begin.

"When the rain comes, and the grass for the horses," said her father.

Henry nodded. The conception was picturesque.

"In September or October, I suppose," pursued Mr. Bruno. "As soon as the veldt is right, old Kruger won't wait for us to send him an ultimatum, he'll send his own instead. He'll say : ' Come on ! ' And I expect we shall send out two more companies of engineers."

But Daphne, momentarily stimulated, was no longer interested. Had all Europe been going to war it would not have found an inch of resting-room in her mind, for her love was a monopolizing and unsociable tenant. Even the thought that this war might prevent their visit to Italy was unimportant now. Italy was nothing. It lay beyond the day when Henry and she should have parted. What mattered was that their few remaining hours were flying, and fate seemed determined that they should never be alone.

And in the next few days they did not meet except in the presence of others. This was all the stranger, since Elsie Detmould had kept to her bed for two days, having taken cold when climbing the Mythen. Henry, one would have thought, would have been freer to seek out Daphne. But he didn't, and she sat on terrace or in lounge, with an unread book on her knees, arguing over and over again her old case. On the Wednesday, three days before he went, he *did* come for a little while and sit beside her—the table between them as before. And all his words, she dared to believe, hinted at warmer meanings behind.

"I don't want to leave this place a bit," he grumbled.

"When are you going? "

"Saturday morning—soon after sunrise. . . . It's—it's not to be thought."

Daphne turned her head towards those meeting mountains where the lake appeared to finish in a dark corner. Up through them, as far as she could remember, climbed the serpentine road to the Furka Pass. She pictured Henry, with knapsack and alpenstock, bending to its steeper slopes, till he reached the summit of the pass and ascended to the ice-fields of the Rhone Glacier.

"Oh, but you'll enjoy going over the Furka. The view from the glacier is too wonderful for words. I can imagine you on the ice."

R

"I wish you were coming too," he murmured.

"So do I. But we're staying here a little longer, and then going to Grindelwald."

"Yes, I know."

"But will your sister be well enough to do all that walking?"

"Oh, yes, that's what she's come for. She was ill in the spring, and was determined to get rid of it. She's always been a dashing sort."

Daphne was now seeing a picture of Henry's childhood, and feeling jealous of Elsie and all those who had known him during the twenty-five years before she did.

"Yes," continued Henry, "I've been looking it out on the map. We shall be only about thirty miles apart, and yet have all the highest mountains of the Bernese Oberland between us."

This could be met only with silence.

The next morning, Thursday, when she was strolling through the hotel, she played on her pains by trying to imagine that it was Saturday, and that Henry had already left. And as she looked at the places where they had talked together, she knew she would not be able to endure the hotel after he had gone; these places would hit her wound too cruelly. Much better to be clear of Brunnen, seeing something new! How could she get away? How could she ask her father to take her away without betraying her secrets? Impossible as it seemed to his incisive eyes, it must be attempted.

She found him on the seat above the empty tennis court with a book and a cigar.

"Daddy," she began, sitting next to him. "Aren't you getting bored with this place yet?"

"Not particularly. Are you?"

She thought it out.

"No. But I'm quite keen on moving on and seeing somewhere else. . . . I'm so afraid, you see, that this old war 'll prevent us doing half of what we planned—you said we'd have to speed up things a bit—so I vote we go on to Grindelwald."

He did not turn and look at her in an enquiring surprise, but studied the tennis court before him; and she knew that he had guessed everything. He did not chaff her, saying, "Let's see, the American boy goes on Saturday, doesn't he?" for he knew (and she could almost *feel* his knowledge) that the matter had passed beyond chaff. Of his gentleness he would erect between them a pretence of ignorance, though each would know that neither believed in it.

"I shouldn't mind," said he. "I'm afraid I *am* rather apt to take root where I can find a garden and book. When do you suggest going?"

"Well, not to-morrow, of course. But Saturday perhaps, or Sunday. I'm awfully keen on seeing the other places."

"Saturday's the day after to-morrow, isn't it? Well, certainly if you order it. You're in command of this expedition."

Dinner that evening showed Elsie back in her place; and Daphne, when she followed the diners into the lounge, resolved to make much of her. She had seen hardly anything of Henry's sister, what with their climbing in the daytime and the attentions of Mr. Clarkson at night. And for some reason she wanted Elsie Detmould to take away with her a liking for Daphne Bruno. So now, since Elsie was sitting alone, she took the wicker chair at her side and asked after her cold.

"I reckon I'd forgotten its existence till you mentioned it," drawled Elsie pleasantly. "Two days in bed 'll finish off the best of colds. . . . But I was determined to be quit of it, as we've all this marching ahead of us."

"Yes, I know. I'm sorry you're going so soon. Must you?"

"Yes, I guess we can't stay here all the time. We want to see other places, and we haven't too long in Switzerland. I've got to get back to my mother, and Henry's got to get back to his wife."

It was as if a revolver had been shot off in Daphne's ear.

But as instantaneous was the conviction that she must keep perfect control of herself and show nothing to Elsie. Elsie had spoken quite naturally and without malice, evidently having seen nothing more than friendliness between her brother and Daphne. Daphne turned and looked at her, laughing.

Daphne Bruno

"I never knew he was married!"

"Married? Very much so. He was married four years ago."

Daphne frowned a humorous incredulity—as if the joke were getting better.

"Four years? He doesn't look old enough."

"He married at twenty-one."

"I suppose he's a father, too. But I simply can't imagine it."

"No, he's not a father yet."

"He ought to have brought his wife with him, on a lovely holiday like this."

"Ah, but she especially arranged that he should bring me. I'm really recuperating from a breakdown."

"Awfully sporting of her," said Daphne.

"Yes, she's a good sort. And I guess she quite enjoys a holiday from Henry. Husbands are a bit trying sometimes."

How Daphne kept up that conversation and her suitable smiling till the moment when politeness allowed her to escape she never knew. There must have been half an hour of it before she found herself in her bedroom with the door closed.

CHAPTER XIX

SHE carried her paralysed thinking to her bedroom. The words, "Never now . . . never . . . never," were behind her lips. Her jaws parted in the dismay of it. The sight of the mountains drew her through her window on to the loggia. Inevitably her eyes turned towards Henry's window; and quickly, though with assumed unconcern, she withdrew into her room : she had seen him standing on his balcony with hands on its railing, and knew that, with a sidelong look, he was keeping her loggia under view.

She undressed, but very abstractedly, and with long pauses when her hand, holding a garment, dropped to her side. "Never now." Never would there be any fulfilment of her love. Yes—though—there were two ways. Probably neither would happen, but it was a slight relief to picture them. Henry and she could go off together one day, accepting the worldly consequences; or he could come to England once every year, and she could meet him for a week of secret, lawless love (she had told Miss Sims she was ready to do that). Ah, all his actions and words fell into place now, especially that jumbled talk about snapping the world's inhibitions—and timidity holding you back—and not hurting others. But it was proof—it was inflating proof that he loved her.

This sudden thought, which brought happiness that quieted despair, she took into bed with her, that she might close her eyes and examine it. Henry loved her, and *she* loved *him* without one lingering doubt, and if at some future day he asked of her anything—*any thing*—she would give it to him. For the shadowy figure that was his wife, she knew not what she felt; sometimes jealousy and anger, sometimes pity. "Oh, I wouldn't have her suffer as I should, if I were never to have him or see him again." No, the best solution would be the hiding of their love and its secret fulfilment in some snatched weeks every year.

Henry was evidently rich, and he would come over to her sometimes. Of course she would do it. And in her case she would injure nobody by giving herself to Henry.

With this vision of the future for consolation she sank into a dream-heated sleep.

Next day, Friday, and their last, on coming downstairs she found that Henry had gone by boat to Lucerne to get money for their departure. It would take him much of the day. So after breakfast she returned to her bedroom, and in a dry despair began her packing. It was manual labour and something to do. But it filled nearly all the morning, for every article was disturbing in its associations, and either she made mistakes that had to be repaired or she lost herself in long musings. When it was finished, except for what would go in to-morrow morning, she let fall the lid of her trunk, and going to the window, looked in the direction of Lucerne, whence Henry's steamer would come.

At lunch Elsie Detmould suggested a last set of tennis. Mr. Clarkson would play and that French girl, Madeleine Louvier. With a quickly-donned brightness Daphne answered, "Rather! Only I'll have to play in this dress. I've packed everything else." The word "packed" pierced her.

Out on the tennis court, with its lead-coloured earth, its surrounding nets, and its pathway climbing to the seats under the chestnut and fig trees—all so achingly reminiscent —they arranged their first set—Daphne and Madeleine playing Mr. Clarkson and Elsie. Sometimes Daphne was inattentive and played badly; sometimes she inexplicably lost herself in the game for a few minutes and played well. It was just as she was beginning her service in the fifth game that she heard a crunching on the gravel-drive behind the trees, and glancing up, saw that Henry had returned. She caught his eyes and, though hers turned away quickly, knew that he had sat down on one of the garden seats.

Self-conscious now, she played erratically, and kept up the formality of joking or even shrieking when she made mistakes or missed easy balls. The sudden sight of him, and then the constant awareness of his presence, had started a dull pain at the thought that this was almost the last time he would be within a few paces of her. As she played and shouted, "Oh, dash!" or teased Mr. Clarkson and Elsie when they were particularly weak, she was really thinking, "Oh, I understand what he meant when he talked about not knowing how to live till the time had passed for living. . . ."

After the seventh game Elsie remembered with dismay something that must be done on this last day, and the set temporarily broke up. Mr. Clarkson offered to pass the meantime by playing against the two girls.

"No," called Daphne," I'll sit out till Elsie returns." It would be obvious to Henry that this meant she wanted to sit by him, but she didn't care. "I'm awfully tired, really. You two have a single."

"Noh, noh," protested Madeleine.

"Yes, *please,*" urged Daphne. "I really mean it. I'd like to sit down a bit."

And, running, she passed through the gate in the surrounding network and climbed the path to the seat where Henry was sitting. He watched her as she ran towards him, and when she arrived picked up her white coat and put it about her shoulders. They sat down together, Daphne staring at the play of Mr. Clarkson and Madeleine, and Henry fiddling with an unread novel that had been beside her coat. He spoke first.

"It was wretched having to go to Lucerne to-day of all days."

"Yes."

"I don't know what I'm going to do about to-morrow. . . . I don't want to go at all. . . . Just got fond of—everybody, and the whole place. . . ."

"Yes, it's rotten."

There was a silence during which several times Henry seemed to take in his breath, as if trying to say something for which he had not the courage. Daphne, without knowing why she made the remark, broke in with :

"But you'll be glad when the time comes to go back to your wife."

"Yes. . . ." He allowed no sign to escape him, any more than she had done before Elsie. "You should have heard me airing my German in Lucerne. I was amazed."

"Why? Did you do it frightfully well?"

"Magnificently."

And again that silence that would not deliver itself of something.

"It's a rotten book, that," said she, after watching him turn over its pages.

"Is it? I——"

But the sharp intake of his breath stopped him.

She told him something of the book's plot, and why it was so stupid, pleased, from some obscure motive, at this acting of naturalness. Then she jumped up.

"Here she is."

"Who?"

"Elsie come back."

He caught his breath again and—before he had time to think, stuttered: "Miss—Miss Bruno, may I say something to you? Oh——" He passed his hand quickly over his eyes. "I wanted to say—couldn't I see you alone somewhere? I shall probably never see you again, and I never get a moment alone with you—quite alone, I mean—and I don't know *how* I'm going to-morrow . . . and can't I see you somewhere this evening by yourself?"

She only stared before her at the game.

"I haven't frightened you, have I?" said he. "I—I don't think I quite know all I'm saying. I don't frighten you, do I?"

She turned towards him.

"No."

"I oughtn't to have spoken, I suppose. It's only despair that made me speak."

Then there was a silence more charged than any. He was obviously waiting for her to encourage him, but she was somehow speechless. Partly because her heart was pounding, and partly because when it came to the moment of encouraging him it seemed the first step in a social disobedience for which she was not competent.

Now Elsie was back on the court and calling:

"Come on, Daphne. We're waiting."

"Righto!" cried Daphne, picking up her racket confusedly, while Henry said in despair:

"May I write you a letter and put it in this book—write what I mean? I'll give it to you as soon as you've finished. May I?"

"Yes," said she, swinging her face quickly to his and back again. "Yes, if you like."

Then she hurried down to the court. And as she played there the side of her eye saw Henry writing something. She trembled to know what it was, and played mechanically at the tennis, longing for it to be over. Yet all the while she provided the necessary banter at other people's failures and explosions at her own. At last it was finished, and when they suggested another set she demurred:

"Oh, no. I can't play any more; I'm not as young as you people. I want to go and write some letters before I dress for dinner."

And rather languidly, with head down, she strolled through the network and up to the seat for her coat. Henry rose and gave it to her. The others, agreeing that they had had enough, were coming up.

"And here's your novel," said Henry.

"Oh, thanks."

She took it in a hand that was shaking traitorously. Calling to the other people, "Well, I've got a lot to do, I can't hang about with all you idlers," she walked—almost ran—towards the hotel entrance. In the vestibule and the lift she kept the book near her shoulder. Along the corridor of her floor she hurried to her bedroom with shoulders swinging. In the bedroom, with the door closed, she nervously opened the book, and saw a half-sheet of note-paper on which was written in pencil:

"Dear,—I must see you for a little while before I go. I simply don't know how I am going in the morning, but I feel if I could have you for an hour or so to myself I could go with greater courage. Dear, there is only one place I can suggest. I would not suggest it if there were any other place or time possible, but there isn't. Trust me, and come to my bedroom after the others have gone to bed. It's the only place where we can be unseen, and you untalked about. Dear, love cannot hurt where it loves. My dear, I have not sought this thing like some silly adventurer looking for a holiday romance—good God, it hurts too much. If I could be quit of it I would. No, though, I wouldn't. I don't know how it came. From the first minute I saw you, I think—with your wonderful little head and your great eyes and your childish clothes. I think I hoped to find you empty of ideas and be cured, but soon I loved your mind and your " (a word had been omitted here) "more than anything else about you. Dear, I do not fully know your ideas about religion and things, but if you see anything in this letter that needs forgiveness, forgive me. I cannot help loving you. If you don't come, I shall understand fully. I hardly know what I am writing about. My love for you fills everything. I can only stare at it. I cannot see before or behind or after it.

"H. D."

She let her hand with the note in it fall to the table-top. For the moment everything was lost in the joy of possessing it. Oh, she would go to him, as he asked. Of course, she would go. Wearied with the strain of it all she lay down upon her bed, holding the note by her side. She floated away on her thoughts, for how long she knew not. She was happy. She could not see beyond that "hour together." All the misery of the next morning's departure was hidden behind it. An hour? It would be no hour, but a long night. How could either, when the hour was over, draw away? Real and awful though she knew her love to be, the romantic aspect of this last hidden union could not wholly fail to please her. To the æsthete that must ever be in her and in Henry it was a fitting climax.

Gradually the fall in the light persuaded her to look at her watch, and she saw that it was seven o'clock. She must rise and dress. It always took her so long to dress when she was lost in thoughts. Slowly, and making many mistakes, she put on one of the "childish dresses," arranged her hair, and clasped a rope of pearls about her neck. Her cheeks had hollowed and her eyes were under-scored with darkness. The tired skin of her face she tried to make good with powder.

When she went down with her father to their table she was able to see, by one of her quick over-shoulder glances, that Henry was already seated with his sister. She had hardly taken her own chair before Elsie came up.

"Are you both coming on the trip round the lake to-night? "

"Certainly not," said Mr. Bruno. "What is it? "

"One of the steamers starts at nine. It's to be

illuminated, and there's to be dancing on deck, and refreshments. It's the very thing for a last night. Come and be really childish."

"It sounds as though it would suit my daughter—not me."

"Well, Daphne, then, will *you* come?"

Daphne was troubled. Did Henry want her to go or to stay behind? Perhaps he would like her to linger in the hotel, emptied by the steamer, and if so, she would be angry with them for having dragged her into their sickly gaieties. But since it was impossible to ask his movements, politeness compelled her reply :

"Oh, yes, I should love it. When do we start?"

"Nine, and back at eleven. It'll be gorgeous."

The dinner dawdled along to dessert and wine and coffee. And at about half-past eight the quiet air of the lake was shattered by an explosion like a gun's. An exclamation came from Mr. Bruno, and Henry walked up.

"That's a signal," said he with a smile that comprised father and daughter. "It means that the weather's favourable and the boat will go."

The explosion came a second time as he said it.

He walked to the window and looked towards the Brunnen boat-landing.

"Yes, the steamer's there; looking very fine with its illuminations. Quite a lot of people are going on board all ready. Some seem to be going independently in rowing boats. They are hanging all round it, and lighting up Chinese lanterns." He turned to Daphne. "You're going, aren't you, Miss Bruno?"

"Yes. Are you?"

"I suppose so. But I guess it'll be cold."

"Go then at once and get a coat," said Mr. Bruno to his daughter.

Daphne hurried to the lift and was soon upstairs. She selected the white tennis coat because of its memories. Then she joined the Detmoulds and Mr. Clarkson and Madeleine in the hall. The night, as they passed into it, was unencouraging. Flaky clouds had floated over the sky, and the few stars that danced between them were ineffectual. Not yet was the moon above the mountains.

Daphne Bruno

On the little boat-landing men and women of all classes were crowding to the gangway; most were hatless; some of the men were in evening dress of British, German, or French design, and their women had veils or mantillas over their heads; other people were in tweeds or Swiss National costume. On the deck, under the Chinese lanterns hung from the awnings, several couples were already dancing, excited to it by four bandsmen, fancy-dressed as Venetian gondoliers, who were jigging their bodies in conscientious gaiety.

Henry, embarrassed, walked with anyone rather than Daphne. Hatless, his hair blowing, he led the party on to the deck. Daphne walked last. There were no unoccupied seats anywhere, so they went and stood against a railing on the farther side and looked at the smaller craft, whose lanterns made a ring round the ship.

"If we can't sit down we may as well dance," said Mr. Clarkson to Daphne. "May I have the pleasure of this waltz?"

There was no escape. She took off her white coat and looked for somewhere to place it. Henry, with set lips, stretched out a hand to receive it. She went off on the arm of Mr. Clarkson, angry with him for dragging her away, and yet glad that Henry had seen her in request. In the waltz she chatted gaily, though always waiting for the moment when their arrival at one corner in the hustled crowd showed her, as her head swung round, Henry leaning against the rail and holding her white coat. The dance finished; but as all the couples clapped, the bandsmen repeated the tune and the merry jigging of their bodies. Her partner seized her again, and she was once more in the dance. Now a slight moving of the floor told her that the boat had started. Cheers came from the shore, and one of the rowing boats shot up a rocket which rained golden fire on the departing steamer.

On her return Henry put the coat round her shoulders, and she thanked him, and, looking up, said:

"Aren't you going to dance?"

"No."

At that moment a Swiss was brought up and introduced to her. He asked her in French for the next dance, and she replied: "*Oui, monsieur.*" And with the band's first notes she accepted his arm and walked back to the dancer's deck. Why she danced she could not tell; her body was exhausted and her mind fixedly miserable. Perhaps it was because the awkwardness and silence of Henry made standing beside him so difficult. And dancing was as good as thinking.

When she returned from this second dance he muttered, as if continuing their last conversation :

"I can't vulgarize what I feel for you by dancing with this crowd."

She sat down on a seat now vacant, and her head drooped. Henry stood by with folded arms, saying nothing. The next dance began and the bandsmen sang as they played. Many of the watchers who were not dancing joined in the song. In the voices of women the singing added to itself an extrinsic beauty from the darkness, the water and the foreign tongue. Daphne kept her head down, partly from the ache of exhaustion in neck and shoulders, and partly from fear of meeting Henry's eyes.

"You're looking done for," said Henry suddenly. "Come and get a strong coffee or something. Let's go downstairs to the saloon and get out of this silly jigging crowd."

She got up obediently.

"All right. It *has* been horribly cold, ever since the boat started moving."

Going in front, he threaded her through the jostling people. They went down the stairs and into the noisy saloon only to find another orchestra playing there while couples danced between the tables.

"Oh, damn !" muttered Henry. "Isn't there a quiet place anywhere?"

He ordered two coffees from the steward and asked Daphne rather fatuously, "Where are we to sit?"

"I don't know," said she. "It's so crowded, isn't it?"

"Foul !"

They wandered among the tables, but nowhere was there a place for them. And before they had decided anything the steward appeared with the two *cafés* on a tray. Henry took it abruptly from him, and walked out of the saloon right away to the stern of the boat, Daphne following. All the seats that they passed were occupied by foolish couples dallying with flirtation between the dances. Henry pushed past their knees till he saw, across an intervening bar, a platform on which rested one of the ship's boats. He stepped over the bar, and Daphne bent her head and went under. The tray he laid on the boat's seat, and pointing to the boat's side, said :

"Sit there. You're tired out."

She climbed on to the side, and this position left her crossed feet dangling. It was true she was tired out. Her body sagged as she sat. She took the coffee and sipped it.

"I am going to speak low," began Henry, "in case any of these detestable people are nearer than they appear and can speak English. . . . My dear, I can't tell what you're feeling or thinking—I simply haven't the courage to ask you for fear of learning that I've built too much on your —oh, but I'll leave that—but I know *I* never want to suffer again what I've gone through the last few days. Sometimes I've wondered what the morning of departure would be like, and how I could stand it. Often I've wished the wrench were over, and I could be away from you. I've said, ' My God, I'm glad I'm going soon. I can't stick it.' "

Her head still hung over the cup in her lap.

"You see—you see," he pursued, stuttering, "I don't know how it all happened. It's an abrupt mystery to me. I seemed to find myself suddenly floundering and struggling in a love—and it was a love such as I'd never experienced before and never expected to. . . . It stands alone, dear, in my life, and always will do. . . . I thought I'd like you to know that much in case we don't . . . lest we never . . ."

He paused long and beat with his feet on the ground.

"Often I wished I'd never seen you at all, and then I thought immediately, 'No, I wouldn't have missed this awful pain.' An idiot's business."

Daphne wanted to nod her bent head as if to show that she understood him; but she couldn't, and she didn't know whether he was looking at her or away.

"I wanted you to know something of the strength—the uncontrollable strength of what I felt for you; so that you could understand that it was something too big for me that forced me to speak. At one time I hoped it'd be enough if I just hung about near you and waited for the end. One might as well have expected one of these ghastly

Swiss waterfalls to stand still. . . . My God, I hate every-
thing about Switzerland, and yet I love it next to you.
. . . I wish I understood anything on earth . . . and what
I'm saying. . . ."

A dance must have finished, for more couples came
towards the seats the other side of the bar. Daphne moved
as if to drop from the boat's side to the ground, but Henry
stopped her with a slight touch of his hand.

"No; don't go. Please don't go. They'll only think
we're sitting out. Stay—stay as long as you can."

They stayed in silence; and when many of the couples
had returned to the deck for another dance, Henry adven-
tured his hand towards Daphne's on the boat's rim, and
touched it with his fingers. She did not move it away or
show any feeling, though at his touch the temperature of
her body fluctuated as in a rigor. His hot, trembling palm
and finger closed on hers, feeling it, pressing it.

Speech yielded to this, and many minutes must have
passed before their silence was disturbed by an excitement
on the boat, everybody crowding to the starboard side and
staring over the water. Many hurried past their retreat.

Henry muttered, withdrew his hand, and looked in the
direction of some pointing fingers. Daphne, hardly moving
her body, also turned her head. They saw that a chalet on
the side of the wooded mountain had been illuminated with
a red flare to greet the passing pleasure-steamer. The red
glow reached its most brilliant and died down, to be succeeded by a pale green flare. On the water under the trees
a rowing boat had also lit a sea-green flare, and its reflection came trilling down the surface as far as the steamer.

"It's the Rutli," people were saying in several
languages. They clapped loudly, the women with their
hands as high as their heads, hoping that their grateful
applause might reach the chalet on the mountain. A boom
from the funnel also acknowledged the courtesy. Automatically and dreamily Henry joined in the clapping, and a
laugh that was rather frightening because so mixed up with
despair shook in Daphne's throat. For a long time the
people watched the alternating lights till they had left the
chalet far on their quarter and its last red flare was like
the glow of a camp fire behind the pines.

"And there's another!" cried an English voice.

Daphne Bruno

The boat was swinging round; and Tell's Chapel, at the mountain's foot, had come into view. Its front was flaring with a crimson light in honour of this advancing boat-load of happy people. And when the boat had completely turned in its course a Brunnen hotel lit up its long façade. Again the grateful people clapped and cheered and the funnel boomed.

Henry turned to Daphne.

"You say nothing, dear. Tell me—tell me this much: does this pleasure hurt you as it does me? "

"A little," she acknowledged. Her hair was blown about in the breeze and she tried to steady and straighten it with her hand.

The flares ashore died down and the people returned to their dancing.

"Hadn't we better be getting back? " ventured Daphne after a long pause.

"Oh, no—*no*. . . . How can you want to go back? . . . The others won't even notice our absence . . . or if they do, I don't care. . . . They'll probably only think we're flirting. . . . God! *flirting!* . . ."

So the silence was resumed, he standing by her, and she sitting on the boat's edge. He did not again seek her hand. Once or twice he broke the silence. "Dear, I want to say this: I don't know what's going to happen in the future, but if—if we never——" The sentence was left incomplete. "I want you to promise never to look back upon what I felt for you and think of it as some holiday infatuation—don't profane it by thinking that. . . . I know when I look back on it I shall never soil it by seeing any folly or wrong in it. . . . It's somehow true, and I'm not ashamed of it."

And later : "Perhaps such a love is too terrible to last— I don't know. . . . I can't imagine now that it would ever end. . . . No, it never could—it must always be there in some form. At present my one wish is to have you evermore and alone. . . . You don't say much, dear."

Daphne looked up at him.

"I'm awfully tired, somehow."

"Of course you are."

Nothing more was said till he exclaimed, "We're pushing into Brunnen already. It's nearly ten past eleven."

She looked towards the shore and saw Brunnen in darkness and their vast hotel with only a few lights in the bedroom windows. The crowd on the boat was already beginning to pack towards the gangway, leaving them alone. She dropped to her feet, but immediately he stayed her.

"No, wait. Wait a little. We've hardly once been alone."

When their end of the boat was quite deserted, he put his arm round her waist and kissed her.

She could not so lie as to resist or reproach him; but she had received only, and not given. They walked towards the gangway—the coffee cups remaining in the boat unreturned, as they were unpaid for. She reflected that neither had said a word about his letter asking her to come to his room; he, doubtless because he had dreaded hearing her say No—wherefore he had kissed lest it were their last privacy; and she because she was shy of saying Yes, she would come.

They found the rest of their party at the head of the gangway and crowded down it with them. On the pier Mr. Clarkson said:

"Come along, children. Are we all here?" And he put an arm into Elsie's and Madeleine's arms and began to walk them along the road to the hotel. Elsie had thrust an arm into Daphne's. Henry walked in front, unlinked, remote. Daphne was obliged to fall into step with the other three as they hurried along to Mr. Clarkson's "Left, Right, Left —Right, Left—Right."

CHAPTER XX

WHEN she got back to her room she sat on her bed with her head down in the same attitude as she had maintained throughout the pleasure-sailing. She could not remember in all her life such tiredness. There was a permanent ache in the small of her back and on her thighs and across her shoulder-blades. Her head was confused and her eyes (she knew) were staring blankly on any object where they fell. Almost she wished she could throw herself straight upon her bed, released from the duty of going to Henry.

What a pity she was so exhausted! It would spoil her "hour" with him. Eyes shut, she drew the back of her hand across her forehead. Then she pulled herself together, stood up, and walked to the drawer where her diary was kept. Taking it out, she opened it and wrote "August 3rd." She marked the date with an asterisk, making the eight-pointed sign with dreaming elaboration, and leaving a long space for filling in details one day.

She walked on to her loggia and looked up at his window. It was alight, and he was standing on his balcony, to all appearance staring over the water, but doubtless looking obliquely at her window. Instantly she stepped back.

"He's waiting for me."

There had been, of course, a light in her father's room next door, and she would have to delay till it had been out for half an hour before she fled up the stairs to where Henry waited for her. And it would probably be a long time before her father extinguished the light, since he always read himself to sleep. She lay down to rest a little that she might not be so tired when she went to Henry. Her curtains she left apart so as to see the disappearance of her father's reflected light. When it should have gone she would get up and do her hair and powder her face again.

She had kept no count of the time when the light snapped out suddenly. Stepping off the bed, she walked to the window, but not so as Henry, were he still on his balcony, could see her. Throwing up a quick glance she saw that though he was not there his light was the one square of brightness on the night.

She went to her dressing-table and did her hair, and with the powder once more made as much as possible of her tired and hollowed face. Then she sat on the edge of her bed to wait a little longer. All this time there would recur in her mouth—on tongue and palate—a bad taste, obliging her to get up repeatedly and take a little water from the glass on the washstand. When it was time to move, she walked again to the window and saw Henry's room still the only wakeful place in the Brunnen night. She walked across the room to her door and opened it.

But courage would not come to enable her to rush along that corridor and fly up the stairs. Supposing she should pass anybody! Supposing her father had suspected something and was watching! She would wait longer. It was a quarter past one. "At twenty-five past I'll make a run for it," she said, and sat again upon her bed.

What would happen when she went to Henry she but vaguely conceived. He would throw wide his arms and she would rush into them. They would sit on a long sofa. In nothing would he hurt her—of that she was sure as she was sure of anything in life. But they would talk of the future. By coming to him she would have confessed her readiness to break with things and to take the lawless road one day. Ever in her mind were his stuttered words about the call of life and the path of danger—words in which she saw, more clearly than some, more mistily than many, a glimmer of truth. And so she thought of her rush to his room as a decisive rush through a gateway towards adventure, experience, beauty perhaps—and wisdom.

When her watch showed twenty-five past she got up and walked to her open door. She even stepped into the passage and took several paces towards the one light that burned over the staircase.

"No, I can't just yet. I'll wait till half-past. . . . . Besides, I wonder if he's given me up, now it's so late."

One part of her could hope he had done so; and for the

hundredth time, as it seemed, she walked back to her window. No, his balcony was still washed in light.

She swallowed some more water to remove the taste on her palate, and sat on the bed again, grasping her knee, to wait for half-past one. A bell from the village sounded the half-hour, and she rose and walked to the door. So tired was she that she supported herself by resting her hand on the jamb. A long way down the corridor burned the dim light over the staircase.

No, she couldn't do it. This was proving itself to her. She wasn't big enough so to break with things. "I simply haven't got the courage." Her mouth was parted as she strolled back into the room. She was too near her child-hood for such a step and too muddled. As Henry had said, one didn't solve the riddles of how to live until it was too late to live.

"Oh, but I must go. I may never see him again and he's waiting for me."

She walked to the door and was summoning courage for the rush when the passage outside seemed to creak with a step. Instantly she shut her guilty door and put out the incriminating light.

This was the end, she knew. She would not go now.

That might have been a night-porter's step, or it might have been Henry wandering along her passage, in which case she had shut the door on him, or it might have been nothing. But the creak, with its reminder of a world looking on, had settled everything. Settled everything. How much of her life, she wondered, did that phrase imply?

"I can't go now. And I think I'm glad. I'm so tired. I think he did frighten me a little with his intensity. I'll be awake at six o'clock in the morning, and wave to him when he goes; and he will understand that I was not angry with his suggestion. He mustn't think that for ever. . . . And now I'll try to sleep. It must be two o'clock."

In her night-dress under the sheet she relaxed her aching limbs and lay on her back and flung an arm on either side. She tightened the closing of her eyes, as if that would help her to sleep. But no sleep would come. Her mind would picture the past evening and the past weeks, and Henry at this moment putting out his light in disappointment. And she would tell herself, "I'm glad it's ending to-morrow. It's too awful—oh, but no, it's worth having been born to have gone through it. . . . But I wouldn't, if I could, have it cut out. . . . Oh, this can't be all. I must be destined to see him again some time. The world is small and time is big."

This last sentence, which had formed itself spontaneously in her mind, pleased her literary sense, and she repeated it to herself for her relief, thinking that in the quiet surrender to the future which it urged she might find some sleep. But sleep hung aloof. She wondered if she would ever sleep again.

It was while wondering this that she saw a huge room, partly hung with pale-blue and pink curtains—a rather sickly room, and yet it was a home that was being prepared for Henry and her—unfurnished as yet except for a wicker chair in which Henry was sitting. She walked towards him and saw that she was walking up a steep country road in England. There was a glow in the sky for a whole village was burning somewhere, and she had no desire to go to anyone's assistance, for Henry was waiting for her somewhere on the crown of the hill. Now, strangely enough, she was not dreaming about him at all—he might never have existed—a thought that was with her as she dreamt—she was laughing in a drawing-room with friends she had known, Trudy Wayne and Miss Sims and Owen.

At last she awoke; and, not at once but very soon, sickened to see the sun pouring through her undrawn curtains. Frantically she looked at her watch. It was a quarter to eight: Henry had started more than an hour ago. A chapel bell was ringing to Mass. An audible moan came from her throat and a rebel's tears rushed to her eyes. Leaping up, she ran to the window as though there were still time to see him. But there were only the mountains hooded in low clouds, and the water filmed and sluggish like a thing unawake.

A wicked and loathsome trick of Chance to make her sleep too long! A moment for blasphemies. Why wouldn't these rebel's tears that had gushed to her eyes pour out? But now she felt dry and hard. Her chief emotion was a desire to insult and injure the inaccessible gods. "Well, I must dress. It's late; it's awfully late." And her clothes immediately reminded her that it was all over—that she was on the other side of the parting. "He's gone." For a minute's luxury of despair she flung herself face downwards on the bed.

Then with deliberation she jumped up to dress and finish her packing; and the courage of it pleased her.

"I think I must be less lacking in courage than I thought. I believe that with an effort of the will I could get up and dress like this on the morning of my execution."

The words reminded her of the old game she used to play when she walked to her death inspired by the verses:

> He nothing common did nor mean
> Upon that memorable scene. . .

And this morning, dramatizing herself as resigned, controlled and brave, she dressed and closed her trunks. At her glass the whiteness of her face, the hollowness of her cheeks and the shadows under her eyes startled her. "I wonder if I'm going to be ill, as people sometimes are on occasions like this."

She ran and knocked on her father's door, and hearing his grunt, "Come in," entered to find him tying his tie.

"I only wanted to see that you were properly up," said she. "It's after eight, and I slept longer than I meant——" Her jaw dropped as she uttered the sentence.

"You would after such a frivolous and racketing night." He had looked at her in his mirror, and at once, in his tact, averted his eyes. The movement told her that he was seeing everything and filling with pity. But he was a wise student of humanity and knew that this was no moment for sympathy, no moment for observing anything at all, no moment for aught but the old chaff.

"I could hear the noise you made on the water till— well, it must have been midnight. . . . Go down and order breakfast. Get some strong coffee and plenty of it. I shall be glad of it too."

"Righto!" She was glad to be alone again.

She wandered down the great stairway, preferring its solitude to the company of the man in the lift. On the ground floor she met other guests who said:

"You're off, I hear."

"Yes," she laughed. "By the nine-thirty boat for Alpnachstad. I'd better say good-bye now, I suppose."

They shook her hand.

"So sorry you're going."

"Yes, so'm I. I've enjoyed it all tremendously. I don't want to go a bit."

She walked along with them to the office of the concierge, and saw in the little pigeon-hole marked with the number of her room a letter. Her heart jumped. It could only be a last letter from Henry.

"Is that something for me?" she smiled at the concierge.

"Yes, miss. Mr. Detmould asked me to give it to you."

He drew it out, absurdly uninterested in what he was handling, and gave it to her. She ran hurriedly with it to the privacy of the terrace where was no one but a man in a green baize apron sweeping. With shaking, uncontrolled fingers she opened and read:

"MY DEAR,—Good-bye. Think of me as one who will carry your memory with him always. The picture I shall try to see most often will be that of you leaving your tennis and coming up the path to me, as you did yesterday. I am glad I have known you. I wouldn't have missed it. I half hoped I should have seen something of you before I started, but you were very tired and slept, I suspect. It was natural, dear. Good-bye. "H. D."

"Oh, I must write to him," thought Daphne passionately, the tears now brimming at her eyes. "I must write and tell him that I wasn't offended at his invitation and didn't mean not to say good-bye."

She ran to the lounge and got some notepaper—glad that it was the hotel notepaper with the picture of the hotel on its top—and started a draft, but soon crumpled it up and started another. . . . Her father appeared, and she crumpled up both drafts and put them in her pocket.

"Ah, ten minutes exactly for breakfast," said he. "Come along, Duffs"

CHAPTER XXI

In half an hour Mr. Bruno and his daughter were on the jetty watching the boat approaching from Treib. Their labelled luggage waited by them. It was a sunny morning now that the clouds and mists had dispersed, but Daphne felt cold and at length put on the white coat which had hung over her arm. She gathered it tight about her for warmth and comfort. Often she looked back at the great hotel and the windows that had been hers and his, and the horse-chestnuts about the tennis-court, and the long terrace where they had sat in the evenings. It was a relief when the boat came alongside and they had to bustle with the crowd on to its decks. They mounted to the higher deck of the first-class passengers, and Daphne, passing the saloon and the engines down in the well, saw with a pang that the ship was a twin to the pleasure-steamer of the night before. There were the same "*Avis aux Voyageurs*" in the alley-ways, and a stairway to the deck exactly similar to that down which Henry, ten or eleven hours earlier, had taken her in search of coffee. Perhaps it was the same boat. On deck she walked straight to a seat in the stern, where she sat sideways, with her elbow on the seat's back, her face in the cup of her hand, and her eyes towards the hotel. She gathered the coat farther about her.

The siren sounded and the boat swung away from the pier. The engines throbbed and the paddles chuffed out on to the lake, while Daphne stared at the hotel to watch it recede. Fast now it diminished and lost its exactness and detail. There was a pulling at her heart and throat, and warmth behind her ears and over the skin of her face.

"The world is small and time is big. Who knows what may happen? . . . Oh, there's nothing *can* happen."

She turned and commenced to talk cheerfully to her father and kept it up for quite a while, till she felt caught in it, anxious to escape from it, and to lose herself again in her pain. Her answers became abstracted, and her father, saying something about the view from the bows, got up and strolled away, doubtless on purpose. Once more her chin went into her hand and her elbow rested on the seat's back, and she stared in the ship's wake—not at the hotel, for it had disappeared, but at the twin points of the Mythen, which could still be seen.

The boat plied from station to station along the lake : from Treib to Gersau and Beckenried and Vitznau and Weggis. Each time it left the station's pier the gazing crowd waved to the departing steamer, and the people on board, whether or not they had friends ashore, waved back. At first Daphne had no heart to wave. Then she remembered how she prided herself on her courage and waved to them regularly.

At Alpnachstad they took the train to go over the Brunig Pass. Their car was an observation car with galleries for viewing the scenery. A kindly conductor came and told them that if they wanted to see the best of the valleys and the pass they should sit on the right of the carriage. So, opposite her father, with her face towards the train's progress, she sat in her corner, her elbow on the window out of which she stared. Sometimes her father ventured a sportive remark, and she looked up and answered with a smile. Sometimes she sank so deep into the gulf of despair that she shook her shoulders and told herself she must have courage. Then instantly, at the effort of her will, all the pain would disappear, and she would want to whistle or hum. . . . But then she missed the beloved pain. It was better to suffer it than to annihilate it with the will.

So she let herself fall back, trying to see again Henry's face and tracing in her imagination the line of his hair, brow, nose and chin.

"Isn't it beastly cold?" she said to her father.

"Not at all. You're getting the first breath from the snowfields."

"Well, I feel shivery," she laughed, and snuggled farther into her coat.

To herself she was thinking, "I wonder if I'm going to be ill. Didn't Dante nearly die when he lost Beatrice? If I'm ill I hope Henry hears of it."

There were two English women in the carriage who

were discussing with enthusiasm their climbs and excursions while staying at Lucerne. Daphne listened to their talk. She envied their capacity to find happiness in scenery and strange buildings; and at the same time she was sorry for them, since their holiday had given them no such ecstasy as hers.

All the while her father's sham wall of naturalness was the very proof of his understanding; and through this humbug tacitly agreed upon, she felt the strength of his support. She could *feel* his unspoken love and rest in it. Once she even caught herself playing up to the part of a cruelly wounded girl; and it struck her as strange and horrible that in the midst of a mental pain which was the most awful that had ever come to her, she could yet be pleased with it as an object of interest to someone else— and to someone, moreover, who was kind.

There was a pendulum swing in and out of despair. Sometimes she felt she would be able to get rid of her harrowing love and that already the healing had begun; she would take an interest in the train's slow climb among the pines, with the valley far below; and then the sudden memory of some movement of Henry's mouth would make her start and cry inwardly, "Never again to see him. . . . Oh, it won't be thought. . . . I can't think it."

At Brunig the train stopped for half an hour to allow the passengers to have lunch at the station restaurant.

"I don't think I want any," said she. "I don't know why it is. Perhaps it's the change in the air."

"Well, have a good stiff *café-au-lait,*" said Mr. Bruno.

Back in the train to proceed to Brienz. She relapsed into her corner seat and her thoughts. The people on the platforms as the train arrived relieved her mind by occupying it. She studied the middle-aged married couples with their children. Too old for first love, these people; they had to exchange this emotion for the love of children. And that wasn't the same; it might be nobler, but it couldn't be so wonderful to suffer and to enjoy. None the less, she found herself looking forward to her own middle age, when all the wounds of love would be healed by time and she could smile and be gay and pleasant. Once she saw a tweed shoulder and the back of a head that gave her a stab and a shudder—it was like Henry's. But no. At that moment he was climbing towards the Furka Pass. . . . Never probably to be met with again.

At Interlaken they crossed to the Bernese Oberland Railway, and this train dragged them to Grindelwald. The snow caps and shawls of the Jungfrau, the Eiger and the Monch came into view. There was a new bracing freshness in the air. And she thought:

"I must get well here. I must drink in this tonic air and make a real holiday of my stay. I'll have some really good weeks."

They were at their station, and she jumped up, feeling quite natural and lively, with only a dull memory of some recent anguish. Immediately she drew back about her the pain she had thrown off. "Oh, not this annihilation of feeling," she told herself as she stepped on to the busy platform. "I would rather feel . . ."

"Now, then," said her father, laying down a bag and looking for his tickets. "Where the devil——?"

But she, holding her properties, was thinking, "I can't stand it. Never will I do what I've often fancied I'd like to do—what I tried to do with Roger—try to make men love me whether I love them or not. The pain is too awful. I wouldn't give it to anyone. . . ."

She followed her father through the exit of the station and up the glaring gravel path of the hotel.

She was shown to her room, and this changed place of sleeping, with its different furniture, stressed her exile from the story of Brunnen. She stood there, staring at the snow-line of the mountains. Soon the porter brought her trunks and laid them on the trestle support and on a chair. Mechanically she opened one and began to take out her dresses. Each carried a memory of some evening on the terrace at Brunnen.

Having hung them mechanically in the wardrobe, she stopped unpacking and stood again to stare vacantly before her. She hardly knew whether she was thinking or whether she had suspended thought; whether this was the uttermost despair or an atrophy of feeling. Once she heard herself saying, "O God, give me some rest—some rest from all this. . . ."

CHAPTER XXII

SHE had no address of Henry's, but that evening she wrote to the hotel at Brunnen, trusting that it would be forwarded to him somewhere. The composing of the letter gave her much mental debate. She wanted to pour out passionately all that she was really feeling—the mere phrasing of love was relief and almost joy; but the old muddle as to whether it was fair to write thus to a man who was returning from her to his wife intervened. And finally her letter amounted to little more than saying, "I never meant not to say good-bye to you." But she hoped he would read everything in her few lines.

There was a moment's afterglow of bygone happiness as she put the letter in the concierge's box. From that moment she encouraged the conviction that he would write a reply to her—just one, before the silence settled. She would stop and stand in the passages of the hotel while she deliberated where he would first be able to write and how long the letter would take to reach her.

Friday morning, she decided, was the earliest she could expect it.

Then, walking on, she would compose his letter.

Now Owen joined them from the camp at Aldershot where the Sillborough Cadet Corps had been training. He was full of the war rumours in England, and Daphne, going for walks with him, pretended to listen. Sometimes she played against him a desultory set of tennis, though the game and everything about it, its cries and its scoring, had a stab for her.

On the Friday morning, when she dared to hope that his letter might have come, she was afraid to approach the pigeon-holes in the concierge's office; and yet, by a will-effort, she walked there quickly, satisfied with her pluck. Sickness took her heart when she saw her pigeon-hole

294

empty and many of the others full. In despairing hope she asked the concierge had that morning's post been.

Yes.

She turned about gaily.

"He hasn't had time to write. Or letters take a long time over these slow mountain railways. I'll give him till to-morrow morning."

Still, at each of the other posts during the day she looked for the letter and suffered the blow of disappointment to see her empty pigeon-hole. Sometimes she would go back and look in the other holes in case her letter had been put in one of them by mistake.

On the Saturday morning she went with a sudden high hope to the place. . . . But her throat was affected and her mouth dried when again the empty pigeon-hole stared at her. There *must* be one. And she asked the concierge merrily :

"What, isn't there really a letter for me?"

"No, Miss Bruno."

And she laughed :

"Oh, what a shame !"

Walking away, she told herself that he was writing a long one and adding to it day by day.

The next morning, as nervously she approached the office, she saw that there *was* a single white envelope in her space. Her heart thumping with eagerness and terror, she said to the concierge :

"There *is* one this time !"

"Yes, Miss Bruno, there's one for you," and he took it out and gave it to her.

The handwriting was Miss Carrell's.

The August days went by, and the pain of going to the office after each post, or of returning from a walk in the hope that the letter would be there, was slowly drugged down by monotony. "He'll never write now. After all, why should he? Mine was nothing but an answer to his good-bye letter."

Only once did her control utterly fail her. It was after dinner in the lounge, and her father, Owen and she were listening to the string band. She had been talking vivaciously, almost happily, to some friends in the neigh-

bouring chairs. Then the band struck up a selection from
Tannhäuser, and the familiar tunes stopped all talk. She
leaned back in her chair and stared at a hunting picture on
the wall. The music, good or bad, well played or badly
played, was stirring up all the pain which she temporarily
trampled down. The Pilgrims' Chorus seemed the very
notes and chords of her despair. And the song "O Star of
Eve" was one of its melodies. As the tune went on
inclemently she felt her breath getting shorter and a misery
rising in her so massed and tumultuous that if it did not
burst in tears it would madden and kill her.

She got up while control was still with her, walked
across the lounge, and once outside the door, rushed up
the stairs to her bedroom. There she flung herself on her
bed, and passionately crying, kept repeating aloud, "I
don't care how soon the end comes. . . . I don't care how
soon the end comes. . . ." At intervals she would stop
her crying and muttering to think, "But no, I don't want
to die and be out of the world where Henry is. . . . I
must be in the same world as he is. . . . If only he would
die and I could die too. . . ."

Mr. Bruno had instantly guessed what her abrupt departure meant. At the end of the Brunnen stay he had
learned with surprise that the American boy whose appearance, even if it held a remarkable mind, suggested a callow
undergraduate, was a married man. And Daphne was much
in love with him. It looked horribly like the real thing.
Her request to be taken away he assumed to have followed
a confession of the boy's, who certainly struck him as a
gentil youth. He blamed neither. What was the good of
telling people not to love if they did? And now Daphne
was in the grip of her tragedy—Daphne suffering! He
must go to her. He mustn't leave her to writhe in it
alone. But he didn't know what to say. Now that he
came to think of it he had never spoken seriously to her
in his life—always behind a veil of banter. "I can't get
through to her. I never have been able to get through
to her."

In the applause after the orchestra's finale he rose from
his seat, saying to Owen, "Keep my place for me, old
man," and walked upstairs. The passage and door of

Daphne's room frightened him, and for a long time he strode up and down wondering what he was going to say. What could he give her of comfort and advice? Though he had written forty books, he had no complete and rounded code of living. And of religion, nothing.

Well, there it was. He knocked on her door. No answer came, though he heard a quick movement inside.

"Daphne."

She did not reply, and he walked back along the corridor, abandoning the task. But at the head of the stairs he stopped.

"No, poor darling, I must go in and see her. I shall find something to say when I'm there."

He walked slowly back, and without knocking, turned the handle of her door. It was unlocked and he stepped into the room. He saw Daphne in the long easy-chair, sitting sideways, her heels drawn up under her, her elbow hanging over the arm but bent to make a support for her head. Her hair was tumbled and falling, her shoulders shuddering.

"Duffy, my darling!"

She did not move, but now her shoulders steadied as if petrified.

"Duffy, what's the matter?"

He was annoyed with his feebleness. How could she answer such a question?

"My dear. . . . I know all about it. . . . Daphne, I can't bear to see you suffering. . . ."

She raised her head and looked up at him, admitting all in a sentence.

"Daddy, how do people stand it?"

What answer could he give to that? The child ought to have some religion—some stay—some hope. He stood there awkwardly with two fingers of his right hand pushed into his waistcoat pocket. Then he began to walk up and down as he struggled to express for her the few things that he believed.

He had searched nature in vain, he said, for a God of pity. All that he was able to see was that *men* had pity. Pity for all things . . . and amazing courage when God or nature was showing no pity to them. And

in spite of modern thought-waves, the unshakable conviction was still with him that men were only at their
best and happy when they were yielding to their pity.
Or, of course, when they were summoning a defiant
courage about them and lifting their heads above their
trouble.

"I'm trying, dear, to give you the minimum of religion
that I have found, and perhaps you'll be able to build more
on it. It's rather a rebel's creed, I'm afraid. It amounts to
saying that men, because they have pity and unconquerable
courage, are greater than God, Who seems to have no pity.
. . . And then I think, if that is so, let us glory in
transcending Him. Let us at all costs keep these things.
. . . I don't know how far I have kept them myself, but
I should like you to. . . ."

His daughter smiled her affection through her tears.

So much of a general code he tried to give her. In
meeting her present need he felt he was happier. Daphne
was staring at him as he spoke with interested eyes. To
begin with, said he, she was much, much better off than
many, because her love had apparently been returned. Many
had loved as passionately but without requital, and had
survived. It would be futile to tell her to cut out her love,
but what she must do was to transmute it. One could
transmute a suppressed love into two things : into service
of others and into art. Didn't Dante transmute his love
for Beatrice into his "Divina Commedia"? So his love was
always with him and always expressed.

"You used to want to write, dear. I hope you will.
You'll find that much of what you are suffering now will
escape into that, and it will be ever so much better than it
would otherwise have been. Remember, there have been
little housemaids in London who have had to suppress their
love and have had no mind to understand these things . . .
and yet they have endured and survived. . . . But I'll tell
you one thing that you must guard against. Books and
Art are very great, and no life is half a life without them ;
but they are apt to become a fixed idea, excluding everything—unselfishness and all the rest. And so you get *set*
as selfish, and only occasionally a kindly impulse in you
shows you what you might have been. . . . So the
remedy, I feel, is to get this other idea equally fixed—

the idea that there is no happiness apart from pity and
service. . . ."

His daughter had risen and was standing before him.

"Daddy, I always think you're wonderful. . . . Don't
—don't tell Owen anything about it, will you? "

He passed his hand over the back of her head, aware
of moistened eyes.

"Don't suffer too much, my Daphne. I can't stand it."

Daphne shook her head and smiled confidently.

PART IV

THINGS AS THEY ARE

PART IV

THINGS AS THEY ARE

CHAPTER XXIII

A DAY in September Mr. Bruno and his children came again to the little garden of firs. The news from South Africa had been such that he preferred to be in France with a view to winding up his affairs there in the event of an early return to England. And Daphne was glad to be out of Switzerland. She had not been able to bear the conversations of guests who mentioned places associated with Henry—the Urirotstock, the Rutli, the Furka Pass, the Mythen. All mountains hurt her.

On the doorstep Miss Carrell greeted the family, inquiring of Daphne:

"Have you had a nice holiday, dear?"

"Absolutely ripping," said Daphne.

And with this sickening lie she carried her wooden despair into the house.

A wooden despair it was, these first weeks. She would take her memories with her on lonely walks in the Montmorency Forest. Its autumnal lights pierced her. She made a pilgrimage to the grave of Geneviève Rollier in Taverney Churchyard; and now more than ever did the tawdry wreaths and the words "A Mon Epouse," "Nous ne t'oublierons jamais," inflate her to pity. She really felt, as her father had encouraged her to feel, an infinite gentleness towards all the world.

"You can't reach to pain fully," said she, remembering some words of Henry's, "till you have suffered yourself." And she was aware of a little pride in her suffering.

She set to work again upon her book "Madame Rolland." There was a whole reservoir of manuscript to be distilled into some last shapely urn. But now, as she studied it—on the other side of her great experience—it seemed shallow, light, unfelt, *invented*. "Invention's the very opposite of creation," Henry had said; and this minute she saw its truth.

The clearer parts of her brain told her brutally what she ought to do. She ought to scrap every bit of this stuff, even though it were the product of two years' brain-bullying, because it had been written when her angle was all wrong, and would only go lumpy and formless if she tried so late to infiltrate it with truth. More, since Henry was always correct, she ought to postpone writing for publication till she had read much more and learned something of "the best that had been thought and written throughout the ages."

But could she do this? Could she scrap it all and postpone, even abandon, the thought of fame? No, the old Daphne of three months ago was too strong to be shed at once by this new creature of selflessness and consecration. She would refashion the book to meet her truer measures, but she must keep her eyes on fame. Next year, or the year after, she must make her little stir whose ripples would reach to Henry.

So she struggled on with "Madame Rolland," though sensible of compromise and conflict. The sceptic in the corner kept protesting, "In spite of me you're heading for one more blunder."

Another subject, besides her book and her settled sadness, found a small welcome at her door. This talk about war in South Africa—it was always dramatic. The letters of Owen, who had returned to Sillborough, were full of it. It was thrilling to read each morning in the English or French papers of the Boers' impudent ultimatum and the British Government's haughty refusal to discuss such terms; of the threatening mobilization in the Orange Free State and the calling out of the reserves in England; of the last dark summoning of Parliament. But this interest was mild compared with her interest in her book. It occupied about the same relation to "Madame Rolland" as a bright little grocer's boy, calling every day, occupies to the mistress of a house.

This grocer's boy, however, came in and sat down in the best room during the days when war was declared. The English papers were better than any drama now, with their huge pictures of Sir Redvers Buller in his cocked hat, about whom she had misgivings because his chin receded, and of that old darling Oom Paul Kruger, who, with his curtain-fringe of beard and chimney-pot hat, was so ugly as to be perfectly sweet. The French papers, with their abuse of the English, were things to be read; and in a moment of patriotic fervour she was anxious to shake off the dust of her heels on such a rude country.

"I vote we go," said she to her father.

And her father shocked her by saying cold-bloodedly:

"But my sympathies, I'm afraid, are rather with Oom Paul than with Tant Victoria."

"Daddy!" she exclaimed, after a shriek of laughter at such a name for the venerable Queen, "how can you say such a thing? You're not a pro-Boer."

But all he did was to smile and murmur, *"Et tu, Daphne."*

"I don't see there's any *Et tu, Daphne* about it. You can't think they're right."

"Neither side's ever perfectly right, dear. But that's no reason why the big man should start to pummel the little fellow and kick his posterior. Little men are always self-assertive or nobody'd notice them much. . . . However, the damage is done. And now it's for us to wonder how long our house and our lives will be safe among these emotional French." (Mr. Bruno knew there was nothing in this alarmist suggestion, but could not resist uttering it. His difference from the ordinary panic-monger was his ability to stand outside himself and laugh at his own delight.) "Supposing they burn our house about our heads."

"Will they really? How ripping! Is it going to be as exciting as that?"

"Who knows? The French are without some principle of balance. However, I shouldn't talk to Miss Carrell about these things; and certainly not to Hollins. Panic is a light sleeper in minds that have never been properly *trued*."

"Oh, no, I won't" promised Daphne, proud to be held of stabler make than Miss Carrell and Hollins, and impressed (as often during talks with her father) at the enormous number of defective people in the world. She was struck, too, at his originality in being a pro-Boer, and wondered whether to learn up the part and be one herself.

"Besides," Mr. Bruno concluded, "we shan't be able to keep up these two homes. No one'll buy any books."

The early and continued successes of the Boers, however, alienated his sympathy from them. It was as if he felt they were going too far. And one morning, on finishing his perusal of a smashing Boer victory, he turned to Daphne and said, "Well, dammit, I think we'd better win now," which relieved her considerably. Then they prepared to return to England. On a day in December, after the incredible defeats at Stormberg, Magersfontein and Colenso, the trunks of the Brunos were packed, labelled, and standing in the hall at St. Leu.

Daphne went for a farewell walk along the roads of the forest. The trees were quite bare, but many of the dead leaves still littered the paths. Though mid-afternoon, the sun-rays, slanting through the boles, had the sad effulgence of evening. Her random progress led her as far as the Pont de Diable and back upon her tracks. It was on this homeward stroll, just as she was nearing the edge of the trees, that she was abruptly withdrawn from her inward thinking by the sight of a man approaching her. The cut of his black overcoat and his height suggested that he was English. On his perceiving her he quickened his steps. It was Roger Muirhead surely. Yes, it was he; and tall and handsome he looked. He was now smiling recognition, and she replying with questioning eyebrows. That he had come in search of her was manifest, and the thought could only please. A rapid wonder passed by her mind: was she to be given at last the opportunity of saying, as she had always wished to do, "It's no good, Roger. I don't love you"? But now, in her dominant gentleness, she had lost the desire to say it. He mustn't be hurt like that. Not more than was inevitable. Less, much less, were it possible. . . . And while she thought these things she was smiling at him with questioning eyebrows.

"What on earth's produced you in these parts?"

Roger lifted his shoulders and looked embarrassed.

"Oh, I was in Paris . . . and thought I might as well

look you up. Your people at the house told me you were here, so I said I'd come and look for you . . . as I've got to go back to Paris almost at once."

"It's awfully nice of you."

"Oh, no, it isn't. . . . At least . . . Oh, I'd better tell you the reason why I've come. (May I walk back with you?) What do you think it is?"

"You've just said: to see us; to see some English friends who happen to be in the same strange land as you are in. I always find that people whom one would hardly know in England, if one meets them in a racket of foreigners, are one's best friends."

Roger gave silence to this as he walked by her side, and she feared she had hurt him more than she meant. So she hastily added:

"It's topping to see you."

"No—no—I . . . Duffy, it was to find you, and you only, that I came." Her heart throbbed. "I wasn't really staying in Paris. I left England on the impulse of the moment last night, and I shall have to get back to-night."

She said nothing, but walked on with him, occasionally kicking at the dead leaves.

"Duffy, I've been in love with you ever since you appeared at that ball. No, please let me go on. I—I'm sure you were meant for me, because each time the first sight of you has been enough to make me fall in love with you. That blasted waltz—I've been humming it ever since, on purpose to work myself into a sad condition."

"But——" she began.

"No, please let me go on. This is what made me come out. I've joined Sinclair's Horse, and I'm going to South Africa almost immediately. I expect my orders for the front any day now. It's all been perfectly glorious except—well, I've been dreaming how splendid it would be if I could go out engaged to you. I can't bear to think of anyone else walking off with you in the meantime. . . . So I resolved to charge straight at it. . . . Duffy, if we were engaged I should be able to write to you. And——"

"Roger, I'd give anything to be able to do what you ask, but I—I can't——" The words "I don't love you" should have come here, but she would not say them. The way of gentleness was to remove his castle brick by brick, not to shatter it at a blow. "I'll write to you, however, regularly. . . ."

They walked on, she diverging him towards an opening in the trees, for he seemed unconscious or indifferent which direction he took. He must speak next; and it was a while before his answer came.

"Oh, Duffy, I know I've jumped it on you rather, but I was forced to, wasn't I? Do take that into consideration, and—I mean, it's a time for deciding things quickly and not spreading them over their usual period. I feel sure— I *know* you're destined to love me—you *did* once—and I don't believe—I never have believed that you are absolutely without feeling for me now. Little things made me think——"

After all her indifference, of which she had been so proud, these words came as a sharp temptation—a temptation to say, "You're as wrong as you can be. I've no trace of love for you"; but she held them back. Sometimes it wasn't easy to be gentle. . . .

"Duffy, do say you will be engaged to me."

"I can't, Roger. . . . We don't know each other well enough. . . ."

"Exactly. I've never had a reasonable chance. I've only had two spells of acquaintance with you. And the very way we've been forced apart each time makes me think we're intended for one another. I believe that a fate waits for every man and that you are mine."

"Roger, you're incurably romantic, aren't you?"

This never offended him.

"Perhaps I am, if it's romantic to believe that. All I know is that I love you with all my heart and soul."

"I'm awfully sorry, Roger . . . but I can't do what you ask. . . . I wish I were able to."

They were now out of the trees and walking down the slope to St. Leu. The nearing of the houses prompted Roger to say despairingly :

"Well, if you can't go as far as that, will you promise not to get engaged to anyone else till I come back or am killed——? "

"Roger, you mustn't be killed. Don't say that."

He scarcely listened to her interruption.

"Duffy, promise me you won't get engaged to anyone till I come back. The war can't last long. If we don't wipe up a few Dutch farmers in six months we shall be a poor set. Wait till I come back so that I can have the chance of a run with the others."

This was the humblest thing he had said, and it went to her heart.

"There'll be no others," she murmured.

"Of course there will be. As I told you once before, there'll always be heaps who want you. That's what makes me mad. . . . Throughout the journey here I was in mortal dread lest I should find you already engaged; and when I glanced at your finger just now and realized you were still unwon I believed in my fate again."

"Roger, you must get that idea out of your head. . . . It's a little sentimental, isn't it?"

This was to put it a different way. To be called romantic was pleasing, but to have his love and his faith dubbed sentimental had clearly injured his pride.

"Does that mean you won't promise me anything?"

"I am afraid so. It wouldn't be fair."

"All right." His face, as she always phrased it, had "tightened." They were at the bottom of the hill, and he put out his hand. "Well, good-bye."

"Come and have some tea with us," she said hastily.

"No, thanks. I must get back."

He took her hand coldly, and after a glance at his watch, murmured something and moved on in front of her. She watched him stride a little way and then, unable to let him go like that, ran hurriedly after him.

"Roger," she called.

"What?" He stopped and turned.

"I don't want you to go like that."

He smiled his wry smile.

"Well, there's no other way to go unless you do what I ask. And I'm not going to pester you for favours. I don't do that sort of thing easily. . . . You're the only person in my life I've ever humbled myself before. I shouldn't have done it if this war hadn't forced my hand. After all, I've kept this to myself for nearly two years."

"But Roger——"

"And I don't ask you to be engaged to me, but only to

309

wait till I come back, so that I may have a fair run with the other fellows. It isn't much. The war won't go on for ever. Besides, I should be invalided or wounded sooner or later; or killed, which would relieve you of your promise."

"Roger, don't talk like that. If you'll promise not to think there's much chance of our ever getting married I'll promise to do what you asked."

"Duffy, you will?" There was almost a note of triumph in his voice. "Oh, thanks . . . thanks awfully. It makes all the difference. You may call me romantic, if you like, but I shall feel now as if I were fighting to—to win through to you in spite of everything you say."

Having allowed a faint haze of falsity to arise it was useless to try dissipating it now. Best continue being kind.

"And you know you are not really bound to go by the midnight boat. Come back and see the family. It's all returning to England to-morrow, and you can meet us in Paris and look after Miss Carrell and Hollins as far as London, while I look after father."

He met this with his grim smile; and, chatting naturally, though sometimes she caught him staring at her in admiration, they walked back to the house.

Roger's visit and request were at least flattering, and she wanted to tell someone about it. Especially since he had been such a success on the journey to London and had looked magnificent. Her father she could not tell, for he had seen her moving on her tragic plateau, and would feel that those who walked up there should walk above vanities. Miss Carrell? Was she right in suspecting that gentleness forbade unnecessary brag to Miss Carrell about offers of marriage? There was Hollins. She must tell Hollins. And in the evening following the day of their return to Old Hall House she begged the old servant to come and sit in the playroom and mend her stockings there. For twenty minutes she discussed a miscellany of topics, awaiting the propitious moment. And when they had reached the voyage of yesterday she asked:

"What did you think of Mr. Muirhead?"

Hollins pursed her mouth at the hole she was darning.

"Not much. I went to the door myself when he come, and before he could speak I thought, ' He's English.'"

They look quite different, don't they? They look gentlemen. But this one struck me as having rather a sort of condescending tone, if you know what I mean."

"Do you know what he came for?"

"He said he happened to be around and knew you but not the master, so I sent him after you."

"You didn't know what you were sending, did you? If I tell you what he really came for will you promise not to tell anyone?"

Hollins, perceiving the glimmer of an interesting revelation, laid down her stocking. What it was she probably had no idea, still thinking of her young mistress as a schoolgirl.

"Of course I won't say anything if you tell me not to."

"He came to ask me to marry him."

"Miss Duffy! Good gracious! . . . But I never knew there was anything between you. I never see him before. Good gracious. . . . I'm sorry I said I didn't quite take to him, first go off, as you might say. It was only his manner, and I suppose it was natural for him to think I was an ordinary servant. . . . Lord. . . . Miss Duffy!"

"Don't get excited. I refused him. . . . But I *did* promise not to get engaged to anyone else till he comes back. He's going to the war, you see."

"But he isn't a soldier, is he?"

"Not professionally. He's Sir Roger Muirhead's son."

"Then what's he want to go out there for?"

"Oh, a lot of men besides the regulars are going now."

"Are they? I don't know what they're up to. Aren't there enough soldiers? It seems we're getting beat everywhere. Well, I hope your Mr. Moorhead'll teach them Boers a lesson. They appear to fight pretty dirty, waving white flags and all that."

"Oh, I think that's largely made up."

"Oh, no, it isn't. I see it in the papers yesterday."

"Well, the French papers tell a very different story."

"They *would,* 'ating us as they do, and being a race of liars, as far as I can make out."

"Personally, I rather admire the Boers and think they're putting up a jolly plucky fight."

Hollins took up her stocking again with an unbelieving smile and a shake of the head.

Daphne Bruno

"No, Miss Duffy, that won't ᴅo. You ain't a pro-Boer, as they say. One can't hold with English people as says the other side is right. Not that I ever met any who did, and I don't believe they're proper English at all. But lor! to think of that young gentleman asking you to marry him!" This was obviously the more interesting subject to her. "To think that all that sort of thing's beginning. . . . Why, it seems only yesterday that the bell rang and the noos come to your father as how he'd got a little daughter. And then when your mamma asked for you to be brought to her, before she passed away—it don't seem twenty years." She stopped her darning to scratch her head with the needle. "Funny you're not in the least like her. She was fair and small and timid like. Lor! I remember I used to say that with your eyes you'd soon have the young men hanging around. And now it's comin' to pass. I used to say your eyes is your trump card. . . ."

"Yes, but they're the only trump I've got," grumbled Daphne. "Otherwise I've a putrid hand."

"It don't look like it, do it?" smiled Hollins, "seeing that there's been one after you before you're twenty. And such a handsome one, too." She folded up the completed pair of stockings and pushed her wooden ball into the heel of one of Mr. Bruno's socks. "What I always says is, Life's a funny business. The noos come that you'd arrived at that there horrible home, and you're brought to the hall door, where I met you carried in; and then time passed with cooking and washing and mending, and you in the house growing so naturally that one hardly noticed your growing at all or worried about it—and now you're going to disappear out of the hall door into another life. Seems strange somehow."

CHAPTER XXIV

THE papers now filled with pictures of Field-Marshal Lord Roberts, who was to proceed at once to the command in South Africa, and of Lord Kitchener, who was to be his Chief of Staff. Of Lord Roberts Daphne had never heard, but she thought his moustache and imperial rather sweet. Lord Kitchener, on the other hand, had been one of her schoolgirl heroes at the time of his return from the Sudan, and she was jealous for him that he should not be in supreme command. Lord Robert, in comparison with Kitchener, was just a toy of an old man, such a one as she always called "a poor little soul." "Still, generals of that sort are often very pure little men," said Daphne comfortingly.

Owen returned from Sillborough for the Christmas holidays, and after the feast spent a mysterious night in town. The next evening he apologized to his father and sister and announced that he had joined the Imperial Yeomanry. He expected to leave for South Africa any day now.

Mr. Bruno muttered a mild oath, but was not displeased with his son.

"I can't say I believe in your war, colonel," said he, "but as my good friend Nietzsche puts it with some originality, 'It's the fighting halloweth every cause.'"

"Lor' bless you, I don't believe in it either," Owen disclaimed. "I only think it's jolly decent—like sin. . . . Don't you?"

As for Daphne, she succumbed to a really bourgeois pride and sentimentality about her brother. Ever since he had shot up six inches above her and could lift her out of a carriage lest her dancing shoes were soiled, she had promoted him to a worldly superiority over herself. It was extraordinary how boys, who were such miserable fowl at ten years old, developed into something much more competent and assured than yourself. She was as excited as he about sleeping-bags, bandoliers, revolvers, grey-coats, field-glasses, riding-boots and badges of rank. And it was a pleasure to write to Roger that her brother Owen was following him and was in the cavalry, so it was possible they would meet.

Roger had left for Cape Town very soon after his hawk-swoop on Daphne in the wood. He wrote regularly and more and more affectionately. It was plain that the loneliness and woman-hunger of soldiering had heightened his love, and that he was picturing her now as much more wonderful than she was. These letters, so courteous, reverent, and yet breathing in every line an impassioned love, raised in her a great tenderness towards Roger, an emotion very different from the humble worship which was her love for Henry.

This was always present: if not actually in her thoughts it was very close, behind a semi-transparent veil. If the veil thickened, making Henry for a space a well-nigh incredible memory, and herself ashamed that her love could quiet so, it needed but the appearance of his figure in a dream for her to awake and find the wound open, aching in sharp air. Or she would look out of her window at night and see the English clouds shaping themselves as mountain ranges, with two points, perhaps, like the points of the Mythen; and immediately any hardening ground would be painfully broken again, and wild sentences arise, "I can't live without you, Henry!" "I *must* have you, Henry!"

This pain swelled her tenderness to Roger; and when he wrote begging, "Please, *please* send me a photograph," she determined to comply; and determined that it should show her at her very best—or better than that. It might be the last picture he would ever see of her. She went to the most expensive photographer's in Brighton, and on the arrival of proofs, opened them eagerly. They were too wonderful—*perfect!* As she studied the picture, large and softened in the latest style, she was (as she said) "astonied, and there was no more bitterness in her." It was she—and yet it was the ideal of her; it was her own dream of herself that she had failed to realize. The longing was in her mind for Henry to see it. Still, there was happiness in sending it off to Roger, and thinking of his joy in its possession, and imagining it on his camp-table throughout the war.

On a May afternoon she rose from her writing-place with a glow of lonely triumph, such as that experienced by Gibbon when he had completed "The Decline and Fall of the Roman Empire." She had written the last word of "Madame Rolland." Whatever happened to this manuscript, she had actually written a book—a story with a beginning, a middle, and an end.

Whether it were good or bad, she could not decide. A few parts she felt sure were splendid, of a great many she feared the worst.

What to do with it now? She could not bring herself to show the manuscript to anybody before sending it to the publishers. Her father she had always meant to surprise by its publication; Miss Carrell was a nonentity, and Hollins, if she struggled through it, would certainly say it was beautiful. And having shut herself within herself of late she had no very intimate friends. Mrs. Montague Jevons was abroad. If only Henry could have criticized it! But her book, she knew, would have been quite different then. Desiring only to earn his commendation, and indifferent to the world, she would not have compromised.

Over what name should it be sent to the publishers? Her own she would have liked. "Daphne Bruno" sounded an author's name.

"But, no. If it's as rotten as I sometimes think it, I should let father down. Besides, it might go a bit on his name, and that I don't want."

"Helen Gilder" was her final concoction. "'Madame Rolland,' by Helen Gilder."

Now the manuscript had to be typed. There was a lady who did typing in Haywards Heath, where she had a little office over a shop in Boltro Road. It would be very pleasant walking the two miles there with the manuscript under her arm.

Half an hour later she was in the office of Miss Elsie Troon, typist, and saying with a mixture of self-consciousness and vanity:

"I want this typed, please; and what is the very soonest I could have it?"

Daphne Bruno

Miss Troon, a stout blonde, was quite unmoved at having an author in her office. She looked at the manuscript, giving Daphne an uncomfortable moment as the title page passed beneath her eyes, estimated the number of words, and named a date.

"I should have liked it before that, as I have got to send it to the publisher's reader as soon as possible."

This sounded excellent, and was reasonably true.

Miss Troon, her blood still unwarmed, promised to have it completed by a day earlier, and Daphne departed, carrying down into the street an anxiety lest any disaster overtook the manuscript while it was out of her hands. Apart from this anxiety, her walk home was very happy, and her sense of work completed made it seem like the first evening of a holiday.

When the day came to fetch the typescript she was almost as excited as if she were going to see her book in print. But she showed no emotion to the phlegmatic Miss Troon, not even examining the work before it was packed up. And in the street, with some idea that Miss Troon might be leaning out of her window and watching, she refrained from undoing the parcel till she was round a corner. But thereafter she walked home along the town and the country road reading it page by page and occasionally walking into other pedestrians or the hedge. It was very well typed, and seemed to have shed some of its amateurishness with this change of dress. Certain corrections she made with her pencil, standing in the middle of the road or with a foot on the hedge.

Her scheme was to send it to the most important publishers first (avoiding her father's lest they recognized the owner's name) and work downward to the smaller people. It was rather thrilling, composing a letter to the firm; writing on the fly-leaf of the typescript: "Property of Miss Daphne Bruno, Old Hall House, Wivelsfield, Sussex," and then making up the parcel. The last knot tied she went out and posted it.

"I only expect to get it back. Of course, I must expect to get it back once or twice."

The first time it returned she took the parcel from the postman's hand with a steady face, and the hope that he would not observe her heightened colour and slight abstraction. She carried it into the playroom and redirected it, with a new letter, to the second publisher on the list. Every morning she watched the postman coming up the drive, and on a day three weeks later saw in his hand the parcel of unmistakable shape. The third time, she was out when it came, and found it in the hall, on returning from a ride. It was a day in July, and the anniversary, so her diary told her, of one of the most intimate conversations with Henry, under the mountains at Brunnen. The fourth time she saw it again in the postman's hands; and lest he should begin to suspect what it was and know her for a humbled failure, she ran out and joked with him as she took it from his hands.

The fifth time it stayed away so long that she thought she might write for information, and did so in a very courteous letter.

"It'll reach them to-morrow morning, and I ought to get an answer the next day after breakfast."

That next day there was, surely enough, a letter for her with the publisher's imprint. This set one's heart going fast and awkwardly; no parcel, just a letter alone. With quivering fingers she opened and drew out the typed sheet.

"Dear Madam (it said),—We desire to thank you for giving us the opportunity of reading your novel, ' Madame Rolland,' but after carefully considering it we have regretfully decided that we cannot make you any offer for its publication. We are therefore returning it under separate cover. . . ."

She tossed down the sheet with the words, "All right, I'll send it to the next, and you'll be sorry some day."

This much of comfort she tried to suck from the letter, that they had taken long to make up their minds. But the sceptic had another view; he hinted that they had not read it at all and, on receipt of her inquiry, had returned it by the next post.

That winter and spring she sent it to three or four more publishers, directing it each time in a soulless, automatic way, entirely without hope, but liking to tell herself that she hadn't given in. She wrote nothing else, and read little.

317

Daphne Bruno

Ambition had drawn into a shell and was hibernating there.
Careless now to whom she submitted it, she tried a Mr.
D. J. Stendal, whose advertisement she had seen in a corner
of a weekly paper. Beneath its tabulated titles it had
added, "Authors Invited Submit Books."

His reply came a week later. It said that Mr. Stendal
was interested in her work and would like to see her at
some time suitable to herself, either at his office in Queen
Victoria Street, or, since he would be in Brighton that
week-end, at the Old Ship Hotel.

Now her heart beat to a tune of high hope again. Ambition leapt from its shell as if it had never been torpid
at all. From Mr. D. J. Stendal's crested paper and offices
in Queen Victoria Street she conjectured that his house
must be in no small way. And Mr. D. J. Stendal was
coming himself. Did this mean that her book was so good
that the head of the firm was prepared to wait on her?
Or was it—was it that Mr. D. J. Stendal, despite his note-
paper, had less standing than—she hurried to look again
at his advertisement. It was certainly a very small advertisement, giving the titles of some poetry books by writers
with unfamiliar names.

Less excited, but still pleased that someone was prepared to publish her work, and fortifying herself with the
words, "Beggars can't be choosers," she wrote that she
would be happy to interview Mr. Stendal in Brighton.

Monday was the day assigned; and it was an April
afternoon, warmer than any that had gone before so that
the spirit of holiday was along the Brighton front, when
Daphne pushed open the door of the Old Ship Hotel and
asked at a counter for Mr. D. J. Stendal.

"He's expecting me," said she to the attendant, wondering if he knew Mr. D. J. Stendal was a publisher, and
would guess her to be one of his authoresses.

While a boy in buttons went to look for her host, she
watched the people as they came and went, and vaguely
pitied them their flat occupations or commonplace holiday.
Not one of them, probably, was at the verge of exciting
things.

"Mr. Stendal's just here, miss," said the returning boy;
and he led her to an ante-room where he pointed to a little,

clean-shaven, sharp-featured man, in a blue serge suit, who was staring out of the window at the sea-front. On the table beside him was an empty cup of coffee, its saucer littered with cigar ash. A disappointingly insignificant little man—but then, what about Lord Roberts. "Let's hope D. J. is just such a pure little man," thought Daphne.

"That's 'im, miss."

Mr. Stendal turned from the window as she drew near and rose.

"Ah, Miss Bruno, I imagine, Miss Daphne Bruno. Yes. It's exceedingly kind of you to give me the opportunity of discussing things with you personally. Won't you sit down?" He smiled. "You're even younger than I thought."

With the quick sensitiveness of an author Daphne wondered what this meant.

"Am I?"

"Yes. Well, you don't mind my cigar, I suppose?—well, we've all read ' Madame Rolland ' with interest, and on certain considerations have decided that we should like to publish it for you."

The "We've all" reassured her; evidently the firm was not small. But it was a shock to hear the title rendered in English as "Maddum Rollend."

"Yes," she said inquiringly.

"' Helen Gilder ' I see you call yourself. I wonder why? "

"Oh, I made it up."

"But why, when—or p'raps you didn't want the name confused with the great Tenter Bruno? "

Daphne flushed.

"Not particularly."

Mr. Stendal now looked out of the window, which had the effect of bringing into the ante-room the sounds of horse-traffic and the footsteps of passers-by and the shrieks of children.

"You're not any relation to him by any chance, are you? "

"Well, yes," said Daphne, with an awkward smile.

"Oh, *relly?* " Mr. Stendal's eyes came away from the window and looked straight at his visitor, whimsically. "Relly? This *is* interesting. Not his daughter, by any

319

chance? Of course, he lives this way, doesn't he? Not his *daughter?*"

Daphne nodded, very red. And Mr. Stendal's eyebrows were surprised and delighted.

"Well, relly. I *am*—I count this interview a great privilege. Yes, and now I come to look, you're not unlike some of his pictures. But why, Miss Bruno—why, with a name to conjure with like yours, don't you publish under it? Your book has a charm, an innocent charm, that pleased me, but "—his lips compressed, as his head shook doubtfully—"the difficulty always is to start an unknown author. You can't get the necessary publicity. And no book, however good, can do much without that. With your father's name we could at least get notice taken of it. We should—I might say, we should be honoured to publish ' Rollend ' for your father's daughter."

"Yes, but that's just what I don't want."

The sensitive Daphne's heart was drooping at the thought that her work was not really good. Doubtless the great houses who only published work on its merits had rightly turned it down. . . . But no, she wouldn't think that. She would believe in it despite everything. It was not that she was a fool, but only that she preferred to be.

"Why don't you want it, Miss Bruno? "

"Because I want it to go in its own strength . . . and father knows nothing at all about it."

Mr. Stendal smiled sympathetically—knowingly.

"I see—I quite see. I quite appreciate your position. It's to be a surprise, eh? . . . And may I ask if—you'll forgive me, I'm sure, for no lady minds being considered younger than she is—may I ask if you're still a minor? "

"Does that mean, am I twenty-one? "

"Yes."

"I was twenty-one last February."

Mr. Stendal smiled benignantly.

"Dear me ! What it is to look sixteen ! You see, you need to be over twenty-one if you're going to sign an agreement. In your own interest I mentioned it."

"Agreement? " Her brows furrowed.

"Oh, yes, there's always an agreement between publisher and author."

"I didn't realize that."

"No? Well, it's quite a simple matter. . . . Now, as regards terms. You mustn't expect to make a great pile of money with your first book."

"Oh, I don't," assured Daphne.

"No. Especially when it's without any particular sting. The great houses find it difficult to sell seven hundred copies of an unknown writer's book. . . . Myself, I make quite a feature of publishing the work of young writers—why, I can't say—they appeal to me, perhaps. But, as I expect you know, it's generally poytry I publish. Now, in the case of poytry, which is even more difficult to sell, the author generally contributes towards the cost of production, and after a certain number have been sold, he begins to get a royalty on each copy." Mr. Stendal smiled benignly. "Now, I don't propose to ask you to contribute anything. Nor do I propose to buy your copyright for a sum down— I always think that's so unfair—if the book was to go, I might make hundreds, while you'd only get your small sum." He then told the stories of several famous novels which had made thousands for their publishers and nothing for their authors, and Daphne was astonished; many of them were books she had read. "Yes, it's pure roguery, isn't it?" nodded Mr. Stendal. "Well, what I suggest is that, after you've sold a thousand copies, you get a royalty on every copy of ten per cent. of the published price. I shall be losing money till I've sold something in the neighbourhood of a thousand copies."

"It sounds all right," smiled Daphne.

"I might even, if you sold, say, five thousand, raise the royalty to fifteen per cent."

"Oh, thanks."

"Yes, I desire to be perfectly fair. Well, now the question of name. I quite appreciate that you don't want your father to know anything about it. If it's a success, you want to be able to tell him that Helen Gilder is relly Miss Daphne Bruno. Whereas, if it isn't a success, you needn't say anything."

"Yes, that's it."

"Quite so. Still, may I suggest that you publish it anonymously? Anonymous books sometimes cause a good deal of talk and speculation—which helps them considerably. Now 'Rollend' is a slight book—very nice as far as it goes—but it can't afford to do without these adventitious aids. ' Helen Gilder ' will do it no good at all. Anonymity might help a little—nothing much, but a little. 'Tenny-rate, I strongly recommend it."

She agreed to this, and, a little later, the conversation terminated in amiable chaff from Mr. Stendal, and the assurance, at the door of the hotel, that he would forward the agreement at once.

Out in the sunshine of the Brighton front her thoughts were a mixture of disappointment and exultation, misgiving and hope : disappointment at the qualified praise of Mr. Stendal and the faint aura of doubts that hung around his person ; exultation because her book would at least be printed and stand on her shelves, which was more than any of these people in the carriages or on the pavements had achieved ; misgiving lest the critics laughed at her work, and hope that they might pronounce it very good.

"I wish I knew if it were good or bad. However, I won't let myself expect it's going to do anything big. . . . But, of course, it's quite possible it might be good and catch on. And then . . ."

She gave herself to the more pleasurable business of imagining the sensation in the papers and the surprise that would be sprung on her father and Owen and Roger. Roger, being an ambitious person, would hardly suspect that she also could do a noisy thing in the world. Probably, though not admitting it, he would be a little jealous. And if it were a success, and published in America, under its author's real name, and Henry saw it !

CHAPTER XXV

OWEN and Roger wrote frequently. They had met at Krugersdorp, as both reported in their letters :

"I struck Roger Muirhead's crowd the other day," said Owen. "My dear, Roger's a great man. He's doing things properly. If you can conceive an amalgam of the Iron Duke, Frederick the Great, Cromwell and Halifax, that's Roger. He's the sort that says : ' My men may fear me, but I think you'll agree they'll follow me anywhere.' I really believe he imagines the British are in the right and the Boers in the wrong; though Heaven knows why. And did you know he was religious? But he is. He never fails to take his men to church if there's a parade. It seems the old boy, his pater, is a tremendous churchman; though, again, Heaven knows why. I blew into his tent, and on a box beside his bed was the same photograph of you as you sent me. Is he still smitten with you, or how did he get it? I'm sorry I don't like him if *you* do. I'll try to; but, honestly, I think him at present rather pompous and superior. He must always disagree with you lest, by agreeing, he should appear to be less than you. I can look into his head and see his motives hopping and popping about, just as if his skull were made of glass, which makes me think I must inherit some of your dear father's insight. But he may grow out of these things. He's very young. And I must say he never misses a chance of being wounded or killed. He's either unco brave, or so ambitious that he's ready to be killed if only he can do some enormously brave deed and have it trumpeted all over the world.

"Love to father, and tell him I met a British officer the other day who had read one of his books. Love to Miss Carrell and dear old Herbert Hollins.—Your hero brother,

"OWEN BRUNO."

Daphne, reading this letter, was more annoyed with Owen than critical of Roger. It was irritating that her

Daphne Bruno

brother should sit in judgment, and contemptuously, on a man who had asked her to marry him.

"After all, Owen, just as much as Roger, has created a character that he tries to live up to—the humorous, cynical young man. . . . When he's been through some pain "—this she thought with a little pride—"he'll be more generous."

Roger's letter had come by the same mail:

"I met your young brother the other day. He's a curious kid. He always seems to want to laugh at everything. I think I've got as much humour as most men, but I like to believe there are some ideals worth holding. If he doesn't believe we're doing a decent job out here, what on earth has he come for? I am afraid I was rather rude, but I can't stick it when people try to make out that every country and every class and every school is right except their own, and I am afraid I'm apt to speak my mind sometimes. It's not as though I was a Tory without an idea beyond my own interests. Like father, who's one of the few capitalists who have ever stood for Liberalism, I'm a Liberal, but I believe in this war and came out to it, though many of my political friends cried shame on me for doing it. . . ."

Now she was annoyed with Roger. "Owen's right: Roger's egotism leaks out everywhere." And even as she said it she remembered that all her thoughts for the last year and more, while men were dying daily on the veldt and the British armies, after an echoing humiliation, were only recovering in a long-drawn tussle, had been concentrated on herself and her desire to do something big.

"I doubt if there's much to choose between any of us; everyone I've had anything to do with has lived in a self-created rôle; Miss Durgon, old Miss Vidella, Miss Sims, Daddy, Roger, Owen and myself. Henry, I believe, did it least of all. Or his rôle was a better one; of itself it destroyed the play-actor. . . . Roger must think me rather a fool, if he imagines I don't see all these things. But ' Madame Rolland ' 'll make him open his eyes."

And then, one morning as she was casually opening the paper, she found herself looking straight at a portrait of Roger. Quick self-reproach hampered her heart; she feared he was dead. It beat again with relief and excitement when she saw beneath the picture : "The Hero of Wittfontein. Lieut. Roger Muirhead, whose heroism is reported on page 5."

Eagerly turning to page five she read under sensational headlines a column in honour of Roger. It was usual enough in those days to see the exploits of English officers illuminated and stressed till they seemed Homeric ; but few had given the journalistic imagination a better opening than Roger. It rushed in a torrent over his deed and lapped worshippingly about his feet. He had been in command of a small post at a place called Wittfontein, which lay across the line of Hertzog's raid into Cape Colony. He and his "handful" of men had been attacked by a large force of Boers who had expected to sweep them up in a morning's work before proceeding to the main column advancing on Britstown. But Lieutenant Muirhead thought differently. Nothing else would satisfy him but to remain undefeated behind their raid, or to delay them by resisting to the last man, while his commanding officer got wind of the position. So all day, though wounded in shoulder and knee and faint with loss of blood, he had crawled among his men, revolver in hand, stiffening the resistance of this "tiny Ladysmith" and refusing to give up the place of command. The enemy had actually abandoned all attempt at capture, although when the British relieving force arrived at the Wittfontein post, *not one of its defenders was found to be without a wound*. Mr. Muirhead was by this time unconscious. The men, now that the Boers had cleared off and left them victors, were in high spirits and full of praises for their officer. Some of their remarks were quoted. "Doubt if we could have done it without him." "He's severe enough, but he don't tell no one to do what he wouldn't do himself." (What music to Roger's ears must this sentence have been !) "He was bound to do something big if the war went on long enough, and he didn't get himself killed."

A thought so unworthy had stirred in Daphne's mind that, in order to drive it back and refuse it foot-room again, she jumped up and rushed into her father's study to find more papers and more accounts of the Hero of Wittfontein ; she took them for proud showing to Miss Carrell and Hollins, and she hurried to her table and wrote to Roger. "Oh, Roger, I'm thrilled. It's wonderful to be your friend." This was expiation, because for a moment she had felt jealousy and disappointment that Roger had achieved his fame before her.

The papers during several days gave space to Lieut. Muirhead. They reported his improvement in hospital, gave a summary of his life, and spoke of his desire after the war to enter politics.

Daphne wondered if his head would be turned, and could not expel the thought that, now he was so big a man, with the world at his feet, he might see fit to drop her as he had done once before. Perhaps the interval between his letters would increase till they stopped altogether. He was in no wise pledged to her. But his next letter, under a base hospital address, began : "My dearest Duffy," which was a phrase he had never employed hitherto. What emotion, in the glow of his triumph, had impelled its use ?

The early part of the letter was studiously occupied with ordinary details of his life; but they were only like a creeper on its real structure, which said :

"You will, I suppose, have heard of the scrap at Wittfontein. I can't think what they are making all this fuss about. It was, of course, a nasty day, but we had to fight whether we liked it or not. The only alternative was to give ourselves up, and that isn't done. I had no use for handing over my weapons and the weapons of my men to the Boers. Hundreds of others would have done what we did and been mopped up. We were saved, and therefore everybody hears about it. And as for all that talk about my keeping command when I was wounded in the leg and shoulder (they might have added the thigh and wrist as well), what could I do? We were surrounded, and I had nowhere to go and get into bed. And I didn't fancy seeing my sergeant take over command as long as I was in my senses. The men were distinctly cock-a-hoop when the Boers melted, and most of the puff in the papers is due to their generous enthusiasm.

"However, I dare say all this praise will please the pater and mater, so I am glad of it for their sakes. But I am still happier if it pleases you at all, because you are more to me even than them. Duffy, I have wanted all the war to do something big, simply to seem worthy of you. And dearest (forgive me for writing that word, but I feel I must, and it can't hurt you), when I first got into hospital feeling frightfully low (emotionally exhausted, I suppose) I made sure I was going to die; and all the time I thought of you as I found you in that wood or left you on Victoria Station, and I didn't want to die, for I wanted, at any rate, to be in the same world as you . . ."

Daphne's eyes moistened; these were words she had used in her thoughts of Henry.

". . . When I picked up that divine photograph from the table beside me I simply longed for you. I would try to imagine you coming through the door into the ward. And when I thought I might be sent home, I was lifted to the seventh heaven at the thought of seeing you within a measurable distance of time.

"I only tell you this because it is proof of how much I love you. If I have achieved any sort of fame, I am happy because I have got something to offer at your feet. I want to say this, Duffy : if you have yet learned to love me, and feel you could marry me, I should love to consider myself engaged to you, and should be only too happy if you cared to tell everybody that we were engaged. But, if not, well, I shall understand, and I expect I shall be home soon enough to plead my cause better."

"Poor, dear Roger," said Daphne, moved. "You thought I'd like to proclaim my engagement to you just now when your name is on everybody's lips. I think it was sweet of you to offer me the chance."

She laid down the letter and walked to the window. Who could say?—had Switzerland never happened she might have learned to love him. He was a little egotistical and pompous, but so was she and everyone else. It *would* have been nice to say she was his *fiancée,* and to have all the papers seizing on to it. And now she mustn't hurt him by too final a refusal.

She spent a long time phrasing her reply :

"My dear Roger,—Honestly, I am awfully proud of your last letter, and think everything in it was splendid of you. I certainly like you better than I have ever done, but not enough to say I'll marry you. You see, I haven't seen very much of you. But it's ripping to hear you are coming back soon. . . ."

Like a moving staircase time carried her towards the date of "Madame Rolland's" publication. Excitement fought with timidity, now uppermost, now under, but generally winning. Often she scanned her father's literary papers, hoping to find a preliminary notice. She saw none, but though disappointed, was not angry. If the story were a success there would be plenty of notices of her next book. The night before publication she took her secret to bed with her, where it kept her pillow hot and her body restless.

With the day she rose and hastily dressed, in a desire to be down before the others that she might separate for herself a few minutes with the newspapers. An advertisement might be there, and possibly one or two reviews. Of course she would not expect big advertisements like her father's—just her book in a column of other titles.

It was a mid-week day bringing several papers and journals. One by one, having found nothing, she laid them by. When the last was abandoned empty her shoulders shrugged and her hand dropped to her side.

"All right," she said resignedly, hardly knowing what she meant by the words, and added : "I think he might have put in a small advertisement."

Restless throughout the day, she decided to go where there were bookshops that she might see if "Madame Rolland" were in the windows. Brighton, of course. She escaped from the house and took the train. And in Brighton she wandered from book-shop window to book-shop window, seeking in vain the cover or the back of her book. At last, thinking desperately that she must have some encouragement to go on with, she entered a shop to ask for "Madame Rolland" over the counter.

It was a nervous business when the young man inquired her needs, and she had to utter the title of her own book.

"Have you a copy"—she coughed, and cleared her throat—"of ' Madame Rolland '? "

The young man shook his head.

"No, miss. Not in stock. Is it an old book? "

"No, no. I think it's published to-day."

"Is it? We haven't heard of it. Who is it by?"

"Oh, I think it's anonymous."

"Indeed, miss? Who publishes it?"

"Stendal. Mr. D. J. Stendal."

The young man bowed, and said nothing. Obviously he did not like to admit that the name was unfamiliar. Daphne, by now, though sanity told her it was nonsense, was apprehensive lest he thought her the authoress, and had no desire beyond getting out of the shop. But not too quickly, or she would confirm his suspicions.

"Yes, D. J. Stendal," she said again.

"Well, we can get it for you, miss, in a couple of days."

"Oh, don't trouble. I'll try to get it elsewhere. Thank you so much."

This inquiry she repeated at every bookshop, and always with the same result. One man, indeed, did find the book mentioned in a list sent out by Mr. Stendal, and she had the satisfaction of seeing "Madame Rolland" in print on a slip of paper.

"Perhaps you'd like to keep that list, miss," said the man—innocently, it was to be hoped.

"Oh, thanks. Well—yes—I will."

She passed out into the crowded Western Road, carrying Mr. Stendal's list. After a few hundred paces her thoughts were disturbed by a strong smell of coffee that seemed to rise from the pavement, and she found herself opposite an Oriental café. It was tempting. A cup would remove the parched taste from her mouth, and the gathering tiredness in her head and eyes. She climbed the stairs to the first floor, and sat at a table by the window. Here she sipped her coffee, or rested her face in her palm, as she watched the carts and buses and pedestrians below.

"It looms so important to me," thought she, "that I can't imagine how microscopically small it is to all these people and everybody else."

Hope sprang afresh next morning when six presentation copies arrived; and in the next weeks she trusted to see some advertisement or review in this paper or that. But nothing could she track till one day, as she was walking on Ditchling Common, a carriage passed her, and Mrs. Montague Jevons immediately stopped her coachman, and

Daphne Bruno

hailed Daphne in a sentence that gave her a leap of delight.

"Hallo! Hallo, hallo! Like father like daughter. I see you've written a book."

Daphne blushed agreement. "Yes, I'm afraid so," and for the sake of something to add, asked: "But how did you know?"

"Oh, I've just read an announcement of it!"

"Have you?" said Daphne—languidly, to conceal her eagerness. "Where?"

"In the *Daily Telegraph*. Just a small notice."

"Oh, I haven't seen that one. To-day's?"

"Yes, this morning's."

"I must look at it. Father's got it. . . . Was it kind?"

"Very. . . ."

As quickly as suited with her mantle of dispassion, she got away from Mrs. Monty and hurried home to see what the paper had said. The *Telegraph*. This was excellent, for the *Telegraph* was an important journal. Only when she was half-way back did she think: "But how did Mrs. Monty know that I wrote it, seeing it's anonymous?" The question stopped her dead on the road. Had it then leaked out that she was the authoress? This might be good news, showing that discussion had played around the book. Or had Mr. Stendal—now her indignation began to rise—carefully divulged her name, in order to stir up talk and stimulate sales?

When she had the paper in her hand, it was a long time before she could light upon the notice. She was looking for a small head-line, and perhaps half a column of criticism. There was no such thing, though one swept the paper three, four, and five times. At length, in a few inches devoted to announcements, she found the lines:

"We understand that a novel published recently, ' Madame Rolland,' is really the work of Miss Daphne Bruno, the daughter of Mr. T. Tenter Bruno. The book has been selling well, the publisher, Mr. D. J. Stendal, informs us, but this interesting news has stimulated the demand."

On the whole she was pleased. The statement that

the book had been selling before the revelation of its author-
ship counterbalanced her anger with Mr. Stendal. But she
was glad that the paragraph was small, and not likely to
be seen by her father, or too many friends. Not yet had it
been declared good, and only if it were good did she want
people to know of it. So she began to get incensed when
she saw in the chatty column of that evening's paper an
extraordinarily flippant paragraph headed, "Following in
Father's Footsteps"; and another, though this was dignified,
in the *Evening Advertiser*.

The constant repetition of her father's name reminded
her of something she had quite forgotten : all of these
paragraphs would be sent to him by his press-cutting agent,
and would probably be on his breakfast plate the day after
to-morrow. If they were, she would not be able to face
him. She would run. Pray that he didn't leave his study
to-day, and meet anyone who would enlighten him !

The well-known envelope of the press-cutting agent did
not appear, however, till three days later. When Daphne
saw it, she went out of the house without stopping for any
breakfast.

She walked along the road towards Haywards Heath.
The impulse strengthened to go up to town and demand
an explanation from Mr. Stendal. She was spoiling to be
rude. The slippery little beast ! Yes, and now that she
was fairly successful, she stood in a new relation to him.
She could tell him what she thought; and she would. All
the way in the train she was framing her insults. They
held allusions to solicitors, and "steps" and adequate
apologies.

In Queen Victoria Street she had difficulty in finding the
offices of Mr. Stendal. Mr. Stendal's number seemed
to be occupied by the headquarters of a patent knife-
cleaner. Then, at the side of what she had supposed to be
a private door, she saw several brass plates; and one of
them, under the heading "Third Floor," read, "Mr. D. J.
Stendal, Publisher." Walking nervously but resolutely up
the dark, iron-bound stairs, she vowed that if the clerks,
as seemed possible, brought a message that Mr. Stendal
was engaged, she would push past them into his private
room.

Arrived, rather breathless, at the third floor, she walked

Daphne Bruno

along a dark passage till she saw a door on which was painted, "Mr. D. J. Stendal." Being called to come in, she turned the handle more timidly than pleased her, and entered a bare, littered room, long enough to hold three tables, at one of which sat a youthful girl-typist, at another a shock-headed man with a stoop, and at the third little Mr. Stendal himself. On deal shelves round about the walls were files, iron boxes, and stray copies of books published by the firm.

Mr. Stendal, recognizing his visitor at once, rose and said pleasantly:

"Ah, Miss Bruno. Mr. Bates, this is Miss Bruno, you know, who wrote 'Rolland.'" He did not introduce her to the typist. "Please sit down."

And he removed some papers off a chair and courteously placed it for her.

Daphne was disconcerted by the presence of other people, and stuttered:

"I rather wanted to see you in private a minute."

Mr. Stendal smiled gaily.

"Well, we haven't another room. But you needn't mind Mr. Bates. He and I really are Stendal's, so I couldn't have a secret from him, if I wanted to. That's so, Bates, isn't it? Do sit down."

She sat down.

"You want to know how your book's going on. Miss Dale, look up 'Rolland,' and see what the figures are, will you? Thank you."

Daphne interrupted.

"I didn't come about that. I wanted to know how it leaked out that I had written it. I especially stipulated that it should be published anonymously."

"I know you did. Or rather, you wanted it published under an assumed name. And you will remember that I recommended anonymity as more likely to stimulate interest. Well, it turns out that I served you well by that bit of advice. You see—to tell the truth—we sold nothing—practically speaking, nothing at first. I don't think we had any orders, did we, Miss Dale? And I thought that, as you had entrusted its publication to me, I had best do all I could for you. So Mr. Bates, who sees to the publicity department, sent round a paragraph—didn't you, Bates?—

and we were delighted the way the papers took it up. Not many, but one or two important ones. I grant I did it on my own authority, but you will appreciate I had your interests at heart. I think you will forgive me when you hear that our manœuvre has created quite a demand; small, of course, but good—distinctly good for a first novel. The shops and the libraries have both bought. What are our sales now, Miss Dale?"

"Twelve hundred."

"Excellent. Twelve hundred copies, Miss Bruno, sold right out. That means we've topped the first thousand, and are now in the second when you get the ten per cent. royalty."

Daphne started to speak, but Mr. Stendal hurried on:

"And what's more, it's really getting noticed and reviewed. Did you see the little notice in the *Times* this morning? And those cuttings that came this morning, Miss Dale; pass them to Miss Bruno to see." He took them from the typist's hand, and gave them to Daphne, who accepted them limply. "There. You can keep those. We've made a selection of quotable phrases—haven't we, Bates? We're advertising the book next week. I hope we may sell at least two thousand copies for you."

Daphne could scarcely say anything, being driven by the desire to get away. The news that the book had sold nothing until the mention of her father's name had been the final blow after a week of buffeting. The sting was taken from her studied insults. She was near to crying, and it must not be done before these people. But something—something that would hurt must be said.

"I told you I had not come to hear about the sales. I am not interested in them. What I am interested in is the explanation why a definite promise to me was not honoured. I see you have no explanation. I must speak to my father about it. He understands these things better than I do, and will instruct me what steps to take."

"Precisely! Exactly!" said Mr. Stendal enthusiastically, though there was a peep of a forked tongue in his enthusiasm. "He will appreciate exactly what we have managed to do for you, considering the—er—the slight nature of your book. He knows the conditions of publishing, and the necessity of all reasonable publicity. And he will see how we've kept strictly within the terms of our agreement."

Daphne moved towards the door, but turned on him and said :

"I think he will appreciate very little of all that, not being a perfect fool. He will appreciate that you have considered nobody's interests but your own. He will certainly appreciate that you have kept within the terms of the agreement, for that is what one would expect from people like you. I imagine it's not too safe for you to venture out of cover. . . ."

Mr. Stendal smiled, as one does when managing a restive pony, and seeing that Daphne was fumbling for the handle of the door, hastened to reach it first. He opened the door courteously.

"There now. We won't lose our tempers. I think you're a little ignorant about the difficulties of putting a book across—the competition, and all that. Especially one that is really nothing out of the ordinary. Believe me, we are doing the best we can for you, and shall continue to do so. Certainly it is in our interests, and in yours too. Good day, Miss Bruno."

In Queen Victoria Street Daphne walked along, purposing to mount an omnibus that would take her to her station, but letting them one after another pass by, as she accompanied her angrily-running thoughts. Still in her fingers were the press-cuttings Mr. Stendal had given her, but, dreading the lash, she determined not to look at them till seated in her train. A gloomy journey that would be, carrying her to the interview with her father. And when she was in her corner seat she waited till the train had actually started before lifting the first and reading it.

"The work of a famous writer's daughter must always be interesting," it said; "one seeks to learn how far the talent of the parent has been transmitted to his children. We cannot say that we are impressed with the work of Miss Daphne Bruno. It is quite undistinguished, and there is no precocious genius here. Her ignorance of life is naïve in the extreme; that, of course, is very pardonable in a young writer, but what is stranger in her father's daughter is her absence of literary palate."

Daphne, who had been setting her lips as she read, was pierced with a fear that this sentence told the truth. Henry was right. Not having read one-hundredth part of the books which the ages had pronounced to be good, perhaps she did *not* know what was true loveliness and what was bad.

The next review echoed the thought:

"A first effort, especially from the hand of a distinguished writer's daughter, invites indulgence, and we shall hope one day to congratulate Miss Daphne Bruno on a better work than ' Madame Rolland ' (Stendal). Let it be said at the start: this is the work of a completely immature writer. We wish we could have added that it was full of promise. But Miss Daphne Bruno has certainly not revealed her promise yet. Were the word not too hard, we should describe the treatment as illiterate, not in the sense that it is grammatically wrong, but that it is the work of one only slightly familiar with great literature, and whose values are therefore false. But let this not deter Miss Bruno from try- ing again after a long intercourse with those writers whose genius is no longer on trial. We imagine that she will then be the severest critic of her first book. One remembers the early work of Shelley, and will be slow to deny promise to any young writer."

"Oh, please don't be kind," said Daphne, as she put this cutting away.

The other reviews agreed; that was the worst—they agreed. They called the work "commonplace," "inno- cent," "shallow," "superficial." Having read the last she sat looking out of the window, her trouble increased by the sudden memory that since nearly all these cuttings men- tioned her father, they would have been in his hands since the morning's post. There was nothing to do but to go straight to her execution. In her mind hovered the old lines, their pronoun changed to meet her case:

> She nothing common did nor mean
> Upon that memorable scene . . .
>   But bowed her comely head
>   Down, as upon a bed.

Daphne Bruno

Mr. Bruno met her in the hall, having seen her come up the drive. His irritability, obliged to simmer all day, was anxious to boil over.

"Where on earth have you been since before breakfast?"

"I've been up to London."

"London? Do you mean to say that you run up to London when and how you like?" Knowing a pang of self-reproach that she should be so unshepherded, and finding the thought ill-timed, he submerged it in anger. "Well, I might have known. It's on a par with everything else. Just come in here a minute."

He led her into his study where the press-cuttings were on the table. Lifting them up and tossing them back again, he demanded:

"What's all this about a book you've written? Why on earth didn't you tell me something about it and get my advice?"

"I wanted to surprise you."

Mr. Bruno again smothered the pity, and made a gesture of impatience.

"Stendal? Who the dickens is Stendal? Why, I know most of the publishers by name, but I've never heard of Mr. D. J. Stendal. Some Vanity Publisher. Nice to have any of my name linked with a firm like that! I suppose he made you pay for the privilege of being published?"

"No, he didn't. I'm getting a ten per cent. royalty."

It was annoying that, while she stood there looking up at him with eyes that were rather frightened, compassion should gain ground from anger. He wanted anger to hold its own.

"Well, are you such a little fool that—can't you see that for your work to be published by a house of no standing is itself enough to damn it. . . . These Stendals and their like only bind up stuff that no one else'll print, for conceited amateurs to circulate among their friends. He only took yours for nothing because he thought that . . . Couldn't I have advised you about publishers and agreements? . . . But I suppose you have no faith in my advice."

"I wanted to do it by myself."

"And you've ended by doing a ridiculous thing. and,

336

incidentally, though it's a small matter, making me appear ridiculous."

"Oh, I didn't want to do that. I said all along I didn't want to let you down. That's why I published it anonymously."

"Anonymously? Then what's all this about?"

He lifted up the cuttings.

"Mr. Stendal deliberately let it out, to make the book sell. I've just been up to tell him what I thought about him."

At this point anger capitulated. He sat down in his chair, and after tossing the cuttings to the back of the desk, turned round towards his daughter.

"Poor child! Doesn't it show how you ought not to have attempted anything without advice?" One of her hands he picked up. "And did you really think you could assault the world with the few arrows that have so far arrived in your quiver? I fancy you must learn much more about books and men. Don't you see that, if you want to compel the world to listen to you, you must convince them that in some respects you know more than they do?"

"What about the Brontës?"

"H'm. . . . Well, Charlotte only came off when she was writing about what she knew—which wasn't often. And the sheer genius of Emily——"

"Well, I'm your daughter, so perhaps I'm a genius like you."

"No, I am not a genius, Daphne dear—only a brain trained and tempered for its work. . . . Besides, this is a more sophisticated age than the Brontës' age. . . . Stands Fiction where the Brontës stood? . . . I wonder some humorous editor hasn't sent me your book to review."

"I don't want any more reviews. I hope nobody writes another word about it. I wish I'd never published it. I wish I could wipe it all out."

He pressed the hand he was holding.

"Poor Duffy! They *have* hit it rather hard, haven't they? But they're an ill-conditioned race, critics."

"Daddy "—it was evident an idea had struck Daphne—"would *you* read it? You're the only critic whose verdict I should consider final."

"Would I read it! Why, to tell the truth, I've been

aching to ever since I heard about it. I'll read it now. Where is it?"

"I hid them upstairs. . . . But you'll promise to tell me exactly what you think, and not try to let me down lightly. An awful lot will result from what you say."

Releasing her hand he told her to run and fetch it.

When she returned, he rose up to meet her and took the thin volume. After studying its shape and print, he went to the book-shelves and, pushing a squad of books towards the right, made a place for this newcomer next to the last of his own works. For a few seconds he studied it in this position, and then took it out again and came back smiling to his daughter, whom he drew against him and kissed.

"I am proud you've started writing too, my dear—which is a remark I might, without loss of dignity, have made earlier. Come now, it's not a small thing to have a book published at twenty-one."

The tears were in Daphne's eyes.

"Oh, but they didn't do it because it was good, but only because I was your daughter. I know it. I know it. And I know I've made both you and me look foolish."

"No, dear. Only to fools. Besides, let me read it. Your court of appeal may reverse the verdict."

Daphne sat upstairs till dinner time, unable to read, for she was trying to imagine whereabouts her father was now in "Madame Rolland." After the first bell she went down— why softly she did not know—and quietly turned the handle of his door. He was no longer reading.

"Have you finished it?"

"Yes, dear."

"Well?"

"You want exactly what I think, as though you were nothing to me?"

"Yes."

"Duffy, young writers always think they can write about people or places or emotions of which they know nothing. It can't be done. Once in your story you strike a vein of truth, and though you have over-written it, the truth can still be seen, and is not a little appealing"—he turned his eyes back to the book. "It's in your love-scenes. And

338

there's a glimpse of vision, promising much despite all these critics, in the episode at the grave-side. But the rest, I'm afraid, is machine-made, which is what they mean by calling it 'insincere.' The result is, you get sentimental, forcing emotions where they would not have been. And there's too much gratuitous ornament, whereas in a perfect work of art ornament and structure are one and the same."

Daphne nodded.

"All that's a long way of saying it's mostly bad."

"It's the work of your prentice hand, dear. . . ."

"Oh, don't let me down lightly. I understand." She turned towards the door. "Come on, let's go to dinner."

CHAPTER XXVI

SOMEWHERE she came across a quotation : "Regretting not yesterday, nor fearing to-morrow." Like a reveille, it called her to that defiant courage of which her father had once stuttered to tell. The reiteration of it braced her like a tonic. "I don't regret yesterday, and I'm not going to fear to-morrow." She was going to begin again. And this time she was going to begin right. She was going to cut out all vulgar ambition, and all imitation of others, and the indolence that prevented her from reading aught but the easy and pleasant. "This time I shall do what Henry tried to make me do. In fact, I shall write for an audience of one—Henry. Or two, perhaps—Henry and me. I shall write what he would have approved. To that end, I'm going to study not only books, but men. Daddy said I must do that, too. So, as soon as possible, I'm going to get out of this cloistered existence and experience the world." It was an inspiring notion. She could feel glad about all that had happened, for it seemed as if one thing in her life—and that the most important thing left to her—was purged of its alloys, and in its direction trued.

Though two years had passed since she had left Henry, she had no real doubt of her love for him. Certainly his figure had gone behind a curtain before which she could dance and laugh and play her part, even sometimes stopping to ask herself, "Have I then ceased to love you, Henry?" but the thought of him was always hazily present, and often, very often, he emerged vivid and solid into her dreams, and she who had questioned her love before would wake up with her sadness, and be satisfied with it.

But *his* love, what of that? For a long time she had dreaded lest it had faded. Surely it must have done. She had been so disastrously ignorant in those days, so *illiterate;* and her beauty was something in which she had never believed. Why should Henry still care to remember her?

Of course, he had said on the ship that night: "Don't profane my love by thinking *that*." But anyone infatuated would have believed so much. Since her good-bye letter he had never written. What was there to show that his passion had stood the test of years? She would never know if it had; for notwithstanding her oft-repeated words, "Time is big," she did not really believe they would ever meet again.

Still, she loved. Quietly, and without wreck. She had just idealized him in her memory. No doubt he had had faults, but she had never seen him except in the rapture of love; she was surprised how little she knew of his real character. To her he was now the idealized portrait of one who would have understood her dreams, guided her work, and received the full measure of her love.

"I am going to reach through to him with a book. It may be twenty years before it is published—it may not appear till after my death; but one day it'll get to him."

So now to work unremittingly, and to live abundantly.

Lowered to a complete self-distrust by the unthinkable press-cuttings, she began her studies with "An English Course for Middle Forms," "The Story of Ancient Greece, Simply Told," Saintsbury's "Short History of English Literature," and "An Introduction to Philosophy." And the initiation of this reading, especially the brain-teasing philosophy, pleased and flattered her. As she pursued it she could almost feel the refining of her brain, and the strengthening of her ratiocination. It made her think of a flower that was opening late.

She had continued to write to Roger, whose return to England had been delayed, and his replies had spoken no more of love, though their tenderness was as implicit as ever. And now he surprised her with a letter sent from London, saying that he had arrived, and, at his request, was to be transferred to a convalescent home at Brighton. "I shall have all the days to myself. Couldn't I meet you, say at Ditchling, on Thursday?"

This letter, in the days of her rejection by the world, filled her with pleasure. She felt affection, nowadays, for anyone who had always liked and admired her. And in the rush of her enthusiasm she wrote:

"Of course. I'll meet you there where first we met. Isn't that out of a song? On the King's Highway, where it runs across Ditchling Common, by the bramble bush. At three o' the clock."

Hesitation, before she sucked the envelope, asked: "Haven't I been a bit too gushing? Offering to meet him like that in that sentimental place. No." The flap went down irreparably. "I've let him do all the gushing so far, and now he's come back I ought to make a fuss about him. . . . I've been mighty high and proud all along, and Lord knows I had nothing to be stuck up about."

This lifted the memory that she had hoped to dazzle him with her fame, and once again the words of the shattering paragraphs troubled her breath, but she recovered herself by repeating: "I don't regret yesterday, and I don't fear to-morrow."

Soon she must give to Roger her final answer, "Yes" or "No." It surprised her that, though she did not love him, the idea of being engaged to him was full of thrills. Or did the thrills lie in just being engaged, rather than in being engaged to Roger? . . . Not altogether.

She must think it out thoroughly, and not let her nature gallop her into any more blunders.

Let her get her motives into the light, one by one. To assist clearer thinking she took an empty postcard and pencil, and drew a bisecting line, printing FOR on its left and AGAINST on its right.

For? She sucked the pencil, pushing it far back on her tongue. She would be perfectly frank with herself. Recent rough handling, like recent reading, had polished away a cloudiness from her brain.

The first and lowest motive was the desire to be an engaged person, with all the notoriety it brought, and the snub for any who had laughed at her.

This she refused to note on the card. But she doubted if this disciplinary refusal amounted to writing it out of her nature.

Secondly, she would rather be married than an old maid. She *liked* Roger, and would never be in love with anyone else, because she was in love with a memory. A girl didn't always get a second chance, unless she was exceptionally beautiful and fascinating. Already she was over twenty-one.

She wrote "Not O. M."

Thirdly, if she married she would rather be rich than poor. Roger's was a splendid offer.

She wrote "S. O."

Then she wanted opportunities for full and varied living. Who more than Roger could give her these? Think of the fun it would be, fighting political battles by her husband's side, and if he got on (as he certainly would, being the sort), what might she not see of government and pomp; diplomacy, intrigue and the pageantry of Courts?

She wrote "Life."

Then, of course, she wanted to experience caresses and passion, and was not displeased to find that, after the idealization of Henry, the thought of Roger's embraces were more stirring to her than those of any man she had ever seen or could imagine.

She was in some doubt what word to write here, for "Love" was not the true word, and "Passion" was crude. She put three dots.

And what really was her attitude to Roger himself, apart from his position and all that he could give her? He was such a magnificent creature that she would be enormously proud of him as a husband. And she wanted to marry something big, not "a poor little soul." His little poses she could always forgive; indeed, she would have to, whomsoever she married, since she had never met a man who wasn't decorated with them.

She wrote "Very proud of him."

Examining these tabulated reasons she was appalled at their selfishness, and sucked her pencil again, while she thought: "But isn't there some motive which is a bit nobler?" She knew there was, and it came into the light. That creed of gentleness, which her father had offered, had been saturating her nature during the last two years, and the disillusion of recent weeks had helped it on its way. Strange how mixed one's motives were! There was joy in the thought that since Roger loved her as passionately as she had loved Henry she would save him from her suffering by giving herself to him.

For this item she wrote, "Not to hurt."

Daphne Bruno

On the AGAINST side she could only write, "Not real love."

But if she waited to write different from that she would never marry.

There was the position. Now one could only intermit thought, and wait for what would happen.

On the Thursday afternoon she dressed with care. Wisdom told her that she had to compete with the famous photograph, and that its beauty was now to be regretted, for it enlarged her deficit. But her glass, before she left it, assured her that if she came second in the competition it was no such dishonourable second.

Anticipation trembled in her as she passed through the "toll-gate" on to Ditchling Common. She had but to turn the curve in the road and she would probably see Roger. She saw him, walking up and down by the blackberry clump, and waved a hand. Immediately he advanced towards her, and she studied his figure as that of one who *might* be her husband. Roger had no photograph to contend with; now that he was older, wider, browner, and perfectly dressed, he was even in excess of her thoughts.

"Coo, he's sure to be disappointed in me," she was thinking.

But there was no disappointment in his face; rather, beneath all his dignity, was he grinning a little sheepishly. He put out his hand.

"And how's Daphne?"

"Daphne's all right, except that she has an objection to being called Daphne."

Roger flushed, lest he had begun by offending her, but parried with a smile:

"Miss Bruno, am I to say?"

"Don't be silly. You know what I mean. Those who really like me call me Duffy."

His smile broadened.

"I have dared once or twice to write so much. And I confess I was primed up to call you by it; but when I saw you my courage leaked away."

"Why?"

"Because you—you are older and more terrifying."

"You're a fine person to talk about being terrified of

344

anything. Besides, I'm nothing like *you*. I'm frightened to death of you."

"Is that so?" asked he, with his enigmatic grin. "Well, where are we going? How long have you got?"

"As long as I like. You seem to forget that I've come of age since you went away."

"Well, let's walk for a bit, and see where we arrive."

They started towards Ditchling. The guiding of the conversation lay with Daphne, for Roger was apt to turn inwards (probably to a rehearsal); and she saved it from the sloughs by asking him scores of helpful questions about himself.

It was a warm afternoon with the sun unobscured; and at last he suggested that they sat somewhere on the grass. He led the way off the road and up the slope towards the trees. At any rough or steep place he held out his hand, enjoying the action, as she could guess, both from his love of gallantry and the touch of her hand. But he was shy of choosing where they might sit together, and it was she who finally declared herself too fagged to go further, and promptly sat down. Roger spread his length beside her. Then there was silence. (No doubt he had gone in to the dress rehearsal.) He stared at the two windmills on the skyline of the downs; and when he spoke again it was without bringing his eyes away.

"Duffy"—he cleared his throat—"I don't know whether it's fair to speak to you like this the first time we see each other. . . . And I'm determined to consider you first in everything. . . . I didn't intend to say anything at all this first day, but somehow your letter consenting to meet me alone made me hope I might——" He turned now towards her, but she was looking at the close grass by her crossed feet. "Duffy, you know what I mean. For nearly four years I've had no doubt of my love for you. I never worried about girls till I met you; my dreams were all of success and fame. But when I saw you the second time at that ball, looking absolutely divine, I was routed instantly. . . . And all through the war I never doubted. It was always glorious to think of you, to picture you, and to look at your photograph, and to hear the chaff of the other fellows when it stood on my camp-table. Duffy, could we be engaged now?"

Daphne Bruno

She had no answer, continuing to look at the grass; but as Roger said no more, pity obliged her to speak.

"But we don't really know each other—only by two years' letters. And you can't know me from letters. One only shows oneself at one's best in letters."

"As I've always told you, I'm old-fashioned enough to believe that somewhere there's a woman made for every man. And I know you are mine."

She smiled at him.

"And as I've always told you, you're an incurable romantic."

"Perhaps I am."

"But perhaps I'm not so sure of my—my love for you. Roger, I think I ought to tell you: I was very fond of someone else some time ago, and I've never quite forgotten."

She had turned to look straight at him as she said this, and saw the pain knit his brow and narrow his eyes.

"When was this?"

"Two years ago."

"And did he ask you to marry him?"

"No."

"Why? Was he a fool?"

Daphne kept silence.

"Do you expect he will ask you to marry him?"

"No."

"Why not?"

"He has married someone else."

Roger said nothing more. And Daphne, frightened by the pause, heard herself inquiring:

"Couldn't we have a month's companionship together? I'll see you every day if you like—and if you wouldn't mind asking me again in a month's time——" She began to be a little afraid lest he scorned to be temporized with. "I'm very fond of you—and proud of you."

To this he gave long thought, unwittingly lowering and raising his jaw.

"Yes," he decided. "I want you so badly that I would rather have you if I were only second best—but I haven't had a chance with you yet."

They spent nearly every day of that month together; and she could only be pleased to see him working to win her love with all the care and watchful labour he might have given to carrying a kopje in South Africa. It was doubly to be valued from one who prided himself on his haughtiness. He was courtesy, consideration and generosity. A merry humour he had always had, and it made him good company. He had bought a car, now familiar sights on the roads, and taken her long, luxurious drives.

As the time drew nearer when she must speak again, indecision harrowed her. This time it would be final; Roger would not go on petitioning for ever. Sometimes she felt she was looking forward to saying, "Yes"; sometimes, when a glimpse of his egotism made her doubt, she would feel that she was caught gasping in a stream, since it would be impossible, after all his kindness, to send him cruelly away.

It fell that he proposed to her again before the month was finished. A late afternoon as she came downstairs, dressed to drive with him as far as the foot of Ditchling Beacon, where they were going to climb the Downs, her father stepped out of his study and intercepted her.

"I suppose you had better see this," said he, and handed her a press-cutting. There was something dramatically despairing about his gesture and his return to the room. She followed him, glancing at the slip of paper on which the cutting was pasted. It named a journal of which she had never heard, *London Carnival*. Type and paper were poor, and the paragraph was signed, "Our Cynical Spectator."

"On the Dissipated Habits of a Great Critic's Criticism," ran the headline; and the smaller print said:

"Criticism, like Charity, should sometimes live at home. But perhaps a happy marriage between these two, and a dwelling together in the same house, is impossible. There's *such* a difference in temperament. And that, no doubt, is why the criticism of the great Mr. Tenter Bruno (as, to be sure, we have observed in the case of other punishing critics) roams abroad, and seldom spends a night at home. Indeed, we might almost say that in his house, Charity, timid maiden, has secured her divorce from brutal Criticism —with custody of the child.

"The child, in this affecting tale, is Miss Daphne Bruno,

the great man's daughter; and only the great man's charity could have allowed her nonsensical little book, ' Madame Rolland,' recently published, to see the light of day. It was a tactical error, of course, for whatever reviewers may be saying in print, those writers who have been lashed heretofore by the great Bruno are enjoying a mild hilarity. We have studied some of the notices, and detect a praiseworthy doubt of the propriety of securing points against Mr. Bruno by lunging foils at his daughter. For ourselves, we are less squeamish, and judge it all to the good of literature that every book should be submitted to the unhampered attacks of criticism, and especially those that only win their publication by the glamour of a famous name. For these have entered with a spurious ticket."

"Oh, daddy! . . ."

Such a note of pain rang in the words that her father came towards her and took the cutting out of her hand. He had known all along that he should not have shown it to her, but had been quite unable to forgo a display of his honourable wound.

"No, darling," he hurriedly enjoined, "don't take it seriously. It's just a low papermaking copy. Nobody who matters reads it, and those who do forget it in ten seconds."

"Oh, it's awful!" she said.

"No, no. If you're going to be an authoress, you must get used to ridicule."

"But, father, I'll write at once, and say you knew nothing about it. Your reputation's much more important than mine."

"Dearest, it's all stuff and nonsense. I showed it to amuse you, not to distress you. You certainly shall not write. People might say that I inspired your denial. And if they think I'm going to disown my daughter——"

His brain condemned the poor heroic; and when Daphne was gone, he stood disquieted to think that vanity could put a stick in a man's hand with which to strike what he loved.

Daphne went out of the house with a head dulled, as by a blow, into confused thinking. In vain she commanded herself to get the thing in proportion—to see that the paragraph was only a drop in the ocean of that day's print, and already forgotten by anyone less interested than herself. The very memory of her words would flutter her heart for a sick second.

And when she met Roger and his car by the Royal Oak, she could not keep up the gaiety of her greeting. Throughout the drive, after formal answers to his remarks, she would relapse into the worrying memory. And she knew that he had observed her depression and was respecting it.

At Ditchling they left the car, and climbed the pleasant turf of the Downs. It was one of those gracious afternoons that, by discordance with melancholy, increase it; an afternoon of sunlight on the great cheeks of the hills, and wide shadows in their hollows, and clear views to the highlands in the north, where the pine-woods were darkly blue under a private cloud.

After a speechless climb, she agreed in mock-merriment to Roger's suggestion that they rested for a while and enjoyed the view. She sat down in the shelter of some tall gorse, saying formally : "This is quite like old times, isn't it?"

Roger did not acknowledge this remark, but, sitting beside her and idly picking the grass, inquired :

"My darling, what's the matter with you?"

In that unauthorized "My darling!" sounded a real pain; it was manifestly the outburst of a heart charged with love and sympathy.

"Me? Nothing," assured Daphne, with a quickly acted smile. Not wholly acted, however; because that note of love had been potent to sound retreat to her shadows. Being loved like this by Roger was the sunniest place in her life.

"You're miserable. You've been miserable ever since you appeared. I can't bear you to be miserable."

"It's nothing, really." To show which, she picked up a small snail-shell and threw it in front of her. "It was only one of those horrible press notices ; rather more pitiless than usual."

That Roger was throbbing with his love for her she knew by his low-pitched answer :

"I wish I could find anyone that would hurt you."

Daphne Bruno

"But they're right," corrected Daphne. She felt quite happy now in the sunny place. "Rather salted, but right."

"Right or wrong, I shouldn't care. . . . But they're not right. No one who ridicules you could be right. You don't know what you are. You're—there's no one fit to hold a candle to you. It sometimes amazes me that you're so innocent of what you are. If only you could see yourself as I see you! My darling, I never *can* see anyone who seems so beautiful as you, just because you're the model by which I test everybody's beauty. If another woman's eyes are not the same colour and shape as yours, they're imperfect. If her nose is a different shape from yours, or the lines of her figure, they're so far wrong. . . . Oh, but I forgot, I've no right, till you give it to me, to talk to you like this. . . ."

His closed fist was lying on the turf by his side, just between himself and her; and Daphne, unable to answer him with words, laid her open hand on his.

"Duffy! That means——! Oh, my darling!" He put his arm about her waist and pulled her gently towards him. "Then may we be definitely engaged to one another?"

She turned her face towards his, smiled, and nodded.

He kissed her, but without passion, as if he would not hurt her by too quickly taking all his privileges.

"Are you happy, darling?"

"Yes. . . . I think it's wonderful that you, of all people, with the whole world to choose from, should love me. And in spite of all you say, I still can't see why it is. . . . I'm awfully proud of it, really."

"And you love me?"

This was to be met with a smile.

"I think so. I want to be close to you. I want to be happy with you, and to make you happy, and help you in your career. And I want you to kiss me."

"Darling!"

This time he gathered her close, and pressed his lips on hers with all the passion that first he had withheld.

"My beloved!" he said, as he drew back his head to look down upon her face. "And you can't see what you are! Why, every time you look up at me, as you did a second ago, with your huge eyes, you make me mad for need of you. I feel I can never have you close enough—

that even hugging you is a poor apology for all that I would have—that though you are as close to me as you are now, you are still too many miles away."

Again he hugged her, and Daphne, in this embrace which seemed never likely to end, found her thoughts running fast; she was already picturing with delight the announcing of her engagement to her father and the others at home; the congratulations that would come from all who knew her; the inspiring future that stretched before her, with election fights and luxurious living. She was bewildered to have reached this point, but excited; and because excited, happy. And when he released her, she said:

"Do you mind if we go home? I'm so longing to tell everybody."

Roger grinned, as might a staid elder amused by a child.

"Yes. Let's go back." He jumped up and helped her to her feet. "Fancy to think we came up this hill un-engaged and go down it engaged. I wonder what we are going down to." He accompanied their downward steps with a chain of such romantic utterances, and then inquired: "But what do I do next? Not having been engaged before I don't know. Do I come back with you and ask your father's permission? I'm all for doing the proper cere-monial things. I've always believed in ceremony. Not, though, that I should let you go if he refused."

"Daddy won't refuse. But let me tell him, will you? Don't you come in at all. I know how to deal with him. I'm sure you'd make a mess of it."

He drove her, as by newly acquired right, to the gates of Old Hall House, and she, escaping before he could kiss her good-bye, hurried excitedly up the drive. Letting herself in, she saw Miss Carrell standing in the lamp-lit hall.

"Is father at home?"

Her voice trembled, and she was grateful for the half darkness.

"No, dear. But he's back to dinner. He can't be long."

"Oh, all right."

She rushed up to her room and dressed with trembling hands. Once dressed she did not know what to do. Her head and cheeks were so burning that she was moved to study them in the glass and trace the visible effects of such heat. It had tinged them with wine-colour. When she heard her father's key she gave him full five minutes by the bedroom clock, during which her heart seemed to beat a million times, and then walked downstairs and burst into his room. He was sitting in his arm-chair dragging on a slipper.

"Please come in," said he.

"Father, I'm engaged to be married."

Mr. Bruno's hand left the slipper, and his foot trod down its heel. The surprise jerked him out of his whimsical port.

"What on earth are you talking about?"

"Talking about being engaged. I got engaged this evening."

"Got engaged? But I didn't know anyone was in love with you."

"Of course you didn't. I didn't proclaim it from the house-tops."

"Good God! First you write a book without my permission, and now you say you've got engaged. . . ." Mr. Bruno perceived that he was recovering the authentic note of badinage. "I am too old—too old to stay the course with you."

And indeed he was confused. Here was his daughter, whom a few hours earlier he had hurt, coming in radiant with news of her betrothal. To think that her movements were so far from him was pain. The pain was sharpened by this unexpected sentence that their days together were to be numbered. But badinage must screen it all. . . . It would hide, too, for her sake, any mention of the American boy.

"Whom are you engaged to?"

"To Roger Muirhead, of course."

He shook an uncomprehending head.

"Don't you remember? He came to tea with us at St. Leu two years ago."

"But how long have you known him?"

"Oh, since he was fourteen. Off and on."

"Has he got any money to keep you with?"

"Money? Heaps. He's got a motor-car."

"Who *is* he? What's his father?"

"Sir Roger Muirhead."

"No? The excellent old merchant who has managed to combine capitalism with radicalism and religion! Good gracious, Duffy, and is his boy in love with you? Let's see, didn't he do something they made a song about in the war?"

"Of course he did."

"And you're engaged to him?"

"Yes, please. If I may."

"You're sure you're not married to him?"

"No, darling. Only engaged. That's to say, if you'll let us be."

He shrugged his shoulders and spread his hands. Then he stood up.

"Well, well. I suppose one kisses you on these occasions. But I must see this Roger of yours. And you're not to be married for a year, do you see? You must have experience of each other. And we must have the war over and Owen back."

"Oh, that'll be all right. I don't particularly want to get married."

But Mr. Bruno wasn't listening. After looking at her with a smile, he said:

"And has Apollo come for Daphne at last? I trust that, like your Greek original, you were not too encouraging, but fled from him into the woods."

Daphne concealed a start. This chance sally, evoking a picture of Roger (who was rather an Apollo) as he came seeking her under the Montmorency trees, was so astonishingly appropriate that for a minute she dethroned hard reason and wondered with him if, after all, there were a destiny behind these things.

CHAPTER XXVII

Daphne was never sure in what proportion her feelings were mixed in the days between her engagement and her marriage. Doubt would tinge her happiness; but it was never very active, and the period, as a whole, was flooded with a bright light of pleasure. The brightness put out every ember of annoyance at the reception of "Madame Rolland." If ever she desired a glowing press, she got it now. "Mr. Tenter Bruno's daughter to wed War Hero," the paragraphs were headed; "The Hero of Wittfontein to Wed." Two of the papers mentioned, "Miss Daphne Bruno is herself an authoress, having produced in her twenty-second year an artless and charming little story." But most, thank goodness, seemed never to have heard of "Madame Rolland."

She was too happy with it all, imagining Miss Vidella, Miss Sims, Trudy Wayne, Winnie Chatterton, and all her scattered friends reading the news, to be more than palely jealous when the majority of the papers occupied themselves with Roger's career or her father's. But in her mind she hid the resolve to create a work that one day—if only after death—would make Roger chiefly famous as the husband of Daphne Bruno.

Roger took her to Porth Wannick, the Muirheads' house in Cornwall. Of the romantic character of this house on the rocks Roger had often spoken; and when she saw it, she declared that it was far more amazing than he had painted it. You turned aside from the Penzance Road, by the ruins of a disused mine, and went down and down a narrow lane, passing the Porth Wannick land on your left, till you reached a smuggler's cove, where you saw in the very rocks the tiny harbours and docks cut by that fine buccaneering scoundrel, old Captain Helco, for his guilty craft. The house, grey like the rocks, rose above the largest of the tiny harbours, which was now a swimming bath for the residents. It was not large, being but a two-storied, rectangular mansion, under a hipped roof. But the windows were mullioned, the central hall door was an antique purchased from a fifteenth-century house, the gardens were laid in terraces above the rocks, and behind them swept the farm-lands of the estate. Here, for seven months of the year, Sir Roger played Lord Bountiful to the natives, experimenting on his soil to see if he could make all their fortunes by growing beet for sugar there; or trying to cure the conservatism of the pilchard fishers by introducing improvements in their methods and their boats.

The placid Lady Muirhead and he received Daphne with a parental delight. It seemed that their son, who treated his father with a sort of feudal respect, had long told them of the girl in Sussex whom he was determined to capture. And now he brought her there with a hint of triumph. Lady Muirhead, probably thinking that such was her expected part, fell in love with "the new daughter" at once; and Sir Roger, who, when you lived with him like this, was found to be surprisingly old, mingled in his attitude jocosity, patronal tenderness, and a garrulous intolerance. Daphne liked them both, only feeling ill at ease at the amount of religion Sir Roger maintained in his house. Never did she dare to shock him or his acquiescent lady by confessing that she had no religion at all.

In truth, she was afraid of Sir Roger, who steam-rolled you out with his talk, though your brain saw a hundred weaknesses in his argument. But you didn't answer him with the incisive replies that occurred to you. It would have been like fighting against a steam-roller with a scalpel. He was only seventy-three, but she suspected that after his retirement from active part in the Muirhead Traders, which was his life's creation, senility was setting in early. She wondered what her father would like.

Mr. Bruno came down to Porth Wannick for a month, and appeared to think a good deal, as his host tossed bits of walnut into his mouth (one bit following another before it was really due), and, chewing them rapidly, announced to his guest the truth on all subjects. Little doubt he annoyed Mr. Bruno by seeing a comparison between the creation of books and his own creation of the Muirhead Traders, and between the fame of a great critic and the fame of a trading firm. "I suppose some of you writers, Bruno, make a good thing of it," said he, chewing one walnut and prospecting in the dish for another.

Mr. Bruno said it depended on what was meant by "making a good thing of it."

"Why, making a living, of course," explained Sir Roger. "What else?"

There were those who interpreted it differently, suggested Mr. Bruno.

"Oh, stuff and nonsense, Bruno, stuff and nonsense," Sir Roger buffered. "I know all that gammon backwards—knew it when I was sixteen. A clever fellow like you knows at the back of your mind that the impulse to acquire shekels and power is what makes the world go round. Give me those fellows who acknowledge it frankly and get on with the job."

"You can have them," answered Mr. Bruno, concealing his restiveness behind a smile; "and no doubt they'll join your Liberal Association down here, and the parish church."

"Yes, and why shouldn't they? Why shouldn't they?" snapped the host, the red light appearing in his eyes.

"Why shouldn't they," echoed Mr. Bruno, "if the harmony is complete?"

"Of course it's complete—complete as you make 'em. Liberalism and Christianity, it's all the same; it's just *Noblesse oblige.*" Sir Roger repeated the phrase: "*Noblesse oblige.*"

As became the wiser man, Mr. Bruno retired from the developing battle with a shrug. And Sir Roger rolled on.

Her father summed up Sir Roger to Daphne, when he met her next morning before breakfast, walking on the terrace-gardens above the rocks.

"Uncouth, dear," said he sadly. "Uncouth."

Daphne nodded, and hinted that Sir Roger was getting old.

Mr. Bruno agreed, and continued without a smile:

"But what an honourable life he can look back upon! He's created the Muirhead Traders, who operate in the East, where very large profits are consistent with Christianity. He was telling me all about it last night. And he's been able to retire with a great income. He's been able to keep his boy out of it—though why he should have wanted to I don't know—and he's going to give him three thousand a year when he marries you."

"Golly!" exclaimed Daphne.

"Yes, a wonderful old man," reflected Mr. Bruno. "I think he must have gone up Sinai once and been given God's final opinion on every subject under the sun."

"Daddy!" laughed his daughter.

"Well, what else can it be, when to criticize anything he says is to verge on blasphemy? It's a marvellous state of mind to get into, when you can so believe in your commercialism that any questioning of it is about equivalent to saying that Christ might have sinned. But the boy's all right—your boy's all right. He has the grace to mix shame with reverence in his attitude towards his parents."

Daphne was looking at the peacock which had appeared on the terrace above.

"Gracious goodness, Duffy!" exclaimed her father, "is that a peacock? What a very appropriate pet for Sir Roger! . . . I am afraid your father-in-law's a little vulgar. Don't you think so?"

It was quite a new idea to Daphne, and worried her for a day or two. But the scales fell to Roger's side again when the news came through of his adoption as Liberal Candidate for the Middle East Division of Sussex. Eagerly they read together the little stack of Sussex papers that reported the meeting of the Liberal Council, or commented on its choice. The Radical *Gazetteer* was gushing:

"The Middle East Division is to be congratulated on their new Liberal candidate. This constituency, predominantly agricultural, is one of the most difficult for Liberalism to win. But now with the adoption of Captain Muirhead, all the signs point to a great and resounding Liberal victory at the next General Election. That desirable event, we hope, will not be long delayed, believing that the Balfour administration is as much discredited here as it is in the great industrial centres. All that was needed was to secure a popular and able candidate. Captain Muirhead has everything in his favour. He has been familiar with the district since childhood, one of his father's houses being situated within its bounds. He is engaged to the daughter of one of its most distinguished residents. His war reputation will effectually quench any pro-Boer nonsense. . . ."

And another paper said :

"If Captain Muirhead is able to wrest this stronghold from its Tory masters it will give him a magnificent start in his Parliamentary career."

And another :

"One must not omit the signal advantages possessed by Mr. Muirhead in his beautiful fiancée. All the world knows that he is engaged to the talented and charming Miss Daphne Bruno. Perhaps it is not for us to express our hope that, when the election comes she will be, not his fiancée, but his wife. If she inherits her father's gifts, and his witty radicalism, she will be an invaluable lieutenant for the gallant captain."

"Oh, I shall never be able to speak in public," interjected Daphne, "if that's what they mean. But I shall love doing everything else."

"By Jove !" said Roger, who did not always listen to his fiancée. "We simply must win, after all this puff."

"Oh, rather !" agreed Daphne. "Let's begin nursing the constituency at once."

He gave her a kiss in acknowledgment of her enthusiasm.

"When will there be a general election ? " she asked, while still in his arms.

He grinned down at her proudly.

"A question that interests me much more is, when will you marry me ? "

"Oh, not yet. I'm much more interested in politics. It's such fun being engaged. There's no hurry, is there ? "

At this Roger released his hold and turned away.

"I can't understand girls," said he. "They seem differently made from men."

Daphne knew that he was slightly hurt about something.

"Why, what's the matter now ? " she laughed. "Oh, I know I've said something wrong."

"Oh, if you don't understand, you don't. . . . That's where the trouble lies. If you wanted me in the way I want you, you would understand."

"Of course I want you, Roger."

"My dear, you don't understand the meaning of ' want.' "

"But daddy said we weren't to get married at once."

"We could have got over that. . . . Well, never mind; it's only another way of saying you're cold."

"Oh, I'm not," denied she, for it was one of her prides that she was an ardent nature. The "Oh, I'm not," a Cockneyism into which she fell when indignant, made Roger frown.

"Yes," she added hastily, "I know I said that like a Cockney serving girl." (She would borrow her father's phrases, and air them as her own.) "I got it from talking too much to the servants when I was a kid. However, what were we saying? I'm not cold. I'm ardent."

Once again he took her into his arms and smiled down tolerantly upon her.

"Surely you're the most innocent girl that ever got engaged."

It was rather annoying, this assumption that she was a fool, and she retorted:

"I'm not innocent at all. I know everything and exactly what you mean."

His hold relaxed a shade, and she realized that this, too, had disappointed him. She was seeing in his mingled thoughts what he himself hardly knew to be there: that while he desired her much, he wanted her to be innocent— for somehow an innocent girl gave more to men's desire.

Panic stirred sometimes as (she supposed) with every engaged girl; but she was too excited and happy, on the whole, to let it come far into consciousness. Once, however, it escaped her guard, and ran about riotously. She had spoken lightly of religion. Roger was annoyed—less, she suspected, from the strength of his own religion than because he thought she ought to be converted, like a princess marrying a foreign king, to the traditional religion of her sovereign's house. And she said forthwith:

"I know I'm going to shock you, Roger; but this is the truth. The only reason I want to be married in church is because it's always done, and a registry office sounds horrid. And I want to wear a white dress and have a crowd of people there."

Roger's features palpably tightened.

"It's no good being angry. . . . You ought to be pleased with me for trusting you and being so open. I could quite easily lie about it. But the plain truth is, that I haven't got any religion."

Roger then began an irreproachable homily on the necessity of some religion in life, but before he got very far, Daphne, irritated, burst in:

"But, Roger dear, frankly now. What's the sense of *you* preaching Christianity to me? I know you for what you are, and I'm fond of you for what you are. And I know you to be ambitious (just as I am), and that you like everything of the best (as I'm sure I do), and that you like to be on top and to flatter yourself you don't easily play second-fiddle. Well, that's all perfectly delightful, but it's not Christianity."

Roger wrinkled his brow to think out an answer; but she had thought it out quicker, and knew what he was going to say.

"I don't know that you're right, Duffy. There must be 'top-men' in the world. Only it's the duty of the men on top to care for their workers and servants all they can, and so to serve them."

"Well, I'll be a Christian, if that's all it is—so long as I'm one of the top-dogs."

He let her rebelliousness pass, only grinning, as if he could afford to wait in the knowledge that the time would come when he, with his stronger mind, would be able to mould her to the pattern he desired. It was rather like the grin one might give to a pet dog who tried to get a stick out of one's hand.

Panic was running in Daphne, while she thought that life seemed to be made up of making mistakes, going too far with them, being too gentle to turn back, and accepting as punishment a ruthless life-sentence.

She was rather frightened, though pretending to be delighted, with the big house in Fettes Gardens, South Kensington, which Sir Roger had offered them as a wedding present. As she walked up its four or five stories, and calculated that it would require a butler and four or five women servants, she wondered how ever she would be able to manage them. She felt very little different from what she had done in Miss Vidella's form-room; and how could a schoolgirl command this battleship? The similar houses to left and right frightened her with a picture of their wealthy and competent ladies. So did the tall well-bred houses opposite, on the other side of the railed-in gardens. " I feel like a pea in a pod too big for it," she thought. But she was careful not to show her feelings to Roger, lest he found her even more inadequate.

"I'll do it. I'll manage it. After all, these terrible women next door, and the dowagers over the road, must have started somewhere."

They married Daphne at St. Patrick's, Fettes Gardens, in the August after the signing of peace with the Boers, when Owen had returned to play an exceedingly important and well-dressed part in the ceremonies. She was very proud of her men. Who there looked like her father, on whose arm she was, or Roger, who took her at the chancel steps, or Owen, who had appointed himself vicar's warden and master pew-opener? At sixty-two her father's hair, not at all to his displeasure, had gone quite white, but his tall figure was as slender and neat as Owen's. She enjoyed the excitements to the full, and only felt a warming of the eyes when, on going to her carriage to drive to the station, Hollins, who had hardly taken her eyes from the bride all the afternoon, cried as she hugged and kissed her, saying : "The meaning 'll have gone out of life, Miss Duffy, with you gone. The meaning 'll sort have somehow gone out of life. God bless you, dear. God bless you." Her father just kissed her, patted her on the shoulder, and made a joke.

He delayed on the steps, however, to watch the carriage receding along the road towards the first corner. That carriage, of which he could see only the hinderparts and the horse's twinkling heels, was taking Daphne out of his range and beyond his call. His jaw jerked forward at the thought. The stream of life, so he put it, had brought her to him where he drifted, and running rapidly on, like the unsentimental thing it was, had floated her away before he had hardly touched her ; and he would never catch her now. Pain and bewilderment sat uncomfortably at his heart. " I missed her. I missed her somehow." A variant of something Daphne had often uttered of late, with crumpled brow, seemed the best expression of what he was feeling :

Daphne Bruno

"I don't know. One doesn't learn how to adjust oneself to life till it's nearly time to die."

The carriage turned the corner, and old Sir Roger called: "Come on, Bruno; it's all over now." (Detestable the way he called you "Bruno," as if he were your equal!) He turned and walked over the doormat into the house. The chaff and laughter of the guests was beginning to sound hollow, and the whole assembly to show its fractures, now that its centre had been riven away. Mr. Bruno thought of his home, and his study, and his books; and made an excuse for returning to them.

CHAPTER XXVIII

DAPHNE, though she concealed it, was very proud of the circumstances of her married life. She was proud of her big house and its fine furniture; of having so much money in her purse (Roger gave her an incredible allowance), of her shopping at the great stores; and of giving her name as Mrs. Muirhead.

These were the pleasures; but there were worries, too. The housekeeping, though she tried to approach it light-heartedly, was a permanent anxiety; she knew nothing about it. Mistress of one man-servant and four women, she had no talent whatever for ordering them about. Instead of issuing commands as one accustomed to authority, she caught herself throwing out hints of what it would be nice for them to do. She could hear the weakness in her hesitating speech, and wondered if they perceived it too, and laughed at her. This nervousness she had tried to conceal from her husband, but one evening at dinner, when she had asked the butler: "Would you mind getting the other cruet? Yes, thank you very much. It's downstairs," Roger said:

"Dearest, I don't think there's any need for you to petition the servants to do quite reasonable duties." The criticism was eased by a kind smile.

Daphne, determined, like him, to avoid any friction in these early marriage days, decided to accept the rebuke merrily.

"But I'm in mortal terror of them."

Roger shrugged.

"Then our household will inevitably be run in a slovenly way. Of that I'm quite sure. I'm the last person, as you know, to suggest bullying one's servants, but I believe it's happier in the end for everybody, if they're disciplined."

"All right," said Daphne, with a slight heart-sinking, "I'll try."

She was as much at sea with her social duties—her calls,

X

and her entertaining at home. Dinners! She had never been to one before marriage. How on earth were they created? She felt sure that she was doing something wrong, and these fashionable women would criticize her among themselves. And they had no right to, she thought angrily; life was something bigger than their silly little conventions, and she had as many brains as any of them—more than most.

Roger made her worse, for it was quite obvious, though he thought it tactfully concealed, that he was putting her through a course in social demeanour. When talking enthusiastically at their meals together, she would emphasize with her arm or point; and he would hint that the best people didn't do that. She spoke too loud when excited, and laughed too shrilly, he said. And certain words such as "Lordy," and "Crikey!" and "Coo!" he ruled out as impossible. In fact, he was evidently pained at this discovery of "no polish" in his wife.

The result was that if her deportment-master came into her drawing-room, she was reduced to the awkwardness of a schoolgirl. His merry conversation and ease of manners she guessed to be partly paraded as a demonstration of how these things were done; and his thoughtful silence when their visitors had left to be the symptom of his disappointment at her failure. Once at a convenient *tête-à-tête* dinner, he said deliberately:

"You don't seem to have much social gift, darling, do you?"

"Haven't I?" said she, hurt. "How do you mean?"

"Why, you never say anything. You look divine, of course; but you seem to have no subjects of conversation."

"Oh, but I think I could talk the hind leg off a donkey with people of my own age, and in an easier setting. But I'm frightened of all your dames. You see, I feel so young." She leaned her elbows on the table. "Do you know, I *can't* realize I'm married. I can't see any difference in myself from when I went to school and played the fool. I feel just the same."

"And you look it," agreed Roger, fetching down her left hand from where it was meeting the right, under her chin, and holding it lovingly on the table. He kept it, till the entrance of the butler obliged him to withdraw his own, guiltily and humorously, on to his lap.

This hand-holding and mutually understood jest were typical of their relation. They were good friends. And Roger was a model (as he meant to be) of courtesy. He was never brusque with her. The way he assisted her from carriage or omnibus, or helped her on with her cloak after the theatre, or considered her needs at meals, or opened the door for her when she left a room (even when they were alone) showed that he delighted to honour his wife as the queen among women And she—she felt grateful to him for having married her, and was resolved that throughout his life he must have all his dues.

And yet she knew that he was always contrasting his own home with others better "run," and her over-awed shyness with the aplomb and ready wit of other hostesses. She knew it more than ever when he appeared to have abandoned the deportment-course in favour of silence.

This silence was like a perpetual rebuke. And when one day he was studying a parliamentary Blue Book, whose very appearance seemed to show the difference between the width of his interests and hers (and perhaps was not unwillingly displayed to that end), she sat alone by the window, and stared into Fettes Gardens.

"Yes, I see where I've failed him. One doesn't see it till afterwards. I never knew I was going to dislike and rather despise the social hum-drum. I am always ready to picture myself in any large occupation, and doing it better than anybody else; when the plain fact is that I am without social gifts. I'm only an artist, like father, and probably a smaller one. . . . But I must get into these household duties. I must get into things, and not let him down. It's only fair to him."

So she set about it with renewed vigour. She kept elaborate books of accounts, drew up exceedingly neat programmes for the servants' labours, bought books on etiquette (surreptitiously), diligently read the papers so as to know what was being talked about, watched with unremitting care over her husband's wardrobe, and at all social assemblies studied the behaviour and the vocabulary of the vivacious ladies who did not disappoint their husbands. And her rapid improvement, manifest to herself, greatly encouraged her.

Daphne Bruno

But the havoc it made of her writing and reading was an abiding disquiet. And one morning at breakfast, when she read in the book-reviews, to which she always turned first, of a young woman writer's triumph, her mouth squared, and, dropping the paper, she sipped her coffee in dejection.

Roger noticed, and rested his hand on hers.

"What's the matter, dearest?"

"Nothing." She looked up brightly.

"Yes there is. You look wretched, as you can sometimes."

"I'm depressed, I suppose."

"Depressed? What have you got to be depressed about?"

Perhaps his features had tightened a little. Had she hurt him by so poor a compliment as to be depressed sometimes? He raised surprised eyebrows.

"I can't see what you've got to be depressed about."

Jarred, she answered with a note of anger.

"I know you can't."

"Well, what is it?"

She slightly tossed her head.

"Oh, sometimes I can't help thinking of all I dreamed I was going to do. And time passes, and I do nothing."

"Do nothing!" echoed Roger, covering his injury with a smile. "Well, you're only twenty-three, and you're married and have a fine house and most luxuries. I don't think you've started badly."

"Oh, but I meant in the writing way. I intended to— to read all the literature in the world and then write. I set myself too big a task, I suppose."

Roger ruminated over his toast and marmalade, and decided after two or three minutes that he was right in being offended.

"Your trouble, Duffy, I think, is that you want all the advantages of married life, and all the advantages of freedom——"

"No, it's not——"

"Please let me go on. *I* accept the disadvantages, and there *are* a few, though you may not think it. There are some things that haven't turned out just as I thought, but I've resigned myself to them philosophically."

She flushed at this frank statement, and said nothing.

With the greater ease that came to her in domestic and social duties, however, she found that, with system, quite a number of hours in the week could be secured for her reading. Yes, she had been a little panicky. And as book after book returned to her shelves read, and not only read but understood, she felt again the improvement in her mind, its finer tempering and wider reach. Her taste advanced with every month, so that the memory of certain parts of "Madame Rolland" made her catch her breath with dismay. And the more she read, the more avenues of learning opened before her, and the more she sought to snatch studious hours from the day. Fancy if she could become equal in knowledge to her father! And to Henry!

And then with a spasm of apprehension she suspected that she was going to have a child. Soon she knew.

It was useless to tell herself she ought to feel differently about it; she didn't, and there was the truth. She didn't want the child. Not yet. For years it would smash up such study and such writing as she wanted to do. And it might be the first of many! No good to tell herself that the feeling was unnatural; she knew it was perfectly natural; the whole force of her had been directed to a different channel. And because of this there had lingered in her mind the flattering conviction, a last romantic delusion, that she was not one of those who bore children easily. It had been encouraged by her early immunity.

That night, when Roger lay by her side and was about to embrace her, she said abruptly:

"Roger, I'm frightfully afraid I'm going to have a baby. Oh, what on earth am I going to do with a baby? I don't want it. . . . I don't want it. . . ."

He removed his arm from her, and said nothing at all.

Knowing that she had angered him, and anxious to hear his voice, she persisted:

"Oh, you might sympathize with me, Roger. What on earth am I to do about it?"

At last he spoke.

"Really, Duffy, you do hurt me sometimes. I always thought that a wife when she had such a piece of news came with joy to her husband. At least, so I've always read. . . . I can't make it out. Either you are different from most

367

women, or women are very different from what they appear in books."

He heard her sigh, and felt sorry for her.

"Why should it upset you so?"

"Oh, Roger, I don't want one just now. Not just now. Not so soon."

He emitted a sound of disgust, and answered vaguely:

"What a humbug it all is! What a fool's paradise we men live in!"

"But don't you see what bad luck it is to me?"

"No, I don't. I confess I can't. . . . I can't see your point of view at all. As I told you once before, you seem to have entered marriage with an eye to all the advantages, and a determination to avoid all the handicaps."

"I think the motives of all of us are pretty mixed; but what's the good of throwing stones, when we're being punished for it?"

"Let me finish what I was saying. A girl who gets married and then whines because a child appears really does drive rather blindly at life."

"Oh, yes. Yes, I know," agreed Daphne.

CHAPTER XXIX

DURING the months of malaise and sickness that followed she was conscious of a relapse from all those things that in the last few years had brought some goodness and direction to her life. She no longer cared for the defiant courage and the pity transcending God's which her father had set before her. She no longer cared about giving a generous return to Roger for all he had given to her, or about excusing his faults because hers were the same in kind. More than this, she not only eluded these motions towards goodness; she actively fought against them. When a clear thought whispered that her rebelliousness was disproportionate to its cause, she silenced and drove it away. If her new habit of combating indolence asserted itself and bade her be up and about a work, she deliberately sat down and did nothing, thus to snub it. All thoughts that would give her the right to criticize Roger she encouraged; he had pursued her remorselessly, and dazzled her out of her senses into marrying him; and she didn't love him—she loved Henry; Henry only and always; her studies and her writing were for Henry—nay, they *were* Henry; and Roger was enforcing his power to snatch her from them. When a moment's interest and a tremor like love stirred for the coming child, she repressed it firmly, resolved to dislike this little jailer of Roger's.

Self-consciousness haunted her as she grew larger. She would keep seated, if possible, when visitors came; she walked very quickly out of rooms; over shop-counters she stooped slightly. Not the smallest of her disappointments was the knowledge that she would never be able to wear her new clothes, because, when she could fit them again, they would be out of fashion. And her figure, which had always been the admiration of her father and Henry, might never be so small again. More children would arrive, and she would become matronly. Roger had made her slough off her youth, and leave it behind for ever. And she was only twenty-three. . . . And Henry might come again.

What did she know about the management of a baby? Not even how they were dressed. She bought pattern journals which showed pictures and gave the patterns of frocks for the new-born child. Dully she went and bought the materials they detailed, and gave up her afternoons to making the robes.

One day her husband came in and saw her engaged on this work; and, picking up the little long robe, with its lace edges and ribbons, he smiled with pleasure and kissed the crown of her head. Probably he was touched to see her doing this work herself, but said no word of approval for fear of offence. He had great ideas of treating her, at this important stage, with the utmost consideration.

That he should think she had abandoned her right to irritation annoyed Daphne, so she purposely said:

"Oughtn't we to think about getting a nurse for this infant of yours?"

"There's plenty of time, isn't there?" inquired he. "There are enough about."

"We want to get a good one." Daphne, needle between her lips, held up the garment, ostensibly to examine it, really to give an ease to her words. "Because I tell you plainly, I'll bear this child for you, but as soon as it's arrived, I'm going to give it up to a nurse who can look after it all day and give it its bottle."

"But, dear——" he began, and stopped.

She laid down her sewing, and asked:

"What were you going to say?"

"Oh, it's no good worrying you yet awhile. . . . I was only going to ask if you weren't going to—suckle it yourself. My mother nursed me. She told me so."

Daphne felt like saying: "But that's about the thing she'd do best. I don't suppose she ever had any ambition in her life apart from you," but she only said, rather timidly, for she had never overcome a fear of Roger:

"Well, I'm not going to. There's not such a great difference between bottle-babies and the others as all that. After all, I shall only be twenty-four years older than my son or daughter, and I've a duty to myself as well as to it."

Roger held his peace, but walked with displayed disappointment out of the room.

"Oh, walk away if you like," thought Daphne.

She completed all the garments and filled a white basket with them, rather proud of her handiwork. Why she had made and broidered every garment herself was not clear; in part, it was self-martyrdom; in part, the simplicity of her childhood made lordly buying unnatural to her; in part, too, and she knew it, there was a concealed idea of self-punishment for the unkind hostility.

Now that the time drew closer, she wished it would come quickly and be over. She looked forward to being small again, and free from sickness and pain. "As soon as it's over, I'm going to have a real good time." A brilliant idea had abated some of the gloom. Hollins! Why hadn't she thought of Hollins before? The happiness it would give old Hollins! Hollins came, and they enjoyed long talks together. The old servant smiled and shook her head when Daphne declared: "Do you know, I dislike this child intensely. I shall hand it over to you and a nurse."

"Shall I tell you something, dear?" said Hollins. "Your mamma used to talk to me about a lot of things she didn't talk to no one else about; and she told me that she hadn't wanted you at all, but she no sooner saw you than—well, she loved you so, she wouldn't 'ave called the queen her cousin."

Daphne looked at the table-top, and then jumped up. "But mother was quite different from me, I've always imagined. She was that sort. No, I shall hand over the kid to you and the nurse and be free. I wish it would come quickly. . . . Yes, I think I nearly hate it. . . ."

"Nearly ain't half-way," said Hollins.

Roger wanted her to be very careful with herself, and to act as the decorous invalid. But she refused to do anything of the kind, going about the day's occupations as if she expected nothing. And he, ever eager for romantic feelings, began to marvel at her courage. This admiration reached its topmost pitch when one afternoon, two weeks before the marked day, as they were sitting together talking, she suddenly got up and said: "I think I'll go and lie down.

371

x*

And, Roger dear, I think perhaps you'd better get the doctor."

He jumped up to help her to her room, but she said: "It's all right. I'm all right. You arrange for the doctor and the nurse," and walked easily and quickly up the stairs. With a rapid heart Roger hurried to his telephone.

Then he walked up and down the dining-room, sincerely feeling all that it was written he should feel at such an hour. Self-dramatization was there, but he was not conscious of it. He was praying: "O God, make it all right for her. Don't let it hurt her too much!" There was no sound upstairs in her room—no periodical moaning, such as he had supposed was usual. Once or twice, fearful lest this silence boded ill, he walked up to the room, and saw her lying in bed and ready to smile up at him, as cosily as if it were a late morning and she too comfortable to get up. Another time he found her out of bed and in the adjoining dressing-room, seeing that everything was ready there for the nurse. No word or strain of feature suggested that she was knowing pain.

The wheels of the doctor's carriage were heard outside, and Roger himself opened the door to him. It was a satisfaction, though unrecognized, to show the doctor the calm and dignity with which he met the threatening hours. But the doctor, by his unhurried manner, seemed to disperse all exaggerated seriousness.

"Your baby's impatient to be up and abroad," said he.

"Yes, it's a bit earlier than we expected," admitted Roger, not quite sure if he liked jesting at such a moment— whether these doctors didn't get rather coarse. But the words "your baby," seeming for the first time to mean something alive, thrilled him. "Yes, two weeks early."

"Quite so. The little blighter!" said the doctor, wiping his boots on the mat.

"I've 'phoned for the nurse."

The doctor nodded.

"I'll take you up, then, to the wife," said Roger.

He escorted him upstairs, and pointed to the door of the silent room. The doctor passed in, and Roger was left on the landing.

Again he prayed: "O God, make it all right for her! And don't let it hurt." The praying worked on him so that he nearly broke up; but he preserved his outward dignity. He heard himself saying: "My little Duffy, my beloved, I can't bear to think of you suffering. . . . My God, I've been hard with you sometimes. . . ."

And as he walked downstairs, he paused sometimes and stood on a step with his hand on the balustrade, staring at the memory of some moment when he had hurt her with his—his discipline. At last he reached the long dining-room again, and, standing by the window with his hands behind his back, gazed into the darkening street. "If the worst were to happen——" But there his power to think broke down, retiring defeated upon itself.

Upstairs Daphne lay in her pain. She was not groaning, through fear of her husband's thinking her a coward; but her breaths, as the pains seized her, were short, staccato intakes, like the breaths after sobs. At the time of the doctor's entry she was in the pull of such a pain. She felt him take her by the wrist, and was disposed to burst into tears. Instead, she smiled a sick greeting, closed her eyes, and continued her short, sharp gasps.

O God, was there ever such pain? Never, never again would she have a child. "I wish I'd never married. I wish I'd never married. I am caught for life. I may say I'll never have another child, but I shall. Unless I commit suicide after this, and escape from life because it's too hard and frightening. Does everyone of my age look back on a life blundered with and blundering? It wasn't all my fault. I'd only been in contact all my childhood with people who never faced up to anything as it really was—excepting father, and he never spoke. . . . So that I ran into things with the comfortable idea that luck would make them all right—instead of seeing that my fate would be mathematically what I shaped it. . . . The love of being talked about and the desire for life and luxury made me marry Roger. It was a blunder, and very wrong, I dare say— but one *does* make mistakes and be selfish at twenty-one . . . the punishment is too unrelenting . . . too everlasting. . . . Henry . . . I'd have gone through this for Henry. . . . Henry, why couldn't we have fought together for the truth of how to live? . . . Does *any* girl reach motherhood with a scheme of living, other than drifting? . . . Oh, my God!"

Daphne Bruno

It was as if all the mental pain in her life had assembled to be present in this culminating agony. "Oh, doctor!"

Over. Rush of relief, so wonderful as itself to hurt. "It's over and I'm free again. She lay with eyes closed in this luxury of freedom from pain. She had forgotten the child, there being no cry to remind her; or if there had been she had not noticed it. At last, sighing with repletion of luxury, she opened her eyes and looked inquiringly for the doctor. He was not in the room, but there was a nurse, a young woman, pleasant and round-faced, who smiled at her.

"That's right. Why, you're a wonder! You hardly turned a hair."

Daphne, pleased with this tribute, answered:

"Oh, it really wasn't half as bad as I expected."

The nurse smiled meaningly.

"The doctor told a different tale. You're so strong, you see."

There came a cry from the neighbourhood of the fire; and it repeated itself, and ceased.

"Would you like to see her?" asked the nurse.

"Oh, is it a girl?"

"I should think it was. And a little beauty."

The nurse walked away to the crib; and Daphne, though unexcited and not free of her former hostility, undoubtedly felt an interest to see what she had produced.

"There!" said the nurse.

For a new-born baby, it was a pleasing face that Daphne saw in the blanketed bundle held above her eyes. There was no frown, nor was it mottled or over-coloured. The lids were down, and the lashes distinctly visible. Something in the lip and chin reminded her of Roger. But the downy hair was much fairer than his could ever have been.

"I've seen worse," she pronounced.

"Seen worse!" echoed the nurse, taking back the baby. "And I was wondering if I had ever seen a better."

Later Roger was brought in, and he kissed her, declaring that she looked in radiant health. She smiled, liking all this tribute to her physical strength and her fortitude. "You'd better go and look at your daughter," said she. And Roger, after staring into the crib for a long time, came back to her bed and asked her what she thought of "the little rat." Probably he was wanting her to express a different attitude to that which she had adopted before its birth, but she replied :

"I suppose, if it were anyone else's, I should say it was rather adorable."

He pretended to smile, unwilling to argue just now.

"And Heaven knows," continued Daphne, "what's going to happen to her with no one to love her. I feel a compassion for her, if that's any comfort to you."

"Well, you mustn't talk too much, I expect. And I think *I*'ll be considering a night's rest."

"Is it night, then?" inquired Daphne, for the room had long been lit, and she had known nothing of the gathered dark behind the blinds, or counted the passing of time in this bright illumination.

"It's only a quarter to midnight," said Roger, as he stooped to kiss her. "Good night, dearest."

"Good night, my dear."

Not at once, not as her mother had done, did Daphne succumb to the thing that trembled within her whenever she saw her daughter's face. The admiration of all who looked at Evie—"Evie" for no obvious reason had leapt into Daphne's mind as the fitting name for this little fair thing—the genuine, sometimes startled admiration of visitors helped it. But it was a remark of Hollins that bade it go forward to its conquest. It was late at night, and Hollins, relieving the nurse, had brought Evie to her mother for the eleven o'clock feed. Sitting up in bed, quite eager for another glimpse of the little face, Daphne took and held her daughter. She stared down at it, bewildered as to who this little stranger was—so complete in every feature, with such manicured filbert nails on the wrinkled fingers. Baring her breast, she gave it to the searching mouth. Then turning to Hollins, she asked with a smile : "How long do you expect me to go on doing this? Not for interminable months, I hope."

"It's worth doing, dear," answered Hollins. "I reckon there are few things better worth while."

Daphne turned her head and looked at Evie again. Her heart quickened, as if something, battened down, had been allowed to well up in it. The plain truth, she knew, was that she loved this Evie with a trembling love. As she admitted the thought, exhilaration glowed in her; and though she felt she suddenly wanted to lie down and meditate on a lot of things, she suspended thought, keeping only the exhilaration.

Then the child was taken away by Hollins, and the light put down, and she could lie and think.

The image of Evie was with her. "She's going to be intelligent. Anybody can see that from her brow and her eyes. She must have all I didn't have—a carefully watched childhood, and an education of the highest, with a proper training of her taste and a proper disciplining of her mind. I must watch her every moment myself." That inherent scepticism whispered: "But probably every parent has had these thoughts. Probably mother did. Probably father did, and wearied. I dare say Evie's story will only be a repetition of mine. . . . But no. I mustn't—I *shan't* go back on this vow. . . . I shall try to get on with my books as well, but if I can't do both, Evie shall come first."

She lay awake a long time, abandoning her mind to those clearer parts that had always been there. She wanted to locate some basic error that was responsible for the most of her blunders. She seemed to find it at last—where, indeed, Henry had found it—in her ever-present sense of the spectator, that mastering sense of a world looking on. One could not be real when the spectator was the first consideration. Did she inherit it from her father? Was it in part a legacy from the poseurs who had surrounded her youth? No, probably everybody in the world was tainted with it. But people like herself and her father, who could see it for what it was, ought to be big enough to shake themselves free. What a subtle poison, and how difficult to trace!—for often the spectator was oneself, and the deluding of that limited audience nearly complete! She could see the succession of "attitudes" it had produced in her life; her early masculinity, her facile adorations, her insincere religion, her wilful publication of "Madame Rolland," her showy marriage with Roger, and so recently as yesterday her pretended dislike of her child. A few things in her life seemed true and independent of it; her humble love for Henry, her new conceptions of her art, and her late ideas of courage, pity, and grateful generosity to Roger. And now, as pure as any, came her love for Evie.

Brilliantly clear it all seemed that night to Daphne, as the clock ticked the hours away. One was only happy when, regardless of applause, one was making something, giving something, or enjoying intimacy with whoso understood. Making—giving—intimacy—these were the real things. Looking at others, instead of others looking at you. So clear was it that she felt in sight of a liberation from her past. If only—if only she could one day lose the spectator, she would shed like a single garment the poseur and the slave.

PRINTED BY
CASSELL & COMPANY, LIMITED, LA BELLE SAUVAGE,
LONDON, E.C.4
20.531